Praise

"Fascinating and quirky characters come together in this excellent collection of short stories...a true hit for Teppo's fans and new readers alike."
—*Publishers Weekly* (for *The Court of Lies*)

"He can write anything, from fantasy to hard SF to satire. For those of you not already in on the secret, this collection is proof that Teppo's one of our best, a writer who understands genre and storytelling at some kind of samurai level."
—Daryl Gregory, author of *Afterparty* (for *The Court of Lies*)

"High concept meets a thrilling pace. Mark brings the big guns to the writing table."
—Ted Kosmatka, author of *Prophet of Bones* (for *Earth Thirst*)

"[*Earth Thirst* is] A provocative new take on one of the longest-running themes in the genre. Teppo looks to be a writer to pay attention to."
—*Asimov's*

"An outstanding historical epic with exceptional character development and vivid world building...In addition to the heroic battles–including swordfights, archery, wrestling, and martial arts–romance, political intrigue, and promises of betrayal and rebellion are suffused throughout this cinematic tale..."
—*Publishers Weekly* (for *The Mongoliad*)

"This off-beat alternate history of Eurasia could be your new obsession."
—*io9* (for *The Mongoliad*)

"Story lines abound but interconnecting them all is the fascinating evolution of sword fighting . . . sf and military-history buffs will devour this genre-bending saga."

—*Booklist* (for *The Mongoliad*)

"Mark Teppo's *Codex of Souls* is fine fantasy noir. If you like Twilight and Supernatural, then this could well be your cup of very black tea."

—Greg Bear, author of *War Dogs* and *Hull Zero Three*

"*The Codex of Souls* is without a doubt one of the most original Urban Fantasy series going right now. It has stepped away from the pack and embraced a different type of magic and a very different sensibility worth checking out."

—*Mad Hatter's Bookshelf*

"Grim and refined, Teppo's aggressive near-noir is rich and strange—heavily and deftly textured. It's got a punch that'll leave you rattled, intrigued, and tasting blood."

—Cherie Priest, author of *Maplecroft* and *Boneshaker* (for *Lightbreaker*)

"*Lightbreaker* is a damn good book. It throws some new curves into the Urban Fantasy ride. I think you've got a big, fat hit in your hands."

—Kat Richardson, author of the *Greywalker* series

"Teppo's choice to place the events of *Lightbreaker* in an alternate modern society is possibly the book's greatest strength, allowing it to draw on an inexhaustible well of occultist mythology as well as the raw inspiration of Paradise Lost . . . Teppo not only bases his masquerade in a host of theological concepts, he also actively combines them to form a singular and fully fleshed worldview. Hermeticism, alchemy, theism, and epistemology are all poured into the same melting pot, creating a solid, diverse, and original discourse."

—*Strange Horizons*

"The plot is nothing short of captivating, with a twisty cast of villains, surprising reversals, and an escalating sense of danger...Teppo's preoccupation with profound questions of human purpose and potential make this deeper and more thought-provoking than your average urban fantasy."

—*Locus Magazine* (for *Lightbreaker*)

"*Lightbreaker* is the best book about magic that I have read since Peter Straub's *Shadowland*. This book is simply amazing. It is a richly layered journey into the occult. It is complex, dark, and a hell of a ride."

—*Monsters of Filmland*

Also by Mark Teppo

The Potemkin Mosaic
Earth Thirst
The Court of Lies (collection)

THE FOREWORLD SAGA

The Mongoliad (co-authored with Erik Bear, Greg Bear,
Joseph Brassey, Nicole Galland, & Neal Stephenson)
Katabasis (co-authored with Joseph Brassey,
Cooper Moo, & Angus Trim)

Sinner
Dreamer
Seer
The Lion in Chains (co-authored with Angus Trim)
The Beast of Calatrava

Cimmaronin (co-authored with Ellis Amdur, Charles
C. Mann, Robert Sammelin, & Neal Stephenson)

THE CODEX OF SOULS

Lightbreaker
Heartland

RUDOLPH!

RUDOLPH!

HE IS THE REASON FOR THE SEASON

Mark Teppo

ROTA Books

This is R001, and it has an ISBN of 978-1-63023-005-0.

This book was printed in the United States of America, and it is published by ROTA Books, an imprint of Resurrection House (Puyallup, WA).

You going to finish that?

Cover art by Ian Pamplona
Edited by Darin Bradley
Book Design by Aaron Leis

First ROTA Books trade paperback edition: November 2014.

www.resurrectionhouse.com

This one is for Cecil and Em, who never stopped believing . . .

Contents

RUDOLPH!

THE LETTER

I

THE NIGHT BEFORE THE NIGHT BEFORE CHRISTMAS, I CAUGHT SANTA CLAUS trying to hack into the Vatican's computer system. He was using his wife's iMac, belly pressed against the edge of her desk, glasses threatening to slip off the end of his nose. The blue light from the computer screen bleached the ruddy color from his skin, making his face look flat and two-dimensional.

A Norman Rockwell portrait of the kid with his hand in the cookie jar.

"What are you doing?" I demanded. "It's after midnight. You should be in bed."

He started, his eyes flicking between me and the computer screen. "Uh, Bernie, I, uh, couldn't sleep."

"You take your Valerian root?" I asked as I walked across the room. Mrs. C's study was all done up in light wood, polished and burnished until it glowed like warm butter. The floor was covered with a large area rug filled with a mesmerizing swirl of reds and greens and oranges. The two windows high on the wall behind Santa leaked grey light; there was a lot of fog over the North Pole at this time of year.

Santa didn't answer my question.

"Look," I said, "you know the way this works. You've got to be ready for Zero Hour. We have just a few simple procedures for you to follow. You don't skip any meals, you stay off the treadmill and out of the pool, and you get at least ten hours of sleep every night. I'm not your mother—I don't want to be your mother—but I am SECO, and I am charge of making sure you're ready to put the red suit on two nights from now."

Santa glanced at me, his blue eyes blinking over the rim of his glasses. "Ah, Bernie, I'm a little keyed up. I was just doing a little surfing, you know, to relax."

I held up a hand. "I don't want to know where you're surfing."

"It's not where you think."

"Come on, Santa, you're using Mrs. C's computer. Why else would you be in here? You don't want us logging the web traffic to your computer."

"I'm not looking at porn," he bristled.

"I don't care if you are." I tugged at the sleeve of his bathrobe. "Fun time is over. You need to—" I caught a glimpse of the screen. He didn't have a web browser open. In fact, it looked a lot like a Telnet window. The letters looked funny, and it took me a second to realize the command line prompt was in Italian. The rest of the words looked a lot like Latin. "*Humani Generis Redemptionem*," I read.

"I'm not looking at porn," Santa repeated, his voice soft and sad. "I'm looking for Suzy Anderson's father."

My retort died on my tongue. I had read the report.

Midday on the 22nd, Zero Hour minus fifty-seven, Santa had been taking his pipe in his office. While trying to stuff his pipe—a new Dunhill Calabash given to him on his birthday by Mrs. C—it had slipped from his fingers and fallen under his desk. Rooting around for his pipe, Santa had found a small envelope covered with gold stars.

It was a Christmas letter from one Suzy Anderson of 1224 Foxtail Lane in Troutdale, Oregon. Written shortly after Thanksgiving of this year, wee little Suzy Anderson, like all young girls and boys, had hand-written a letter to Santa Claus. In little Suzy's case, she was asking for her dad back for Christmas.

No big deal, right? I don't think I'm going to surprise anyone when I say that we've misplaced Christmas letters before. Come on, an organization this size? I'm surprised we've not lost more of them. Finding a letter this late in the Season is not a reason to panic. The North Pole Consortium—the organization of elves that manage and run the entire North Pole operation—is well equipped to handle such emergencies. In this case, a couple of elves held Santa down, another one got the letter from him, and when I got the call, I came up and told him everything was going to be just fine. "Don't panic," I had said. "We're trained professionals. I've got a team of four working on it right now. It doesn't matter where Suzy Anderson's father is. We'll find him. We'll get him on a plane. We'll get him home in time for Christmas. It's not a problem."

Easy to say; harder to solve.

Santa was watching me closely now, peering at me like he knew what I knew and was waiting for me to acknowledge that I knew that he knew that I knew what he thought he knew. The ole Saint Nick eyeball trick, which has never worked on me.

The report on Mr. Anderson had been routed straight to the top, with copies to SECO (Senior Elf in Charge of Operations—me) and EOD (Elf on Duty—my boss). It had a big "Eyes Only" banner across the top, which meant that under no circumstances was I to tell Fat Boy—internal code name for Santa—what the team had discovered.

And yet, the ole Saint Nick Eyeball and a Telnet window to somewhere with an Italian command line. Odds were Santa already knew something . . .

You see, David Anderson had been involved in a four-car accident on I-5 over the Thanksgiving weekend. Just outside of Wilsonville. Slippery road. A semi going too fast. The accident had made the local eleven o'clock news. The following day's edition of the Portland *Oregonian* had included a small mention that, along with three other people, David Anderson had died in the accident.

Getting Daddy home in time for Christmas was a little out of our jurisdiction.

"I found the *Oregonian* article, Bernie," Santa said.

I swallowed. "Yeah?" I tried to stall. He hadn't blinked yet, and the letters on the computer screen kept distracting me.

It wasn't the fact that Santa was poking around the Vatican network that was worrying. It was the fact that he had gotten that far already.

"Is there something you want to tell me?" Santa asked.

I covered my eyes and wiggled my head, shaking off the ill effects of the Santicular Evil Eye. "Nope." I fumbled for the sleeve of his robe, tugging at it when I found it. "Come on, Santa. It's late. You should be in bed. I'll have Nigel send up something to help you sleep."

He pulled his sleeve free of my hand. "I don't want to sleep." He started tapping the computer screen with his finger, and he didn't stop until I opened my eyes and looked up. "Did you know that this office has been doing Christmas deliveries for four hundred and ninety-three years. And in that time, we've never missed a request. Not one."

"We're working on it," I squeaked.

"How?" he growled.

I shrugged. "They haven't told me. I'm not part of that loop."

"How can you not be? You're Senior Elf. There's nobody between you and EOD."

"Senior Elf in Charge of Operations," I corrected. "I'm the one who is charge of making sure you're ready for Flight Night. I run the Zero Hour prep squad, and our job is to watch your weight, your sleep habits, and to make sure you're not overly stressed." I nodded towards the computer screen. "This qualifies as stress, and I want you to stop this nonsense right now and go back to bed. It's very late."

"Stop patronizing me. I'm not a child."

"No, you're my charge. I'm trying to do my job."

Santa ground his teeth. "So am I."

I raised my hands. "Do I need to make a call? Do I need to get someone to escort you back to your room?"

Santa reached into the large pocket of his robe and pulled out a yellow and black stun gun. He put the flat mouth of the device in my face. "Go ahead and try."

I kept my hands up.

"Do you know what this is?" He lowered the weapon slightly and put a little pressure on the trigger. A red dot appeared on my chest. "It even comes with a laser sight. Though, at this range, I don't think I'm going to miss. It delivers an electrical signal designed to override the central nervous system and directly assault the skeletal muscle structure. It's got two probes that will deliver a burst of—"

"Yeah," I interrupted. "I'm familiar with the specs."

Santa nodded. "Good." The mouth of the stun gun didn't waver.

I sucked in a big lungful of air. "Can we talk about this without the Shockmaster 3000 in my face?" These things were all the rage this year among the security conscious, and I did know the specifications of the weapon. The Shockmaster Series was rated at twice the power of its closest competitor. Too many nut jobs out there had the mental acuity (or drug-induced lack thereof) to monster their way through the nominal levels of electric current offered by other electroshock personal defense weapons. The Shockmaster Series bypassed the brain and went right for the more basic informational pathways of the body: a blast of white noise to jam all circuits, followed by an overwhelming surge of current that makes your muscles lock up tight, leaving the brain wondering who shut off the lights. Meant for your basic three-hundred-pound violator of the restraining order, I wasn't quite sure what it would do to an eighty-seven pound elf.

"Are you going to listen to me?" Santa asked.

"And my other option is?"

He smiled.

I tried to look bored as I glanced at my watch. "Five minutes." I tried not to think too hard about the failure to clear Santa's robe of advanced hardware.

"What is the Consortium doing for Suzy Anderson?"

"Making a video tape," I said, dredging up the details of the Eyes Only report. "I think they're pulling as much video as they can scrounge, along with a bunch of photos. Some kind of life retrospective."

"That's not what she asked for."

I shrugged. "Yeah, well, the guy is dead. Not much we can do about bringing him back from . . . you know . . ."

Santa shook his head. "Four hundred and ninety-three years, Bernie. That's an awfully long run."

"And you've done well. The odds of being able to fill every request every year for nearly five centuries have got to be astronomical at this point. It's a simple matter of math, Santa: sooner or later, you're not going to get the roll you want. You do what you can. It's no reflection on you or your ability to execute the office. You can't take it personally."

"I do."

I shrugged again, though this was more of a 'well, what can you do, you over-achieving nutbag?' sort of shrug.

"Maybe some of my predecessors were inclined to accept substitutions, but I'm not," Santa said. "You let one kid down, you might as well not bother with any of them."

"I'm glad you're taking this so well, and haven't wandered out in the dark lands of depression," I quipped.

Santa's grip tightened on the stun gun. I stretched a little higher for the ceiling. *Defuse, Bernie, remember what they taught you?* It's not my job to take him down. I just have to defuse the situation. Get him to put the gun down. Get him relaxed. And then make a call. Get a few of the Burly Boys in here and let them sock Santa full of Thorazine and Vicodine. Hey, let's just keep Fat Boy on ice until Zero Hour. Remember the prime directive: keep him calm and get him in the air for Flight Night.

"Look," I said, licking my lips carefully. "Maybe I'm going about this all wrong. What can I do to help?" Calm. Keep him calm.

"I'm looking for David Anderson," Santa said. "I'm trying to find out where he's gone."

Maybe a six by three plot in the Troutdale cemetery? Noticing the pitting around the twin holes in the muzzle of the Shockmaster 3000, I kept that answer to myself. I focused on the computer screen instead, paying a little more attention to the Italian and Latin on the screen. "You think the Pope knows?"

"No, I don't think he knows, but someone above him might."

I'm usually not this dense, but I was operating at a handicap, so it took me a few seconds to figure out who—and what—Santa was talking about. "Heaven?" I squeaked.

"There's got to be a manifest somewhere. There's got to be a list. Nothing happens without a list, Bernie."

"And you think you're going to find this *list* on the Internet?"

"Why not?" he asked. There was a slight catch in his voice. I looked at his eyes and saw the tiny crack in his armor. "You can find anything on the Internet, can't you?"

It wasn't much, but it was just enough of a question that I saw my opportunity.

"Yeah, sure," I told him. "You can find anything." Except for a decent chocolate chip cookie recipe. "How about this: I help you look, you put the cattle prod down. Deal?"

He thought about it.

"Come on," I pressed him. "If there is anything, it's going to be in Latin. You need my help."

He frowned. "I can read Latin."

"Yeah, sure," I said. "Who writes your Christmas card to the Pope every year?"

I had him, and he knew it. His hand went down, and I tried not to look too relieved.

I reached for the keyboard. "Let's see what we can find."

II

IN MATTERS OF BELIEF, I AM A PRAGMATIST. YOU PUT SOMETHING IN FRONT of me, give me a chance to get some sensory data off the object, and I'll settle for three senses out of five. Just because something is on the Internet barely qualifies as visual representation of an item's reality. There are no filters on the Internet; it's just the huge Jungian collective made real through one part the American fore-fathers' foundation of free speech and one part the eructation of Freudian neuroses and self-congratulatory psychoanalysis and one part university-funded experiments in memes and viral prop-agation of code structures.

Do you believe everything you read? Maybe not. But can the words you read make you believe?

The tiny clock on Mrs. C's computer reads a little after 3 AM. Less than forty-five hours until Zero Hour and Flight Night. Santa is wide awake, and his hands are on my shoulders, his fingers digging into my flesh. I'm reading the same words he is, and like I said, my bullshit filters are heavily engaged.

He, evidently, doesn't have the same reservations about the Internet.

We were staring at a command line prompt that blinked at me like an innocent lamb. I'd just tagged a machine claiming to be an outward facing interface of purgatory's firewall, and as much as I wanted to think otherwise, I was inclined to believe it. My palms were dry. Santa's breath was whistling behind his teeth. His beard was brushing the top of my head, and it was driving me nuts, but I can't take my hands off the keyboard. They feel like they're glued on.

"It's here," Santa said. "We've found it."

"We haven't found anything," I said. "It's just a command prompt." *Denial, denial, denial.* I was frantically trying to figure out how I could get myself out of this situation. I couldn't unplug the machine. Santa had already seen the automated response scroll past. Even in Latin, there were a couple of words that were pretty obvious. Like *"Purgatorium."* And *"Tabulae Publicae."* Now it was just saying, *"Eadem Vis."* And the damn cursor kept blinking.

I panicked. I didn't have a plan. I just yanked my fingers off the keys and started thrashing at Santa's beard. He yelped and jumped back—and okay, so maybe I was pulling pretty hard. He dug in the pocket of his robe for the Shockmaster. "What are you doing?" he demanded, waving the gun in my face.

I put my hands on my head, my fingers working my scalp like I was trying to work in a hair tonic. "I'm just—" It was all a vain attempt to stimulate my brain into coming up with some workable plan to get Santa to put the damn stun gun down.

"Stay in the chair," he said.

"My head—" *Distract. Distract. Distract.*

"Don't touch anything. We're too close, Bernie. Don't do anything."

I let one hand drop to start pulling on my earlobe.

"Stop it." His voice was tight, and his hands were tighter.

I felt like I was trying to do that thing where you pat your head and do Wise Strokey Beard at the same time. "I just need—"

"That's it, Bernie. I know it is."

His hands steadied for an instant, and I suddenly forgot about my cartoonish behavior. Santa's finger twitched, and the gun popped. There wasn't much chance that I could avoid the Shockmaster's tiny darts, but just sitting there like a spotlight-dazzled amphibian while a couple of thousand volts surged through my tiny elf body wasn't on my bucket list, so I dove for the floor.

Either I was faster than the Shockmaster or Santa jerked his hand too much when he pulled the trigger, but both darts went over my head. I heard the tiny click of the darts against the computer screen behind me, and then there was an ugly stink in the air as the darts discharged, and Mrs. C's iMac reacted poorly. There was an explosion behind me, and I thought to look but then realized I should be paying more attention to the floor, which came up quick. I bounced once, rolled over, and caught sight of the chair as it tumbled forward. I had a moment to reflect on how stupid this accident report was going to read, and then the chair smacked into me and my head hit the floor. Lights out.

I slipped through gauze filled layers of consciousness. Had I dreamed the whole thing? The Internet, Santa and his illicit stun gun, the Neiman-Marcus cookie recipe, the computer that would allow us access to purgatory? Was it all just a bad reaction to the shrimp I had guzzled down the night before?

The tightness in my stomach and the acrid taste in my mouth wasn't of the bad shrimp variety. I had swallowed some blood. My synapses were reluctant to connect, memory coming slowly and only with great concentration. Blood in my mouth. Probably related to the fat lip that was a pulsating knob of heat on my face. Which, in turn, was probably due to the edge of Mrs. C's chair smacking me. And so on, and so on. The connections lined up slowly. Blood. Lip. Chair. Desk. Computer.

Purgatory.

I wished again that it was just a dream.

I heard voices. Underwater voices, like I had stumbled into the last quatrain of an Eliot poem. I thrashed about; or, at least, I imagined thrashing about. I received no confirmation from my limbs that they were in any mood to obey my instructions. I could be a bodiless head swaddled in sixteen layers of sweat-soaked gauze for all the response I was getting from my extremities. I would be notated in the NPC annals as "EH"—Elf Head: the first elf to lose all his appendages while on the job.

That wasn't a pleasant thought.

Maybe it was a dream of multiple layers. That seemed like a better thought, and I hung on to it as I passed out again.

III

MY NAME IS BERNARD ROSEWOOD. I AM AN ELF. I WORK AT THE NORTH Pole. I am one of the Senior Elves (there are a bunch of us), and my division is tasked with shadowing Santa Claus between Lockdown (the day after Thanksgiving) and Flight Night (Christmas proper). Zero Hour is calibrated out of a North Pole Consortium station on Beccisa Island in the Pacific Ocean.

It's all kind of like you imagine it: Santa in the sled, the reindeer pulling the sled, Rudolph in the lead. That's how it happens. At Zero Hour, we switch on the Time Clock, and the second hand stops at one second past midnight. Santa is in the air, and everything is frozen at that one click into the new day while he delivers all the toys.

It all leads to that instant of time. All our preparation. All the planning and organizing. The North Pole Consortium functions solely to ensure that Christmas happens every year on the 25th of December. Christmas doesn't just happen by itself, you know. It isn't just a matter of putting crayon to paper and entrusting your letter to your local postal service. All those requests have to be received, read, entered into the system, catalogued, filled, and packaged back to their requestee. You think Santa does all that himself? Seriously? The man's color blind for one thing.

Enter the elves—the little, round, merry folk who do all the hard work. We've been unionized for several generations now, and it is our organization that really makes Christmas happen. All the technology and information systems advances in the last hundred years are derivative knockoffs of R&D done by the NPC. Automated package tracking? We've been doing it since the mid-20th century. High-speed materials duplication? Twenty years before that. Ceramic and polymer based alloys? At least a decade. Our Elfnet predated Arpnet by a good three years, and data warehousing was last year's buzzword five years ago. Frankly, we reached the 21st century about six years before anyone else, and we're about halfway to the 22nd already while the rest of you are still thrashing your way through the early teens.

Santa is the seasonal mascot. Ever since some wise-ass in the marketing department had the smart idea of putting Santa in a fur-trimmed red suit as part of their promotional outreach during the 1930s, we've had no choice but to keep Fat Boy on the payroll.

The Technology Management team has tried at least three times in as many years to shift RPF—Request, Procurement, and Fulfillment—to an e-commerce style system. Internally, the North Pole has been paperless since the early '90s, but we still recycle over two hundred tons of paper waste every year. TM has been pushing a cloud-based system for Christmas requests: children would e-mail Santa instead of sending their traditional paper letters; the North Pole, in return, through a number of partnered commerce sites, would procure all Christmas presents on a local basis. Utilizing the existing ground mail system, we could fulfill Christmas without having to send the red sled into the sky or turn on the Time Clock.

I'm a people person; I'm not proficient in the sciences for the basic reason that my wee elf brain just didn't have the synaptic connections suited for comprehension of quantum mechanics. Those who did, well, the Clock made them nervous. Supposedly more stable than the Nuclear Clock, we used the Time Clock to freeze the forward motion of Time on Christmas morning so that Santa would have enough time to deliver all the presents.

I know, mind-boggling. Would you want to be operating in a null-space that exists outside the dimensional restrictions of Time? Yeah, me neither. That's why we keep Santa Claus on the payroll.

Most of the year is spent getting ready for the following Season. Production cycles don't really hit their stride until after Labor Day when the Sales and Marketing team present their annual report on the Toy Hierarchy for that year. R&D finalizes a lot of their technological upgrades at this time, and the software daemons start assembling the List. The reindeer, who range across several thousand acres of unoccupied land during the off-season (we call it the Park), are brought back to the North Pole, and SECO goes South to retrieve Santa from the Caribbean where he spends most of the summer fishing for marlin.

Upon return to the North Pole, SECO institutes the hardcore diet and exercise regimen necessary to get Santa in shape for time under the Clock. Proper preparation takes several months of rigorously monitored protein intake as well as a regimented dosage of liver tablets, powdered Mexican yams, blue-green algae tablets, Boron, Smilax, Yohimbine, amino acid supplements, Choline, Ferulic Acid, and medium chain triglycerides three times a week. He only *looks* fat.

SECO is more than just Santa's physical trainer. This elf is also his therapist, his appointment secretary, his bridge partner, his golf caddy (the North Pole has a nine-hole ice course that is a fairly tough par 34), his confidante, his shadow, the guy who says "Gesundheit" when he sneezes, the guy who gets the pickle jar off when he gets his hand caught, and the guy who brings the new roll of toilet paper when Santa is on the can and the paper runs out. SECO—me—is the elf who keeps Santa grounded.

Right.

Why did I feel like I was flying?

IV

"TURN TO ONE-FIVE-SEVEN. SWITCH TO SPECTRUM OSCILLATION. IT'S A straight shot from here. Open her up."

It didn't sound like any of the dialogue from *The Wizard of Oz*, so I eliminated *Kansas* as one of the possible answers to the question that was blinking on and off in my head. I felt like I had been stuffed with cabbage and left out on the roof for about six days. I was still hearing things like I was underwater, yet the voice was familiar.

I was having a little trouble getting a spark to leap across any of the millions of synaptic connections in my head. There was a sensation worming its way into my body, and I grabbed that sensory data like a drowning man and held on. Something was pressing against me, pushing me against something else. The second something was cradling me, like a soft hand or a leather chair.

Bingo. One down.

The first something was gravity, or rather, a force of acceleration.

I opened my eyes as it suddenly dawned on me that I could very well have just been in and out of Kansas in the time it took for me to realize what I was feeling.

I was in the sled, and the clear canopy over my head was filled with the dark blue of the high atmosphere. There were no points of reference by which to gauge the speed of the craft, but my brain did a quick rewind and came back with "open her up." Judging from the constant pressure on my chest, it would be reasonable to guess that we were traveling well past the speed of sound.

And like a bunch of colored dominos, my thoughts tumbled along in a clumsy rush. "We" was me, Santa, and probably nine reindeer.

I tried to move and found myself restrained. I thrashed around a bit before I realized the straps across my chest were part of the seat harness and not some homemade BDSM restraints. I was making enough noise to be heard over the constant rumble of the sled, and Santa looked away from the instrument panel.

"Ah, Bernie," he smiled. "You're back."

He was wearing a black flight suit, and his face was streaked with camouflaged grease paint, streaks of white and black swabbed over a thick layer of olive green. He looked like a moss-covered tree stump.

"Where are we?" I managed. My heart was pounding. I wasn't sure if it was from all the thrashing around or the dawning realization of the situation.

"Mid-Atlantic somewhere." He waved a hand at one of the monitors set in the panel in front of him. The Mark V Sled had a surveillance system arrayed about its outside. There wasn't much to see port or starboard or aft—just pale blue that disappeared into a layer of frothy white—and the forward camera showed the small blisters of the reindeer cockpits along the handle of the sled. The bellycam was filled with more of the thick froth. "Pretty heavy cloud cover," Santa said. "Comet snagged a US Weather Service report that said the whole Eastern seaboard is busy getting another three to six inches of snow. There won't be a break in the cloud cover until we pass Florida." He glanced at a chronometer. "Another twenty minutes or so."

I tried to turn in my chair, and realized there was something on my head. It knocked against the frame of the seat when I wiggled. A helmet

Santa grinned. "Bet you wish you had been wearing that last night."

"I'm not sure why I'm wearing it now."

"We weren't sure when you were going to come around. Didn't want to leave your noggin unprotected, you know, in case we hit turbulence."

The Mark V sled was the latest prototype out of R&D. We hadn't planned on using it this year, as there were still some issues with cargo space. Otherwise, the craft packed all of the latest technology: a Time Clock Wave Generator, stealth armor, chameleon configuration, auto-gyroscopic thrusters, two Harrier turbines, an onboard sixteen processor RISC system, radar, microwave, infrared, ultraviolet, 5G-ready, smartwear piloting and targeting systems, and a full GPS scan of the entire globe with a real-time holographic projection system with resolution down to one meter. There was even a 1.6 cubic meter refrigerator, a bagel toaster, and a cappuccino machine. "Turbulence" was not a word that cropped up much during the design and construction phases.

"Where are we going?" I croaked.

"Purgatory," he answered.

Asking *why* was either going to be considered rhetorical or it would cause Santa to wind up and soapbox me for the next half hour, belaboring me with a whole lot of crazy talk that would include the rationale for kidnapping me, stealing the prototype sled, and hauling ass with the reindeer on a trans-global flight.

"Look," I said, licking my dry lips, "we should talk about this."

Santa shook his head. "I'm not interested in talk, Bernie. That's all you guys do. Talking and meetings and regulations and SOPs. There is no action. "

"It's an incredibly complex situation, Santa. Christmas is too big for just one person any longer. We need the organization—the procedures—otherwise the whole thing would fall apart. We need SOP documentation in order to regulate quality and ensure that any member of the staff can perform—"

"Stow it," Santa snorted. "I've seen the Blue Book. You've got procedures for making sure that the water I take my vitamins with is the proper temperature."

"The human body absorbs the nutrients from the supplements at maximum efficiency in a fluid environment of 99.3 degrees. We spent a lot of money doing the research."

"I remember when we put the first microwave in. It had two settings: *on* and *off*. And before that, I used to heat water on the stove. A gas stove. You think I bothered to put a thermometer in the kettle, or did I just wait until the damn thing started whistling before I poured the water?"

"You probably waited . . ." I said.

"And did all that hot water kill me?"

I shook my head. "That's irrelevant. Systems of codified behavior and operational policies are mandatory for the efficient functioning of any complex production environment," I said. "You can't have individuals working without systematic work-flow structures. It would be—"

"The early twentieth century?"

"Anarchy," I finished.

He laughed. "Anarchy? Please. I'm not saying that we should tear everything down. I'm just operating outside any of your procedure documents, Bernie. You're all snow blind. I'm the only one with a decent pair of goggles."

I wanted to raise a finger in argument, but I discovered that the restraints weren't just in place to keep me from falling out of the chair. Santa watched me struggle for a minute. "Can't have you doing something foolish, Bernie," he said, softly. "It's too important."

"Why bring me at all?" I asked.

The intercom pinged, interrupting his reply. "Snow White to Prince Charming."

Santa toggled a switch on the console. "Charming. Over."

The sled comms were all fiber connections between the blister pods where the reindeer rode and the cockpit—I'm not even sure why the reindeer insist on using code names when it's all hard-wired like this. The gravely voice was crystal clear, though, and it sounded like the reindeer was in the small chamber with us. "Eyes downside, Charming," Rudolph replied. "A scenic vista awaits."

Santa leaned over and toggled the bellycam to the heads-up display that ghosted over the cockpit canopy. The cloud cover beneath the sled was patchy, streaks of distant blue peeking through the rents and tears. We shot across the edge of the storm front and the view went from white to blue. On the right edge of the display was a narrow edge of dark green and brown. Santa adjusted a dial and the camera tracked right and stepped down through several magnification stops until the tiny marks became gantries and towers poking up from the flat landscape. "Canaveral," Santa said.

He moved a white cursor over the image and clicked on a specific launch pad. The imaging system performed a GPS lookup, locked onto the object, and started tracking that location as we streaked overhead. He magnified the image one more step and I could make out the slender shape of a booster rocket. "SLS," Santa said. "NASA's next generation launch system. They're going out farther than the International Space Station. They're going to try for the Moon or Mars, one of these days." He turned away from the image and looked at me. "What happens then, Bernie? What happens when they establish a lunar base and take their families to the moon?"

"I don't know, Santa."

"Christmas will still happen on the moon. Am I going to have to make the trip?"

I swallowed. "I'm sure there is a team monitoring the progress of the Space Launch System. I'm sure a feasibility study is being done right now."

He snorted. "A study. Email traffic for six months, capped off with a bulleted presentation that will send 99% of the audience to sleep. You're missing the point, Bernie. You're all missing the point."

"I'm trying," I shouted. "But I'm finding it a little hard to concentrate after I've been shot at, assaulted, bagged up, and tied down." I burned off a few more calories going epileptic on the straps.

Santa watched until I wore myself out. I was breathing hard, and I worked a few nostril flares into the power grimace I was sending his direction.

"You going to behave if I untie you?" he asked.

I thought about it for a few seconds. "Maybe."

He glanced at the instrument panel. "We're over ten thousand kilometers up, Bernie. We just hit Mach 3. You think you can just step off?"

"I could bite your ankles."

"Would that solve anything?"

"Make me feel better."

He waited until I sighed.

"Okay, I'll behave."

He made two cuts in the nylon straps with a red-handled, black-bladed knife and then got out of the way as I thrashed out of the restraints. He kept the knife in hand until I was done making sudden motions. I pointed at the refrigerator. "Can I get some water?"

"Sure," he answered, folding up the knife and putting it away. "That's sounds good. Grab me a bottle too, would you?"

The cockpit of the Mark V was about three meters by six meters. At one end of the rectangle was the pilot's chair, the main instrument board, and the navigation station; at the other end was the hatch to the sled's cargo bay. In between was what we called the No-Fly Zone: the only things within reach in this part of the sled were the espresso maker, the toaster, and the refrigerator. Standing there, you were making snacks; you most certainly were not piloting the sled.

I grabbed two mineral waters from the fridge, handed one to Santa, and sat back down in my chair. We sucked water quietly and watched the bellycam track across the eastern edge of Florida. It was barely dawn down there, and the frantic shopping activity of the day before Christmas hadn't started yet.

And speaking of shopping . . .

"So what do you expect me to do?" I asked after I had done a little hydrating.

He wiped his mouth. "I need your fingers, Bernie. You're the one who found it. I may have a subscription to *2600* but, you know, I really don't understand half the articles. And Blitzen and Cupid, while they're pretty sharp, they've got hooves and can't type for shit. We're going to need you to access the computer when we get there."

"Purgatory."

There. I said it. SECO training did include a couple of basic psych courses. One of the things they teach you is that you should never give credence to the patient's delusional state. You should never allow the patient to draw you into his mental fugue, never willfully participate in the fantasy environment. Of course, when it came time to write up the several-thousand-page report I was going to have to file when I got Santa back to the North Pole, I was probably going to skim over this whole bit. Frankly, when you've had as rough a morning as I was having, most of the psych stuff seemed like an awful lot of bullshit.

"We know where the entrance is," Santa said. "Blitzen and Cupid did something with some log files and figured out where you went. They found that same web address, but they couldn't get in. They said there was no way to hack into it externally, but if we could get to the terminal itself, then maybe we could do something."

"Like what? Look under the keyboard for a sticky note with the password written on it?"

Santa shrugged. "Sure, if that's all it takes."

"You haven't thought this through very well, have you?"

Santa was quiet for a minute. "We need access, Bernie. I just couldn't wait around for you to wake up. We're on a tight schedule here." He pointed at the chronometer on the instrument panel. "We haven't got a lot of time to find David Anderson before Zero Hour."

Well, I guess that was a bit of good news: this psychosis was going to be temporary.

V

In the nineteenth century, the French engineer Gaspard-Gustave Coriolis discovered that the rotation of the Earth had an effect on the direction of the streams of air that swept across its surface. Dubbed the Coriolis Effect, this observation on the part of old G-G detailed the fact that, because the Earth spins to the east, objects in the Northern Hemisphere have a tendency to turn to the right when they are moving on a straight path, while objects Down Under gravitate towards the left. While this has an effect on the water in your toilet bowl, it makes no difference to circular thinking.

Somewhere over the Tropic of Capricorn, I went Stockholm on Santa. I hadn't gotten anywhere with logical arguments and rational reasoning, so I figured I might as well take advantage of his steady diet of pop psychology from TV and pretend to be swayed by his arguments. Santa wasn't going to be deterred from his mission, and all the noise I was making to the contrary was just giving him a headache. The first thing I do to get rid of a headache is to remove the object or sound that is causing me pain. By going friendly, I'd decrease the chance of getting dropped out the chute like an express delivery toy. And if I could turn the old Stockholm Syndrome ploy to my advantage . . .

Besides, he was bigger than me, and he was packing hardware. I could cite either one as an excuse on my thousand-page report, and no elf would fault me on the decision to play nice.

Santa was napping—supersonic flight didn't seem to bother him in the slightest. Once we passed the equator, he started getting comfortable in the chair, and when we crossed the wide mouth of the Amazon, he started snoring.

I didn't bother with the controls. The autopilot was on, and I knew the reindeer were monitoring the flight status. There were redundant controls in their pods, and any attempt on my part to alter the path of the sled would alert them.

I amused myself with checking email back at the North Pole.

There were more than a hundred unread messages in my inbox, and only half of those looked to be from the office of EOD. I figured the Network Jockies in TM had flagged my account to sing like a fat canary the moment I touched the network so there was no point in pretending that I hadn't seen all the exclamation points in my inbox. Since most of those emails were going to cover the same ground, I replied to the most recent one. Old school telegraph style. Just to let them know I was holding it together.

"Am Fine. Stop. Gone holiday shopping with Fat Boy. Stop. Be back in time for Zero Hour. Stop. He's not holding a gun to my head. Stop. But he does have one. Not sure where he got it. This is *way* outside my job description. Stop."

In addition to all the other amenities that the Mark V sled packed, it also contained a great deal of surveillance counter-measures. If Santa didn't want to show up on radar, he wouldn't. The NPC usually tracked the sled during Zero Hour through a network of relayed GPS coordinates that the Sled's navigational system uploaded to our high orbit network, but I was pretty sure the reindeer had figured out how to switch off that relay. A couple of them are pretty clever, and Rudolph—well, he survived the Cold War after all; he's had a long time to master the art of selective paranoia. The Network Jockeys would probably do a packet trace on the reply I just sent back to the mail server at the North Pole, but all they'd get would be the address of the satellite that the sled had tapped to send the email. There were something like fifty-two of these little communication and positioning satellites parked in geosynchronous orbits, each scanning approximately 1/50 of the Earth's surface at any given time for incoming signals. That's a lot of square kilometers, and at the rate we were moving, they'd never get enough of a fix to be sure where we were heading.

Not that I was all that sure myself. Santa and the reindeer were on a course for purgatory—or what they thought was the entrance to purgatory. Sure, I had found a computer address on the Internet. Sure, it indicated there was a machine out there running some kind of firewall software and it might have some other data structure local to it. But you couldn't make the jump from there to the positive existence of life after death.

David Anderson had been involved in a car accident on November 27th of this year. The funeral had been held on December 7th. There was a plot of land in the local cemetery in Troutdale that contained a box and stone, one with him in it and the other with his name on it. Now, if I believed those two details—and since they were true, why shouldn't I?—then there weren't a whole lot of options.

1) Little Suzy had a fascination with dead things that couldn't be certified by any psychologist as "healthy," and what she wanted for Christmas was for us to dig up Daddy's head, slap a red bow on it, and roll it under the Christmas tree.
2) Little Suzy's fascination with biology and botany and Wade Davis meant that she was hoping that we'd dig Daddy up before the zombie powder that had been sprinkled on him before they put him in the ground wore off.
3) Life did persist after death, and we were going to knock on the gates of heaven and ask God to give us David Anderson back.

Okay. Now for the rebuttals.

1) Too weird, even for this elf.
2) Nobody noticed Daddy wasn't really dead when they embalmed him? Filling Daddy full of formaldehyde would probably constitute a money-back situation with the funeral home, but it certainly wouldn't make his resurrection from

a Voodoo-inspired, medicated state any easier. Flag it as highly doubtful.

3) Well, as a famous detective once said, when you eliminate the possible solutions, what remains—however unlikely—must be acknowledged as a very likely solution. And a couple hundred years prior to that fellow, another wise man once said: "*Pluralitas non est ponenda sine neccesitate.*" Keep it simple, stupid.

The autopilot said we were heading south—all the way south. And what did we hope to find there? The entrance to purgatory, which—if I was going to keep things simple—appeared to be somewhere near the hole in the ozone layer over the Antarctic.

VI

SANTA TURNED OFF THE AUTOPILOT AS WE CROSSED THE ROSS ICE SHELF, and shortly thereafter he adjusted a couple of dials and pulled back on the sled's stick. Our heading changed, and the sun, perpetually parked overhead at this time of year, filled the cockpit with its orange glow. The material of the cockpit blister filtered just about every sort of wavelength but the visible spectrum, and even under that radiant bombardment, it polarized sharply to cut the glare. Santa flipped a few more switches, and then hit the red button that switched on the Time Clock Wave Generator. The TCWG was a localized field generator that kept the sled and team in sync with the Clock at Zero Hour. It shouldn't have done anything without the Clock on—the wave generated by the device would collapse almost instantly on its own—but Santa directed my attention to the column of white light that was now visible. "There," he said. "That's the way."

"Yeah, I see it," I replied. I didn't know what else to say, really. The Time Clock wave had shifted us out of sync enough to reveal the entrance to purgatory—the quintessential tunnel of light. It didn't disappear into infinity; in fact, it didn't look much longer than the car wash at any local gas station. As Santa piloted the sled into line with the glittering mouth of the tunnel, there was a wrenching sense of vertigo as I looked up the shaft of light. From the mouth of the tunnel, it certainly looked like it went on to forever.

Santa maneuvered the sled right into the center of the tunnel, and toggled the afterburners. The Mark V rumbled beneath us. Everything went black for an instant as the intensity of the light increased and the polarization sensors in the cockpit tried to compensate. There was an awkward sensation of weightlessness coupled with the disorienting panic of all the individual cells in my body trying to move in eighteen different directions at once, and then the ride became smooth again. Ridiculously smooth, even.

Transparency returned to the cockpit blister. We weren't over the South Pole any longer. There was no sky, no cloud cover below us, no hot sun sizzling in space over head. Everything was white. There was no horizon because there was no sense of ground beneath us. It was all just white.

Expect for a small patch of green and brown off to our left.

Santa had already spotted it, and he adroitly turned the sled towards the splash of color. I found the controls for the camera systems and pulled up the nose camera, dialing in the magnification. There was a small field of green grass, and sitting primly in the center of this seemingly unsupported green field was a small brown house. Large windows looked back at us and there was a wide set of double doors. Illumination spilled out from the interior of the building, revealing a pleasant arrangement of comfortable chairs. Some of the seats near the windows were filled with people in white robes.

Santa carefully brought the sled down toward the lawn, and there was a tiny rumble beneath me as the landing gear reached out and made contact with the ground. "Well," he said, pushing the sequence of buttons that locked the sled in place. "It looks like we're here."

"Here being a relative term," I pointed out as he cycled the hatch. The air was cool and there was a lingering smell that reminded me of the way the Residence smelled when Mrs. C was baking something in the kitchen. Santa let me go first, so I went carefully, not quite sure what I was going to step on. It looked like grass and seemed to be supporting the weight of the sled, but part of my brain still thought I was going to fall right through the illusion as soon as my foot touched the ground.

The grass was firm but spongy, kind of like the surface of a well-groomed Chia Pet. I took a couple of hesitant steps, wondering if the sensation in my knees was what Neil Armstrong felt when he first cavorted on the surface of the moon.

"Nice lawn," someone said. "Seems familiar, though . . ."

Rudolph was big, even by reindeer standards, and his dark body was completely hairless. His horns were bone white and sprouted out of his head like awkward tree branches caught naked in the midst of winter. Back in '64, there had been an accident with the old Clock—the nuclear powered one—and we had lost the entire reindeer team. Santa had been down in a house at the time or he would have been baked into Santa Strips. Rudolph should have died with the rest of the team too, but for some reason—maybe he had been far enough away from the Clock that the radiation dose hadn't been enough to kill him outright—he survived. Though, if the Eyes Only NPC reports filed by the Old Quacks from that era were to be believed, he was permanently irradiated. There was no question he stopped clocks when he passed—delicate machinery broke down if it spent too much time in close proximity to him, and if you left a frozen burrito in the same room with him for ten minutes, it'd be warm and ready to eat. He could—if he wanted—make his nose glow, just like the kids expected. Of course, he usually set the drapes on fire and rendered the dog sterile when he lit up, but hey, everything's got a side effect these days, so why should being bathed in the ruby glow of a reindeer's nose be any different?

He was, like the rest of Santa's reindeer, a complete pain in the ass. More so, because he was like that stereotypical old fart who was always yelling at the damn kids to get off his lawn. He wasn't our favorite reindeer.

Well, Mrs. C liked him. And no one really ever said "no" to Mrs. C.

I ignored Rudolph and his weird black humor, and stumped towards the pair of doors. Santa chuckled behind me, but even his famous joviality seemed subdued. The doors of the building opened smoothly as I approached, and I paused on the threshold as the warmth and smell of the shop washed over me.

"Smells just like—" Rudolph began.

A robed figure with sandals and close-cropped white hair swooped up to meet us. He looked like one of those vampire kids that were still popular among the teen readers—seventeen going on a hundred and sixty—and his teeth were somehow whiter than his robe. Pinned over his left breast was a tiny sword-shaped brooch. The blade was outlined in orange. On his right pectoral was a tiny stick-on nametag. It read: Mike.

"Hello," he gushed. "Welcome to Café Perkatory."

"—coffee," Rudolph finished.

"Are you here for a beverage?" the old young man asked. "I don't mean to brag, but our coffee is simply the most divine blend."

"Shade grown on the hills of Oaxaca?" Rudolph asked.

The greeter wrinkled his nose at the hairless reindeer. "Good guess, but no. We carry GOB, exclusively." He waved a hand over towards the counter. "Right over there. Just tell the barista what you want. Latté, mocha, cappuccino, brevé—whatever you desire, they can make it for you."

"GOB?" Santa whispered to me out of the corner of his mouth.

"God's Own Bean," I whispered back, somewhat appalled that the translation of the three letter acronym had come so quickly to me. That said something about how long I had been in the corporate world. Talk about purgatory.

Our host was still chatting with Rudolph. "If I had to guess," Mike said, "I'd peg you as a quad grande skinny extra whip caramel mocha."

Rudolph let out a short bark. "Oh, you can see right through me, can't you?" he tittered in a voice that made my sphincter pucker. Seriously? Do not tease the irradiated reindeer.

Santa—exuding some of that natural serenity that made standing in line to get your picture taken on his lap seem like the most pleasant afternoon ever—laid a hand on the reindeer's tense flank. "Do you offer other services?" he asked. "Is this café wired for the Internet?"

The greeter flashed his pearly whites again. "Absolutely." He pointed towards the far wall where a computer monitor sat on a walnut desk. "The terminal over there is plugged right into a 10GbE backbone. No firewall filtering, anonymous remailer services, no cookie presets, no popup advertising, and—" he winked at Santa "—no site or download restrictions."

He smiled down at me. "And you, young man, what about you? Are you here for Passage?" There was something in his eyes—was it a touch of sorrow?—as he asked.

"No," I stammered. "No, I'm not." I jerked a thumb at Santa. "I'm with him."

The moment of human empathy passed on Mike's face, replaced by a confused expression that made him seem younger. He looked out at the spoon-shaped sled parked on the lawn. "None of you are here for Passage? Someone still in your conveyance, perhaps?"

Rudolph shook his head. "Well, we do have some friends along but they wanted to wait in the car."

Santa's hand moved to my shoulder, and he pushed me towards the monitor in the back of the room. Rudolph stayed behind to torment the greeter. "It's the craziest thing," I heard him say, "none of us are dead. I don't know where we took the wrong turn, and I'm really surprised you don't recognize me . . ."

Santa kept me on course through the maze of plush chairs. A large fireplace was quietly chewing through a pile of logs. The trio of individuals behind the counter were dressed like the host— just as androgynous and just as perfectly formed. In addition to offering espresso drinks, they also had a fully stocked bakery and ice cream parlor. The people scattered about in the chairs all had full beverage at their elbows and were contentedly thumbing through glossy magazines. None of them appeared too concerned with the large red "Now Servicing" number on the wall—and I did a double-take when I realized it was showing a rather large number in scientific notation. And no one even glanced at the unmarked white door at the back of the room. To me, it was almost impossible not to look at. Was that the door to . . . ?

Santa pulled me back from the door and shoved me into the chair at the computer station. "Okay," he said, his hands resting on my shoulders. "This is what we came here for."

The screen saver was the floating logo of the coffee house—a flat-rimmed espresso cup with wings—and it vanished when I touched the mouse. I poked around on the desktop and checked out a few menu options. It seemed like some homegrown UI over a modified LINUX OS, but I hadn't seen the variant before. Santa's hands tightened on my shoulders when my movements faltered. "What is it?" he hissed.

"It's a dummy terminal," I said. I pointed at the thick cable that ran from keyboard into a port in the wall. "There's no computer here. It is just a keyboard and monitor that do I/O for a larger system that's somewhere else." I lifted the keyboard and showed him the blank top of the desk. "And there's no sticky note."

"But what about the computer that this is connected to?" Santa asked.

I poked around a bit more. "This is just a glorified Internet browser, Santa. There isn't much else here."

He bent over and his voice was tense in my ear. "Can you get a terminal window?" His hand was a claw digging into my collarbone.

I fussed around a bit, and discovered that I could—in fact—get a terminal window open. "Huh," I said, somewhat surprised at the glaring hole in the system's security.

"That's it," he hissed. "Come on, Bernie. I know that's all the opening you need. I've heard the stories. I know you can do this."

I looked up at the glittering light reflected in his eyes, and felt the tension in his fingers. This was one of those defining moments, wasn't it? Nothing else mattered, and what happened next would shape untold generations to come. Or some such silliness. Right here. Right now. You either took the chance, or spent the rest of your life wondering what would have happened.

A voice in my head—the part of me that was holding out against the whole Stockholm Syndrome scenario—tried to get my attention. Something wasn't right . . .

I took a deep breath, pushing that voice away, and put my fingers on the keyboard.

VII

It only took me a little over an hour to break into purgatory.

Rudolph grew tired of playing with Mike and had joined us at the terminal. With both he and Santa blocking the view of curious onlookers—should any of those in the café show the slightest inclination to be curious—I was able to focus on doing some pretty illicit hacking. The sort that Santa had heard stories about.

I hated to admit it, but Santa had been right: this terminal did connect to the purgatory mainframe. While most of the UI was all about shoving a browser at you, command line access was available, and like Santa showed us every year, all you need is an open window. The rest is just being smarter than the code separating you from the data. We elves may be small, but we make up for that lack of stature by knowing how to play dirty. No one would call my ad hoc code pretty, but it worked. *Pluralitas non est ponenda sine neccesitate* and all that.

"Okay, here we go," I said as my tiny terminal window took over the entire monitor and data started spooling past. "The data warehouse here appears to hold records for every being that has received—well, for lack of a better word—Passage. Which makes—"

"The café is a waiting room," Santa said.

"Yep," I said. "It certainly looks that way. You have your tunnel of light, a cozy waiting area while your life is being weighed and

36

considered, and then"—I glanced over at the white door—"off you go. Headed for your final destination." I tapped a few keys, making the data stop and start.

Rudolph snorted. "One express elevator to hell coming up."

Santa ignored him. "How long, Bernie? How long do you sit out here before you go on? What happens next?"

I wasn't entirely sure what the data was telling me. Some of the fields were a bit cryptic. "It looks like there's a transition period," I said. "Thirty days or so."

"Thirty days," he said, his face breaking into that quintessential grin. "It takes thirty days before you complete Passage."

"I think—" I started.

"He's still in there," Santa said to Rudolph. "We can get him out." He tapped his throat comm several times, and his smile dissolved. "Comm link is dead."

"Figures," Rudolph snorted. "I bet this whole place is a giant Faraday cage." He turned toward the front door of the café. "I'll get the others."

The last line of data on the screen started with "David Anderson," and I quickly memorized the long alphanumeric sequence that followed.

Santa laid a hand on my shoulder. "Thanks, Bernie. I know I've put you in a bad position, and I promise I'll make everything right with the NPC when we get back. I'll tell them that you were coerced, that you strenuously argued against this course of action. Just relax here. Get yourself a cinnamon roll or something." He nodded towards the white door. "The reindeer and I can take it from here." He glanced over his shoulder and lowered his voice. "We're, you know, going to bring him back."

Like I hadn't been paying attention. I hit a complicated key sequence, and the terminal window vanished. "And how you propose to do that?" I said. "Do you know where he is?" All my code was gone from local memory. I hit three more keys and the screen saver came back on, the winged cup banging around the edges of the screen like a blind turtle.

Santa's eyes went from my fingers to the screen. "Wait. What happened?"

"It's time to go home, Santa. This has gone on long enough," I said. "It's time to head back to the North Pole. We've got to get ready for Zero Hour."

Santa looked at me closely, studying my eyes. I tried not to blink. "Bernie. Why did you wipe the screen? I need to know where he is."

I shook my head. "Not on my watch."

"Make it come back," he said.

"No."

"Bernie," he said, looming over me. He tried to glare at me, but it didn't take, and after a second, he tried a different tack. "It doesn't matter," he said. "We're going in."

"And what's going to happen in there? Do you have any idea where David Anderson is?"

"We'll find him."

"How?"

"We'll figure it out," Santa growled. "Rudolph and the others will come up with something."

"Seriously? You're going to let them figure out how to extract a dead guy from heaven?"

Santa squinted at me, suddenly catching a hint of the angle I was playing. "This isn't part of the plan, Bernie. I can't be responsible for anyone who isn't totally committed."

"I will be committed when I get back. They'll stamp my chart *Certifiable*. But until then, I'm riding along." I tapped my head. "You could hack in yourself, but it would take you and the reindeer, what, a couple of hours? I don't think you have that kind of time. Right now, I've got that information in my head, and the only way I'm going to share it is if you take me along."

Rudolph clattered up, a leather satchel slung across his withers. "Hey," he said. "What's the hold-up? It's going to get a little crowded in here in a second. Someone is going to get curious about all of—" He jerked his head toward the parade of reindeer that were wandering into the café.

Santa turned his head. "Bernie wants to go along."

I nodded. "That's right. You two need a chaperone. Someone with a lick of sense."

Rudolph rolled his eyes. "Great. Munchkin here wants to sit at the Big People table. Can't we just clock him on the head again?"

"You could, but I've got David Anderson's location up there. You want to risk scrambling it?"

Rudolph looked at Santa. "You didn't write it down?"

"There wasn't time," Santa said. "I didn't think he'd pull this stunt."

"I warned you, didn't I?," Rudolph said. "But you never listen to me, do you?" Behind him, reindeer were queuing up at the white door. They were covered in white sheets, looking like lumpy ghosts with horns. "We're going. There isn't time to stand around and yak like a couple of cows." He nodded at me. "Get the information from him or bring him along. Those are your choices. Quit talking about it."

"He won't tell me," Santa said. "What do you want me to do, torture him?"

"Worked for the Inquisition."

"I can't torture an elf, Rudolph."

"You're soft, Fat Boy," Rudolph snapped. "We should leave you behind too. Are you going to be a liability in there?"

Santa shook his head. "But what about Bernie? He's baggage, and we're traveling light. We don't need him."

"Sounds like we do." Rudolph stamped his right hoof. "Get on, Bernie. You're with me."

I gulped and pushed the chair away from the desk. Using the chair as a step ladder, I clambered onto Rudolph's broad back. His skin was warm and moist to the touch. I wrapped my hands in the satchel's leather strap. My mouth was dry.

"This is a bad idea," Santa warned.

Rudolph snorted. "Just add it to the list of bad ideas you've had tonight." He clattered towards the white door, and with deft placement of a hoof, he swept the door open. "Come on," he said, looking back at Santa. "Clock's ticking."

I winced at his choice of words as the reindeer started filing through.

Santa was the last in the reindeer train to cross the threshold, and he glared at Rudolph as he stomped past. Rudolph shouldered the door wide and clattered after him. Behind us, I heard someone's voice calling out. "Ah, excuse me? Excuse me?" It sounded like Mike, but whatever else he had to say was cut off as the door shut solidly behind Rudolph.

"Don't be a pain in the ass," Rudolph said to me. "Be useful or I'll leave you here. Okay?"

I swallowed. "Okay." I noticed there was no handle on this side of the door.

The room beyond the café was white. Not as white as the atmosphere that we had flown through, but still whiter than any antiseptically sterile hospital ever built. Of course, the angelic host probably had on hand a fleet of ascended housekeepers who actually enjoyed their work, and I was willing to bet the solvents in heaven were a little stronger than the kind you could get at the local drug store. Still, it was white enough to induce a headache.

The reindeer shrugged off their draped sheets, and I stared, slack-jawed, at what I saw. Each animal sported a strange assortment of machinery and wires arrayed throughout their horns. All the cables and wires led back to sleek pods, slung like saddlebags across their backs, but with more straps and buckles to hold them in place. Each pod had one or more nozzle or barrel poking out of its front. Vixen turned his head towards me, and I caught the glare of laser light from a rangefinder attached to one of his horns. With a tiny whine, a translucent orange panel slid in place over his right eye. He looked at me, and a nozzle on one of his pods extended slightly and pointed in my direction. "Check," he said.

The rest of the reindeer powered up their gear too, calling out as their systems came online.

"Right," Santa said. "Let's go."

Rudolph—and I—took point, trotting down the single hallway that led away from the entry room.

"You going to tell me where we're going?" he asked.

"That's a lot of guns," I said, my attention still caught up in all the machine guns, flamethrowers, rocket launchers, and who knew what else the reindeer were carrying.

Rudolph shrugged, a slight bump in his gait. "Be prepared. That's our motto."

"That's the Boy Scout motto."

"Who do you think gave it to them?"

"Who are you going to shoot?"

He turned his head so I could see the look in his eye.

"Never mind," I said, suppressing a shudder. "5.CXLIII. XLVIII.2.LXXVIII.XXI."

"You know what it means?" he asked.

"Location code, I assume."

We passed into a large octagonal chamber with high ceilings. Diffuse light dripped from the porous stone overhead. The hall-ways leading off from this room looked identical to the one we had just traversed.

Santa was bringing up the rear, and when he reached the chamber and saw the seamless similarity to all the passages, he dug out a stick of the camouflage grease paint and made a mark on the wall next to the passageway leading back. "Which way?" he asked.

"Bernie?" Rudolph asked.

It occurred to me that Santa's choice of the black BDU and camouflage grease paint hadn't been the best fashion choice for this mission. The only parts of him that blended in at all with his surroundings were his hair and beard. Rudolph caught me staring and sighed. "I know. He's like this at the mall too; can't blend in for shit."

There was another mark on the wall, though—one that hadn't been put there by Santa. Above the lintel of the portal near Santa was a recessed number, and as I looked around the room, I saw that each door had a number. They ran from zero to eight. *Keep it simple*, I thought, running through the sequence of numbers I had just rattled off to Rudolph. I pointed to the door marked with a 5. "That one."

Rudolph whistled to the rest of the team as he jumped for portal number five. There was something strangely non-Euclidean about the hallway. It was about the same width as the previous passage—not much more than two reindeer wide—and appeared to run straight forever, but my stomach made strange motions like it was being pulled in different directions as Rudolph jogged along. Illumination seemed to increase just ahead of us, and looking back, I could see about ten meters behind Santa, who—I noted—had already fallen a bit behind Dasher, the last reindeer in the pack.

Rudolph stood, sniffing the air, as we waited in the next chamber for the others to catch up. Santa trotted in a good ten seconds after Dasher, and unlike the reindeer, he looked like he was getting a good workout. He leaned against the wall a little longer than necessary when he made his mark.

Blitzen wandered up, the open muzzle of his mini-gun brushing my leg. "I don't think Fat Boy's ready for the New York Marathon," he pointed out. Unlike the other reindeer, he was wearing a pair of actual glasses. Black, horn-rimmed. Like he was some sort of librarian or something. A tiny data feed streamed along the bottom of each lens.

"It's not part of his regimen," I said. "More strength training. Not that much cardio."

"He's going to keep falling behind," Blitzen said. "And if we have to sprint . . . "

"You want to carry him?" Rudolph asked.

"Just making an observation. I'm not volunteering." Blitzen nodded at Donner. "That's his job." Donner was larger and broader than Rudolph, and he wore a red bandana. Unlike the others, he wasn't carrying pods—he had a pair of what looked like Hellfire air-to-surface missiles. I suppose maybe the bandana was a way to let the other reindeer know he was not to be messed with. In case the Hellfire missiles weren't warning enough. Donner saw us looking at him, and after a quick glance back at Santa, rolled his eyes and shook his head.

"We keep this quiet; no one will have to worry about breaking any land speed or dead lift records. Okay?" Rudolph said.

Blitzen gave us the librarian glare over the rim of his glasses as I did a quick scan for the shadow numbers over the portals. There were only six portals in this chamber, and I couldn't see any reason why we were short two. As I was squinting in the perpetual light, a watery aquamarine light started to fall, a thin rain ghosting not far from Comet's head. He jerked away from it, the twin muzzles of his guns whining as they targeted the glow. The light remained innocuous, hanging in space, filling and emptying like a recycling waterfall. It took a bit of imagination to see it, but I could make out two numbers flowing through the blue, one bleeding into the other like an hourglass chamber empties and fills again when you invert the glass. One number was a V and the other was CCXXV.

And as if made more real by my apprehension of it, the blue light started to fill the room. It wasn't a gas or a mist, but rather a sensation of change that seeped into the chamber. As the room filled, turning everyone a slight shade of blue, a sharply delineated series of floating cubes became visible—their edges touched and gilded with a dark indigo. This cube of cubes floated in the center of the chamber, and the reindeer moved back unconsciously from the floating grid, especially after Dasher brushed one and its center turned a vibrant orange. The other cubes in the block faded, as if trying not to draw attention to themselves.

"Okay, smart guy," Rudolph said. "You're the expert."

"Me?" I wondered. "How am I the expert?"

"Virtue of having a number in your head. You were the one yammering about having geek knowledge. Time to share."

This chamber had fewer ways in and out, and I read the numbers over the six portals again, reading the Roman and Westernizing them in my head: 0, 218, 219, 226, 232, and 233. And, finally, I spotted the last two numbers I had been expecting. They were on the ceiling and floor: 176 and 274, respectively. Once I had seen them, I could make out the faint shape of the closed doors. These doors weren't open portals like the others but rather slightly wavering rectangles of heat stroked air.

Rudolph and the rest were all still waiting for me to crack this mysterious code, and I kept getting distracted by Cupid, who was sniffing at the floating grid structure. The cubes glowed and faded as his nose moved back and forth between individual points on the outer edge of the shape, and I realized it was a seven by seven by seven shape. "It's seven cubed," I said. "Seven to the third power."

"Seven is the number of religion," Blitzen said, quickly jumping at the opportunity to talk about one of his favorite subjects. "The relationship of Man—his spirit and soul—to the universe is represented through the cube—a seven-sided figure."

"There are only six sides to a cube," Cupid counted.

"There are seven points, seven facets, in fact," Blitzen said. "The outer sides and a inner center point. The correspondences depend on your religious inclination, but they can be reduced to a rather archaic axiom: the center is the father of the directions, the dimensions, and the distances."

Dasher snorted and shook his head, as if all this knowledge was making him sneeze. "I liked it better when we didn't have Internet access at the Pole," he said. "He was much less obnoxious when all we had was Mrs. C and her library card."

"Yeah, but that would mean no streaming TV," Dancer pointed out. "We'd have to wait for it all to come out on DVD."

"The seventh point is the center," I said, hauling the conversation back to the topic at hand. "What do you put in the center? What do you put in a box?"

"A soul?" Santa offered.

I nodded at him. "That's it. These numbers are like IP addresses for computer systems. Each individual, each cell, has a specific address that is unique to his or her location. The series of numbers tells you exactly where that person is within the larger structure." I pointed to the flickering numbers. "We must be in the 225th chamber of that grid, and from here we can get to other points in the structure. Each layer contains forty-nine chambers, and there are seven layers." I did a little bit of math in my head. "Which puts us on the fifth layer down. Right on the outer edge."

Cupid was pretty good with the new math too, and he figured out which cube I was talking about and approached it carefully, lighting it up. "From here," I said, "we can move along this same plane." I pointed at one of the doors. "Which is why there are only six doors, five directions from here—north, northeast, east, southeast, and south—and one door back the way we came. If we wanted to move up in the grid to the fourth layer, we'd go through the ceiling."

Santa nodded. "And if we wanted to reach the sixth layer, we'd use the floor." He continued to bob his head. "Think in three, lads."

"Three," as in three dimensions. Of course Santa would orient himself to the grid layout. He had to have a keen sense of navigation in order to find his way through some of the more modern urban landscapes. "So where are we going, Bernie?"

"One forty-three," I said.

Santa snapped his fingers at Cupid. "Up two levels and into the SE corner," he said without a second's thought. Cupid skirted the wavering rectangle in the floor to nose at a higher block on the outer edge of the other side of the floating cube.

"This one?" the reindeer asked. Santa and I both nodded.

Direction and destination. Everyone likes to know where they're going on a field trip.

VIII

"**D**OES IT BOTHER YOU THAT WE HAVEN'T SEEN ANYONE?" BLITZEN ASKED AS he jogged alongside Rudolph. We had just left 5.CXLII, on our way to 5.XCLIII.

"Why would we?" I asked. I had been doing some math while Rudolph had been trotting along the endlessly unremarkable corridors. "If there are seven layers, and each one contains up to 343 chambers, we're talking about more than 2,400 chambers. And the location address has six values, so if the same ordering system persists, you're talking a very large number of single points." Somewhere along the way, the math had gotten hard, and I had started dropping numbers. Not enough fingers. "Billions, I suppose."

"Like, a one-to-one ratio for every soul that ever lived," Blizten pointed out with a knowing nod, as if he had been waiting for me to catch up.

Rudolph skidded into the next chamber and nodded towards the glittering water droplet that formed in the air. "Looks like we're here. Now what?"

"A one-to-one ratio," I said, still grappling with the implications of what Blitzen had just said. "You know how immense this place must be?"

Rudolph twitched his shoulder, trying to shake me out of my mental rabbit hole. "You must have been one of those kids who tried to think about what it was like to own a million marbles. How big would your house have to be to hold to them all."

I bristled. "Yeah, maybe. So?"

"You could only hold fifteen in your hands at any one time, so what did it matter how many you could pile in the corners?" He snorted. "Focus, Bernie. We only want one guy. Not the entire historical population of China."

"Right, right." I tried to get away from the all-encompassing hugeness of the structure. I had an address. There was no way to craft a linear system to store all this information, a three-dimensional shape was required. But even that was too limiting, too finite, when you got right down to the math. I mean, you would run out of numbers eventually, right?

The rest of the team was piling into the chamber as I slid down from Rudolph's back and approached the center of the chamber. The grid of cubes was glowing in the faint light, the indigo edges of the shapes flickering and turning in the light. "Five. One forty-three." That's where we were, but the numbering system continued; there were still four levels to go.

"Forty-eight," I said, pitching my voice across the room. The cube of cubes shivered and spun, turning on its horizontal axis and pitching itself towards me. It rotated sharply, the top line peeling open, and when it reached a ninety-degree rotation, it stopped. The top plane was leaning toward me, and a single cube on its surface was glowing orange. It was within reach, and like a child who has never been burned before, I touched it.

The orange glow increased as the rest of the structure around it began to fade. The indigo edges separated and sprang outward in geometrically predetermined paths. I stepped back as the orange glow filled the now two-dimensional shape. There was a click that I felt in the bones of my jaw, and then the orange light vanished. All that remained was a door—a one-sided door, but a door nonetheless. "Forty-eight," I said, pointing at the faint notation carved into the door at the top. "Halfway there, is my guess."

"We're supposed to go through that door?" Comet asked, peering at the back side of the free-standing door.

"I suppose so," I said, glancing over at Rudolph.

"You first," the reindeer said.

I sighed and reached for the doorknob. I was expecting some sort of shock, but the handle was cool and turned easily. What I saw on the other side looked like an identical chamber, but when I stepped through, all of the reindeer vanished. I could see Rudolph and Comet when I looked back through the open door, but the rest of reindeer and Santa—who I knew were clustered around the door but out of direct sight—weren't there.

I was somewhere else, but I hadn't felt any sort of transition or change as I had crossed the threshold. I was just . . . here now.

I got out of the way as the others filed through. There were seven doorways leading off this room, the eighth being the one through which we had all just come. Over the door was an orange-tinged "0" and the other doorways were marked "1" through "7."

"It's just like the beginning," said Santa. He snapped his fingers at me. "Bernie, you said we were halfway there. That was a six point location code you were spouting earlier, wasn't it?"

I nodded and rattled it off for him again.

He pointed to the second door. "It's a layer within a layer. I got it now. Seven series of seven by seven by seven. And once you pass through the orange door, it repeats itself. It's like a Mandelbrot structure: the greater the magnification, the more area you discover. We need to hit the second cube, the seventy-eighth chamber of that lattice—" He flashed us a tired smile. "—and there I'm guessing we'll find another floating cube with another three hundred forty-three chambers. And it'll be the twenty-second one that will have our boy."

"Dig," Cupid concurred. "It's like God's Own Pachinko machine."

I grabbed the strap of the leather satchel on Rudolph and scrambled onto his back. "Let's keep moving," the hairless reindeer said. "We'll have all year to unpack the theory." His hooves clattered against the floor as he made for the door that would take us to the second lattice.

IX

I HAD TO GIVE SANTA CREDIT. HE CERTAINLY SEEMED TO HAVE FIGURED OUT the organization of the lattices of purgatory. Entering the second cube, we found ourselves in chamber LVII, and it was pretty easy to follow the Roman numbers on the walls to LXXVIII. We all gathered in the last chamber as the blue light outlined the floating grid of the last numbers in the location code series. 5.CXLIII.XLVIII.2.LXXVIII.XXI.

Santa approached the hovering shape and said the number that he wanted. The cube twisted and opened under his touch and dropped a hanging door in the center of the room.

This door was locked.

The edges of the indigo outline still held some of the orange coloration, sparking and jetting tiny strips of color. Centered in the smooth portal was a large seal, infinitely textured and raised in a very specific pattern.

Naturally, Blitzen recognized it.

"Great Seal," he said. "Kind of like the ones in the last chapter of the Big Book."

"Which book?" Cupid asked.

"Revelation. You know, the seven seals that are opened on Judgment Day."

Santa looked at me. "I thought you said purgatory was a holding station. They held them for thirty days, and then they go to their final destination."

49

I raised my hands as I slid off Rudolph's back. "Wait a minute. That's what the system said."

"You sure the thirty days wasn't referring to the transference of paperwork?"

I opened my mouth, closed it, and opened it again, but no words came out.

"Great," Rudolph said, "the bureaucratic elf makes a paperwork error. Anyone surprised?"

I wasn't sure: that's the only thing I was sure about. Yes, it took thirty days for the request for Passage to be processed. But Santa was right. What did that mean? Was the paperwork a formality? Had I made the mental jump to pay $50 and get out of jail at the end of three turns on my own?

"That's what Judgment Day is all about," Blizten said. "Judging."

"Really?" Rudolph asked.

Blizten ignored him. "All the souls who haven't been formally condemned or accepted are granted release at that time and they pass into the next realm when the final trumpet sounds." He nodded at the Seal. "This may be one of those. His paperwork is in transit, but David Anderson may be waiting for the Final Judgment before his Passage happens. This door may not open until then."

"That kind of puts a damper on things, doesn't it?" Cupid pointed out.

"How long till Judgment Day anyway?" Dasher wanted to know.

"More than twenty-four hours," I said, my eyes on Santa. "It's got to be past midnight," I said softly. "It's got to be Christmas Eve now. It's time to go home."

Santa didn't reply, which wasn't terribly surprising, given the situation. He stared at the seal, chewing on the end of a mustache. I could see the frustration clearly in his eyes. To have come this far and—

"Hey, code warrior," Rudolph snapped.

"What?" I turned toward him. "Me?"

The big reindeer dropped his head and pointed at the door with his antlers. "Front and center. You wanted to tag along and be useful. Now's your chance."

I deferred, pointing over my shoulder at Santa. "No, I wanted to keep him from hurting himself."

"That's what you'll be doing by getting that door open," Rudolph said.

"Open?" I squeaked.

"Look at Prince Charming there. You think he's going to call it quits now?"

I didn't need to look at Santa to know the answer to that question. "How am I supposed to open it?" I asked.

"Try using the razor sharp power of your intellect," offered Rudolph. "Come on, binary monkey. It's just a lock. We're heard about you and security systems."

My ears burned. "It's a hobby," I said.

"So's masturbation," Rudolph replied, "But not nearly as useful right now."

He had me there.

I stepped up to the door and examined the Great Seal: two concentric circles , divided by a ring of unknown script. The inner circle was cross-hatched with more symbols—lines and whorls that, if I had to guess, probably said: Do not open until Judgment Day.

"I'm not sure where to start," I admitted after a few minutes. Sure, I have a facility for languages, and most of the stories they tell about me breaking into things are true, but this script? It meant nothing to me. The only thing I had figured out was that the writing was textured differently than the smooth surface of the door. It was extruded like scar tissue on a Barbie's shoulder, and I reached out to touch it.

The electrical discharge knocked me across the room—a violent flash of blue fire that limned the outline of the Seal in an angry glow. I bounced off the far wall and rolled a few times, the seams of my clothes smoking. There was an immense ringing in my ears, and my vision was filled with wavy lines.

Comet leaned over, nosing me with his muzzle. A tiny spark leaped between us upon contact. "You okay?" he asked.

I had bitten my tongue hard enough to draw blood, and could only manage a thin squeak, like air leaking from a Mylar balloon.

"Well, I'm glad we got the obvious out of the way," Rudolph said. "Anyone one else have any bright ideas?"

No one said anything for a moment, and I pushed myself upright. The reindeer were standing around the floating Seal, and they were all trying not to look at each other. Comet looked like he was trying to calculate how many days until Judgment Day.

"Prancer," Santa said suddenly, firm and decisive—the way he sounded during Zero Hour flinging presents around. "Are those cutting lasers on your antlers?"

"Yes, sir," Prancer replied. "Nd:YAG."

"Perfect," Santa said. He snapped his fingers at the Seal. "Cut us a hole, son."

Prancer stepped up to the door. He turned on the laser cutters attached to the tips of his antlers and leaned in to situate the fiery points just outside the Seal. He rotated his head left and right, inscribing a tight circle, and the laser cutters left a dark mark on the door. A smell like scorched sand filled the room.

Prancer clicked the lasers off as he stepped away. The rest of us moved back as he put some distance between himself and the shining symbol. "Fire in the hole," he shouted as the pod strapped to his back irised open, and a slender tube popped out. There was a spark of fire back by his tail, and an RPG lanced forward in a gout of smoke.

There was a sound like lightning hitting the large tree out in the yard, followed by enough smoke to fill a goth concert in an underground bunker. I held onto the floor, waiting for it to stop rolling. Shapes moved in the smoke—shapes I assumed were reindeer. Comet lost his balance trying not to step on me and banged his head against the wall. A hoof caught me on the hip as he tried to stay upright.

A hole opened in the smoke, a whirlwind of moving air that revealed the shattered portal. The Seal was gone, and the door was open. Standing on the other side of the threshold was a thin man in a white robe. "Hello?" he said. "What's going on?"

Rudolph appeared out of the mist, and the guy startled at the sight of the hairless reindeer. "I'm Rudolph," he said, "I'm here with Santa."

The man's eyes were wide already, and they got wider. "Excuse me?"

"Santa Claus," Rudolph explained. "The guy in the red suit who delivers presents at Christmas?"

"Yes," the man said, "Yes, I know who Santa Claus is. But . . . but what are you doing here?"

"Your daughter made a request," Rudolph said. "We're here to take you home."

"Suzy?" His eyes watered. "My Suzy?"

I really wanted to enjoy this tender moment, but there was a persistent buzzing that kept distracting me. Almost like a flying insect. I brought up my hand and felt something prick my palm. I jerked my hand away from the sting.

A tiny winged cherub about the size of a large orange buzzed my head, stabbing at me again with his tiny sword. I ducked, trying to swat him away without getting stuck by his sword. There was a tiny trickle of blood on my palm where he had tagged me once already.

Comet danced past me, bumping me with his shoulder. A targeting eye-piece was lowered across his left eye, but the cherub was too small for him to get a decent lock. He couldn't get a clear shot.

The tiny angel came at me again, chattering and hissing like a deranged mouse.

Santa appeared out of the smoke, his cap gone and his white hair in wild disarray. The camouflage paint had run into his beard, and his sleeve was on fire. But his hand was steady. "Get down," he said, the large muzzle of the .45 pointed at my head.

I dropped to the floor as the gun went off. A tiny echo followed the report of the pistol, a thin whistle like someone had forgotten a tea kettle on a hot stove. The only remnant of the angel was a pair of tiny feathers drifting in the haze and a fading gleam of light.

"They know we're here," Santa shouted. "Go to Plan B."

"There's a Plan B?" Comet said.

I brushed the cherub feathers from my shoulder. "Run like hell is my guess," I muttered.

A keening buzz like a thousand hornets singing backup for an Irish pipe band filled the room. Tiny bubbles started to pop in the smoky air, bursting like soap in a Calgon bath, and each bubble released an angry, sword-wielding cherub. A squadron of the miniscule angels dive-bombed Comet, and he reared back, triggering both of his mini-guns.

The cherubs moved like hummingbirds on crack, but their rapid ability to shift direction wasn't enough to avoid every single bullet thundering in their direction. He fired off four times as many rounds as there were chubby angels, and all that came down on him was a cloud of angel feathers.

There was more gunfire from across the room, and Prancer fired another RPG round, making lots of noise and smoke. Santa's hand fell on my shoulder. "Come on," he said. "Time to go." Rudolph grabbed a mouthful of David Anderson's robe and pulled the man out of his processing chamber. The hairless reindeer dragged him for a few steps until Mr. Anderson got the idea and found his own motivation to move.

Vixen triggered his flamethrower, illuminating the far side of the octagonal chamber and burning away some of the smoke. Something larger than a cherub caught the brunt of the blast, becoming a pillar of fire. The larger angel came on, and Dasher caught it from the side, tracers from his mini-gun rounds cutting holes through the smoke. The angel twisted and bucked, knocked around by the force of the bullets. The assault must have finally breached its body because it came apart suddenly, opening up and imploding like a balloon popping. For a split second, all that remained was an amber light, burning where the angel had vanished. Then it was gone.

The ruined portal to David Anderson's cell wavered then transformed back into the tiny cube within the floating grid as Mr. Anderson moved farther away from his waiting cell. The floating grid was quite evident in the smoke-filled room—the indigo outline of the boxes made each cube stand out. Rising up through the insubstantial lattice structure were more angels like the one the Dasher had just popped. Seraphim—if I had to guess, all clean, white marble wreathed in white streamers with stoic faces frozen with hard expressions.

We fell back from the 78th chamber; Dasher and Prancer brought up the rear, their weapons sporadically going off as a seraphim got too close. Rudolph slowed down long enough for me to get one foot in the strap of the satchel and he was off again, running down the hallway. Mr. Anderson was riding Vixen, and Donner didn't seem to be bothered by Santa's additional weight, even with the large missiles on his back.

I caught myself wondering if two Hellfire missiles were going to be enough . . .

We reached the outer edge of the second cube with only a couple of altercations. The cherubs were acting as spotters for the seraphim. When we entered one of the chambers, there was invariably a pair or three of the tiny winged angels, and they would immediately start piping their celestial alert. Santa had evidently been spending some time at a target range because he rarely needed more than a single shot to dispatch a cherub.

But they were waiting for us in the first room: a full rank of seraphim ranged in front of a line of solid stone pillars. Stubby wings jutted from the top of these massive columns, tiny wings that didn't look like they could lift a hamster, much less a three-hundred-pound block of stone. Blitzen was leading the team, and he slid to a frantic stop. "Thrones," he shouted. "We've got thrones."

"Get out of the way," Santa yelled from behind Rudolph and me. Rudolph put on a burst of speed and, as he entered the room, executed a tight turn. I stayed low and held on tight as centrifugal forces tried to tear me off his back. Rudolph didn't slow down; he dashed for the first door—the passage to the first cube—and Blitzen was right behind him.

Donner fired both of his missiles.

My head hurt from the sound as they streaked into the large chamber and impacted the assembled host. My skeleton ached as the shock wave threw me from Rudolph's back, and a good two years worth of memory cells in my brain burned out in a flash as I slammed against a hard surface. My sense of smell took an extended vacation, and I couldn't feel my toes. I just wanted to lie on the floor for about six weeks until my bones stopped hurting.

Blitzen kicked against the rippling wall, shaking his head. The mini-gun enclosure hanging across his left flank was twisted and bent. He frowned at the damaged gun. He couldn't see that his left ear had been torn as well, and it looked like the pain hadn't registered in his brain yet.

Rudolph had been scorched across his back, and he was favoring a rear hoof. He worked his jaw like there was something loose in his mouth that he couldn't quite get at. The leather satchel slung across his chest was askew and red light was bleeding from the top of the bag.

"You're leaking," I said, raising my voice over the ocean of sound still hammering in my skull.

Blitzen looked at Rudolph. "What is that?" He was shouting too. Or least it looked like he was. I could barely hear him.

The hairless reindeer looked down and saw the light. "Must have been cracked by the explosion."

"What? What cracked?"

"The old Clock," he said.

Blitzen took a step back. "The Nuclear Clock? I thought that had been dismantled after the accident."

Rudolph shook his head. "You think anyone knew how?"

Blitzen moved even farther away. "What are you doing with that?"

"Insurance policy. Donner shot off both his missiles," he said to Blitzen. "We're out of heavy armament. They're going to cut us off at the exit again. They'll be waiting. We're going to need an edge." Rudolph looked down at the bag, the red light shining against his nose. "Get the others. I'll lead."

"Don't worry. I'll definitely be behind you," Blitzen said. He nodded toward me. "Bernie, get this gun rack off me. I'll be your taxi."

"No argument there," I said. The Nuclear Clock had burned a whole team once before. I really didn't want to be anywhere close by when Rudolph decided to turn it on again.

X

BLITZEN EXPLAINED THE ANGELIC HIERARCHY TO ME AS WE DASHED ACROSS the first lattice of purgatory. The little ones were cherubs, evidently the messengers and scouts of the order. The larger ones with the long streamers and the unformed faces were seraphim, the first order of angelic creatures that were based on the shape of man, or rather, the template which God used when he formed mankind. Next on the list were the thrones, those creatures who were used to tear open mountains and hold back the seas.

After that would be dominations, was Blitzen's theory. And he was right.

And they were bullet proof.

Donner's Hellfire solution had cleaned out the top room of the second lattice, leaving long gouges in the walls and floor. The rainbow-colored streaks on the ceiling were the only remnants of what must have been the corporeal shells of the angelic host that had been waiting for us. Evidently a pair of AGM-114F Hellfire missiles with anti-ship HE-blast warheads was all the emphasis one needed to make your point in purgatory.

After that, the angels kept their distance, massing in large blocks on either side of our path. The dominations were tall and thin, and they shined like polished ceramic. The first time we encountered a foursome of them, Comet diverted from the group and let loose with both barrels. The room was filled with the spattering sound of ricocheting rounds as the tall angels stood firm and reflected all the metal being slung their way. They didn't come any closer, and Comet, not nearly as bulletproof, opted to not waste any more rounds. They made their point: beyond the dominations was out-of-bounds.

We were being herded towards the first chamber where the host would be waiting for us again. And I knew who they would be: the greeters.

All three were there, taller and more beautiful than they had been in the café, and their broad white wings stretched nearly to the ceiling of the chamber. Their robes sparkled with light as if they had been spun from strands of diamonds, and their eyes were filled with the visible spectrum. They had flaming swords and their expressions were resolute.

Michael—Mike—held up his hand as the team dashed into the room. The reindeer slid and scampered to a halt. "You may not leave," he said. "No one leaves purgatory."

"We're on a tight schedule," Rudolph said, and he ducked his head toward the flap of his satchel, catching the fabric in his teeth and tearing the bag open. A red radiance spilled out, followed by a narrow metal container. The cylinder had three bands of fading orange paint about its column, and the top was surmounted by a pair of large switches. The device hit the ground with a clang, and Rudolph kicked at the switches. "This is an express run. No stops, no services."

The Clock engaged, and everything froze for an instant. The air was thick and heavy. The red light spilling from the base of the cylinder took on a tactile weight, an ooze that leaked like blood across the floor. The flames of the angels' swords slowed to frozen streams of orange and yellow light.

"I don't know how long it'll run," Rudolph said, his voice slipping and slurring. "But I'm not sticking around to find out." He made a dash for the exit, past the trio of angels.

We were all slowed by the Nuclear Clock's field—its bubble outside of Time was only partially effective here. We weren't completely untethered from Time, but we were certainly operating at an angle to it, an angle much more acute than the angels'. Their movements were even slower than ours.

They could clearly still think just as quickly as we could because their movements shifted from completely clumsy to marginally accurate as they tried to stop us. A flaming sword, lined with slow fire, cleanly missed Comet's head, but Dasher had to dodge the angel's backswing. Santa caught an angelic blade on his pistol, and the weapon slowly spun out of his grip. Donner ducked the angel's arm and drove a heavy shoulder upward, knocking him aside. The angel fell back in slow motion, his wings curling around his body like a flower closing at night.

Michael wasn't at the top of the hierarchy because of his consummate skill at greeting folk at the door. He corrected quickly to the Time shift, and his aim became true. His hand came down on David Anderson as Vixen ran past, and the man had only a moment to open his mouth in alarm before he was pulled off the reindeer. Vixen felt the man's weight shift across his back, and he tried to turn around, but the angel's swift sword stroke brought him up short.

The other reindeer couldn't fire their weapons for fear of hitting David Anderson and they faltered, unsure how to proceed. David Anderson was trying to wriggle free of the angel's grasp. Santa was shouting something from the hallway back to the café. Vixen pranced about just beyond Michael's reach.

Rudolph came back at a full gallop, his hooves barely touching the ground. He leaped, clearing Michael's raised sword, his head nearly smacking into the ceiling. As he sailed over the angel's head, he kicked back with his hooves, striking Michael hard between the wings. He landed on the far side of the trio of angels. "Go!" he shouted. "There isn't any time. Go!" His face was flush in the light from the bleeding Nuclear Clock.

Vixen grabbed David Anderson while Comet and Dasher dropped crosshairs on Michael and opened up. Archangels were equally bulletproof, but the force of the rounds was enough to keep him off balance. Long enough for the rest of us to get into the hallway that led to the white door and the café.

The red glow faded as we ran, and the reindeer stumbled out of the Clock's field, and the ambient sounds scaled upward. Santa slid off Donner as we reached the end of the hallway, and the muscular reindeer lowered his head and plowed through the handleless door.

The team followed close on his hooves, leaping through the hole he had made. We were calling Michael's bluff.

It was chaos in the café: the patrons all scrambling for cover as Cupid emptied the rest of one of his guns at the big windows, clearing an easy egress for all of us. The reindeer bounced off chairs and tables, their hooves knocking against the wood and recklessly knocking aside cups and saucers.

I looked back as Blitzen jumped through the window. Comet and Dasher were right behind Santa. Smoke was billowing out of the ruined door, white and pink. The red light from the Clock was getting brighter. Santa dove through the window, tucking and rolling like a twelve-year-old Olympic gymnast as the back of the café exploded into a fountain of light.

"Move! Move! Move!" Santa shouted as he came to his feet, the security dongle from the sled in his hand. He auto-started the vehicle and shoved the staring Dasher towards the sled. "Don't look back, you idiots. Don't you read the stories?"

I hadn't, or at least, I didn't remember which stories Santa was referring to. I kept looking over my shoulder.

The fountain of light crackled and sparked as it ate the restaurant. As I watched, the computer station vanished, followed soon after by the bakery counter. The coruscating light snarled as it devoured everything it touched, like the sound of glass being ground beneath a steam roller, though magnified a few hundred times. The patrons of the café just stared at the light in wonderment as it rolled over them, dissolving them into its incandescent arc.

Santa shoved David Anderson up the steps of the sled, hollering at me at the same time. He didn't have to bother; I was right behind him. He shoved the other man into the navigator's seat on his way to the pilot's chair, and I hit the buttons to close the sled while grabbing the nearest protrusion to try to anchor myself. Santa yanked back on the stick, the powerful engines of the sled howling in protest. The sled tilted up as the roaring ball of light came after us, thrashing and glittering.

I felt the back end of the sled lurch suddenly, and then we punched through the film surrounding purgatory. The sky changed, and we were over the South Pole again, the white clouds beneath us, the black ceiling of night overhead. Just astern of the rapidly moving sled was a wound in the sky, a cascading stream of argent color. "Atmospheric phenomena," Santa said to David Anderson who was still staring at the play of light behind the craft. Santa punched the coordinates for Troutdale into the navigation system and throttled the engines fully up. "It's just a light show."

I couldn't look at it any more. I kept thinking about Rudolph.

XI

It snowed in Troutdale last night: three inches of fluffy stuff covering the trees with a coating that looked like powdered sugar on French toast. The orange and red light from the burning wreck of the Mark V sled pushed back the shadows fronting the houses along the road. Santa was halfway up the walk to the house, cradling his right arm against his chest. I had torn a long strip from Mr. Anderson's robe before shoving the befuddled man towards the front door of his house.

Santa pushed me aside as David Anderson stood on his own porch and rang the bell. There was already a light on upstairs. Santa's block-long crash landing had made quite the Christmas night racket.

We had made it to the 45th parallel before the engines flamed out. The reindeer bailed out, and Santa had managed to turn the last sixty miles into a long power glide. The sled had only bounced twice on the road before it was abruptly stopped by the pick-up truck. There was enough electrical equipment in the nose of the sled that it hadn't taken long for a stray spark to find the truck's punctured gas tank.

The porch light came on, and the door cracked open. David said something, and the door swung wide in response. A small girl, her red hair askew and her pajamas twisted, stood on the step. She was still half-asleep, but as Mr. Anderson bent down and swept her up in his arms, she came fully awake, shrieking with delight.

Santa smiled. There were tears in his beard, and I pressed the strip of white cloth against my face, forgetting that I had meant to offer it to Santa as a makeshift sling. The smoke from the fire was getting in my eyes.

Lights were coming on in the other houses as people crawled out of bed to see who was making all the clatter. I lowered the cloth and looked at the snow-covered street. The reindeer gathered around the burning wreckage, looking toward the house. Santa—streaked with soot and camouflage, his holster empty, his hair wild about his bare head—slumped to his knees, completely enraptured by the reunion on the front porch.

I heard sirens in the distance. "Uh, Santa," I said. "We need to go. We're kind of making a scene."

He sighed and winced as his arm moved. "It's Christmas, Bernie. Don't rush the miracle."

THE CRUSADE

I

THE STAFF OF THE LE GRAND COURLAN SPA RESORT ON TOBAGO RAKE THE beach before sunrise, and if you're the first guest out on the sand, it's like you're the only one in the whole world. You can slather on the sunscreen, lay out your towel, and get nice and comfortable before anyone else can shatter the illusion of absolutely perfect isolation and anonymity. I had been at the resort for two weeks, and this was my third day of snoozing the morning away on the bench. I had . . . well, I had many more days of this bliss ahead of me. And the best part about Tobago? It's near the equator. The weather never changes, even when the leaves change in the Northern Hemisphere and stores start putting up their—

"Santa wants to see you."

The voice wasn't from the hotel staff. None of them knew my background. I had come to the hotel during the flurry of guests showing up for the Heritage Festival, and I stayed when they all left. I was just an anonymous little person who was content to sit in the sun and drink caipirinhas all day. I tipped well; they left me alone. It was working out pretty well.

I tilted my head back and cracked open an eye. The large shape blocking the sun was four-legged, but I didn't see any footprints on the beach other than mine. It was as if the reindeer had plummeted straight down from heaven.

Which was more than a little true.

"Go away," I said, making a languid shooing motion that I had picked up from watching the European women by the pool. "I've retired, Rudolph."

"Is that what you're calling it?" Rudolph snorted as he ducked his head toward my glass. He tried to get at my drink but the mouth of the glass was somewhat narrow and his tongue was rather broad. "I heard the NPC has erased you from the boards."

"Semantics," I quibbled, frowning at the sight of all that reindeer tongue on the rim of my glass.

Rudolph bit off a chunk of the top and chewed the glass noisily.

We weren't sure what had happened in purgatory after Rudolph stayed behind to hold back the Heavenly Host while we made our escape. The week between Zero Hour and New Year's Day had been a blur: I was either numb from the endless interviews with Internal Affairs, or I was sitting alone in my room, numb from the grief of having lost Rudolph. I hadn't even liked him all that much, but his absence was a deep, dark hole in my soul.

And then, on New Year's Day, there he was, in the Parkwith the rest of the reindeer, as if nothing had happened. Sure, there were some burns on his hide, and a few of the points on his rack had been snapped off, but unless you had spent a lot of time with him recently, you probably wouldn't have noticed. And with the NPC in total Cover Our Collective Asses mode, *no one* noticed.

Rudolph bit off another section of my glass, and his tongue snaked down into the remaining liquid, questing for the wedge of lime at the bottom. "I wasn't going to finish that anyway," I said with a sigh.

He was different, though. Still irradiated. Still irritable. But there was something about him that was, for lack of a better word, purified. Like bits of him had been burned away during re-entry. Plus he appeared to have the stomach and appetite of a super goat.

"Santa's sick, Bernie," Rudolph said, garbling the words around a mouthful of glass. "Real sick."

I still dreamed of the snow, but it was only a dim recollection of the frozen miles between the North Pole and the smoke-stained edges of civilization. I was an elf without a home. The NPC had, in fact, stripped me of my union card, and I had been informed that

I was no longer welcome past the 60th parallel. They took the cost of a one-way bus ticket out of my last paycheck, and I had made the journey south like any other land animal.

Whatever. I was done with Christmas anyway.

Yet, here was Rudolph, dropping out of the sky like a lost satellite and ruining my vacation. What did I care about Santa being sick? Was he dying? Had he sent Rudolph to fetch me so that he could impart some final secret from his deathbed?

"I don't care," I said, though the gnawing burn in my stomach said otherwise. And it wasn't because I had had too many strips of bacon with my brandied crepes and peaches during breakfast. Sure, I had lost my union card and I couldn't work up north anymore, but it wasn't that. I had made someone a promise once.

At the Academy's graduation ceremony, Santa had personally given each one of us our pin. And I could recall that day clearly. He had been on his knees, working his way down the line of graduates. He put the pins on each of us, shook our hands, and looked us in the eyes when he said how proud he was to have us as Little Helpers. Yeah, I was young and eager and full of enthusiasm about being part of the team that made Christmas happen, and the whole ceremony was a bucket full of popcorn schmaltz, but I really felt like he meant what he said. To each and every one of us. And I had made a promise that afternoon in front of all my peers and my mom. I made a promise as I shook Santa's hand that I would never—never—let him down.

I felt the subharmonic ping in the base of my skull as we passed the outer markers at the 85th parallel, and Rudolph began his descent through the perpetual layer of clouds that wreathed the high latitudes. I was strapped to his back like a piece of cold pork, though I felt little of the outside temperature as I was wrapped up in a thermal radiation suit that was only a dozen sizes too big. After a few minutes of gliding, we broke through the clouds at the top of the world. Way off to the left, I could make out the tiny lights of some jumbo airliner on the polar route between America and Europe. We were only a few minutes from where Peary once thought he had reached the North Pole. I leaned forward, peering ahead for the telltale outlines of the Residence and the rest of the North Pole against the packed ice cap.

What I hadn't expected was a low-slung star hanging over the Residence. It couldn't be more than a hundred meters up, floating in place like some high-flying kite suspended perfectly overhead. As Rudolph flew closer, I could see that was some sort of glowing figure—like something that wouldn't have been out of place at the Macy's Thanksgiving Day parade.

Except this one had wings and a flowing white robe.

"Our own Star of Bethlehem," Rudolph quipped as he flashed over the southernmost fence of the Park and buzzed the floating figure. The glowing radiance was coming from the white halo parked over its skull like a ring of lucent fire. The smile painted on the helium-filled face was lopsided, which made it resemble something made by a team of asylum inmates rather than a cadre of dedicated kindergarteners.

The Residence was an eight-story knockoff of Frank Lloyd Wright's Fallingwater, though the interior looked as if it had been designed by Antoni Gaudí. While it was the primary residence of Santa and Mrs. C, it was also the central hub of the entire North Pole operation. There is a wing of guest rooms for visiting dignitaries, a conference hall/3D IMAX theater, an indoor swimming pool, tennis court, and four bowling lanes down in the basement. Radiating out from the Residence were the endless warrens of the entire production complex of the NPC. There wasn't much to see aboveground, but trust me when I tell you that the entire polar cap was riddled with tunnels. The Residence, however, was the only building architecturally designed for people over five feet tall.

Rudolph came around the floating balloon angel once more as he floated down to the balcony jutting out from the third floor of the Residence. He landed gently, and it felt like falling into a pile of fluffy snow. For a large reindeer, he moved with astonishing agility. He stepped lightly through the recent snowfall, and the security system of the Residence, reading his rather unique heat signature, opened a reindeer-sized door.

I fumbled with the zippers on the thermal suit as the warm blast of the climate-controlled environment melted the layer of ice on the suit. Inside, the Residence was dark, lit only by the reflected light coming in through the windows from the miles of snowpack surrounding the Residence as well as the dim glow from the angel's halo. The inside air was still, and I felt like we were secretly entering a hidden chamber in one of the pyramids at Giza.

Rudolph headed for the second floor. I had half-hoped that Rudolph's words had been a scam—a shameless attempt to retrieve me for other reasons—but as we came off the stairs, that hoped-rained away. We were heading for the infirmary, and the door at the end of the hall was partially open. Rudolph paused before the door, illuminated in the weak antiseptic light coming from the room beyond, and I felt his body tense beneath me.

I was suffering from a similar shortness of breath.

I thought of Schrödinger's experiment with the cat. The one where he posited that any observer couldn't know whether the cat was dead or alive until someone looked inside the box. What lay beyond the door in front of us was in that same quantum state—neither alive nor dead—until we entered the room. As soon as we peeked, the state solidified, and, well, in Schrödinger's case, the cat died.

Rudolph pushed his head against the door, and with a heavy step, we entered the infirmary. The walls and floors were ethereally white, and the bank of machinery next to the narrow bed was silent, the lines crossing the scopes flat and unmoving. Mrs. C sat on the edge of the bed, and she was as pale and devoid of color as the walls.

She raised her head as Rudolph came up to the bed, and her eyes were frozen chips of bent glass. "You just missed him," she said. "He might have been out there in the hall . . ."

I slid off Rudolph's back and approached the bed. Santa's skin was the color of fireplace ash, and his mouth hung open as if the muscles of his jaw had been severed. He had lost a lot of hair and most of his beard. His right hand stuck out from under the blanket, and it looked like nothing more than the bent wire frame of a toy that hadn't been run through the papier-mâché machine yet.

Mrs. C touched my head. "He asked about you," she said quietly. "He wanted to know if Rudolph was bringing you home."

I didn't argue the use of the word. This wasn't the time. "Yeah," I replied. I leaned forward, unwilling to come any closer. "Rudolph brought me back. You hear? It's me. It's Bernie. I've come back."

There was no response, and I felt a lump in my throat that I couldn't swallow away. I gulped air as if I was drowning. "How?" I finally asked.

"It started right after Christmas," Mrs. C said. "The letters started coming. More than a hundred thousand before Valentine's Day."

"What letters?" I had been on administrative leave by that point. IA was done talking to me, though the inevitable farce of a summary meeting hadn't happened yet. We all knew the NPC was going to yank my card—it was just a matter of when—and all my friends had long stopped pretending to know me.

"Christmas wishes. They started writing early this year. In the US, they wrote letters to Santa before they filed their income taxes."

Rudolph's voice was cold, like the bitter taste of a chain link fence on a winter morning. "One wasn't enough for them. They begged. They pleaded. They demanded that Santa bring each of them a Christmas miracle. Like he was some circus pony that would perform a trick on cue."

"He began to regret last Season," Mrs. C continued. "He began to doubt that he had made the right choice in bringing Mr. Anderson back." She stopped, and stared down at her hands. "And then—" she said softly, "—then the angel showed up."

"What angel?"

"The one on the rooftop."

I remembered the helium-filled figure floating over the village. "The balloon?"

Mrs. C shook her head. "No. That's just the reminder. The real angel is on the rooftop. The day after he appeared, Santa didn't get out of bed. At first, he just said it was a late summer cold, but it didn't pass. A week later, we moved him in here and started an IV-drip to keep him hydrated. He said he felt like an empty jack-in-the-box, like you could wind him up and he would pop open, but that there wasn't anything inside." Her voice dropped to a whisper. "Nobody wants an empty jack-in-the-box."

"What about the others? What about the rest of the staff? I thought the medical staff were all graduates from the best schools in the Northern Hemisphere."

"They're gone," Rudolph snapped. "They've all left."

"What?" Questions were beginning to collide in my head. "Why?"

"Holy Quarantine, Bernie. The North Pole has been shut down."

I sat down heavily on the edge of the bed. "Christmas has been canceled," I murmured, looking at Santa's skeletal visage. "So, there's nothing between Thanksgiving and New Year's now. Just a lot of cold days and cold nights."

"And they're going to get colder," Mrs. C said softly.

"This is how the next Ice Age starts," Rudolph explained. "This is how it begins: despair and the death of the holiday season. The nights are long, Bernie. They are very long. And if you can't push it back with extended shopping hours, then it will come into your house, into your heart. We can't let it end this way, Bernie. We can't."

My heart was already cold. "It's already started, Rudolph. It's too late. You—" I wanted to say that he came too late, but what would it have mattered if he had come and found me a month ago? "We can't—" I stopped. There was no point. This was Divine retribution for what we had done.

"Who says we can't?"

I looked up at Rudolph. The reindeer's eyes were dark and light like shutters were blowing open on the furnace inside his head. "Oh no," I said. I knew what he was thinking. Santa may have wanted to see me, but Rudolph came to fetch me for something else entirely. "No way. I'm not going back there."

"Why not? We know the way. What more can they do to us?"

"You're out of your mind."

Rudolph laughed, and I flinched. Rudolph wanted to go back to purgatory. He wanted to make another raid on heaven for another soul.

Santa's soul.

‖

I WENT OUTSIDE TO CLEAR MY HEAD. SPECIFICALLY, I WENT UP ON THE ROOF. The angelic balloon hovered perfectly over the North Pole, its white fire halo bleaching the landscape. There was a line keeping it in place, and I traced the thin thread—losing it several times—down to the rooftop of the Residence.

On the far side of the climate control tower and the row of satellite dishes was a small lean-to made from bubble wrap and the plastic rods we got in bulk from a German weapons manufacturer. The same stuff that goes into those new H&K replicas carried by all the latest action figures. A worn lawn chair sat beneath the ragged structure, and a portable heater was partially submerged in a pool of tepid water beside the chair. A deep-sea fishing rod rested in a brace, and the line from the rod went straight up into the sky.

A man dressed in a long, white cloak was sitting in the lawn chair, reading a paperback novel. He looked up as I approached and gave me a dazzling smile that was more teeth than lip. His hair was cut close to his scalp, and his skin was a dark bronze. His eyes danced in his face like tiny sparks, and his fingers were long and finely boned. He reminded me of a wet seal.

"Hello," he said cheerfully, dropping a bookmark in place.

I nodded in return. The last time I had run into angels, they had been trying to kill me. I was—understandably—a little cautious.

"I didn't realize any of the little folk were left," he said breezily. "I had heard that most of you went to Alaska for the salmon fishing season."

"One assembly line to another," I murmured.

He shrugged. "Some are more suited to it than others. I'm glad they found work."

"How about Santa?" I asked. "You glad about him?"

The angel caught the edge in my voice and raised an eyebrow. "I'm sorry. I don't think I quite understand."

"Santa's dead."

Something flashed in his eyes, and his lips pressed firmly against his teeth for an instant. "Ah."

"You can get the hell out of here now," I said. "Your job's done."

The angel shook his head. "I'm afraid not."

My hands balled into fists. "What's left, you parasitic leech? The North Pole has been shut down, everyone's been driven off, and Santa's dead. What's left for you to pick through?"

He pointed skyward. "Orders from on High. You've been placed under Holy Quarantine. This whole area is subject to enforcement. You can go about your life if you like, but the office of Santa Claus has been shut down until further notice."

"How long is that?" I asked.

"Further notice?" he shrugged. "Substitute the word 'eternity' if you need a little help on the bigger picture. Do I have to quote chapter and verse for you?"

"But why?"

"You might ask yourself that question, Mr. Bernard Rosewood. The last elf to be Senior Elf in Charge of Operations." He smiled at the expression crawling across my face. "Yes, I know who you are. You're a bit of a celebrity in heaven."

His fingers folded around themselves in a manner that seemed to bend space, and when they stopped, he was holding a folded sheet of paper. He held it out for me to see that it was not unlike the FBI's Most-Wanted posters you see in the Post Office. There were two pictures on the page: one of me, and one of Rudolph. Rudolph looked like someone had just slapped him with a salmon, and I looked like I was auditioning for *Sesame Street*. Typical.

"You were on duty that night, weren't you?" he asked. "It was your responsibility to avert crises, forestall disaster, head off certain catastrophe."

"But I did—"

"What did you do?" He caught me trying to read the fine print on the page, and his fingers did that trick again, making the paper vanish.

"I . . . I helped, I guess," I said.

"Bingo, Button Boy. And as an official Little Helper—" He flashed his grin at me again. "You still have your pin, don't you? As a Little Helper, you go down with the ship. So to speak."

I took a menacing step towards the seated angel. "Now just a minute. We were helping. We were bringing light. Not like you. Not like you towel-wrapped, feather-dusted, blood sucking—"

The angel clapped his hands. "Ooh. Name calling. This is grand. Are you going to hit me next?"

I stopped, my clenched fist dropping to my side. Taking a swing at him wouldn't solve anything. And anyway, he could blow me off the roof with even his tiniest exhalation.

I had wandered aimlessly out of the infirmary; Mrs. C and Rudolph hadn't tried to stop me. I was in shock. I was hurt and angry, and I wanted an explanation. My feet had brought me to the roof in search of that explanation, and my hands wanted to wring it from the angel. But my brain kept trying to be rational.

My eyes rested on the paperback in the angel's lap. It was a thriller by a famous writer who had died recently, but I didn't recognize the title. "I don't think I've read that one," I said conversationally, trying to resurrect that feeling of languid torpor that I had been trying so hard to perfect at the hotel.

"You haven't," the angel smiled. "He just finished it last week." He leaned forward, his voice dropping to a whisper. "There are no long publishing lead times in heaven."

My spine wanted to melt into my shoes, but I tried to keep the quaver out of my voice. "Maybe I could borrow it when you're done." I tried to affect a bored yawn, though it felt like my jaw would crack and fall off.

The angel laughed. He held out his hand. "We haven't properly met. I'm Ramiel."

I stared at his outstretched hand. Rational brain or no, I wasn't going to take that hand. We had gone toe-to-toe with the Host and had made them look bad. So, okay, maybe we had been asking for it by busting David Anderson out, but there was no way I was going to be that civil. Santa was . . . well, yeah, what was the point of being civil now, right?

I thrust my hands behind my back so he couldn't see how tight my fists were. "Okay Ramiel, now that we're on a first name basis, why don't you tell me the 'chapter and verse' version of why you're here."

Ramiel cast his eyes heavenward in a 'give me strength' manner. "Which 'thou shalt not' would you like to hear first? Okay, let's start with 'Thou shalt not worship any images but Mine.' I realize most of you don't remember much of the Old Testament, much less which Commandment that is, but the basic problem is that you performed a miracle last Christmas. On the day before the birthday of Jesus Christ, you performed a resurrection. How many people hoped that you would go one better and bring back the King of Glory on his birthday?"

"Elvis?" Rudolph interjected. He had come up like a silent fog and was standing in the snow behind me.

"The other King," Ramiel said politely, though his tone was crisp. "The point is that Santa performed a capital-M Miracle. Now, there are some things that you can get away with: being out of range of your dog when it shakes itself dry, making a parking meter stick, winning the lottery twice in a row, always getting the short line at the grocery store, and so on. But a resurrection is an entirely different class of miracle, and those are reserved for direct agents of the Man Upstairs." Ramiel spread his hands. "I barely get to influence parking, and I'm one of the Seven. Santa Claus is, let's face it, a minor deity. At best. This effected a huge swing in the balance of belief structures.

"What do you think would have happened this coming Christmas if we let you go unpunished. 'What did you get for Christmas?' Suzy Anderson's schoolteacher asked her after the holidays. 'I got my Daddy back,' she said. And after the school psychologist called Suzy's house and actually talked to dear old Dad, little Suzy brought him in for Show-and-Tell."

Ramiel waved his arms and dropped his voice an octave. "'Hello kids, my name is David Anderson, and I was brought back to this mortal plane of existence by Santa Claus and his reindeer as my little girl's Christmas present. Does anyone have any questions about the afterlife?'"

"So what's your point?" I asked just to be difficult. I wasn't that dense. I had gotten the point pretty clearly, but somewhere during Ramiel's monologue I had snuck a peek at Rudolph, and I could tell from his body language that it was going to be impossible to talk him out of his damn fool plan. The one that required me to drink the same Kool-aid. If I let Ramiel ramble on enough, then maybe Rudolph would see the futility of his plan and back down. They might not have been expecting us the first time—God's attention to detail notwithstanding—but there was no way we were going to catch them by surprise a second time. And without that precious element, I didn't see how we had any chance at all. Less than a snowball's chance, in fact.

Ramiel was enjoying having an audience. If we were in grade school, he would have been the big kid who would have talked about what he would do to you if he had the time, but since recess was only fifteen minutes long, he was going to have to settle for beating your head against the tetherball pole for twelve of those precious minutes. But those other three? He would definitely fill them up with as much self-aggrandizing prattle as possible.

"My point is this," Ramiel said. "You minor leaguers have always coattailed on the important dates for the majors. And you couldn't be satisfied with that. You got a little greedy." He lifted his hands. "I can understand that. Hubris can happen to anyone. Just ask the guy who took the Long Drop. But you were supposed to have learned from his example; instead, here you are, trying to horn in on our territory like some overzealous vacuum cleaner salesmen."

"What if we apologize?" I asked, out of sheer curiosity more than any real hope. "A big press release apology. And, you know, a couple thousand Hail Marys and six lifetimes worth of community service? Can we get Santa back?"

Ramiel shook his head. "It's too late for that. Even if Santa was returned to this plane, what do you think is going to happen the day after Thanksgiving?"

"There won't be any parking at the mall?" Rudolph tried.

"No, it'll be the first day that the Church of Santa Claus will be open for business. And every mall across America—across the world—will have their own little altar and High Priest for you to visit and deposit your little prayer—your little tithe for something 'extra-special' to come your way. What'll it be next year? Loved ones two years gone? Your favorite cat—Fluffy—get hit by a car? No problem, just drop on by the First Church of Claus and put in an order to get them back. Don't you worry your pretty little head about a thing. Santa always delivers. Who cares if your grandmother's been dead ten years. Santa always comes through for good little girls."

Ramiel leaned forward. "Look, I'm not trying to downplay what you guys did. It was a splendid thing. But you acted without thinking about the consequences. There's an order to this universe. There is a Plan. Didn't either of you read Revelation? Bringing back the dead has always been part of the agenda. It may seem like you did a little thing, but in ten years, will it be so little anymore? Where does it end? Who decides what Santa can't bring you for Christmas?"

I felt something crack in my spine. "What? You couldn't just come down and talk about it? You couldn't drop by and ask Santa to keep his gift-giving to more secular fare. Who gave you the right to shut us down and kill Santa? Is that justified by what we did? Is God that much of an asshole?"

Ramiel refused to get ruffled. "There's no need to be rude about it."

"Oh? We're just supposed to take this? We're just supposed to roll over and say 'thank you' for this display of wisdom and justice?" The venom in my spine flooded my body. I realized I had been holding a lot of things back since that circus sideshow that had been the NPC investigation. First I lost my union card, and now Santa was gone. The venom flushed through my cheeks. "I did my job. Do you think that mattered? Do you think anyone cared? I lost everything—my apartment, my pension, my union card, my life—everything!—because I wanted to bring some happiness to someone's life. That little girl was hurting!" I was shouting now, screaming at the angel. "Hurt and lost and she wanted someone to help her. She turned to us. Why did she turn to us? Because no one else would listen to her. No one did anything to help this little girl's pain. What were we supposed to have done?"

Ramiel's voice was like steel beneath a bolt of silk. "Maybe nothing at all. Did you think of that?"

I jumped him. Rationally, I knew he was immortal and invulnerable and all those other 'i' words that you use to describe angels, but I wanted to be sure. And if we were all wrong, then I wanted to be the one who broke his nose first.

III

I SAT IN MRS. C'S PRIVATE OFFICE AND NURSED MY BLACK EYE. SHE HAD a new computer—one with lots of RAM and a giant widescreen monitor—and I had a dozen windows open on a dozen different systems scattered across the world. Last time I had been going for stealth; this time I was using brute force. My code was busy gathering zombie machines and rerouting services, and there was nothing for me to do in the meantime but sulk and try not to fuss too much with the ice pack.

Rudolph had yanked me off the angel before things had gotten too out of hand, though Ramiel had totally taken a cheap shot as the reindeer hauled me away. A little sucker punch right in the face, burying a knuckle right in the corner of my left eye socket. Maybe he had been trying to egg me on, trying to get me to do something stupid enough that he could toss me off the building with impunity, but Rudolph lowered his horns, and the angel had backed off.

I had resisted at first, but when the pain from the angel's love tap forced its way through my anger, I relented and allowed Rudolph to lead me back to the stairwell down into the Residence. I had stopped at the door and looked back at the angel. Ramiel had never even gotten up, and he was calmly reading his book as if nothing had happened.

"I'm in," I had said to Rudolph. "Let's go find Santa."

"Give us some coordinates, Bernie," he had said. "We'll do the rest."

I had hacked into purgatory's system once. I could do it again.

Naturally, the Network Jockeys had forced a system wide password change as soon as we had gotten back last year, and some middle manager somewhere had been given a task force and a mandate to crawl all of the code to make sure there weren't any backdoors into the Elfnet. My fall from grace had been spectacular enough that someone had thought to be proactive and make sure I couldn't get all spiteful afterward. They had done a good job too. I couldn't fault them for missing the drop box in a Miami post office as well as a Platinum American Express card—the payments for which were coming like clockwork out of a union slush fund that no one remembered setting up. They had been worried about internal security, after all.

Like I said, I hadn't been planning on coming back. And while they could take away my union card, I was due a decent retirement plan. I gave a lot for the cause, after all.

It only took me a half hour to hack the electronic trail from that credit card account to the NPC accounts payable system, which was such a freaking black box that I knew none of the NJs or anyone in Technology Management had any idea what went on in the guts of that system. Which is where I had hidden my back door.

Spiteful? Me? No, just a careful planner. Like Rudolph said: always be prepared.

I had to assume that heaven's IT staff had done the same sort of audit after my last excursion, which meant a sledgehammer approach had a better chance of success this time around.

Ramiel had mentioned hubris, and I suppose you could apply that word to my *the world is a nail and I've got a planet-sized hammer* approach. But it's not my fault, truly. I blame technology. Technology screwed everything up. Sure, there are some truly labor saving devices out there (and I'm not talking about the Segway), and medical science has done a great deal in assisting humanity to a more prosperous, idyllic life on this planet, but, mostly? We've invented a lot of tech that does nothing but facilitate a ridiculous indifference to the world around us. Not to mention a rather unbecoming avarice and self-absorption.

It had happened to Santa, after all. If you want to talk about hubris, let's be honest about what happened last year. But it goes back farther than that, really. Back when your parents' parents were children, technology was a little slipperier. In fact, Santa was just coming out of what could be considered the Slippery Age. Christmas, more often than not, didn't happen overnight. It took anywhere from a couple of days to three weeks, depending on the surface mail or whatever horse and buggy routine the local carriers used. It was easier when half the world didn't believe in Fat Boy. Sure, the popular mythology says that bad kids got coal, but the way it actually worked was that bad kids (read kids who didn't believe) got nothing. It was easy, it was simple, and it drove the point home. If you believed, if you allowed yourself that tiny smidgen of imagination, then you made Santa's List. Well, the world got smaller, and the List got bigger, and the old methods weren't going to cut it anymore. Not only did these kids believe, but they believed that it happened on the night of December 25th. We didn't have the luxury of spreading it out over a week or two anymore.

We needed an angle, and the Trinity explosion in July of 1945 gave us that. We had a team inside Los Alamos, and while everyone was going all googly-eyed about the explosion in the desert, we were trying to figure out how to harness it. And with the help of a couple of big-brained pranksters from the labs, we did: we built the Nuclear Clock.

You remember *Miracle on 34th Street*? The film starring Maureen O'Hara and John Payne? You want to know the real reason it did so well when it came out in 1947? Well, think about it. The first time the Nuclear Clock had been used was the 1946 Season. Boom! Presents everywhere in one night! Santa's popularity exploded quicker than it takes small children to unwrap all of their presents under the tree. Sure a lot of social historians like to claim that the war being over was the root cause of all that festive year, but come on, the real reason? Santa Claus.

And when the Clock slipped in 1964, did we roll up the shutters and slink off? No. We made another clock—a better one—and kept going. Yeah, we lost some reindeer, and Rudolph became the strange thing that he is, but Christmas kept coming. Year after year after year. Nothing could stop Santa. The tech got better and better, as did the ability to deliver exactly what each and every kid wanted for Christmas. Capital M miracles aside, we were in the wish fulfillment business, and we got really good at it.

So good in fact that when the impossible request came in, Santa hadn't balked. We had gone into heaven and gotten a soul back. Because he could. Because he had the technology to do the job.

And that was why he died. Technology killed him.

If the world had been a simpler place, then it would have remained populated by simpler minds. And, frankly, simpler minds accept the mysterious and inscrutable as being just that: mysterious and inscrutable. They don't poke and prod and try to peek behind the curtain. You let the brain swell to fill the available space in the skull, and it starts to dream all sort of big dreams. Giant telescopes that can see to the edge of the expanding universe. Microscopes that look so far in the other direction that the fabric of reality can be measured. With these marvels, simplicity is left dead by the roadside, and the only companion you've got left in the vehicle is Complexity and his buddy, Fatal Error.

My windows started beeping, signaling that the code each had been running was finished. I had my army of slaved processors. I moused over the nearest window and typed the command that would launch my unified assault on the firewalls of purgatory. But my finger hovered over the 'Enter' key for a second, not quite ready to commit to this course. I was about to launch such a denial of service assault that no one would be able to stream anything anywhere for at least an hour. All so that heaven's attention would be on their firewalls, and no one would notice the extra payload being slipped through on the back of the normalized data packets.

Complexity. Fatal Error. Hubris. While my zombie horde was tromping through the front part of the house, breaking the furniture and making a mess of the rugs, I would be casually perusing the books in the library, looking for a very specific volume.

There was still time to walk away. Still time to tell Rudolph that we weren't meant to do this—that we had been given a warning and left alive as an example to others.

But I knew what he would say: we were meant to make a different example.

And with that in mind, I pushed the button.

IV

At first nothing happened, and then, after five minutes, the cursor blinked and the line fed. I stared at the cursor for a long moment, wondering what had just happened—or not happened, as the case might be—and then I remembered I hadn't bothered to put any error checking in my code.

The code had worked. My query had executed. Purgatory was there, as expected, but my stealth request had come back empty. As in *no data found*.

It would take a Silicon Valley hotshot IT department a couple of hours to break up my DDOS attack, and adjusting that time for supernatural agency meant I had about ten more minutes before the spectral swords of purgatory's defense system eviscerated my hack. Time enough to try at least one more query, and so I tried 'Kris Kringle.'

Same result: a line feed and no data set returned. I got desperate and opened up a couple more windows so I could try every possible combination in the time I had left: 'Father Christmas,' 'Nicolas of Myra,' 'Sint Klaes,' 'St. Nicolas.'

They all came back empty.

I hesitated a second, wracking my brain for one last query, and then realizing I overstayed my welcome, I started to unload my code. But it was taking too long, and suddenly paranoid, I reached around to the back of the computer and yanked out the power cord. The screen went dark, and I sat there in the near-darkness, wondering what I had missed. But I knew my code had been good, which could only mean one thing: Santa Claus wasn't in purgatory.

"Keep it simple." The voice spoke directly into my left ear. I jerked upright in the chair, banging my knees against the underside of the heavy desk. My heart pounding, I glanced around, but there was no one in the room with me. The only sound other than the harried echo of my heart in my ears was the distant tick-tock of the old upright clock in the corner of the room.

"Rudolph?" I said. Just in case he was hiding—I don't know—behind the drapes or something. "Comet?" Of all the reindeer, Comet was the most prone to practical jokes, though even this sort of game seemed a little out there for him. Especially now.

A ghost light flickered across the monitor, and I squeaked in fright. And then immediately berated myself for doing so. It was just a phantasmal effect that some monitors had—a flicker of color through the pixels as the screen started to cool down. There was nothing there. There was no one else in the room. I was just spooking myself.

"Keep it simple," I whispered to myself. The oldest rule in the book. Good old William of Ockham. Maybe it was his ghost reaching out to tell me to stop spooking myself and actually apply some brain power to what I did and did not know.

"Okay," I said, nodding. "What do you know, smart guy?"

My code was good, as was my theory. So that meant the problem was on the other end, which meant 1) the data structure in purgatory had changed over the last year and I had been querying the wrong fields, or 2) Santa hadn't reached purgatory yet and no record had been entered into the vast data warehouse of heaven for him yet, or 3) he wasn't there.

Okay, rebuttals.

1) Doubtful. Nothing in IT is ever changed. If it is changed, it takes at least five years and many millions of billable hours to even rename a field much less change the existing data structure.

2) A lack of speedy data entry suggested that the dead could be in, what? limbo for some time before actually reaching

purgatory. Okay, entirely possible, but I was willing to bet Santa Claus wasn't one of those who got turned away at the door. Yeah, old man, come back in a few hours. We're not quite ready to process you yet.

3) Where else would he go if he wasn't going to heaven?

Well, now there's a thought. *Which thou shalt not would you like to begin with?* I didn't remember my Commandments all that well, but I was pretty sure that neglecting one precluded you from going to heaven. It was one of the incentives to *not* break them.

I heard a sound like someone dragging a line of sleigh bells across a metal tabletop, and a smell reminiscent of melting chestnuts assaulted my nose. I glanced around Mrs. C's office. The room seemed a little darker.

My tongue was thick in my mouth. "Santa?" I croaked.

Near the doorway, a gentle snowfall sparkled. It melted before it touched the heavy carpet. My heart was making that loud noise again, and I tried to mentally shush it as I slipped off the chair and approached the small snow flurry. I heard the sound of sleigh bells again as the tiny snowstorm drifted toward me. I reached up to catch a snowflake, and my hand touched something cold. The tiny flake lay frozen on my fingertip, a perfect star shape. I withdrew my hand, and the flake melted, turning to a dot of water that ran down the pad of my finger.

And then I heard the voice again, and I knew it was him. "The gates of heaven are closed, Bernie." It was like a winter wind, teasing and tugging at your hair. "They won't let me in." The snowfall glistened.

Suddenly the door burst open, and a young reindeer bounced into the room. He hurtled right through the falling snow, and the storm scattered like a flight of dark birds, nothing more than shadows bouncing off the walls and ceilings. The reindeer was just as surprised as I was, and he bumped into me before he could stop himself. Fortunately, his horns were merely tiny buttons growing out of his skull, and the impact between his head and my stomach was only like getting hit by a Major League fastball instead of a being skewered like a slab of beef.

I landed on my ass and tried to catch my breath. The young reindeer rebounded like he did this sort of thing all the time, and he danced around me. He was covered with tinsel—it looked like it had been taped onto him in wide stripes—and his nose was quivering like a cube of Jell-O as he examined me. A mesh bag filled with ceramic canisters was slung across his withers.

"Gotta go. Gotta go," he squeaked.

"What?" I asked, still trying to ease my cramped stomach.

"Rudolph wants you. It's time to go."

"Go? Go where?"

I didn't know this reindeer. There were others outside the normal team, of course. Up to a hundred or so could comfortably range across the Park, and this youngster looked like he was still growing his first year's velvet on his horns.

"Launch bay," he explained.

I glanced around the room, half-hoping to catch sight of the column of snowfall. "I'm not done," I protested. "I don't . . . I haven't finished my research. I don't have all the information I need. I can't leave."

He grabbed the end of my trousers with his mouth and tugged. "There's no time," he said through clenched teeth.

I pulled back and discovered that even a young reindeer was stronger than me. The muscles in his neck bunched as he tugged me across the floor. "Wait. What do you mean there's no time? Time for what?"

He let go and cocked his head as he recited his instructions: "Find Bernie: ten minutes. Time before they leave: fifteen minutes. Time it takes to reach an altitude of five thousand feet: another five minutes. Commence dive bomb attack: ten minutes after . . ." His tongue wiggled in the corner of his mouth. "Subtract four . . . carry the one . . ." He shook his head. "Nope. You doing more research? That's what there's no time for."

"Hold on. Dive bomb attack?"

The young reindeer did a little jig in the doorway. The ceramic canisters rattled in the bag across his shoulders. "I'm the diversion," he announced proudly.

Rudolph. He was taking the team and heading for the South Pole. With or without me. This reindeer was right. I was out of time.

❄

"You're late," Rudolph announced as I tumbled off the pneumatic carrier that ran between the Residence and the launch bay. He was standing on the dark pad, impatiently tapping a hoof against the control panel that raised and lowered the pad.

The launch bay could very well be turned into a historical museum if Christmas remained canceled. Each generation of the Sled was housed down here. Well, those that were still intact. The Mark V hadn't come back last year, and there was a version of the red sled from the late 1890s that had been lost in the Arctic Ocean. But the rest were here, lined up in chronological order, covered with plastic, and permanently moistened with grease on the off-chance that they would be needed.

The launch bay was the only area underground that the reindeer were allowed to access. In fact, a service tunnel ran straight from the bay to the barn out on the Park, which made it easy for them to come and go when it was time to fly. And they were all here, standing off to the side of the pad, waiting for me.

They were covered in white and gray greasepaint, wearing their assault rigs. There had been some advances since the last time I had seen this gear. The cumbersome targeting visors had been replaced with a variation on the glasses Blizten had been wearing last year, though with a bit more theatrical flair in their wraparound style and dark lenses. We had dropped in on purgatory, bristling with guns and rocket launchers and flame-throwers like hardwired Visigoths out for a weekend of empire burning; now, with this next-generation gear (which looked like it had been designed by H. R. Giger and molded by Samsonite), they could pass as Elvis-impersonating Cold Warriors flying in for a black bag job before picking up their dates for a fancy costume ball.

"What's the rush?" I asked after I got done gawking.

"Mrs. C," Cupid supplied. "She's gone gray. Whatever Santa had, she's got it too." His grin seemed a little strained.

"You find Santa?" Rudolph asked.

"Uh, no. Not exactly."

He glared at me. "Bernie," he said menacingly. Vixen and Prancer shuffled a few paces away from Rudolph at the tone of his voice.

"He's not in heaven," I blurted out. "There wasn't any trace of him in purgatory." The other reindeer stared at me. Blitzen shook his head, adjusting his librarian nerd glasses with a hoof. "Look, I think we've made a bad assumption." When I was tearing down the back stairs to the basement, inspiration had hit—a clear blast of enlightenment that had forced my feet back up the steps to the library. I held up the book that I had gone back for.

Rudolph peered at the worn cover. "*Inferno*," he read. "We don't have time for obscure literary games, Bernie."

"Dante's *Inferno*." I tapped the cover of the book. "Santa's in hell," I explained. "We broke one of the Commandments. We don't get to go to heaven anymore."

Cupid couldn't stop his gruesome chuckle.

Rudolph stared at the book for a long moment, chewing on his lip. "Fine," he said, tapping an access code into the panel on the console. "We go to hell instead."

"Wait a minute," Donner interjected. "No one said anything about going to hell."

Rudolph lifted his head, and his eyes were gleaming. Like I had seen in the infirmary. "You got a problem with that?"

Donner nodded. "You're damn right I do. Raiding purgatory is one thing, but hell is . . . well, hell is . . . hot."

It was a bit more than that, but we all got what the muscular reindeer was trying to say.

"Bring a wet towel," Rudolph said as he punched the final button on the panel. Somewhere beneath us, distant machinery rumbled. High overhead, the domed surface of the launch area cracked open, and a thin layer of snow drifted down. As it coated Rudolph, he gave off a neon gleam.

"Look, Rudolph," Prancer interjected. "We've gone up against angels. We can handle them. But the minions of hell? I, uh, I don't think that is a good idea."

"Why not?" Rudolph wanted to know. "If you're scared, say it. That's all right."

"It's not a question of being scared. It's a question of suicide," Blitzen interjected. "We're too old to be caught up in some damn fool crusade. Twenty years ago, maybe. But not anymore."

"You're all scared. You're all terrified that you might be killed trying to save Santa."

Blitzen snorted. "And you're not?"

Rudolph shook his head. "No, I'm not."

"You're lying."

"Am not."

Blitzen sighed and looked at the other reindeer. "We've played poker with you for too many years, Rudolph. We know your tell. We know when you are bluffing."

The glow on Rudolph's skin became a little brighter. "I am not bluffing."

"Thanks for ruining it, Blitzen," Cupid pointed out wryly. "I had been pretty happy with the extra cash at Christmas every year."

It was the glow, I realized. That was Rudolph's tell. "How long have you guys known?" I asked.

"Hey, we let him play. It's not our fault he kept coming back." Cupid shrugged. "Look, Rudolph, we understand this macho posturing. We get it. We really do. But you don't have to keep proving yourself. You don't have to kill yourself to show that you're worthy of being one of Santa's reindeer."

I felt something nuzzle under my arm, and I started. The young reindeer who had been sent to fetch me had wandered up, and he had just stuck his head under my arm. I glanced down at his young face and realized there was at least one reindeer here who would follow Rudolph anywhere. Even to hell.

I rubbed the cover of Dante's book with my thumb, feeling the coarse stitching of the binding. The little guy wasn't the only one. I would go too. It was that nagging feeling that had been haunting me ever since Rudolph had interrupted my morning nap. That reminder that there was an unassailable responsibility that came with working for Santa—be it as one of his Little Helpers or as a reindeer—a responsibility you couldn't shirk. Sure, Santa was just a guy we shoved in a red suit every year, but he was a symbol of something bigger. He was what stood between us and the cold nights. And if Santa fell, well, then it was our job to take his place, wasn't it?

Mrs. C had said as much. The nights were going to get colder. And when I looked at Rudolph, I could see what the young reindeer saw. I could see that whatever fire had been started that night in 1964 was never going to go out.

"I'm going," I said. The reindeer all stared at me. "It's not about being worthy," I told them. I rubbed the young reindeer on the head and walked over to the sled pad.

"It's not about being scared," I said. "I'm scared shitless of going to hell. But I can't let that stop me because there is something I'm even more afraid of. I'm terrified of the expression on every child's face on Christmas morning when they find out Santa hasn't come. I'd rather face anything hell has got to throw at me than answer to every mother and father with a tearful child in tow come Christmas Day."

I laughed at the irony of what I had just said. "I'm even afraid of trying and failing. But does that mean I don't try? Does that mean that I let fear rule me?"

My question hung for a moment, and I thought again of the tiny snowstorm in Mrs. C's office. A little bit of Christmas struggling to make itself heard.

Cupid shouldered his way to the front of the group. He walked across the bay and stepped onto the pad with me. "Count me in, field mouse." He stood next to me, a tall reindeer with an entire platoon's armament strapped to his back . . . and Elvis glasses wrapped around his head. I felt like I was in some weird David Lynch version of *The Night Before Christmas*.

Blitzen nickered gently. "Better to fall in hell," he said, "Than cower before heaven." He joined us on the pad. I wasn't quite sure who he had been quoting, and I don't think anyone else knew either, but the words sparked something in the rest of the team, and they crossed as a group and crowded onto the pad.

Rudolph looked up at the cloud-covered sky. "God bless us all," he said. "Every one of us." He pushed the green button on the console, and the pad jerked into motion, rising up toward the surface.

"We're going to need it," Cupid cracked.

"Amen," answered Donner.

V

"YOU SURE ABOUT HELL?" RUDOLPH ASKED. WE WERE STANDING ON THE southern ridge, just past the Park. The rest of the team was hidden in the snow behind us. Rudolph had brought a more elf-sized thermal suit this time, complete with a Batman-style utility belt. And a hat too. A floppy baseball cap with a Boynton reindeer cartoon on the front. Someone had stitched SECO across the back. Rudolph denied any familiarity with a needle and thread. He only glowed a little when he said it.

The hat was a little too big, but I wore it anyway, turned backward so the bill wouldn't get in the way.

Rudolph wasn't wearing an assault rig. We all knew what he would do to the electronics in the gear before we made it even a kilometer from the Residence. Instead, he wore a harness so that I could ride him, along with a sleek pack. When I had stashed the copy of *Inferno* in the pack, an ordinary-looking thermos caught my eye, but I hadn't had a chance to ask Rudolph if it contained soup or whisky. Instead, I snagged the pair of high-powered binoculars.

I dialed in the magnification on the glasses, trying to pick out the angel on the roof. "It's a little late to wonder about that, isn't it?" I asked.

Rudolph snorted. "Better now than when we're trapped on a plain of lava."

I reflected on the visitation that I may or may not have imagined in Mrs. C's office. "Well," I said, "I'll have to be that much more convincing then, won't I?"

Something sparkled off in the distance—a thin glint of reflected moonlight. I tried to focus on the glittering object, but it was too small (and too shiny) to identify. If I didn't know better, I would easily think that the flying object was a small aircraft.

But I knew better.

"Who's the youngster?" I asked as I watched him turn and dive toward the roof.

"Name's Ring," Rudolph supplied. "Got a stripe of enthusiasm longer than the coast of Iceland. Thinks he knows something about flying."

"There weren't any open slots at Top Gun?"

"Hasn't been since that movie came out in '86."

"Just as well," I said. "The North Pole has got nine flight jockeys that think they're the best. What would we do with another one?"

I turned my attention back to the roof, and I caught sight of the angel as he stood up. Something flickered on the roof, obscuring my field of view, and I dialed back the magnification. Somehow I couldn't keep the angel in focus.

"He's getting bigger," Rudolph said. And he was right: Ramiel was elongating like a living Stretch Armstrong doll.

Ring had the stellar hoof-eye coordination of the young, and the first canister he dropped was right on target. Ramiel, large enough now that we could see him without the binoculars, reached up and casually closed his massive fist around the tiny object. Rudolph made a warning noise in his throat, and I quickly looked away. Even still, the flash of light made my eyelids glow.

Whatever was in the canister made a lot of light, and I was guessing a commensurate amount of heat. I blinked a few times, trying to clear the afterimage of the supernova flash, trying to see what was happening on the roof of the Residence.

Ring had already come back around for a second pass, and as I watched, a galaxy of stars bloomed on the roof. The youngster had dropped most of his load, and I didn't blame him. It wasn't like he was going to get many more chances. The sound of the detonations finally rolled over us, a rumbling reverberation that felt like being strapped to the undercarriage of a '86 El Camino. Ramiel stood in the center of the exploding cloud of stars, the remnants of his right arm still upraised. His thunderous, unearthly howl finally reached us.

"That's got to hurt," Rudolph chuckled.

A tiny shape buzzed the belly of the clouds on our left, and I tried to focus in on it through the glasses. Ring was circling like he was going to make another run. "What's he doing?" I muttered.

"Come on," Rudolph growled. "Come on."

I swung the glasses toward the roof and realized he wasn't talking to Ring. Ramiel was tracking the tiny reindeer, but he wasn't moving.

"What are you waiting for?" Rudolph whispered.

Ramiel hadn't moved. He was still on the roof.

Ring made a third pass, and his aim wasn't as perfect this time. The stars exploded in a line toward the angel, and Ramiel finally moved, striding toward the edge of the roof. He only had to take three steps, and as the last bomb blew apart the tiny lean-to where he had been sitting, the angel launched himself into the sky after Ring.

I watched the angel come close to Ring, the fingers of his remaining hand nearly reaching the flying reindeer, but then the gap widened. The angel was falling back toward the ground because, well, that was how gravity worked.

"He jumped," I said. "He didn't fly. He just jumped."

Rudolph didn't seem terribly surprised. He looked over his shoulder and whistled to the rest of the team. "Ring'll stay out of his reach," he said. Behind us, I heard the soft sound of reindeer leaping into the night sky.

Through the glasses, I watched the one-handed angel leap again, sailing through the air after Ring. They were both getting smaller as Ring led the angel away from the North Pole.

"Time to go," Rudolph said, pulling me away from the show. "That book have a map?"

I lowered the glasses and folded them up. "Dante?" I said as I put the glasses away. "Sort of."

Rudolph gave me a look that—six months ago—would have made me quiver in abject fear. Now, I just shrugged. "Look, Dante wrote *Inferno* more than seven hundred years ago. Like three hundred years before Mercator was even born. Plus it's all in verse, which is great for metaphors but crap for specific directions. It's a map *of* hell; it's not a map *to* hell."

Rudolph snorted and pounded the snow pack with a hoof. "Our choice of direction from here is *south*," he said, nodding toward the distant specks of the reindeer team. "But after awhile, they're going to want something more specific. Time to come up with something, Bernie."

I nodded, my tongue racing around the edge of my teeth as I thought quickly. "How about Germany?" I offered. "There's got to be an old entrance that is still open."

Rudolph shook his head. "Most of the camps were plowed over and are farmland now. Though, I can't imagine what grows there. And there probably aren't signposts, either."

"Blitzen doesn't have a Brimstone-o-meter or something?"

"Not his department," Rudolph said. "That's little people R&D. And no, there wasn't anything like that in the Wish Lab archives. He checked."

There was a distant trio of explosions behind us, a reminder that Ring was buying us time—time that we were, in turn, wasting. I wracked my brain. We needed an entrance to hell, though maybe it wasn't a physical gate that we needed.

"What if . . . ?" I started, thinking out loud. "Look, Dante wrote about hell in ornate and flowery prose. We should just follow his lead, right? What's the metaphorical equivalent of his dark wood? Someplace like—"

"Vegas," Rudolph said.

"Okay, yeah. Vegas," I said, nodding.

What can I say about Las Vegas that hasn't already been said by clowns more gifted and more infatuated with the pulsating neon experience of that glittering oasis in the desert? We weren't there for the tinkling ring of spilled coin, or the tremulous shout of an early winner, or even the cacophony of air horns, fireworks, and applause that made up the soundtrack of the sin-swept city. We were there for the hollow spots: the ugly alleys yawning behind every casino, behind every shining facade; the foul-smelling dumpsters where the mountains of buffet scraps went to die; and the cheap hotel rooms far away from the lights where the wallpaper peeled down on drunks too destitute to care they were being absorbed by the city.

The reindeer rode the Jet Stream down along the curve of Alaska and the Rocky Mountains. Somewhere near the gray smear that was the Great Salt Lake, they turned across the Sevier Desert for the Nevada border. "*Fiat lux*," I whispered as we sped through the half-light near dawn, and there it was, snaking across the empty sands: the argent and rainbow glow of the Strip.

"Vegas," called Comet from the point position. He affected a dry British accent as he banked and fell towards the only dark spot on the Strip. "There never was a more wretched hive of scum and villainy. We must be careful."

The reindeer watched a lot of TV and old movies during the off-season. It was better than the alternatives. Like gambling. Or rolling drunks in the parking lot of Canadian bars.

The reindeer came down in the construction of a new casino on the northern end of strip, and once Rudolph was on the ground, I told them to stay out of sight as I reconnoitered the situation. I used hand signals straight out of any prime time action drama, just to be sure they got it. Dante and I went for a stroll. There had to be something we could use as a stand-in for an entrance to hell. There was too much expiring hope in this city—there had to be some way to make the crossing. Too many dreams spattered from sixteen stories up; too many grand designs lost in the ill tumble of a silver ball or a pair of dice. Despair was never far from the surface of anything here.

I stood on the pavement outside the construction zone and flipped open the book. The pages were lit by the flickering red and blue light of the Strip, and I felt like I was standing on the edge of a crime scene. "*Relinque spes*," I read, tracing my finger along the Latin inscription that Dante said was written over the doorway to hell. *Abandon hope all ye who enter here.*

"This going to take long?" Rudolph was at my elbow. Cupid wandered up to the edge of the sidewalk, ogling the gaudy lights across the street.

I glanced behind me, expecting to see the rest of the team. "What part of 'let's keep a low profile' was confusing?"

"The part where we stood around, sniffing each other's butts while you figured something out." Rudolph nodded up the street where a pair of giant galleons floated in a man-made lagoon.

"Reindeer don't sniff—"

"So what are we supposed to do?" Rudolph asked. "Light a fire? Sacrifice a goat?"

"We're fresh out of goats," I said.

"Where's Ring when you need him?" Cupid wondered.

A late-model convertible slowed to a stop in front of us. A large gentleman with slicked back hair and mirrored aviator glasses sat behind the wheel. There were three women in the car with him, and the one in the passenger's seat was wearing what looked like a private school uniform, and I couldn't help but wonder what school allowed blouses to be cut that low as she leaned out of the car.

"Hello, sailor," she said breathlessly.

I was momentarily flustered. "What? How? I'm not—" I couldn't fathom how she thought I had just gotten off a boat. The thermal suit didn't look anything like nautical gear.

"Maybe she thinks you work on a submarine or something," Rudolph suggested.

"Do you see any body of water deep enough—" I started.

"Like on the missile tube cleaning crew," Cupid interrupted, trying to be helpful. "You know, they put you in and . . ." He rotated his head around in a circle.

The woman's attention was drawn to the reindeer doing the stupid *look at me, I'm an elf in a missile tube* gag. "Look at you," she said with a smile. "A pair of fancy sunglasses and you're the King of Rock and Roll." She winked at Cupid. "How's it hanging, King?"

"I'm ah . . . I'm feeling a little lonesome tonight," he said in his best Elvis Presley voice.

"What a shame," she said. Her two friends in the back seat giggled and nudged one another. They were staring at Rudolph. The driver was tapping his fingers on the steering wheel in time with the music. He had given us a onceover and seemed unimpressed.

The schoolgirl in the front seat wiggled around on her seat until she was on her knees. "I can't believe the King of Rock and Roll is standing here all alone," she said to her friends, who both giggled again. She put her hands on the car door and leaned forward. "Can I get your autograph?" she said, her voice husky enough to pull a dog sled.

"Absolutely, ma'am," Cupid said, bumping me aside as he approached the vehicle. "But, I have to admit that the King is traveling without a pen."

She pouted, a lip motion that made me forget something important. One of her friends rummaged around in a purse the size of a postage stamp and produced a tube of lipstick. The schoolgirl took it, and her frown turned upside down. "But I don't have anything to write on," she sighed, leaning forward again and doing a magical little wiggle with her shoulders. The motion made one of the buttons on her blouse slip out of its eyelet, and even more of her became visible.

"That's not exactly a flat surface," Cupid said. "But I think I can manage."

She smiled and carefully rotated the bottom of the lipstick until it was fully extended. The entendre wasn't lost on me, and I was starting to get a little uncomfortable.

Cupid leaned in for the tube of lipstick. "You know," he admitted, "I'm not really Elvis."

She smiled and ran a finger along the edge of one of his ears. "That's okay, sugar. You really didn't think I was a school girl either, did you?"

Cupid took the lipstick in his mouth. "Well, since we're clear on all that," he said around the obstruction, "I think I'll sign 'em both."

"Hang on," I said, tugging Cupid's tail in an effort to get his attention. He dropped the lipstick, and it fell into the car. He leaned forward, fully intending to go after it. "We're not interested," I said, yanking harder.

The schoolgirl was sitting on her knees on the car seat, and she wrapped her hands around Cupid's head as he nosed around her lap. He said something, but his words were muffled.

"We've got other plans," Rudolph said, and his voice was flat and hard enough that it killed the mood. Cupid wasn't so lost in his quest for the missing lipstick that he didn't hear Rudolph's tone, and he backed away from the car so quickly that he nearly trampled me. "All that we really require is some directions."

The driver had heard Rudolph's tone too, and his right hand had dropped off the steering wheel, drifting toward the loose fold of his coat. But his hand stopped when he saw the look on Rudolph's face.

"Look," I said, shoving my way past Cupid. I raised the heavy book and showed the frontispiece to the four in the car. "'Abandon hope,'" I read to them, "'all ye who enter here.' That ring a bell for anyone?"

The woman sitting behind the driver leaned forward and tapped him on the shoulder. "Didn't we just see that movie?" she asked him.

A thin smile touched the driver's face. "Yeah," he said, his right hand returning to the steering wheel. "At the Bellagio. A couple of nights ago."

Rudolph clicked his tongue noisily. "We were thinking something a little different. Maybe written on a sign or something."

The other woman in the back curled a ringlet of her hair in a finger and started twisting it in a mesmerizing motion. "How about Treasure Island?" she suggested, languorously pointing across the street. "On the bridge. There's a board there. Maybe it says what you're looking for."

"It's from Dante." We all stared at the schoolgirl in the front seat. The driver even lowered his glasses. She shrugged under our scrutiny. "St. Mary's Finishing School for Girls. You think uniforms like this are easy to come by?" She waved a scarlet fingernail at the book. "*Inferno,* right?"

"Yeah," I said. "Yes, it is."

"The sign isn't important." She smiled at me as if we shared some secret. "You might want to try the Mirage."

The driver nodded, seconding that suggestion, and he revved the engine as he dropped his hand to the gear stick. The schoolgirl produced a business card and offered it to Cupid. "Call us," she said.

He took it carefully between his teeth, and as the car started to roll forward, she let a long finger trail along his jaw. The two women in the back blew kisses to Rudolph.

I took the card from Cupid's loose jaw as the convertible drove away. It was slightly damp, and I wiped it off on the thermal suit before dropping it into the book. If we managed to get Christmas back this year, I'd see about getting them on the List. A special holiday Dispensation.

Cupid didn't notice the missing card. "I think I like schoolgirls who can quote Dante," he said.

Rudolph glared at Cupid. "We're not on holiday," he said. "Focus."

"What?" asked Cupid. "I was helping. I just thought it would be easier to get into hell if a couple more Commandments were busted along the way."

"You're thinking of adultery," I pointed out. "Fornicating, though *evil*, isn't necessarily Commandment-quality."

"Maybe she was married," Cupid tried.

"Yeah," I said. "Maybe the guy driving was her husband."

A look of confusion crossed Cupid's face as Rudolph whistled for the rest of the team.

"There was a guy in the car?" Cupid said.

The volcano exploded. The Mirage—not to be outdone by the combative sideshow going on next door at Treasure Island—featured an erupting volcano outside the casino. Every fifteen minutes, the mountain spewed ash and fire, and the flaming detritus from the explosion fell into the lake surrounding the mountain, bubbling and steaming like a witches' cauldron.

We stood on the boardwalk beside the lake, and the reindeer's glasses were filled with reflections of flickering fire. Nearby, a trio of very drunk tourists were arguing about who was going to pose first with Cupid, and none of them were having much luck figuring out how to work the cameras on their smart phones. Cupid was playing up the Elvis impersonator angle to such an extreme that I thought he looked more like Mr. Ed than the King of Rock and Roll.

Not that any of the drunk trio were old enough to remember Mr. Ed. Nor Elvis, for that matter.

"Anyone have any idea how to open a gate?" I asked. I glanced at the others. "I don't suppose you brought along a Time Clock Wave Generator, or something?"

Donner shook his head. "R&D hasn't figured out how to make a portable one yet."

"So, what then?" I asked. "Wishful thinking?"

"This was your idea," Donner reminded me.

The faux lava flow lessened, and as the steaming water subsided, Blitzen spoke: "'What if the breath that kindled those grim fires, awaked, should blow them into sevenfold rage, and plunge us in the flames.'"

Everyone was quiet for a moment.

"That wasn't Dante," Prancer finally said.

Blitzen shook his head. "Some other poem about sinners and sin."

We stood around some more, each of us lost in our own thoughts. Blitzen was probably reciting more poetry to himself; Donner stared at the water like he was waiting for a fish to jump out or something; Prancer started to whistle a Christmas carol, but broke off when no one else seemed inclined to join him; and Rudolph—well, Rudolph had only one thing on his mind.

Someone screamed off to our left, and at first I thought one of the inebriated photographers had suddenly realized Cupid was actually a reindeer and not an Elvis Presley impersonator. But, when I glanced over, the trio were all looking at something below the mountain.

Maybe there was something to what Blitzen had quoted after all . . .

Floating on the center of the lake was an ancient barge, a bent shell of a boat whose timbers appeared half-rotten. A tiny railing—no more than a few inches high—ran edge of the deck like a line of fractured teeth. The lakewater boiled, and I could swear there were flames underneath the barge. Swirling smoke obscured the back of the vessel, but through plumes, I spotted a figure hunched over the rudder, a black rag bent like an old twig. As if it knew we were all looking at it, the figure raised an arm and beckoned.

The three drunks bolted.

The flames beneath the boat brightened, sending sweaty fog across the boardwalk.

"I guess this is our ride," I said.

No one moved.

I nudged Blitzen. "You first."

"Me?" Blitzen snorted.

"You're the one who called this cab," I said.

He did a little dance on the boardwalk and then leaped over the railing, landing easily on the deck. The rest of the team followed, and when we were all on the barge, I slid off Rudolph's back, somewhat unsure of what I was going to be standing on.

Wood. Warped and old wood, but wood nonetheless.

There was a thrum of water beneath the wooden belly of the barge. The steam thickened, rising around us, and Vegas started to vanish. The boatman leaned over his rudder, sweeping it to the right, and the boat began to move on an unseen current. The fog enveloped us completely.

From the bow, one of the reindeer shouted a warning, and a small shape catapulted out of the fog, skipping across the deck. It was a reindeer—a small one—and his fur was matted with sweat. A few of strips of tinsel were still stuck to the back of his head. He spotted me and bounded over. Before I could stop him, he started licking my face like I was a rapidly melting ice cream cone.

"Just . . . stop," I sputtered, trying to get away from the tongue bath.

"I found you," Ring chortled. "I made it."

VI

We argued about Ring, which was ultimately unnecessary because there was nothing we could do about his presence now. We were moving steadily, caught in the course of an other-worldly current, and anyway, we couldn't see anything beyond the barge. When we had crossed over to purgatory last year from the South Pole, the journey had been nearly instantaneous, but the passage to hell took longer apparently. It was almost as if we were under the aegis of the Time Clock, but not quite. We argued about Ring because that was easier than reflecting on where we were going.

Ring stood in the stern, staring into the thick fog. He was pretending not to hear us talking about him, but I could tell by his twitching ears that he was listening to every word.

"I'm not baby-sitting him," Donner argued. "This is no place for a kid."

"Young goats are 'kids,'" Blitzen pointed out. "He's not a goat."

"What?" Cupid said defensively, even though no one was looking at him specifically. "I was just kidding earlier."

Rudolph cut to the chase: "We have two choices: take him with us, or kill him and dump his body in the river."

Blitzen blinked heavily. "Did I miss a memo? What happens if Klutzo here"—he nodded at Prancer—"puts his foot in a gopher hole and tears a ligament? You going to put a bullet in his head and leave him too?"

Prancer snorted. "Not before I dust your ass first, bookworm." One of his laser rangefinders clicked on and danced a red dot across Blitzen's forehead.

Blitzen tweaked his head to the side, and nearly caught Vixen in the face with his antlers.

"Hey!" Vixen squawked, raising a hoof to clout Blitzen.

"Wait a sec—" I started.

"Enough, Rudolph," Cupid interrupted. "We've had enough of your attitude. Just because you've been on-team a generation longer doesn't mean you get to decide who lives and dies. What do you think this is? Some sort of post-apocalyptic YA coming of age novel?"

Rudolph bristled. "You think I like being the one who survived? That I outlived the entire team?"

"Outlived?" Cupid said. "They're still around, Rudolph, because you can't let them go."

"You weren't there, pal. You have no idea what it is like to see your friends get fried."

"You're wrong, Rudolph," Blitzen interjected. "We're their name-sakes. We know damn well how they died."

"And we're not in a rush to join them," Vixen snapped at Rudolph.

I tried to get their attention again and was nearly trampled for my effort when Rudolph stamped across the circle of reindeer to bump his chest against Vixen. "We're all going to join them," he snarled. "As long as you stay soft on the hard choices. We're going to join them real quick."

I backed away. There was very little I could do—kilo for kilo— if things got physical. I bumped into Ring and wrapped an arm around his shoulders. He was shivering. "I shouldn't have come," he whispered.

I shrugged. "Nothing we can do about that now."

He smiled shyly, ducking his head. "I dunked him," he said with a touch of pride. "I led him out to where the ice was thin, and cluster-bombed him into the ocean. I dunked an angel."

"You did good, kid," I said, in a species-neutral sort of way. I rubbed the side of his head with my knuckles. "How'd you find us?"

He wriggled his nose. "Smelled you."

"Me?"

"Sunscreen." He licked my cheek. "It's very buttery."

❋

"How far is it to . . . wherever we're going. Limbo?" I asked tiredly. I considered resting a foot on the decrepit railing, but I feared it would break under my weight and I'd tumble off the barge, so I crouched on my heels instead. The boatman didn't answer. His cloak was even more worn than I had first thought—it was patched and spattered with mud and . . . something darker, more vile. His hood was a narrow peak between his shoulders, and its crest drooped to obscure the front of his head. Like a floppy magician's hat past its prime. His skeletal hand was steady on the long, primitive rudder, though it was hard to tell if he was doing much to keep us oriented—if he even needed to.

There came a splash off the bow–the sound of some large, graceless creature, something unaccustomed to the cold touch of the air, yet curious to see what rode on the ferryman's barge. What water I could see through infrequent gaps in the persistent fog was as black and viscous as India ink, and we glided across it with nary a ripple.

The reindeer argument hadn't come to blows, though a lot of heated words had been exchanged before it had worn itself out. Ring had been forgotten early on, and after everything had been said, the reindeer each tried to put as much distance between themselves as they could. Ring sat on the deck near me, his chin resting on the railing. He stared at the curling mist, dejected and forlorn. Rudolph stood in the bow, staring ahead, and I could tell he was still agitated by the way his tail flicked back and forth. The rest of them were exhausted, and several were lying on the uneven deck, fatigued by the weight of their tactical gear.

We were all strung out. I hadn't gotten any sleep in nearly twenty-four hours, and I didn't know much the others had been getting, but I was willing to bet it wasn't very much. Our nerves were frayed, and many of the reindeer were like powder kegs with single-second fuses. I was having trouble concentrating. The more I tried to focus, the more my thoughts flitted off to visions of feather beds and sugarplums.

"It's the river," the boatman said without preamble. His voice was softer than I would have expected. He let go of the tiller with his right hand and wiggled his fingers, producing something that, at first, I thought was an extra finger bone. But when he raised it to the dark opening in his hood, I realized it was a cigarette. A thin flame sprang from the tip of his index finger, and I tried to get a glimpse of what lay under the hood as he lit the cigarette. He shook his hand, extinguishing the flame, before I could get a good look, and then he exhaled a plume of white smoke that curled around his head like a reluctant fog.

"A lot of lost lovers sip from these waters," he said. "It brings them peace, but only for a few days. And then the pain returns. Stronger because it has been remembered. The experience always grows stronger when dipped in memory."

He held out his hand, revealing a wrist broken and scarred, and nestled in the palm of his hand was a faded and crumbled pack of cigarettes. The brand name was *Old Bones*, and I reconsidered the idea that what he was smoking was an actual cigarette.

"I don't smoke," I said, as politely as I could. The logo on the pack really did look like a pair of finger bones.

His fingers curled around the pack, and both disappeared into his long sleeve. "Most don't," he said. "And those that do always tell me they are trying to quit."

"A last ditch effort at salvation?" I tried.

"To the last." He blew a large smoke ring that slowly floated over his head, reminding me of a halo before it dissipated like the last light at nightfall. "Don't get called by many," he noted. "Most are surprised to see me. And none ever pack baggage."

"It's just a day trip for us," I said.

He laughed—a wet sound like pigeon wings snapping. "The last who said that was a young man with light bleeding from his wrists and ankles." He spat over the rail. "Some called him the Harrower."

"The Harrower," I breathed. There is an episode of Biblical apocrypha that describes Jesus's descent into hell following his crucifixion and burial. It is documented in the gospel of Nicodemus— one of the lost books of the Bible. An ambitious student in Wales had hypertexted most of the oeuvre of some crazy English occultist, and while I had been researching my attack strategy against purgatory, I had stumbled across the story of the Harrowing of Hell while on some hyperlink rabbit holing.

Jesus goes down into hell to retrieve the lost souls—the abandoned prophets of the Old Testament who have been left by the side of the road as mortal man thunders towards Apocalypse and Judgment Day. Jesus did this great trick, or so the story goes, where he slipped down through a secret tunnel into the dark places under the earth. He just popped on through the gates of hell like they weren't there, and had a bit of a wrestling match with Satan before liberating Adam and Noah and Moses and all the others who deserved seats in heaven.

"And did he?" I asked. "Did Jesus only come down for an afternoon?"

The boatman blew a pair of smoke rings that morphed into skulls and crossbones.

"Don't believe everything you hear," he said. "Some stories are meant to give you hope, but there is no hope here. Not on this river."

"Abandon hope all ye who enter here."

He nodded gently. "Ah, that was what the Italian poet kept saying." The boatman said something that sounded Italian, but it was from a time and place I didn't know. "You don't know the original, do you? You've got a translation, but that's not the one I remember." He was quiet for a moment. "Ah, yes. The one done by the writer. Sayer. *Lay down all hope.* That was how she said it. *Lay down all hope, you that go by in me.* Every generation phrases it different—sometimes it needs to be in order for it to be understood." He shrugged and took another drag. "Abandon. Lay down. *Relinque.*"

"Heard 'em all." I said, offering a tentative smile. "But I don't believe everything I hear."

He laughed again. "That's twice now, Dreamer. Twice you have made me laugh." He spit over the railing.

"Is there a prize for the third time?"

"There are no prizes on this river."

There was some catch in his throat that tripped up his words. Even more curious, I took a step closer. He did not move as I approached, and when I reached up and grabbed the back of his hood, he made no effort to stop me.

I revealed the white bones of a skull, jaw locked in a rictus, eye sockets filled with gray ash. His half-smoked cigarette was clenched between frozen teeth. But there was something lopsided about his face, something about his eyes that was out of place. There were tracks down his bony cheeks; tracks inscribed by a flow that had gone on for centuries. Tear tracks. "My God," I realized. "You're just as much a prisoner as everyone else."

He reached up with his broken wrist, and pulled the cigarette free. He flipped it at me, and I took a step back to avoid it. He raised his hood, hiding his tear-streaked face, and when he spoke, his voice was now muffled by the hood. "Your stop is next, Dreamer."

Before I could say anything, Dasher shouted from the front of the barge: "Land ho!" The rest of the team clattered over to see.

I felt the barge tip as they all bunched along the port side, and for a second I thought the barge might tip over. The ferryman pulled on the tiller, and the back of the barge swung outward, angling the barge toward the bank.

The mist had taken on a yellow cast, like something from an Eliot poem, and it carried a scent of melted polyester and charred cardboard. It was as if the smell was masking something else, a top note that hid the stench of rotting flowers or the breath of dead babies.

A rocky shoreline gnawed at the bottom of the barge, and we got hung up for a second, slowly spinning around an obstruction in the water. Then, with a grinding noise, the barge surged across the rocks beneath us, and we were free.

Something bobbed in our wake—something dislodged from the murky riverbed. It rolled over slowly, and I caught the rounded curve of some great creature's ribcage. Bubbles broke around the swell of the thick bones, and the carcass disappeared beneath the disturbed surface.

A gangly pier appeared in the yellow mist, a ragged spit of wood jutting from the broken line of rock that made up the shore. The boatman leaned hard in the other direction, and I felt a reverberating scrape as the rudder slowed our movement in the shallow river. The barge bumped against the pier.

Donner leaped over the leaning railing and clattered across the rickety pier. The rest of the reindeer followed like a series of nocturnally imagined sheep springing across an equally imaginary turnstile. Ring hung back, approaching the front of the boat with some reluctance. He stopped at the railing and glanced back at the ferryman and me.

I coughed, and then extended my hand to the ferryman. "Thanks for the ride," I said.

He was busy lighting another cigarette, and he ignored my hand. "You shouldn't trust that map of yours too much. Dante was prone to metaphor and hyperbole."

"Is that freely offered advice?" I asked. "Am I supposed to believe you?"

He spat into the river again. "Belief is what you make of it."

"But didn't you tell me not believe everything I hear?"

"You have to believe in something," he clarified. He nodded at me and then toward the reindeer. "Your heart. Them."

He started to push the tiller in the other direction, slowly shoving the barge away from the dock, and I took the hint. Ring waited for me, and after I jumped on his back, he leapt over the railing onto the ramshackle pier.

Behind us, the barge slipped away, vanishing into the thickening fog. The ferryman's cigarette glowed, a light that pierced the gloom. "I took him back," the ferryman called. "The one who bled light. I took him and his baggage back to the other side."

"Why?" I shouted, turning around on Ring in a vain effort to see and hear more plainly what the ferryman was saying.

"He made me laugh," the ferryman said. "Once for each day he lay dead."

The boat was almost lost in the fog. "Will you do the same for us?" I shouted after him. "Will you take us back as well?"

The boat was gone, and I nudged Ring to get closer to the edge of the pier. The wood groaned under the young reindeer's feet, and I strained to hear anything over the complaining wood.

His voice came faintly from the distance, almost as faint as the sound of a flower petal falling on cool ground. "There is no hope on this river."

VII

THE WOOD PILINGS AND BOARDS OF THE PIER HAD BEEN A WARM OAK COLOR once, but they had been stained dull ochre from an eternity of contact with the yellow fog that swirled along the bank of the black river. The fog had a cloying weight to it, like it was reluctant to let go of my clothes and hair, and it made my skin crawl. What floated over our heads was lighter in color and less dense—a mist more than a fog, for the meteorologically inclined—and somewhere between sky and ground, the two melted into a damp inversion layer. Dasher tried to go airborne as the team assembled on the spongy ground beyond the pier, but he fell back to the ground almost immediately, coughing and choking.

"Looks like we walk from here," Rudolph said as Ring and I joined the group. The reindeer had already powered up their tactical rigs, and several were pawing the ground with adrenaline-fueled eagerness.

"Here" being limbo, aka Not Quite Hell—in much the same way that purgatory wasn't quite heaven. But you could certainly feel that it was close by. The ferryman hadn't named the river, but he had said it was a sister to Lethe; in *Inferno*, Dante and Virgil crossed the river Acheron where they reached the first circle of Dante's vision of hell—the circle where the unbaptized went. Here we would find the souls of those men and women who would have gone to heaven if they had just been recognized properly by the

Church before they died. Dante gave the impression that it wasn't such a bad place to go if you had to go to hell.

My eyes were starting to sting, and the fog was making my throat itch. There were indistinct humps and lumps dotting the mist-shrouded landscape, like enormous piles of mashed potatoes that had passed through the twin stages of 'rot' and 'decay' several weeks ago.

Clearly, Dante hadn't stuck around for long.

"Well," said Comet, "I guess the limo isn't coming."

He trotted away from the pier, disappearing almost immediately in the miasma.

"Last one there is a rotten egg," he called.

Ring's shoulder shuddered as he fought back bile. "It smells like rotten eggs already," he whined.

I breathed heavily through my mouth. The smell got worse as we moved away from the river, and I couldn't imagine what sort of olfactory torment the reindeer were going through. Especially Ring. If his nose was sensitive enough to have tracked the scent of my sunscreen all the way from the North Pole, well, I didn't want to truly imagine what this place smelled like to him.

"Fan spread," Rudolph called to the team. "Double up and watch to the middle. Let's not get lost in this muck." I climbed down from Ring, and scrambled onto Rudolph's broader back. As soon as I was settled, Rudolph started off after Comet, setting the pace for the rest of the team.

Ring followed, through he kept his distance from the other reindeer. I glanced back and saw the dejected droop of Ring's head. It wasn't just the smell that was bringing his mood down. I tapped Rudolph lightly on the back of his neck. "You could apologize," I said softly.

Rudolph glanced over his shoulder at Ring. "No one ever apologized to me," he said.

"Yeah, and look how you turned out," I said, looking back at Ring. The small reindeer's face was pinched, and his ears were tucked against his head. "Quit being so defensive."

Rudolph snorted, and his next step jostled me enough that I had to grab on or slip off. "What have I got to be defensive about?"

"The kid dunked Ramiel," I said. Loudly enough that Ring heard me. His head came up, and his face was all eager beaver. Rudolph saw it and snorted again, but this time neither Ring nor I felt that he meant it. Ring trotted closer, coming nearly abreast with Rudolph, and I gave him a wide smile.

It felt good. Like I was breaking some rule here in hell, which only made me want to smile more.

We passed the first mound. It was black and sleek like stone that had been melted into a slick bubble of polished curves. There was no sign of Comet, and Rudolph gave the mound a wide berth, but Ring—emboldened by the almost-apology from Rudolph—trotted up to it, leading with his tiny, bouncing nose.

There was a tiny *snick*, and Ring jumped back with a squeak. A piece of the mound was flopping out at an awkward angle. Like a tiny hatch had popped open. Rudolph paused, and we both watched as Ring double-sniffed the dangling bit. "I didn't touch it," he said. "I didn't touch anything."

The sound came again—a metallic *snick* like shears closing—and I saw the dangling piece move. *Scissoring.* "Move," I shouted at Ring. "Get back!"

The little reindeer jumped sideways as the piece of dark material twisted and struck at the reindeer's flank. I saw it more clearly now: the upper half was a curved blade; the lower half was a jagged jawbone. The pincer snapped at Ring—*snick, snick*—like a pair of sharp scissors slicing cleanly through a yard of cloth.

Where there had only been one pincer, there were suddenly many as the mound exploded into a writhing mass of demonic crustaceans. They wriggled and crawled over one another, their large pincers reaching and snapping for the small reindeer. They had long flat bodies and thin legs like stalks of rotting asparagus. If they had eyes, I didn't see any; all I saw were enormous mouths with rows of sharp teeth and pairs upon pairs of arms. The larger sets—the ones that ended in the snapping pincers—were meant to grab prey; the smaller ones had three digits and resembled T. Rex arms—they were responsible for grabbing and shoving food into the mouth. These creatures had been evolutionarily optimized to feed their eternal hunger.

"We got company," I shouted at the other reindeer as Rudolph backpedaled from the tumbling morass of hungry demon crabs. Ring leaped into a short glide as an eager monster dashed for his flashing legs, and its outstretched pincer snipped off a piece of a back hoof. Ring stumbled as he landed, and Rudolph's gait slowed to let him catch up.

An eager crab outdistanced the rest, scuttling and snapping for Ring, and Rudolph intercepted it. He reared, and put both hooves right in the center of the crustacean's shell. One of its pincers nearly caught Rudolph in the neck, but the big reindeer bore down, and there was a loud crack as his hooves broke the shell. The crab screamed—a human enough sound that my skin went all goose-bumpy—and all four thrashing arms went limp. Rudolph leaped free of the dead crab, his front hooves dripping with a pale slime, and with a hissing noise, the body of the crab started to melt.

"Okay, that's gross," Ring said. He had stopped when Rudolph intercepted the leading crab, and he actually leaned toward the melting corpse, his nose working.

The rolling mass of crabs was close, and my jaw dropped with surprise as one of the crabs actually pounced. Rudolph wasn't as surprised as I. He dropped his head, spearing the crab on the points of his horns, then he shook his head ferociously a few times. The crab tumbled free, leaking from the holes in its shell.

"Run, you idiot," Rudolph snapped at Ring.

Ring snapped out of his naïve curiosity and started running. Rudolph trotted backward, which I greatly appreciated. I'm sure it was because he wanted to keep an eye on the crabs, but it also meant his horns were between me and them. I was trying to count them all, but they scuttled over each other with such alacrity that it was hard to keep track.

Another one leaped, and before I could warn Rudolph, a missile shot overhead and intercepted the flying crab, turning it into a fiery shower of crab bits. The crab-mob veered to the right, boiling over another mound. More crabs geysered, the second mound joining the mob from the first, and then all of them swarmed after us again.

"Oh, great," I said. "They have friends."

Another missile streaked past, and this one hit the front rank of the crab-mob, making a hot, noisy mess of crab beasties. Cupid appeared beside Rudolph and me, miniguns whining and chattering. The leading edge of the mob bucked and wavered under the assault, bullets shattering shell and pincer alike.

"Did you miss me?" he shouted over all the noise.

The rest of the team appeared out of the fog, falling into a tight formation around us.

"Where did they come from?" Comet wondered. I was glad to see the fog hadn't eaten him whole. "I didn't spot anything on my pass."

"Ring woke 'em up," I said. "The mounds. They're just crabs. All molded together."

"Oh, boy," Comet said. "There's a lot of those mounds up ahead."

Donner and Prancer dropped back from the rest of the team. Donner laid down a thick line of orange foam between us and the crabs, and when he came back for a second pass, the crab mob had already rolled over the line of expanding foam. Prancer opened up his flamethrowers. The foam ignited with a roar, and the black mob scattered. The surrounding fog was lit by dancing bits of fire as the burning crabs fled.

"Running away or going for reinforcements?" Vixen wondered. "Anyone want to guess?"

"Let's not stick around and find out," I suggested. As Donner and Prancer rejoined the line, the team reoriented themselves and picked up the pace. We had no idea how many mounds there were, but no one was interested in doing a survey.

Clinging to the harness on Rudolph's back, I kept an eye on the tiny fires. One by one, they went out. "Ah, team, I think we have a problem . . ."

Crabs started boiling out of the fog from all directions. Comet and Cupid each took a side with their miniguns; Dasher and Dancer kept our route open with tactical missile strikes. Donner kept up a steady stream of naphtha foam behind us, and Prancer and Vixen made sure it all burned bright and hot with their flamethrowers. Blitzen had some sort of short-range laser system that drilled neat holes in crabs who thought they could fly. Rudolph trampled any that got past all that.

But they kept coming, wave after wave of scuttling black bodies, their pincers rattling and snapping at us.

"Hole!" Ring shouted, and the team veered as one, dodging a dark spot that opened suddenly ahead of us. Comet was on the outside edge of the team, and he leaped over the hole instead of going around it, and as he passed over, a stack of crabs spewed out of the hole like a jet of dark vomit.

Comet kicked at the pair of crabs snapping at his hooves, as small slots along the underside of his pods opened. A handful of oblong canisters dropped out.

Like the ones Ring had been carrying.

The canisters exploded, a burst of hot light that illuminated the crater in the ground, and jets of sparkling white smoke shot upward, making a brief hole in the mist overhead. Shards of crab carapace scattered through the air, and a piece whizzed past my head. It sizzled as it went by, the accelerant from the grenade still eating at the crab shell.

The ground around the hole was littered with gouts of white-hot flame, and the rim of the crater was on fire. A thin stalk of crabs climbing over each other struggled to grow tall enough to reach past the fiery rim of the hole, but it leaned over and touched the rim before it could grow tall enough. The crabs scattered, falling back into the crater, and as I watched, the hole started to shrink, a wound closing on itself in an effort to stem the pain. The fires weren't going out on their own; they were going to be smothered.

Dasher played wingbuck as Comet did his run and jumped over other holes. On our right, Cupid and Dancer did the same. We kept running and gunning across the first circle of hell. I scooped up a jagged piece of lower pincer somewhere and hacked about myself with it on the few occasions that Rudolph found himself in pincer-to-hoof combat with the crabs.

My internal compass was all screwed up; it had been since we had boarded the barge, but Rudolph ran like he knew where he was going. Single-minded. Focused. Running on a straight line away from the world of sunlight and snowfall, deeper and deeper into places of darkness.

Comet, our perpetual point deer, spotted it first: the white line that marked a change in terrain. It wavered through the fog, like a mirage of a damp oasis in the desert, and the crabs, as if they could sense the edge of their realm, redoubled their efforts to bring us down.

Everyone switched to full auto. There was no point in trying to conserve ammo.

VIII

THE WHITE LINE TURNED INTO THE EDGE OF A SANDY DESERT. I HAD NEVER been so happy to see sand dunes in my life, but my elation was cut short as a bubbling wall of crabs started to rise between us and the desert.

"They're cheating," I whined. "How did they get in front of us?"

"It doesn't matter," Rudolph snapped. "We go through regardless."

I did a quick check on the other reindeer. Donner and Blitzen were the only ones still wearing their rigs. The rest had ditched theirs as they had run out of ammo. "How?" I asked. "We're running out of options. Blitzen's not punching reindeer sized holes in anything, and Donner's foam isn't a projectile weapon. I can run faster than it can spew."

"We go over then," Rudolph said, galloping faster.

"But—" I squeaked, and then caught myself.

What other choice did we have?

Rudolph whistled at the rest of the team and did the herky-jerky galloping two-step that signaled his intentions to the others. Cupid looked at me, wide-eyed, and I merely shrugged.

Donner slowed slightly, cutting across our back trail, his nozzles spewing orange foam. They ran dry, and he did a weird shimmy, popping the restraints on his rig. The whole thing came apart and bounced along behind him. The rig was overrun by the crabs, and it self-destructed after five seconds, going up with a teeth-rattling *whomp*. The line of orange foam Donner had laid down went up too, creating a wall of flame. The tsunami of crab crashed into the burning wall, and some of the crabs spilled through, their shells slick with sizzling fire, their pincers burning like the torches of an angry medieval mob. The wave crashed, creating several firebreaks in the wall, and crabs poured through.

The wall of crab ahead of us was leaning as if it was going to fall over on us as soon as we got close enough to be smothered. Just as I thought it was going to topple, Blitzen fired his laser weapon, cutting a line through the crabs just below the smeared mist line. A surgical slice. Crabs fell, no longer connected to the wall, and the ones that still had working legs started to scuttle in our direction.

Rudolph's chest heaved as he sucked in a lungful of air, and then he jumped. I did the same—sucking in air, that is—and I held on tight as he went airborne on a steep climb.

We hit the mist, and my eyelashes curled. Tears bled from the corners of my tightly closed eyes, and every inch of my skin was doing the frantic spider dance, shouting *Get it off! Get it off!* My chest ached, and I wasn't sure how much longer I could hold my breath. Rudolph kicked his legs, knocking something away, and then . . .

Rudolph passed through the apogee of his leap, and I felt the change in the air as soon as he started descending. My skin stopped freaking out. My lungs stopped panicking when they realized they might actually get good air soon, and when I felt Rudolph land on solid ground, I opened my eyes.

We were through.

The second circle of hell was an endless desert. We went from spongy fog-shrouded darkness to orange sky and pure white sand. There was no sun, just a sky the jaundiced color of a rotten orange, and the sand looked like it had been heat steamed of all color over the course of several millennia.

I gasped for air, and started choking as my lungs filled with hot air.

So that much was true: it *was* hot in hell.

"A towel wouldn't have been enough," Donner gasped as he landed behind us.

My gaze was drawn to the line between the two circles. The wall of crabs was coming down as the crabs lost their cohesion. The burning ones kept crawling forward, and as soon as they crossed the line, they flash-burned to ash, creating a thickening haze of drifting ash.

Of the team, only Rudolph was unaffected by the temperature. Blitzen was still wearing his rig, and while the reindeer moved a little more sprightly without the weight across their backs, I could tell the heat was taking its toll.

"Let's get moving," I said to Rudolph.

Rudolph nodded and moved out, trotting on a course perpendicular to the line between the circles. We kept to the ground. While flying would get us off the hot sand, it took concentration and a reserve of energy that none of the team had. Tongues dangling, the rest of the team followed Rudolph and me across the second circle of hell.

Dante claimed this circle was the prison of the lustful, where they were held captive by winds created from their own lecherous desires, but as we crested dune after dune, I started to think that Dante had gotten this one wrong. A wind had blown here once, because sand dunes didn't arrange themselves, but it hadn't blown in a long time. The sand was pristine and unmarked—not unlike the beach sand at the Le Grand Courlan Spa Resort.

The boatman had warned me against trusting Dante. The first circle certainly hadn't been as dull and boring as the poet had led me to believe. Unless the crab creatures were some demonic interpretation of being unbaptized, but I wasn't sure how you went from "Whoops, I forgot to get dunked in the river" to "OMG! I am teh hungerzz!"

"Maybe Dante got it backwards," I mused out loud.

"How's that?" Rudolph asked.

"Dante said the first circle was where the lost souls went. The second was where the lustful were imprisoned. But it sort of seems like he got them reversed," I said.

"Great," Comet groused. He was near enough to have overheard our conversation. "So the map is wrong."

"I never said it was right," I countered. "It's a metaphor. We interpret hell in our—"

"Bla bla bla," Comet interrupted. "This isn't a poetry—"

His leading hoof disappeared into the sand. He stumbled forward, trying to catch himself with his other hoof. That leg sunk into the dirt as well, and he barely managed to avoid a full faceplant. He struggled to pull himself out of the sand, but the ground shivered around him, sucking him down.

"Grab him," Rudolph shouted as he pranced close to the sinking reindeer. I wrapped one hand through the harness straps and leaned over, straining to reach Comet's rack.

The dune was shifting around Comet, trying to bury him at the same time it was sucking him down. The ground beneath Rudolph's hooves remained firm though, and I managed to wrap my hand around Comet's antlers. "I got him," I said to Rudolph, who started to back up. Comet stopped thrashing, and I groaned as the tug-of-war between the quicksand and Rudolph stretched me tight. I was suddenly aware of just how sweaty my palms were.

Donner charged over, sliding to a stop next to Rudolph, and he locked his antlers in Comet's, adding his incredible strength to Rudolph's. It was enough to overcome the pull of the sand, and Comet slid out so quickly it was almost as if something had spit him out. The dune quivered, grains of sand tumbling in a narrow wave, and then stopped.

I looked, and looked again. But I couldn't tell where the quicksand began. It all looked the same. The other reindeer crowded around, wondering what had just happened.

"It was right there," Comet said, nodding at the sand. "Something grabbed me."

"Where?" Blitzen said, his nose cautiously stretched toward the ground.

"There!" Comet said, and when Blitzen stopped moving, he amended his answer. "No, to your left."

"Here?" Blitzen tapped the sand lightly with his hoof, and nothing happened. He moved his hoof to the left and tapped again. "Here?"

"Yes," Comet said, struggling upright. "It was right there." He stomped over, ignoring my squawk of alarm, and banged his hooves against the sand. "It was . . . right . . . . It was right here!"

He glared at us. We stared back. Nothing moved on the desert. And no reindeer sank.

"Okay," Rudolph said. "It's a mystery, but let's not dwell on it. Keep moving. Watch your step. You know the drill. We're easy targets when we stand around like this."

My arms ached, and I leaned against Rudolph's neck. His skin was warm, and I could feel a distant quiver in his muscles. He was tired. We all were. "We're easy targets anyway," I murmured. "Anyone watching can see us coming for kilometers."

Rudolph leaped forward suddenly, and my head snapped back as I tried to hang on. He pranced about, bouncing me around on his back. "St-st-st-stop it," I chattered. "What's wrong?"

A tiny whirlpool turned in the sand where he had been standing. It stopped as I watched, filling up and smoothing out until there was no sign anything had happened.

"We're surrounded," Vixen muttered. "They're under the sand." He squawked in surprise as the sand sucked at his front hooves, dragging him down to a kneeling position. The others leapt to his assistance, dragging him out of the quicksand, and he stood gingerly a few meters away from where he had been standing. We all stared at the flat sand, squinting for some sign that something had actually disturbed the sand.

"There's nothing here," Ring said. He nosed my leg and directed my attention to the way we had come. "All it wants is to stay that way."

All sign of our passage across the desert was gone. There were no hoofprints.

What happens to the lustful when they finally give up?" Blitzen asked. "What becomes of them then?"

"Despair," Ring answered.

Blitzen nodded. "They lose hope, and that's when the sand claims them." He pawed the ground. "How long has it been since Dante wrote *Inferno*? More than seven hundred years. None of the souls here lasted that long."

"What? You mean eternity came and went, and we missed it?" Comet was still stepping gingerly, as if he expected the ground to open up at any moment.

Blitzen shook his head. "No, they may still here. For centuries, they were tormented by what they didn't have, and after a long time—a very long time—they gave up. They couldn't sustain that desire any longer, and that's when the sand took them." He tapped the sand. "They're down there somewhere, entombed in this sand by their own hopelessness. An oubliette of eternal despair."

"That's depressing," Prancer said.

Blitzen cocked his head. "Don't dwell on it," he said. "I'm not, and that's why I'm still standing."

"That's only because using words like *oubliette* makes you all tingly," Comet said. He titled his head and tried to shake out some sand that had found its way into his ear. "Okay, Mr. Sunshine, if you're right, then all we have to do is keep our mood up, and we'll be fine."

I stared off at the endless ridges of sand dunes, and Rudolph snorted at me as he quickly pulled a back hoof from the cloying sand. "Sorry," I said. "The idea is a little daunting. We have no idea how long it's going to take to cross this desert."

Rudolph kept moving as the sand kept trying to suck him down. "Knock it off," he growled. "Or you're walking."

"Carols," Ring giggled. "We can sing carols." He pranced around Rudolph. "Oh, you know Dasher and Dancer and—"

"Not that one." Rudolph glared at him.

Prancer nudged the bigger reindeer with his shoulder. "Loosen up, you old stick in the . . . uh, sand," he said, trotting off and nodding for Ring to follow him. "Come on, kid. I'll teach you a new one. "Ambrose the amber-assed antelope had a very shiny ass," he sang in a clear contralto. "And if you ever saw it . . ."

Ring skipped along beside Prancer. "Saw it. Saw it. Saw it," he sang.

I slapped Rudolph's flank gently, starting him out of the mood he was in. "Made of brass," I said. "You'd say it was made of brass. Come on, you know how it goes."

Rudolph exhaled noisily, and the stern flick of an ear in my direction was the only acknowledgement I got that he had heard me. He fell in behind the rest of the team as they followed Prancer and Ring, though he didn't join in with the other reindeer games.

He had a different way of maintaining focus. As always.

❄

After carols came an extensive Elvis retrospective. Throats were past parched as we hit the last years of the King's life, but the reindeer kept on, their voices falling to rattling whispers as they trotted and staggered across the hot sand. I lay flat on Rudolph's back, soaked with both mine and Rudolph's sweat—and well past caring about it.

I had long since given up on trying to keep track of how far we had gone—counting dunes was just asking to get clobbered by a depressing thought. Depression was tantamount to giving in, and we all knew what happened then. The team was tired, and the idea of having to pull someone out of quicksand was almost enough to open up the sand right then.

Prancer was teaching Ring something like the fifth alternate version of "The Twelve Days of Christmas" when the young reindeer squeaked.

"Lookit, lookit, lookit," Ring crowed.

I raised my head and glanced at the prancing reindeer on the top of the next dune. The team staggered up the slope and spread out, and when Rudolph reached the top, I struggled up.

In the distance, past a very finite number of dunes, a dark line ran along the horizon.

"Hooray," I croaked. "Something new."

"We made it," Ring sighed.

"Almost," Rudolph said. He went ahead, stepping and sliding down the far side of the dune. The others followed, slowly.

Still, step by step, the dark line got darker. And thicker.

IX

THE LINE BECAME A BANK OF BLACK CLOUDS STRAINING IN CHAOTIC MOTION at the edge of the desert. There was no sign of any ground, and when we reached the verge of the second circle, we saw why: the desert simply ended in a sheer cliff. Comet walked to the edge of the cliff, ignoring Blitzen's warning, and sniffed the boiling clouds carefully.

"They're just storm clouds," he said. "You can smell the rain." A bolt of lightning flashed somewhere within the cloudbank, and thunder shook the cliff.

Comet backed up, and we all watched part of a dune quiver and slide over the edge of the cliff. The white sand was picked up by the winds of the third circle, and the clouds swallowed the grains instantly.

Rudolph was eyeing the tall plumes of clouds, and I knew he was wondering what the air was like up there. There was a definite temptation to fly over the cloud cover, as they had so many snow-storms during Zero Hour. But it was a dangerous temptation to succumb to.

Ring strayed close to the edge, his nose working. "It stinks," he whined. "Like Brussels sprouts."

"Where?" Comet joined him, testing the air too. "I didn't—oh, yeah, there." He made a face, sticking out his tongue. "Oof. That's not good."

"We have to go down," I said, mostly for Rudolph's benefit. "You descend into hell. We can't fly over this." I had pulled out the book, speed-reading to figure out what Dante had written about the third circle.

And I had just hit the spot where he talked about the guardian of the third circle. The big one.

Rudolph lowered his horns grimly, as if he were going to charge the storm. "Down it is," he said.

"I'm not going first this time," Comet said. Whatever was down there, he had smelled it too. And he looked a little green.

I glanced at the others. We were haggard and exhausted, and this was only the third ring. I didn't have the heart to tell them how many more there were. Blitzen caught me looking at him, and I quickly gazed back down at the book.

I saw the word my finger was resting on—*misery*—and I quickly closed the book. That wasn't helping.

Blitzen sighed, reading something in my sudden panic about the book, and lowered his antlers. He gently prodded Comet in the rear.

Comet danced forward in surprise and then realized he'd been suckered as he danced right off the edge of the cliff. He took it gracefully though, and turned his moment of shock into a some-what graceful leap. The clouds embraced him, and we heard his caterwauling shout as he dived.

Blitzen jumped off next. Cupid shook his head as the second reindeer vanished. "Lemmings," he sighed as he followed the first two. The rest followed in quick succession. Once a couple go, the rest follow. Reindeer stick together like that.

Ring backed away from the edge until he bumped into Rudolph. "It really stinks," he said.

Rudolph walked around Ring, and glanced back when he reached the edge of the cliff. "You can't stay here," he said gently.

"I could," Ring protested. "I could wait for you right here. I'm good at waiting."

A ghost of a smile touched Rudolph's lips. "No you're not," he said. "You didn't wait for us to come back to the Residence."

Ring hung his head. He took one step forward, and then his nose started working again, and he backed up two steps.

He was quivering from nervous exhaustion, and I was struck by how young he really was. The others were old Zero Hour veterans. They had done the impossible more than once. They might not like what was asked of them, but they knew how to push themselves.

"Come on," Rudolph said. "We don't leave any behind."

"But, on the barge . . . ? You said I was expendable."

The smile vanished as a ghost of old memories darkened Rudolph's eyes. "No one is expendable," he said. "I was making"—he shrugged as if it didn't really matter what he had been trying to do—"Come on, little buck. It's time to fly."

Ring still balked. He knew what Rudolph was saying, but his hooves refused to cooperate. He was a sniffer, that one, and he couldn't turn his nose off. The noxious odor assailing him was paralyzing the motor function center of his brain.

Rudolph snapped at Ring, baring his teeth, and the little reindeer spooked. Ring bolted—in the wrong direction at first, but he corrected quickly and nearly flew past Rudolph as he sprinted off the edge of the cliff. He dropped soundlessly into the clouds.

Rudolph didn't move. "There. I apologized. You happy?"

"I'd pencil in a note to be thrilled later," I croaked. "Right after my note to fall down in stunned amazement. Hang on. Let me see if there's a pen in my utility belt."

Rudolph took two steps forward, and as soon as we left the white sand, the wind rose around us. "You can write your memoir later," he said as he flew into the storm of the third circle.

There are reports that Venus harbors a horrifically violent atmosphere beneath its gently swirling cloud cover. I've read a couple articles in *Sky & Telescope* filled with graphs and charts comparing our pleasant Earthly weather to the raging hurricanes that blow night and day across the barren face of Venus. Somewhere between the two extremes fell the weather of the third circle of hell. The weather was only tempered by the fact that if the wind was blowing *that* hard, you couldn't really enjoy the stench rising from the landfill that lay beneath the storm clouds.

Rudolph's descent was initially an out-of-control freefall defying the laws of physics and gravity that shoved my stomach between my lungs and spine. We didn't fall that long—or maybe it was forever, and my brain blocked it all out—and when we broke through the layer of clouds, the wind dropped in intensity to a good, stiff kite-flying sort of breeze.

My ears were ringing, and I felt like I had just been wrapped in burlap and trampled by a herd of musk ox. The ground, which I smelled well before I got a good look at it, came up quickly, and Rudolph botched the landing. He smashed through a mound of garbage, and I lost my grip on the book as a banana peel tried to force its way up my nose.

I tumbled to a stop in a mountain of used coffee pods, and I lay there for a minute, trying to figure out how to breathe without actually breathing. I heard Rudolph groan nearby, and eventually he appeared in my field of vision. Dark stains—like rotten jam and old 40-weight oil—smeared across his withers, and he moved like he was favoring his front left leg. "We can do that again if you like," he offered.

"I don't think I pass the height requirement on that ride," I said, extricating myself from the coffee pod mound. The top layer was loose trash, but the layer was fairly shallow. Looking for the copy of *Inferno*, I scuffed a few microwave pizza boxes out of the way and found packed garbage beneath. Hard, like granite, but still aromatic as only a landfill can be. One that was being baked by eternal fires deep below.

While Rudolph hobbled around, trying to determine whether he's suffered a cramp or a sprain, I kept looking for the book, even though I knew it was lost in all this trash. Hell wanted me to lose my mind over the book, and I had to fight that urge.

I focused on finding other things instead. Like the rest of the reindeer. They all knew to ground themselves in inclement weather. I found a pile of garbage that was solid enough to support my weight, and climbed high enough to take a peek at the landscape.

The terrain wasn't flat. There were ravines and trenches as if centuries of wind and rain had slowly carved courses through everything we've ever thrown away. The Grand Canyon of Trash. Off to my left, movement caught my attention, and I waved when a pair of reindeer crested a nearby ridge. It looked like Dasher and Dancer.

The wind shifted slightly, blowing an especially fetid effluvium of rotten vegetables right in my face. I clamped a hand over my nose and mouth and tried my best to not breathe.

"Here," Rudolph said, and something tapped me on the head. He was offering me a long candy cane. Still wrapped in plastic.

"Where did you get that?" I gasped as the words forced me to inhale.

"I packed some treats," he said. He twisted and rummaged through the pack on his back, producing another candy cane, which he ate—plastic wrapper and all.

I fought with the plastic for a second, and then managed to free the end of the candy cane from its wrapper. I licked it cautiously, and a tingling sensation crawled up my tongue. My head cleared almost immediately, and the pressure behind my eyes eased. I rolled the plastic up and took a large bite, and somewhere in my chest, my stomach started to crawl out of its hiding place. "What's in these?" I asked.

"Natural ingredients," Rudolph said, mouth full. "Totally organic. Hand-shaped by joyous volunteer children."

"The NPC doesn't let children work in the factories," I pointed out.

"I never said they were locally made," Rudolph said. He jerked his head toward the pack on his back. "There are more. Hand them out to the others. We could all use a pick-me-up."

Still sucking on the curl of my cane, I rooted through the pack on Rudolph's back, taking a proper inventory: nearly a dozen more candy canes, only two of which had broken in all the chaos; the plaid thermos I had seen earlier; and a walnut case without hinges.

"What's this?" I asked, hefting the case.

"Oh, that. Yeah, it's for you," he said.

"Celebratory cigars?" I asked, shaking the box slightly.

"Don't—" He shook his head. "You're not supposed to shake presents. Don't they teach you that?"

"You got me a present?"

"Yes. Well, no. I was just being prepared, and I didn't know . . . just open it."

The box was nicely made—all of the edges were rounded and smooth—and it took me a few moments to find the seam along the top. Once I found it, opening the box was easy.

"Oh," I said when I saw what was inside. "You shouldn't have."

Inside the box were a pair of pistols, delicately cradled on a bed of purple velvet. They looked like something René Lalique would have made if he had been hired to make the props for a Flash Gordon serial. Silvered glass and polished metal. Elf-sized too. The grips were insulated, and the pistol was heavier than I expected. I would probably have better luck clubbing someone on the head with the gun than actually shooting them.

"A little short on ammo," Rudolph said. "Which is why I didn't tell you about them earlier. They wouldn't have been much help against all those crabs."

"How short?"

"Four, I think. They're a bit unusual."

"How unusual?" I asked. The barrel of the pistol was cold, and I realized why the grips were insulated.

"Nitrogen pellets. Cold kiss of Absolute Zero with those puppies."

"And you could only manage four?" I scoffed.

Rudolph shrugged. "Hey, four in each. Everyone else only got armor piercing rounds. I don't see what you're bitching about."

I wasn't quite sure where I was supposed to put the gun. I didn't relish shoving it down the front of my thermal suit. The trouble with experimental weaponry was twofold: one, it probably hadn't been tested; and two, someone had identified a target that might require this kind of firepower to vanquish. And pointing that sort of firepower at my crotch didn't seem like the best idea.

Rudolph reached over and deftly snagged the piece of forgotten candy cane in my left hand. "Pose for *Guns and Ammo* later," he said, crunching. "There should be some holsters in the bottom of the box. Let's get moving."

I lifted the corner of the velvet case—there were, indeed, some holsters. Shoulder holsters, in fact, and already rigged for someone my size. As I struggled into the rig and slipped the pistols into their leather holsters, Rudolph trotted off to meet the pair of reindeer.

His gait was solid. Whatever had been troubling his left leg was gone.

❄

"There's something out there," Donner said. Unlike the others, he was a sucker, and he still had several inches of candy cane left. Donner had been the last to rejoin the team, and he looked like he had been running awhile when we had found him.

"Rodents of Unusual Size?" Blitzen asked.

"Larger," Donner replied. He nodded at Ring, who was nursing a bump on his forehead from tangling with a kid's bicycle when he had landed. "Bigger than that one."

"Big enough to eat him in one bite?" Cupid wanted to know.

Donner shrugged. "Would it really matter if it took one or two bites?"

I ignored them, focusing instead on the problem at hand. What had Dante said about the third circle?.

Prancer called out to Rudolph: "That's a dead end," Prancer called out to Rudolph, nodding toward the narrow gap between two pillars of trash. Rudolph had been about to slip through the gap; he paused, eyes narrowing as he considered our options.

Rudolph's innate sense of direction was better than my map, and we had been following his lead as we wandered through the canyons of garbage, picking up the rest of the team. I could tell that Rudolph wasn't pleased by the idea of backtracking as it meant we weren't moving directly toward our goal, but I couldn't think of any other way. We had tried to stay up on the top of the ridges, but the smell had been worse up there, even with the tingling menthol afterscent of the candy canes in our nostrils. It was easier down in the canyons, but the route wasn't going to be direct, which was making Rudolph grumpy.

"Did you hear that?" Ring asked.

"What?" I asked, straining to hear anything other than the distant sound of the wind as it murmured through the canyons.

"It's big," Donner reminded us.

Rudolph glared at the muscular reindeer as he starting trotting back the way we had come. The reindeer fell in line, moving quickly to keep up with Rudolph, and I hooked an arm around Prancer's shoulder as he came by and swung up onto his back.

We followed Rudolph as he ducked through narrow openings and led us down wide trenches. I gave up trying to make sense of our wandering. It was like following a route in a forest that had been cut by a schizophrenic woodsman with an inner ear imbalance. Rudolph was getting more and more frustrated. He knew where he wanted to go, but there wasn't a direct path; turning away from his goal was like forcing the compass to point south.

When we ended up in a box canyon with sheer garbage walls, I called for a conference. We huddled up while Rudolph stared angrily at the wall in his path. "We need to think about where we're going," I said. "There's got to be a key of some kind."

"This is hell," Blitzen pointed out. "There may not be a key to this maze."

Rudolph took a running leap at the wall in front of him, zooming up to the top of the cliff like crazed hummingbird. As soon as he reached open air, the wind caught him. Rudolph bared his teeth, and his muscles stood out in stark relief on his bare skin as he strained madly against the wind. He made a valiant effort, but the wind was too strong, and when his hooves stopped dancing, he was thrown back like a leaf. We watched as he sailed overhead, and then he dropped below the upper edge of the cliff and neatly swung around to land on the ground nearby.

"It was a nice effort," Cupid offered.

"I hate mazes," Rudolph said. His skin was slick with sweat. He glared at me like the confusion of garbage was my fault.

I ignored him as I tried to think. Dante had written a long poem about visiting hell, and as I had said a couple times to the reindeer already, it was just a metaphor. While our journey had obvious parallels to his, it wasn't the same. I might as well have brought a foldout to the Super Mall of the Americas. It would have been filled with tiny graphics of stuffed animals and floating hamburgers and would have been just as useful.

We came from a different time than Dante. We were different. Our cultures were different. Our hells wouldn't match, and as long as I kept clinging to the notion that we were making the same journey, we'd keep getting lost. Sure, Dante's third circle had been a mass garbage heap—a prison for the slothful and gluttonous—just like the one we were in now, but there weren't any trapped souls.

In fact, other than the hunger crabs, our trip so far had been suspiciously free of any tormented spirits. The only torment was our own, and that was being heaped on us by the environment.

"It doesn't matter," I said, the thought forming in my head. Hell wasn't a place. It was an idea—a fluid environment that only became solid as we brought our own perceptions and apprehensions to bear on it.

"I thought Dante would give us directions," I said, "but all Dante really did was show us where the door was. Everything else has been different. Well, sort of the same, but different, you know?"

"Not really," Blitzen said. "You're rambling a bit there, Bernie."

"What is hell built on?" I asked him.

"Torment and frustrated desire," he said without hesitation. "Founding principle of Satan's misery."

"And each circle is a new iteration built upon the previous one, isn't it? The first was hunger—lust—a totally uncontrolled urge to consume. And then came despair, right? The sudden realization that you could never consume what you truly wanted, that you could never aspire to what you dreamt about. And after despair?" I waved my hand around me. "Confusion. Discord. The discarded refuse of your cast-off dreams and feeble attempts at creative accomplishment. This garbage heap is everything that we ever bought, ordered, or had manufactured that wasn't quite what we wanted."

"Are you heading somewhere inspirational with this speech?" Cupid asked. "Because you're not off to a very good start."

"I'm thinking out loud."

"Well, talk faster then."

I was watching Ring's ears and nose twitch, as the little reindeer alternated between smelling and listening. "What's the key to the fourth circle?" I asked. "What's the key to every circle? What keeps us moving forward? We keep thinking there's something better out there. We keep hoping that we're going to find the inner core of hell."

"No, seriously," Cupid said. "You should just stop talking now."

"Temptation," Blitzen said. "It's all about temptation."

"What?" Cupid looked at Blitzen. "How did you get there from his blather?"

"There has to be some moment that gifts you with momentary illumination," Blizten explained patiently. "We have to have reoccurring epiphanies that lure us into thinking that there is still some hope. Every failure is not absolute; there is always some tiny nugget of hope that makes us get up and try again. It's nothing more than temptation. The Temptation of the Infinitely Unobtainable."

I grinned. "Which makes your next failure even worse, doesn't it?"

Blitzen nodded. "The pit keeps getting deeper and deeper."

I waved an arm at the walls of garbage. "That's why the walls are higher, and why the wind is stronger."

"So, wait a second," Cupid said. "I'm not following this. It's going to get worse, every step we take?"

"Of course it is," I said absently. I was becoming mesmerized by Ring's nose.

"And there's no end to it?"

"None at all," I said as I wandered over to the small reindeer.

"Okay, so what's the point then?"

Ring caught me staring at his nose, and he stood stock still, his tail vibrating with the effort to keep his nose from wiggling. "What?" he squeaked.

"What do you smell?" I asked.

"Garbage," he said. "And Brussels sprouts."

I wrapped an arm around his shoulder. "No, you don't," I said. "There's something else, isn't there?"

He wrinkled his nose and shook his head. "Come on," I urged him. "Tell me."

"It's rotten," he said quickly, lowering his head. "Like a tub of Santa's sweaty socks."

Vixen made a choking noise, and Comet hung his tongue out of his mouth.

"It doesn't smell good, Bernie," Ring whined.

"I know," I said gently, patting him gently. I looked over at Cupid. "It's all about temptation. The key to every circle, or the key to the only circle. Do you get it? I thought we had to cross all these circles of hell to reach the center, and I convinced you all that was the right path, but it's an endless path, isn't it? We're going to wander each circle forever. But it doesn't have to be that way. We made this hell; we can unmake it too. We can get right to the heart of it. But to do that, we have to dream really big. We have to think really hard on the single thing that we want more than anything in the world."

I hugged Ring. "Come on, little one," I said. "What do you smell? What do you want more than anything in the whole world?"

Ring acquiesced finally, lifting his head and opening his nostrils to the horrible effluvia whirling through the air. The little reindeer's knees shook, and his eyes started to water, but he didn't stop trying. He didn't shirk from smelling as hard as he could.

"Come on," I whispered, hoping that I had guessed right. Hoping that the heart of an innocent reindeer was the purest of them all. "Let yourself be tempted."

His eyes widened suddenly. "Mrs. C's peanut brittle," he squeaked. "I smell it. I smell it!"

My stomach grumbled, and the back of my throat seized with sudden hunger. How long had it been since I had eaten anything other than a candy cane? "That's it," I whispered. "That's our ultimate temptation. Follow that smell, Ring. Follow it."

I let go of Ring, and the small reindeer bounced around me, his head up and nose tracking the most elusive of smells.

"You sure about it?" Rudolph asked, his eyes dark.

I shivered under that gaze, but I kept my apprehension under control. "Hell is supposed to draw us in. It's like the Hotel California. Sure, Satan's got an eternity to wait for us to show up, but there's a fast track. Because it's not the trip in that he wants. It's having us stuck here, knowing that we can never leave. And we've been wandering around, thinking that we just have to get to the center where we can get Santa's soul back, but come on, that's our job, right? That's not what we really want, is it? What is it that we really want? More than anything else in the world?"

"Lunch," Ring squealed suddenly, and he galloped off, lead by his nose.

"Off you go," I said to the others, signaling that we should follow Ring before he left us all behind. Cupid gave me a hairy eyeball as he passed, not quite sure that anything I had just said mean sense, but he followed Ring's lead. Lunch was lunch, after all.

Rudolph waited for me. "That was a pretty good trick," he said as I climbed onto his back. "Will it work?"

"I hope so," I said. "Remember Persephone? She craved a pomegranate. Imagine the lure of a pound of Mrs. C's peanut brittle."

"So the real trick is going to be stopping them from actually eating any," Rudolph said. "Who is going to tell them they can't have a bite?"

I patted his warm skin. "That's your job," I said. "They already expect you to be the killjoy. Might as well live up to it."

X

Mrs. C's peanut brittle was an old family recipe, gleaned from the hand of her Norwegian grandmother, and it had the texture of soft gold. She usually made it after Halloween, and I stuffed myself stupid on it more than one night while writing FitReps for Santa during the run-up to Zero Hour. I had the dullest nose of the team, but after following Ring for about an hour, I could smell it too. It was almost like that vapor trail you see in the old cartoon, the one that lifted you up and carried you.

And finally, we found the source of the smell: a silver portal at the end of a long canyon, not unlike the one where we had conducted our confab. But this one was more imposing, longer and deeper. The walls curved inward as they rose overhead, blotting out the dark clouds thrashing in the sky. The sound of the wind rose in pitch as it faded, crying and wailing in anguish as we approached the portal.

Ring was waiting for us. "Come on," he whined, shaking with excitement. "It's just through there."

The portal shimmered suddenly, silver motes rising from the bottom. Prancer saw the tiny sparks before Ring did. "Look out," he cried, shoving the little reindeer out of the way.

A large shape catapulted through the portal, and Prancer was knocked aside, his body twisting painfully. The monster landed heavily, its weight shaking the ground, and we all stared at the three-headed beast that had just appeared.

I knew his name because, before I had given up on Dante, I had read about him. Cerberus. The three-headed guardian of hell.

Hercules faced Cerberus once. His twelfth and final labor was to retrieve the hound from hell, and the stories say that Hercules admitted that he couldn't have accomplished that deed without the help of Hermes and Athena. Dante used Cerberus as an allegory for the uncontrolled appetite which haunts the gluttonous, their punishment for a lifetime of excessiveness. The Disney animators turned him into a gigantic black beast with flaming eyes and jaws that dripped lava.

Maybe they hadn't done the lava dripping part. But they should have, because that was certainly how he was.

He was tall enough to stare down a truck driver behind the wheel of an 18-wheeler, and his teeth gleamed like polished chrome. His three heads perched atop thick necks that looked like the trunks of old-growth redwoods. His tail bristled with rattles and spikes—and maybe a tambourine or two for all I could tell. A mane of hissing serpents rose from the peak of his massive shoulders. Fire bled from his eyes, and what dripped from his black and pointed tongue burned a hole in the garbage beneath him.

Prancer was lying very still not far from the hound's massive paws. One of his legs was bent painfully under his body. His eyes were open, but he was doing his best not to look up at the beast towering over him. Cerberus's leftmost head was eyeing him, considering whether or not he would make a good snack.

"Nice doggy." Comet had been next in our file, and he was directly in front of the growling beast. "Anyone got a spiced ham or something?"

"I don't think a whole cow would slow him down," Rudolph muttered. His shoulders twitched. He wanted me off, but I didn't want to move. He shook me again, and I slid down reluctantly. I got it: I was small enough that Cerberus probably wouldn't consider me a threat, and Rudolph could move faster without me clinging to his back. But I wasn't going to outrun the big dog, not with my short legs. My stomach was hiding behind my lungs again, tapping out an SOS on my spine.

The central head dipped lower, drooling. The ichor hissed as it melted the garbage; somewhere in the packed trash, something ignited, and a lurid glow illuminated the beast's jaw. Its teeth gleamed, and it shook its head, scattering drool. The tiny fire crawled out of the hole and sent out runners of flame, chasing the scattered drops of magma spit.

Ring, who had been standing closest to the door when Cerberus had pounced through, made a noise like a startled fruit bat as he sailed up from behind the large hound. He buzzed the three heads in a *Top Gun* fly-by, and I made an involuntary animal noise myself at the risk he was taking. Cerberus's right head snapped at the flying reindeer, its teeth clashing together with a sound like two dump trucks colliding. Ring made a beeline for the nearest wall, flying close enough that he could skip along the packed garbage.

Whether he planned it or not, his run led the attention of the three heads right to Rudolph.

The hairless reindeer lowered his antlers and pawed the ground. "Come on, doggy," he said, mimicking Comet's tone. "How about a game of fetch?"

One of Cerberus's heads barked, and hell's guardian charged. The rest of the team scattered like frantic shoppers hitting the mall at opening on the morning after Christmas. I hunkered down, trying to pry up something to hide beneath. The left head snapped at me as Cerberus thundered past, its teeth closing noisily over my head. Along my sleeve, the material of the thermal suit started to bubble and hiss.

I batted at the melting fabric with a glob of cardboard, trying to scrape the spittle off before it ate through the insulating layer. I got most of it off, and after quickly checking on the rest of the team who were playing a deadly game of cat and mouse with the hound of hell, I ran over to check on Prancer.

He was struggling to stand when I reached him. He got upright, and his ankle held, but judging by how he clenched his teeth, he wasn't about to join in the game.

"Can you hobble?" I asked. I gingerly checked out his ankle, noting that it was already swelling.

"How far?"

I nodded toward the portal.

"Yeah, I can do that," he said. He offered me a wry grin. "There's peanut brittle on the other side, right? I can do anything for some peanut brittle."

I didn't have the heart to tell him. "Just get out of sight," I said gruffly, pushing him gently in the right direction.

"He came out of it," Prancer said, bobbing his head toward the portal. "I bet he can go back through it too. I'm not going to be able to run."

"You won't have to," I said, reaching for one of the pistols hanging beneath my arms.

Prancer hobbled toward the portal, and when he stepped through it, silver streamers smeared his body into a dancing cascade of light. For a second, I saw through the portal: a plain of fire. But then the vision and the reindeer were gone, and all that remained was the fading echo of a church bell and the tinkling laughter of small children.

The reindeer swooped and darted like overweight hummingbirds around the snapping jaws of the hound. Donner came in low and speared Cerberus in the backside with his antlers and was nearly caught by a huge paw for his audacity. The muscular reindeer sped away, his hooves tearing at the trash as he went directly up a nearby wall. Blood dappled the tips of his antlers.

Cerberus leaped after him, its paws digging and tearing at the slope. Donner had slowed as he neared the top, unaware of how close Cerberus was behind him. Vixen shouted a warning, and Donner reacted without looking back. He lunged forward, cresting the top of the wall, and the wind caught him immediately. He was slammed against the edge of the shelf and tumbled heavily down the side of the canyon.

Cerberus dug in to the wall as its right head snapped at Cupid, who was trying to draw all three heads from Donner, who was sprawled on the canyon floor, dazed. Cerberus let go of the wall, and slid to the base, where it sprang toward the downed reindeer.

I ran, even though my too-short legs were no match for the large hound's ground-devouring pace. The rest of the team was coming too, but it looked like Cerberus was going to reach Donner first.

Unless . . .

I saw Rudolph flying straight up, and when he crested the top of the canyon, the wind grabbed him. He didn't fight it. Instead, he let it carry him, and then he dove, hurtling down at Cerberus like a falling asteroid.

Rudolph landed directly on Cerberus's back. The middle head howled as Rudolph's hooves beat at the hound's spine, and the dog's mane of serpents struck at Rudolph's flashing hooves.

Cerberus went down, its back legs buckling under Rudolph's sharp blows. It thrashed on the ground, and then rolled, trying to crush the reindeer. Rudolph waited until the last moment to leap away, and one of the serpents tore at his flank, leaving a long scrape.

Rudolph's attack allowed the other reindeer to reach Donner. They formed a tight semi-circle around him, their horns lowered like a wall of spears.

Cerberus scrambled to its feet, two heads growling and snarling at the circle of reindeer. The left head was looking for Rudolph,, and it found the hairless reindeer just as Rudolph delivered a powerful back leg kick to the left head's jaw. The head snapped back, smacking into the middle head, making a sound like a couple of coconuts smacking together. "Get Donner out of here," Rudolph shouted at the team as the hound staggered, its heads yowling and snapping at one another.

Blitzen got his head behind Donner, and the groggy reindeer staggered upright. As one, the team started moving backward, toward the portal. They kept their antler wall pointed at Cerberus.

The right head snarled at the retreating reindeer. That head wanted to take a shot at breaking through the wall, but the other two heads wanted a piece of Rudolph, and they pulled the third head with them as they pounded after Rudolph.

The reindeer passed me as I slowed to a lung-heaving walk. I waved them on when Cupid made some noise about getting behind their pointy bits. "You heard Rudolph," I gasped. "Keep moving." I transferred the pistol to my left hand, and tried to wipe the sweat off my right.

I watched as Rudolph danced and taunted Cerberus. Without a bunch of other flying targets to distract the individual heads, Cerberus was getting closer to Rudolph with every snap of its jaw and swipe of its paw. It was going to tag Rudolph sooner rather than later.

I put several fingers in my mouth and whistled loudly. Rudolph heard my signal, and left off teasing the hound. He got a running start and took off, flying below the rim of the canyon. Executing a tight turn, he came back around toward the reindeer and me. He had to pass by Cerberus, and he tried to keep as much distance between himself and the hound as possible. But Cerberus took a run at a nearby wall, and then sprang off the vertical surface, sailing through the air. Rudolph tried to dodge, but a large paw caught his shoulder and shoved him into the wall of garbage. Rudolph kept Cerberus at bay with his antlers as they both slid down the garbage wall.

Rudolph landed sideways, and before he could scramble out of the way, Cerberus steam-rolled him. Rudolph rolled a few more meters, his limbs flopping limply, and then he was still. Cerberus turned around quickly, and ran over Rudolph again.

My shout was lost in the thunder of the hound's paws against the ground. I started running. My hand was both cold and sweaty, the grip of the pistol sticking to my skin.

Cerberus slid to a stop, and slowly stalked back toward the downed reindeer. The middle head was drooling, igniting fires in the trash again. The left head laughed at the sight of me running toward it.

Rudolph's legs kicked feebly. He raised his head and tried to focus on Cerberus, but his neck was too wobbly.

Cerberus stalked toward Rudolph, all three heads now focused on the downed prey.

I wasn't going to make it in time.

I slid to stop. My chest heaving, I raised the Flash Gordon pistol and aimed it at the large hound. "Hey," I shouted, trying to get its attention.

The middle head growled, fire dripping from its jaw.

I pulled back the hammer on the pistol with my thumb.

The left head barked at me.

"Bad dog," I said.

The pistol recoiled lazily as I pulled the trigger, and the bullet took its own sweet time leaving the barrel. *Jut a leisurely afternoon jaunt*, it seemed to be saying. And then everything sped up again, and Cerberus's left head snapped around as the bullet went into its open mouth. An explosion of ice crystals came out the other side of the dog's head.

Cerberus staggered, unsure what had just happened. The middle head gnashed its teeth, spittle flying, and the right head—having caught sight of the damaged left one—raised its muzzle toward the dark clouds and howled. Some other time and place, I might have felt sorry for him, but I could see Rudolph kicking and twitching as some of the acidic spittle fell on his bare skin.

I squeezed the trigger a second time.

Cerberus bellowed like an angry furnace as my second shot went under the chin of the righthand head and buried itself deep in his fiery core. It came apart in an explosion of icy crystals, and when I blinked the frost from my eyelashes, there was nothing left of the hound of hell but a scattered spray of melting icicles.

Rudolph raised his head as I came up to him. "Once upon a time," he said slowly, "all you got for being bad was a lump of coal in your stocking."

XI

WHEN I STEPPED INTO THE PORTAL, I FELT A COLD HAND TOUCH MY BACK. It started as a gentle caress, and as it worked its way up, its touch grew warmer and warmer, until fingers of fire were squeezing the back of my neck. I pushed my way through the portal, gasping as sweat ran down my back, and then I popped through to the other side.

And I stared.

"Hey," someone said behind me, and I blinked. I hadn't moved more than a meter, and Rudolph was awkwardly filling the space between me and the glittering portal. "Could you take a few more steps forward?" he asked.

I blinked and swallowed. "Yeah, sure. Sorry," I said, making room, and when he limped away from the portal, it started to shimmer and twinkle. I raised my pistol in alarm, but nothing else was coming through. The dancing lights lessened, and after a few moments, there was nothing left on the sandstone wall but a wet smear.

"I guess we're done back there," Rudolph noted. He looked past me. "Oh, wow," he said.

We stood on a small shelf that jutted out from immense cliffs. A polished trail wound down from our position, leading to a landscape that was utterly out of place in hell. It was the quintessential hidden paradise. El Dorado. Shangri-La. The Savage

Land. The version of Xanadu where the roller-skating muses live. A sparkling river traced a line across verdant fields as if its course had been drawn by an indolent giant. Off to my left, a forest of blazing orange and red leaves resembled a swath of delicate fire that burned all the way to distant foothills below hazy mountains. A quaint little village—its houses arranged in neat rows—was arranged along the shore of a placid lake as blue as the sky. A white clock tower anchored the town.

"What is this place?" Rudolph asked, a shudder running through his frame.

I inhaled deeply, filling myself with all the great aromas of fall: cinnamon, warm berry compote, apple pie, freshly cut hay, the perfume of young ladies. I could smell Mrs. C's peanut brittle too. "I'm not sure," I said. "I think we made it."

"Ah," he said. "Persephone and the pomegranate."

I nodded. "We can't eat anything. That's the trap."

"I'm not worried about you and me," Rudolph said. He nodded toward the distant town square, rapping a hoof on the ground to get my attention. "Vixen, especially. You can't take him to the food court at the mall. All those free samples?" He shook his head.

I climbed up on Rudolph's back, and he started to trot down the path. He picked up speed quickly, which did wonders for my nerves.

We were still in hell, after all.

A white sign at the outskirts identified the town as Maple Valley, and while there weren't any logos saying as much on the board, it looked like the construction of the quaint town had been under-written by J. Crew, Williams-Sonoma, and Restoration Hardware. Kids, prancing down the street in synchronized delight, were poster children for the fall lines at The Gap and Eddie Bauer. Signs—*Slow, Children at Play*; *Barn Dance This Thursday*; *Bake Sale in the Square!*—were hand-painted and festooned with streamers and lace trim, of course. The bake sale sign didn't mention a date, which I took to mean that the bake sale was always happening. There wasn't a stray leaf in sight. It was as if the fall colors had come, but none of the leaves were in a rush to leap to their deaths.

The whole town was perpetually poised on the edge of the equinox—that half hour between summer and fall, when everything was just *perfect*. The bubbling laughter of the children flowed around us as Rudolph trotted toward the main square, and somewhere in the distance, a radio looped love songs from that time in history when no one was worrying much about megalomaniacs convincing entire countries to take up arms against their neighbors.

The main square was filled with rows of booths, almost like a miniature version of the town itself, and I caught sight of the some of other reindeer as Rudolph and I wandered around. Dasher was off to my left, letting himself be chased by a small boy in blue pants with a water gun. Blitzen was mesmerized by a taffy-pulling machine, and three young ladies wreathed in taffeta looked like they were trying to convince Donner to participate in a dunk tank.

Ring appeared, scampering in circles around Rudolph. "Isn't this great?" he gushed. "You've got to come see it! It's Mrs C's peanut brittle. I found it. I did!" He made another loop and darted off toward a cluster of booths that appeared to be the bake sale's ground zero.

Rudolph let out an agonized whimper, and my stomach answered with an eager growl of its own. If I hadn't been sitting on Rudolph, I would fallen to my knees and crawled towards the sweet-smelling stalls. There were rows of apple pies, ice cream cones stacked taller than the tip of Rudolph's tallest antler, a sizzling vat of oil that was producing deep-fried deliciousness on a stick, bacon on bacon sandwiches, and there at the back of this first row of booths was a Nordic-looking woman ladling sparklingly chill lemonade out of a block of glacial ice.

This was just the rank of booths I could see. Even more splendid food and drink lay beyond. My stomach knew it. It didn't need silly sensory data from my eyes and nose. It knew.

I really wanted to believe it. I wanted there to be a joyous little valley in the middle of hell where the bake sale went on for eternity. But I knew it wasn't true. I knew it couldn't exist. I knew we had made it ourselves. I had asked Ring to imagine Mrs. C's peanut brittle, and everything else had come from that desire.

This was the fourth circle. After lust and despair and sloth came greed. This was the temptation that would undo us.

A little boy ran up to Rudolph and me, a stick of cotton candy in his hand. "Hello, magic horse," he said to Rudolph, holding up his stick. "Would you like to share with me?" The sweet perfume coming off the whirled cone of spun sugar reminded me of the sugar icing spray the NPC used on stockings. The little boy's face was flushed with excitement, and his eyes gleamed with unhinged joy at the sight of such a marvelous *horse* in his town.

Rudolph shook his head politely. The boy kept shoving the stick of cotton candy in his face, and Rudolph backed away a step. "Make him go away, Bernie," he begged, his body trembling. "Make him stop."

I wasn't quite sure what the big deal was. It smelled delicious— summer sunshine spun into wispy sugar strands by magical silk spiders. Were we being rude? Not even a tiny bite? My tongue ached. The little boy looked at me—a Rockwell-perfect image of Midwestern civility and early-century innocence.

I managed to wrench my gaze away from the plume of cotton candy and watched with mounting horror as the man at the taffy booth detached a long strand of freshly pulled taffy. He held it out to Blitzen, who was staring at it like he had been blinded by the sun. His mouth gaped open, and his tongue lolled like he was trying to make room for the entire strand of sticky taffy.

Persephone had only eaten four pomegranate seeds. Four little seeds, and she was condemned to spend a third of the year in hell. What would a bite of taffy get you? Or a mouthful of cotton candy? Or a slice of Mrs. C's heavenly peanut brittle?

I turned back to the little boy with the apple cheeks and the stick of cotton candy. His smile broadened as he saw me straighten on Rudolph's back. I reached under my arm for one of the pistols and drew it out of its holster. When I shot him in the chest, he exploded in a blinding blast of ice crystals.

Someone screamed nearby, and a shudder ran through Rudolph as he shook off the cotton candy glamour. A woman ran toward us, nearly stumbling and falling on an icy patch left behind by the boy. "You killed him," she screamed. "You killed my little Billy."

I shot her too, for good measure.

Everyone started screaming, a cacophony of sound like a flock of angry birds in a threshing machine. The sound swelled and swelled until it became an unending shriek—a hundred fingers clawing at blackboards. Gritting my teeth, I dropped the now-empty pistol and put my hands over my ears.

A pinhole opened in the center of the square, and the entire town started to smear as it was sucked away. The booths vanished, the apple pies and ice cream cones and bacon sandwiches sliding away in a long liquid pull. The white clock tower bent in the middle and then zipped away like it had been sucked through a straw. The tree-lined avenues lost their integrity one line at a time, turning into a stiff backdrop before bleeding into a rushing wash of color.

The sky went black, and the ground became a beaten deck of rusted metal. Statues—melted and twisted as if caressed by someone with lava fingers—rose up around us. Tiny winged creatures with long toenails capered across the shoulders of these statues, and their shrill voices were the dying scream of the now-vanished town. Beyond the monuments, there was nothing but a vast space filled with flying rocks. Somewhere far below this suspended plate, I could imagine a furnace like the belly of a dying star, and hot air rising from that furnace was what kept the plate floating and what spun the rocks. Collisions were rough, shattering events where chips as large as elephants were knocked free and spun away in crazy orbits.

The reindeer were all there, stunned by the rapid transformation. I tried to check each reindeer's mouth. Had any of them taken a sample of what hell had offered? Vixen wasn't chewing anything; Cupid's mouth hung open. *What about . . . ?*

In the center of our haphazard circle, a sparkling rain of fire fell. It twisted and slowly assumed the form of a tall man. His eyes were a blazing blue, and his smile was a dazzling display of expensive orthodontistry. He wore a silk smoking jacket with velvet lapels, a red shirt with black buttons, and pair of crisply pressed pants. On his feet were Italian slip-ons. Ferragamo's, if I had to guess.

Probably the python moccasins that had been all the rage last Christmas. A cigar burned casually in his left hand.

He did a slow turn, looked at each one of us as he pulled heavily on the cigar, the tip glowing like a malignant Cyclopean eye. When he came back around to Rudolph and me, he pulled the cigar from his ruddy lips and tapped it once. A thick block of ash fell free. It struck the metal plate, and a spark snapped at the contact.

One of the reindeer screamed. I tried to see which one it was, but the sound was cut off nearly as soon as it had begun. There was a flash of light as flesh and blood and organs vaporized in an instant. In the horrible emptiness that followed the scream, we all heard the sound of the loose bones as they rattled against the plate.

It had been Prancer. Silly goofy Prancer who knew all the songs. Who had even warned me that he'd do anything for a piece of peanut brittle . . .

XII

"Welcome," Satan said, puffing on his cigar again. "I hope my entrance wasn't too ostentatious. I attended a seminar once where the speaker really stressed the importance of making a good first impression. It can totally set the tone for the whole relationship." He flashed his perfect smile at me as smoke plumed from his nostrils in even jets.

And that was when it hit me: that crushing weight of true despair. We had come so far, fighting our way through hell on this crusade to rescue Santa's soul. We had pitted our might and our brains against the unholy realms and had nearly made it. But it had all be for nothing. *Hubris*, I thought bitterly. What had we really won? Here, in the center of hell, Satan's power was absolute. With a mere flick of his cigar, he could reduce us all to ash. We had been led here by our own gullibility. While our persistence kept us from being swallowed by the desert in the second circle, it gave us false hope. It was a ghost light that lured us on, leading us into a hell of our own creation. The oubliette of eternal despair, as Blitzen had called it.

The rest of the team looked as depressed as I was, and our expressions made Satan laugh. "Oh, such abject misery. You all look like orphans out of a Dickens novel. So very, very sad." He clucked his tongue lightly as he tilted his head and looked at me. "And for what?" he said.

He flicked the end of his cigar again, and we all flinched, but there was no ash to dislodge. "Nothing," Satan said, a touch of mocking disappointment in his voice. "There is nothing here for you."

Rudolph hadn't moved. He was standing square, perpendicularly lined up with the Devil's face. It was a classic martial arts stance, altered slightly for reindeer physiology. He didn't seem concerned about the hulking demons crowding us. "We came for Santa," he said quietly. "We're taking him home."

Satan laughed. "Santa? What makes you think I have him?"

"He's not in heaven."

"He's not here." Satan spread his hands. "You're welcome to look." And when Rudolph didn't move his head, Satan looked Rudolph in the eye. "You don't believe me," Satan said.

"Why should I?"

Satan made a face. "Please, that is so tired. I lie no more than a fifth-grader with Pokémon cards in his pocket and a copy of *Playboy* stashed under his mattress." He pointed at me. "I don't need to lie, my dear Rudolph. Your friends do that quite well on their own."

"Bernie," Rudolph growled.

I thought frantically, and all I could come up with was the glittering snowfall in Mrs. C's office. "Oh," I said, realizing what it was. Rather, *who* it was. "He never left," I whispered. "The gates of heaven were closed. That's what he said. He couldn't get in. He's still there. He's haunting the North Pole."

"And you're here," Satan said, spreading his hands. "Oh, the irony is making me all tingly. Down th—"

"Then who killed him?" Rudolph interrupted. "Who killed Santa Claus?"

"Bird flu, perhaps?" Satan offered. "Maybe Ebola is making a comeback. I hear that bats are carrying it now." He shuddered, a motion of his upper body that became a quaking movement on his shoulders. "Oh," he sighed. "I'm so awful at keeping secrets."

His well-manicured hand dipped into the pocket of his smoking jacket. "Maybe"—he smirked as he pulled out a thin vial—"maybe it was this." He shook the tube and held it up.

The agitated liquid changed color, changing from a rich hunter green to a cherry red.

"I thought there would be more of it," Satan said, peering at the tube. "But I guess it doesn't last long when it has been drawn off. Some sort of biochemical reaction to the atmosphere down here, I guess"—he shook the vial again—"but you'd have to ask a real scientist. I'm just—"

"A liar," Rudolph said.

Satan rolled his eyes and shook his head. "Look closely," he said, holding the vial out for us to inspect. Tiny bubbles floated in the red solution, and I would have sworn they looked like tiny Christmas ornaments.

"It's Christmas," I breathed. "He's stolen Christmas."

"Not *all* of it," Satan clarified. "Just what was keeping the old man upright."

"His spirit," Rudolph said.

Satan raised his shoulders. "I suppose you could call it that." He shook the vial again, making the bubbles move. "But I'm inclined to be more generous than that. I mean, we could dash off to a lab somewhere and get this analyzed, but I don't think it'll last that long. So let's just call this the very spirit of the season, shall we?"

"You son of a bitch," I spat. "That's why Santa died, and that's why Mrs C is dying too. You've stolen their . . . their . . ." I sputtered to a stop. Their hope. Their spirit. The *Spirit*.

"It's an unfortunate side effect, I'm afraid," Satan said, a thoughtful expression marking his face. "I'm afraid you can't take it without ruining the host." He shrugged. "But, I've never been one to lose much sleep over things like this. Guilt? Nah. Not for me. Too much baggage."

He flipped the vial in the air, catching it easily. "Look on the bright side, boys. Do you know how long it's been since I've made Santa's List? It's going to be a lovely Christmas for me this year."

He smiled and raised his head as a fiery rain started to fall on the statues surrounding us. The statues started to twitch and wiggle, animating in jerky motion like leftover frames from *Fantasia*.

"You've gone and shown real pluck and effort," he said, "but really? You've lost. You're here, and you're going to stay here for the rest of eternity. I'd love to stay and chat more, but I do want to enjoy my present to myself before it evaporates. Maybe I can round up a few Princes of Hell later, and we can play Go Fish or something."

Rudolph shook his head. "We're not done yet," he growled. He was unfazed by the statues coming to life around us.

Satan cocked his head and looked at Rudolph, a bemused expression on his face. "Excuse me?" he said.

"Bernie," Rudolph said. "Open the pack. Get the present."

"The *what*?" Satan and I both said.

"Get it," Rudolph said.

Bewildered, I pulled open the pack and rummaged around inside. The only thing left was the red and blue thermos. "This?" I asked, lifting it out of the pack.

"That's my thermos," Blitzen said in a surprised tone of voice.

"Not anymore," Rudolph said.

"Are you regifting me?" Satan asked, a dangerous note entering his voice. "Are you giving me someone else's gift?"

Rudolph shook his head. "I'm not very good with wrapping paper and tape," he explained. "And it fit nicely inside the thermos."

"*What* fit?" Satan growled.

"A tactical nuclear device," Rudolph said, and I dropped the thermos as if it had burned my hand.

It clattered to the deck, and several of the leering demons flinched as it rolled across the plate. Satan looked down as it pitched up against his python-leather clad foot. "A thermos," he noted. "You expect me to believe that you've got a nuclear device inside this thermos."

"A *tactical* nuclear device," Rudolph repeated. "Small yield, but highly radioactive." He turned his head slightly. "Bernie. In one of the pouches on your belt, there's a detonator. The code is '4-4-6.'"

My hand strayed unconsciously to my belt, feeling for the zipper on one of the pouches. I moved my fingers and felt inside, touching a rectangular shape. I pulled it out carefully, and turned it over. It looked like a solar calculator, but when I hit the ON button, the display actually lit up.

The Devil snorted, and a tiny line of smoke drifted from his left nostril. "You're actually threatening me with a nuclear device?"

"It probably won't kill you," Rudolph said. "And, in my state, I might even survive. But everyone else is dead. Turned into water vapor and blasted into component atomic particles. That includes your little vial of Christmas Spirit."

Satan's eyes flickered towards the tube in his hand.

"If the children don't get Christmas," Rudolph said, "you don't get Christmas."

I pushed the 4 on the keypad, and that same number showed up on the display. Just like you'd expect with a calculator. Or a calculator that had been modified to send a short burst of radio signals when someone pushed the ENTER button.

My eyes strayed towards the back of Rudolph's head. I had to know if he was bluffing. I knew his tell. The reindeer had told me. He glowed when he bluffed.

My throat closed, and I struggled to breathe.

Rudolph wasn't glowing.

"It's a simple deal," Rudolph said. "You give us the vial and safe passage out, and we don't detonate the device."

"What if I said *yes*, but lied?" Satan puffed on his cigar, affecting an air of utter indifference.

Rudolph laughed, and I flinched. It was the same laugh I had heard in the infirmary at Santa's House. Everything was simple to Rudolph. Black or white. On or Off. Go or Stop. Success or Failure. He didn't believe in anything else. And his laugh was the sound of perfectly distilled madness—the purity of knowing something that no one else could ever imagine.

Satan stared at Rudolph, his gaze equally unyielding. "Go ahead," he said. "Set it off. I don't think you have what it takes to destroy everything you've ever loved."

"Bernie." Rudolph's voice was a clear chime. My finger trembled, but I managed to press the 4 again.

Some of the demons in the assembled rank shifted nervously, but I noticed the reindeer were all standing tall.

"You don't think that nuclear death isn't something visited upon those trapped here?" Satan waved an arm towards the crashing rocks. "You should visit the ninth circle. Nuclear winter would be a summer's day there. Your threats are empty, reindeer."

"Are they?" Rudolph asked.

Satan licked his lips, his tongue black and forked. "You're bluffing. There's nothing in that thermos that you couldn't buy in a can at the supermarket."

Blitzen moved beside Rudolph. "He doesn't know how to bluff," he said. "I should know. We play poker together. Every Friday night." I could feel a slight tremor from Blitzen.

Cupid marched up to Rudolph's other side. "After saving Christmas, Santa let me see," he sang "Satan begging for pity." He leaned toward Rudolph and nudged my hanging leg. "Do it, Bernie. Don't let them say we didn't try."

I pushed the third button. The display read '446.' My hand drifted towards the ENTER key.

Satan's eyebrows came together, and his face darkened. "This is my domain," he hissed, growing a few centimeters as he spoke. "How dare you threaten me in my own realm." He held the tube tightly in his hand, and his knuckles went white. "Who do you think you are?" he demanded, stepping forward until he was almost nose-to-nose with Rudolph. "James Bond? Robin Hood and his band of Merry fucking Men?"

No one said a word for a long moment, an expanding second that seemed to stretch to the end of Time and back. Rudolph and Satan stared at one another. And, at the end of that second, Satan blinked.

"I'm Rudolph," the reindeer said. "And we're Santa's team."

And then he head-butted Satan.

XIII

THE DEMONIC HOST WAS CAUGHT OFF GUARD BY RUDOLPH'S SURPRISE ATTACK. Satan staggered back from Rudolph, his forehead bleeding. His grip on his cigar loosened, and the thick cylinder fell towards the deck. Cupid spun and lashed out with a hoof. It was a NFL-worthy kick; the cigar flew the length of the deck, and vanished over the edge of the plate.

Blitzen lowered his head and charged the nearest rank of demons. He caught one in the belly with his rack, and it howled loudly, clawing frantically at his antlers and raking free long strips of velvet. When Blitzen shook his head, the demon popped like a water balloon, dispersing in a smear of dank smoke.

The rest of the team leapt into the fray with equal abandon.

Satan, blood streaming down his face, tried to clout Rudolph with a fist, but the reindeer reared back beyond Satan's reach. I dropped the detonator and tried to grab the harness, but my hand closed on nothing, and I slid off Rudolph. Satan ducked under Rudolph's flailing hooves and drove a shoulder into the reindeer's chest.

Ring got in a good shot, smacking his head against the back of Satan's thigh. Satan stumbled, his center of gravity disturbed, and Rudolph caught him in the face with an upward antler swipe. Satan stood on his toes for a second, his head cradled in Rudolph's antlers, and then he tumbled to the deck.

When he scrambled back to his feet with a roar, the vial was still on the plate. He kicked it accidentally as he sprang at Rudolph, grabbing the reindeer Greco-Roman style, and they strained against one another, titans wrestling for the fate of the world.

I dove for the vial, trying to get my hands on the last of the Spirit of Christmas before someone trampled it. Something grabbed my feet and pulled me back. My chin rebounded against the deck, and I felt a sharp sting as the contact drew blood. I struggled as I felt the thermal suit tearing around my ankles. A gangly demon covered with spikes was clawing at my legs, his cracked nails shredding my thermal suit. Soon, those nails would be doing the same to my flesh if I didn't get him off me.

A large hoof hit the deck next to my head, and I froze. Reindeer, like most four-legged creatures, will instinctively not step on living things in their path, but I didn't want to press my luck. Especially with a reindeer the size of Donner. The demon hissed at Donner, who took it as an invitation and charged. There came a satisfying thud, and the demon let go. Donner lifted his head, the howling demon caught in his rack, and heaved the flailing monster toward the edge of the plate. It scrabbled and flailed as it bounced along, but its nails were no good against the metal, and with a final howl of outrage, it went over the edge.

I stayed low, scanning the plate for the vial as the demonic host went back and forth with the reindeer. I couldn't go toe-to-toe with any of big demons, and so I had to be small and quick as I darted about in search of the vial.

I nearly had it when a squat demon backed over me. He fell on his ass, and I banged my chin on the plate again. Vixen had been chasing the demon, and he poked at it with his antlers, forcing the ugly monster to scuttle away on its backside. Lying on my stomach, I reached for the vial, catching it with a finger at first and then flicking it around so that I could a good hold on it. I half expected someone to suddenly step on my hand or kick my fingers—that's the way these sort of things went, right?—but my fingers closed around the vial without mishap.

It was warm to the touch, and the liquid turned from green to red when I shook it. I fumbled with the pouches on my belt, dumping it in the first pouch I could get open. It wasn't quite a lead-lined, Kevlar-covered, gelatin-filled capsule, but it would do.

The reindeer had been giving as good as they got, and I would have guessed the odds were pretty even, but the arrival of a pack of large winged monstrosities with more teeth than brains was tipping the scale. These flappers harried the reindeer from above, which forced them to split their attention.

And then the odds went from bad to worse when Satan caught Rudolph with a haymaker that knocked the reindeer down. As I watched, Satan jumped on Rudolph, straddling the struggling reindeer, and delivered punch after punch.

Ring darted up and head-butted Satan with his tiny knobs, and when that didn't get Satan's attention, he started flailing away with his hooves, doing a pretty good meat tenderizer impression. Annoyed, Satan stopped punching Rudolph long enough to twist around unnaturally. He caught one of Ring's legs and pulled the young reindeer close. He raised his other hand, fingers spread, and pressed it firmly against Ring's chest. There was a crackling flash of smoke and Ring flew across the plate, his fur burning.

Rudolph tried to buck Satan off, but Satan held on tight, riding Rudolph like a prize rodeo rider. When Rudolph started to tire, Satan wrapped his hands around Rudolph's neck. Rudolph squirmed, trying to get his antlers in play, but Satan ducked his head and leaned in close, his hands squeezing.

I caught sight of Prancer's bones, and my gaze was drawn to the circular shape of his skull. He didn't have the largest rack of the team, but he had always been one of the most obstinate. *Dense,* even. I darted across the deck, grabbing at the short rack of antlers as I ran by. *Hardheaded,* I hoped.

Rudolph's eyes were straining, and his tongue bulged out of his mouth. Satan wasn't exactly having an easy time of strangling the big reindeer; I could see the corded strain of the muscles in his arms as he bent to his task. It wasn't going to be a quick death.

"Yo, Scratch," I shouted, and Satan swiveled his head in my direction. His eyes gleamed with excitement, and his smile was filled with hellfire.

He never should have looked.

I wound up and swung Prancer's skull like I was aiming for the center field triangle in Fenway Park.

The v-shaped weapon was not unlike a turkey wishbone, and I made my wish as the heavy object smashed into Satan's face. I kept my grip, even though my elbows went numb, and the other half of the antlers splintered off as Satan was lifted off Rudolph and sent sprawling across the plate. He flopped over once and lay still, his nose mashed flat on his face. It was going to take all the plastic surgeons in Beverly Hills to make that face pretty again.

Rudolph was flopping around too, and even though he was having trouble breathing, he was still in better shape than Satan. "Grand slam," he wheezed as he struggled to his feet.

I hefted the remnants of Prancer's skull and antler rack. I still had the bigger piece. "Sometimes," I said, "you get what you wish for."

"You've got to think bigger when you do that, Bernie," he said, looking past me. I looked, and saw more flappers approaching. "You should have wished for an entire carrier battle group."

"You want to threaten them with the thermos again?" I asked.

Rudolph shook his head painfully. "You can only fool 'em with chicken soup once."

I stared at him. There was a matched set of fingerprints bruised into his throat, and blood from a nasty cut over his left eye was painting his muzzle and throat. "You *were* bluffing," I said. "The others said you glowed when you tried to bluff at cards. That was your tell. That's what gave you away."

He smiled. "Hey, they let me play, didn't they?"

Donner whistled from the far end of the plate, calling the team to formation. The others started to disengage, falling back toward the muscular reindeer. Donner kept the edge clear of demons, and the reindeer charged for the gap, laying about themselves with antlers and hooves as they ran. I swung up onto Rudolph's back, both of us wincing painfully at the contact, and he limped towards the opening.

Donner was wrestling with a monster three times his size as we approached. Ring darted past us and butted the demon in the calf with his head. The monster slipped, and Donner yanked his head to the left, throwing the demon off the plate. Just like that, there was nothing between us and the edge. Rudolph stumbled slightly as he tried to run, and I leaned forward, hanging on tightly as he went over.

The worst dive ever, but neither of us cared. We were off the plate, and it only took Rudolph a second or two to orient himself and start gliding on the super-heated air rising up from the furnace heart of hell.

"There!" I pointed out the rest of the team to Rudolph. They had found a floating rock that was relatively flat, and were already landing on it like tiny snowflakes. Rudolph spiraled down, and managed a landing that was about as bad as his dive.

"Nice—"

I didn't finish as clawed hands wrapped themselves around my head and pulled me right off Rudolph's back.

I squirmed in the demon's grip, but I might as well as have been a biscuit for all the good it did. This demon was enormous, and I had no idea where he had come from, but he was on the rock with us now. Holding me aloft with one hand, and forcing Rudolph's head down with his other. He was kneeling on Rudolph's back, bending the reindeer's spine in a direction it wasn't meant to go. He was the size of an office building, swollen with dark fluid and shaped like a Cubist's nightmare. He had six eyes in his massive head and his tongue looked like the rainbow tassel on the end of a winter cap.

My vision swam—no, more like it was drowning, going down for the third time. I could barely make out the other reindeer, and I dimly tried to figure out why they weren't helping us. They were all on the far side of the rock. Half of them were crouching and Ring was actually bouncing up and down. Blitzen was at the point of their loose formation, and when he looked back at us, I realized what he was doing.

The demon giggled—a sound of crumbling boulders—his attention on Rudolph's flexing back. The big reindeer was trying to squirm out from beneath the demon's weight before his spine snapped. Neither of them were paying much attention to where our floating stone was heading.

Blitzen was changing the course of our rock by altering the distribution of weight across it. Ring's Tigger impression was making tiny corrections to our course as we hurtled across the sky. I stopped squirming, and shoved one of the demon's thick fingers out of the way enough to see where we were going.

Rather, what was heading for us.

A rock, twice the size of our flying boulder, was on a collision course.

Blitzen was going to scrape us along the belly of the bigger rock. Not enough to take off a layer of stone, but enough to clothesline the big guy squishing Rudolph. And If he was still holding me at the time . . .

My kingdom for a witticism, I thought fleetingly as the air in my lungs vanished. My mom had imprinted me with a great deal of Shakespeare when I had been too small to get away, and it had a tendency to bubble to the surface when everything else fled. What I wouldn't give for a tongue sharpened by a serpent's tooth or a brief gift of Puck's gab or Mercutio's rapiered repartee. Or even the Riverside edition to bludgeon this monster with.

The large rock loomed like a falling planetoid, and I closed my eyes, unwilling to watch the end as it arrived.

Out, out, brief candle . . . was my final thought. Well, not my final thought. My final thought was: *Really? The Scottish play? That was how I was—*

XIV

"STOP SQUIRMING," DONNER ADMONISHED THROUGH CLENCHED TEETH. HE was biting down on the upper part of the thermal suit, and I was—thankfully—still in the lower half. I had no recollection of how far I had fallen or what had happened after . . .

Blitzen had piloted our floating rock perfectly, close enough to the tumbling asteroid to have turned Han Solo's hair white. A melted spire jutted out from the surface of the bigger rock, and when it hit our asteroid, the demon had other things to worry about. I was tossed aside as the spire cut a large gash through our rock, tearing up the layers of basalt like a piece of bread in the hands of a cholesterol-hungry butter-lover coming off a five day detox.

The spire missed the demon, but it got hung up on a hunk of something hard in the core of our rock. Rudolph tumbled across the stony ground as the two rocks snapped toward each other, the hook holding them tight. The smaller rock flipped around the hook, and smashed itself against the bigger rock, crushing everything between them.

The impact had been noisy, and shards of stone flew off both rocks. I tried to figure out if any of the flying chips were actually tiny reindeer, but I was busy falling.

It's a long drop into the furnace of hell. Long enough to get maudlin, and I had been starting to really feel sorry for myself when Donner swooped down and snagged me.

I felt like a lion cub being dragged home after having been caught wallowing in the week-old carcass of a zebra, bouncing and dangling from my mother's jaw.

It was a great feeling, actually.

I caught sight of a glimmering rectangle lit by fire. "Satan's awake," I shouted up at Donner. "And he's putting out a call for all of his friends."

Donner flew faster, and I stopped looking behind us and started looking ahead, trying to figure out where Donner was headed. We passed the smashed together rocks, which were still spinning end over end, and kept going.

Going where? I wondered. *How were we going to get out of here?*

There was a different glimmer far ahead. A ribbon of light flowing through the endless sky. Like a river.

Styx?

Other shapes floated up around us, and I did my best to not squirm as I looked at them. Dasher and Dancer and—

My heart skipped a beat.

—and Vixen. And Comet and Cupid and Blitzen and Ring.

"Is that a river?" I shouted at Blitzen.

"We hope so," he shouted back. "How many rivers are there in hell?"

Three actually, I thought. Styx, Cocytus, and Acheron. According to Dante, Cocytus ran around the ninth circle, spilling over into the pit. Acheron ran between the worlds, and that was the one we had come in on. Which left Styx. Where had Dante put the river Styx?

"What about Rudolph?" Ring cried. "We can't leave him."

Blitzen shook his head. "He's gone, kid. He didn't make it."

Ring stiffened his legs. "No," he wailed.

Donner and Blitzen slowed too, and the rest of the team streaked on, heading for the river. Behind Ring, who was trailing all of us, appeared a dark line limned with fire.

Satan's host was coming.

"The collision flattened anything larger than a dust mite," Blitzen told Ring sadly. "Rudolph wasn't in any shape to fly. He didn't get off in time." He nodded toward the thickening line behind us. "They're coming, Ring. We don't have time to go back and check."

"No one gets left behind," Ring said coldly and wheeled around, streaking back towards the two embracing stones.

Blitzen watched the little reindeer swoop and dart back towards the spinning pair of rocks. "I'm too old for this," he muttered. He looked over at me and shook his head. "Not one word from you," he admonished. "You've got the vial. You're going home. Don't wait for us." He shot off after Ring.

Donner was a good soldier, and he listened to Blitzen. I kept my mouth shut and my hands wrapped tightly around my chest. There was a burning ache behind my ribs. Prancer. Rudolph. Ring. Blitzen. How many were we going to lose?

The river was a flat Möbius strip winding its own course through the rock-filled air. A large stone shot through the ribbon, and water splashed outward in an explosive arc, the huge droplets falling as hissing rain. The hole in the river remained for a second, and then the water filled it in. There was an invisible channel cut in the sky, and the river continued along that path as if nothing had happened.

We flew up and over from the side, the team gliding onto a path directly over the river. From above, it looked like any body of slow-moving water, deep and wide enough to move with languid grace towards its final destination. I glanced up and down its length, trying to spot anything floating on its surface.

The boatman had said there was no hope on the river. And I expected the same was true for Styx as it was for Acheron, but I had hope all the same. I remembered reading that all the waters in hell came from the same source: a large stone statue hidden in a black grotto. The rivers came from the mouth of this chiseled king, and all the waters were tainted by the eternal tears that flowed down his cheeks. Metaphor and hyperbole broke the rivers up shortly thereafter, taking them on their own routes around the lands of hell.

I looked up and down the river, and hoped. I hoped the boatman hadn't lied to me, that he wanted to hear another story.

That he wanted to laugh. I hoped the vial shoved in my belt pouch was going to be enough to save Christmas.

"Boat ho!" Comet shouted, and he dropped to the left, angling for a mist that was now bubbling on the water. There was a familiar shape at the edge of the mist: the most bedraggled barge in all the world. The rest of the team banked like a flight of dark crows and followed Comet. Donner let go of my collar as he touched down on the barge's deck, and I quickly stumbled to the hooded scarecrow hunched over the tiller.

"So, Dreamer," he said softly. "Have you come to tell me a story?"

I bent over my knees, trying to catch my breath. "It's a good one," I managed. Between gasping breaths, I spun him a fantastic tale about reindeer and the hosts of hell. The rest of the reindeer weren't all that interested, and I stuttered for a second when I realized what they were looking at.

There were tiny shapes tumbling toward the river. It was hard to be sure against the boiling cloud of smoke and flame hot on their heels, but it looked like three reindeer.

My heart beat quickly in my chest, and I inhaled, rushing through the story. I had to finish it before hell caught up with them.

Rudolph and Blitzen and Ring were flying as fast as they could, fleeing before the thundering line of the howling host. There were little ones that looked like half-chewed lumps of bubble gum; tall ones that dwarfed the one that had landed on our rock; creatures made from bone, and some formed completely from flame. They howled and screamed and wailed as they filled the sky behind the flying reindeer.

The ferryman's face was invisible inside his hood, so I couldn't tell whether he was enjoying my story or napping on his feet. I got impatient and skipped over the discovery of the little town, jumping right to our showdown with Satan. I started to babble, the words tripping out of me.

The three reindeer plummeted into the river, bobbing up on the disturbed surface and paddling desperately for the edge of the barge. The team shouted encouragement as the sky overhead filled with the swarming mass of the host of hell. Demons fell out of the sky, and plumes of steam rose from the river as they hit the water.

Donner kicked out a section of the barge's railing to make it easier for Blitzen to struggle onboard. Rudolph was bobbing behind Blitzen, but he kept slipping under the surface like he was having trouble staying afloat.

I waved my arms and danced about, recreating the battle with the demons in a crazed community theater style. The ferryman hadn't laughed at the bit where Rudolph clobbered Satan in the head—which I had thought would have sealed the deal, but this room was tougher than I thought. I was getting desperate for a laugh, which is the worst situation any stand-up entertainer can be in.

Rudolph didn't have enough strength to climb onboard. He could barely keep his head out of the water. Around him, the river was foaming and boiling as demons thrashed toward him. Ring paddled around Rudolph, trying to help push him onto the barge, and as I got to the part of my story where Satan was choking Rudolph, the little reindeer took a deep breath and dove underwater. Rudolph had managed to get one hoof and leg on the barge, but he was clearly exhausted and couldn't manage to raise himself any higher. Suddenly, his rump lifted out of the water, and he heaved the front half of his body onto the barge.

As Rudolph dragged his dangling rump and hind legs onto the barge, Ring popped up in the boiling water. The little reindeer gasped for breath as he paddled furiously. He disappeared under the water for an instant, coming back up a second later, paddling with some urgency. The disturbances in the water were getting more pronounced.

"And . . . and th-th-then I hit Satan in the face," I said breathlessly. "Like I was swinging at the last pitch of the last inning of the last game of the World Series. Down by two. Three men on. Count is full. One last pitch." I mimed the motion of hitting the game-winning home run.

The ferryman said nothing for a long minute, and then he leaned against the tiller. "Did you leave any marks?" he asked.

"I broke his nose," I said.

The ferryman chuckled, and he leaned back, pulling the rudder of his barge. Instantly, a curtain of fog and fire surrounded the barge, and the host of hell howled with impotent fury. The barge started to drift sideways to the current of the river, and I knew the host couldn't touch us any more.

"I like that part," the ferryman said, raising a bony hand to the opening of his hood as if indicating his nose. "He was obsessed with that face."

I stumbled across the boat to where the team was clustered around Rudolph and Ring. Rudolph was on his knees, still coughing up river water. He was covered with scratches, and part of his left ear was gone. He was having trouble focusing, and he stared at me a long time before he seemed to recognize me. "Did you get it?"

I tapped the pouch on my belt. "Yeah—" I started, but the words died in my throat when my hand came away wet. I fumbled for the zipper, and dug in the pouch for the vial. It was slick to the touch, and my hand shook as I held it up. There was a hairline crack near the bottom, and most of the Spirit had already run out.

Rudolph's head fell forward until his forehead touched the deck. "So close," he whispered.

"Take it," I said to him, lifting his head. He tried to pull away, but I held his jaw firmly. I pushed the near empty vial at his mouth. "Once this is gone, it's all over. Take it so Satan doesn't win."

He opened his mouth painfully and accepted the narrow vial. I pushed his mouth closed and his jaw moved sluggishly around the glass cylinder. I wrapped my arms around his neck and held him tightly as he chewed and swallowed the last of the Spirit—glass tube and all.

Christmas was going to live on, even if only in the belly of a reindeer.

But Satan wasn't finished. He had a parting gift for us, a final chunk to carve out of our souls.

The rest of the team made room for me as I pushed through their ranks. Ring looked up at me as I knelt beside him. His eyes were wet with tears. "Don't shoot me," he pleaded. "It's not as bad as it looks." Satan's handprint was still visible on Ring, burned into his side, but protruding from the center of the mark was a jagged piece of bone. Some monster had hit Satan's target with perfect precision. Ring coughed and there was blood on his lips. "Don't put me down."

I stroked the rough fur of his sweaty head. "I won't," I said.

"Promise?"

I shook my head. "You're going to be fine. We're going home. We'll get you fixed up."

Ring struggled to sit up, and Donner put a heavy hoof on Ring's rump, holding the little reindeer down. Vixen made room as Rudolph dragged himself to join the group. "I did good, didn't I?" Ring asked, looking at Rudolph.

Rudolph nodded. "Yeah, kid, you did good."

"I dunked an angel," Ring said proudly. "I dunked him in the ocean." He coughed heavily, pink froth coming from his mouth. "I was the diversion." I put his head in my lap, and his nose quivered as he smelled the damp pouch on my belt. He smiled and closed his eyes as he thrust his nose into the pouch, like he was rooting around for a piece of candy. Some of the tension left him then, and I felt his breathing slow.

Blitzen was crying openly. "Hey, kid," he whispered. "You can't go. We need you on the team."

Ring struggled to open his eyes. "The team?" he asked, his voice somewhat muffled by the pouch.

Blitzen nodded. "Yeah, this Season. We're going to need you out in front."

Ring's legs scrabbled against the worn logs of the raft as he raised his head. "But . . . but that's Rudolph's job."

Rudolph's face was just as wet as everyone else's. "Not anymore. I don't have what it takes to show the way anymore. You do. You showed us all."

Ring sat up, and this time Donner didn't stop him. "I'm going to lead the team," he said as if he couldn't quite believe what he was saying. "I'm going to lead." His legs rattled against the wood again, and I knew he was thinking about snow-covered rooftops. Then a long shudder ran through his body, and he put his head down in my lap again. "I'm going to be one of Santa's reindeer," he told me, and it was the last thing he said.

On the river of sorrow, somewhere between hell and the North Pole, a young reindeer died.

XV

THE BARGE SWEPT OUT OF THE FOG AND GROUND AGAINST A WHITE PLAIN OF ice. I stood at the back with the ferryman. "Where are we?" I asked, my breath fogging from my mouth.

"As far north as the free water goes," he replied. His hood was pushed back from his bare face, and he seemed to be enjoying the cold air. "I'm just the pilot," he said. "My passengers chart the course. Some journeys are short. Some are long. But almost every destination is possible. It is just a matter of where your heart wants to go."

My heart was a lead brick in my chest. I was surprised it hadn't directed us right back to Satan's doorstep.

The ferryman nodded towards Ring's body, which looked so small on the deck of the barge. "He's not for me. His final destination isn't a place I can go. I'm sorry. I know that isn't much consolation."

I smiled sadly. "It'll do." I held out my hand, and he took it carefully. His grip was firm and dry. "Thanks for coming back for us."

He nodded. "It was a good story."

Donner helped me carry Ring off the barge, and we laid him down carefully on the ice. The rest of the reindeer filed off the barge in solemn single file, and none of them looked at Ring as they passed. Rudolph was the last, and before he came off the

169

barge, he went up to the ferryman and lightly bussed him on the check. "Merry Christmas," he said.

The ferryman's hand went to his face, his pale fingers covering a brief flurry of red and green light that flickered across his skin. He stared after Rudolph as the reindeer limped off the barge and joined the rest of us on the ice.

"What?" Rudolph asked gruffly. He twitched his tail in that *Get On My Back, You Annoying Little Man* sort of way.

"Nothing," I said, grabbing a strap of the harness and hauling myself up. Rudolph's bare skin was cold, and I stuck my hands under my arms to keep from touching his back. I was used to him running hot.

The ice groaned as the barge shifted, slipping into the fog that was rising out of the glacier we were standing on. I looked back, but the ferryman was already obscured by the fog. I heard his voice though. As the barge slipped back onto the waters of Styx, I heard the ferryman start to sing.

"He's got a good set of pipes on him," Rudolph noted. "Who knew?"

It sounded like he was singing "White Christmas."

The reindeer gathered around Ring's body. We had gone to hell and back and looked the part. It was hard to say who had the most scraps and burn marks, and all of them looked haunted beyond belief. In comparison, little Ring looked like he was pleasantly sleeping on the ice. A tiny blot of crimson staining the ice under him was the only indication that he wasn't going to wake up at any moment.

"Go north," Blitzen said. "We'll take care of Ring. You two need to get to the North Pole. If Bernie's right and Santa's still up there, the only thing keeping his ghost there is Mrs. C. You've got to find a way to save her. You've got to find a way to bring him back."

"You going to be okay?" Rudolph asked.

Donner shook his head. "No, but we're Santa's reindeer, and we will bring our own home."

I had no doubt. Woe unto anyone that tried to stop them.

Blitzen looked me in the eye. "Be careful," he said. "It may not be over yet."

"What do you mean?" I asked.

"We only made it to the fourth circle of hell, right?"

"Right," I said. "Satan met us halfway. And then we got out."

He shook his head. "Remember the other circles," he said enigmatically. "Not every journey is a linear one, and nothing is as true as you think it is."

I nodded as if I understood what he was talking about, and Rudolph and I turned away from the group. There was a chronometer-compass in my belt, and I glanced down at it as Rudolph slowly started trotting up the gentle slope of the glacier. The compass needle and Rudolph's nose pointed in the same direction. North. The Pole. The Residence. I felt it in my belly too. A distinct tug toward the top of the world. The Pole still called to me. As much as I had tried to leave, as much as I had tried to bury it all within me, and as hard as Satan had tried to blind us all with despair and desolation, there was still some spark inside of me. A tiny flame of hope that couldn't be extinguished. My promise, made to a jolly fat man many years ago.

Rudolph picked up speed and finally launched himself into the sky. I held tight to the harness as we flew north to see if there was any Christmas left to save.

The North Pole was cold, colder than it had ever felt before. The chill stole in through the torn ankles of my thermal suit, and no matter how I clenched and bunched the front of the ruined suit, the wind blew in and tickled my spine. Rudolph was shivering too as we came over the last rise and dropped below the lip of the valley. The angel balloon still floated over the Residence, but its light seemed weaker. Or maybe the shadows slithering along the walls of the Residence were getting bolder. Rudolph flew close to the ground, his hooves nearly touching the graying snow.

He landed on the upper balcony, and I slid off his back. We both stared at the reindeer door he brought me through previously. It hung half-open, and a snowdrift was already creeping into the Residence.

Merry Christmas, Herr Schrödinger. Thanks for the thought experiment with the cat. We'll always have this moment:

caught on the cusp of not knowing whether Christmas was alive or dead.

"Come on," I said. "We have to find out."

We had to look inside the box.

We found Mrs. C in the infirmary. We walked through nearly visible lines of arctic air as we entered the tiny room. Santa was still on the bed, his white hair spread out on the pillow around his gaunt face. The sheets were tucked in tightly around him, and a plastic tarp had been wrapped around the base of the mattress. He looked like a king in repose, awaiting final passage on the reed boats through the passages of night that led to heaven. Mrs. C was curled up in wingback chair pulled up next to the bed. One of her hands was stretched out and resting on Santa's covered shoulder.

She didn't look much better than he did. Her skin was gray, and her hair was brittle and colorless, like strands of ice. She was wearing a simple house robe that seemed several sizes too big, and one of her slippers dangled half-off, revealing a thin and skeletal foot.

She stirred as we approached the bed, and her eyelids fluttered as I touched her lightly on the shoulder. She sighed heavily as she opened her eyes, as if the effort was too much to manage. She stared at me for a long time, and I watched her pupils slowly shrink to a more normal size.

"Bernie," she whispered, her voice barely more than a weak exhalation of glacial air. "You've come to say goodbye."

I shook my head. "No, ma'am."

She frowned. "You always were too formal, Bernie. Don't be like that. Not now."

I swallowed heavily. "We're back," was all I could manage.

She lifted her head slightly, my words warming their way through the frigid lock on her brain. "Back?" she asked slowly. "Where have you been?"

"Hell," Rudolph said.

She nodded. "I thought you were going to purgatory."

"We were," Rudolph replied. "We had a change of plans."

"That's nice," she said distantly. "Remember to feed the fish, will you? I don't think I can do it anymore." Her voice faded on the last syllable. Her hand slipped off the bed, and she didn't seem to notice.

I shook her. "Mrs C!" The sound of my voice frightened me, and it didn't sound any less frantic when I repeated her name again. She didn't respond, even when I shook her harder.

"No, no, no," Rudolph moaned. "No, goddamn it. This isn't fair. We beat Satan. We got the Spirit of Christmas back."

He swept his antlers at the rack of monitors next to the bed, knocking them over with a noisy clatter. The machines beeped and sparked.

"Why aren't you waking up?" he shouted at Mrs. C. "We got the Spirit back. It's inside me. Listen to me! We can still do Christmas." He kicked at the industrial frame of the bed, putting a solid hoof print in the metal.

Mrs. C's head fell forward, and I grabbed her before she fell out of the chair entirely. Her head flopped back, and her mouth gaped open. A tiny sigh escaped.

Rudolph went wild, savagely drumming the scattered machinery with his hooves. Monitors cracked, knobs were knocked off, and dents appeared in the cases. I wanted to join him, but I was holding Mrs. C who had suddenly become very heavy. I dragged the chair closer to the bed with my foot, and arranged her so that she wouldn't fall forward again. Her eyes were closed, but I turned her head so that when—if—she opened her eyes again, she would see Santa.

And if he ever opened his eyes and turned his head, he would see her looking at him.

And since there was nothing else for me to do, I went to the far corner of the room and pressed my face against the wall, so Rudolph wouldn't see my tears.

He gave up on beating the machines, and I heard him collapse heavily on the floor beside the bed. "Remember when we lost the others?" he said softly, and I knew he was talking to Mrs. C. "You were the one who found me. No one went looking for me. They thought the Clock burned us all."

I pulled myself away from the wall, and slowly wiped my tears.

Rudolph was sitting on the floor, his head in Mrs. C's lap. One of her hands was almost touching his muzzle as if she were about to wipe his tears away.

"You found me in the blackberries. I hurt so much, and I just wanted to stay there and let the bramble grow over me. But you pulled all the branches away. Your hands were so scratched, and your coat was torn. But you didn't stop. You brought me back to the North Pole, and then you came to my stall every day and read to me. I didn't know where I was—I didn't even know if I was going to live—but I would always wake and hear your voice. And every day you reminded me that we were one day closer to Christmas, and that there was a space for me on the team. Santa had found a new team, but he hadn't filled my spot. No one was going to lead the team but me, you kept telling me."

He was weeping now, large reindeer tears touched with soot and grime. "Did you know Ring? He learned to fly this year. He reminds me of another reindeer, equally young and reckless. Ring came after us—followed us all the way to hell, in fact. He wanted to be part of the team. All he wanted was to fly with us during Zero Hour, delivering toys and snacks, buzzing all the air control towers. He wanted to be one of Santa's reindeer because it meant something to him." Rudolph sniffled loudly. "It meant *everything* to him. And he died because he believed in Santa Claus."

Rudolph ran out of words, and he lay there, his head in Mrs. C's lap, waiting for her to say something. His breathing slowed after awhile, and his legs settled on the cold floor. He closed his eyes, and my heart stopped as I realized he was about to give up. He was going to chase after Santa and Mrs. C. No matter where they had gone, he was going to find them. No route was going to be too torturous for Rudolph to—

In a flash, I suddenly realized what Blitzen had been talking about. There were nine circles of hell. We had gone through four when we had met Satan, and I had thought we had merely found a shortcut or that Satan had gotten bored waiting for us. But Blitzen had intimated that our journey hadn't stopped there. Had we been crossing the circles of hell as we had run from Satan and his host?

I racked my brain for the other circles. The fifth circle had been where the wrathful had burned. What was the sixth? Indolence? No, heresy. And suddenly, I saw the pattern that Blitzen had figured out. Anger. Heresy. Violence. We had gone farther into hell instead of coming out as we fought our way to the river and the ferryman. And the last two? What were they?

Fraud, I thought. *And treachery.*

Santa had never left the Residence. His spirit was still here. Mrs. C's spirit was still here. It had to be. She wouldn't leave him behind. She hadn't left Rudolph behind. She wouldn't leave Santa either. And Rudolph? When had he ever given up?

I took a breath to say something, and in my excitement, I gulped air down the wrong pipe. What came out of my mouth wasn't words but a hiccup. A burp.

It tasted funny. Like peppermint.

What was the last time I had eaten anything? At the resort? No, it had been after that. I had had a candy cane. In the third circle of hell.

I touched my lips, and my fingers tingled. I snatched them away and stared at the fading whorls of red and green staining my fingers. It was the same stain that had touched the ferryman's cheek where Rudolph had kissed him.

The Spirit of Christmas. Rudolph had said it was inside him. I had given him the vial and he had eaten it, ingesting the tiny bit of Spirit that had been left. The rest of it had soaked into the pouch on my belt, and it must have gone through the thermal suit as well. The Spirit was in me too. I burped again, and this time I tasted roasted chestnuts and candy-coated icicles.

Rudolph stirred. "Bernie," he groused, his voice low and thick. "What are you doing?"

I sucked air into my belly, trying to remember how to belch on cue. It had been a long time since I had done this. But, right now, it was the only way I could think of to keep Rudolph from slipping away. I scrambled over to Mrs. C and Rudolph, and leaning in, let loose with the biggest burp I could muster.

Rudolph jerked his head up, his eyes rolling around in their sockets. He snapped at me, and I backpedaled. He didn't look all there, and I didn't want to be on the receiving end of a reindeer head-butt. I tripped over a piece of medical equipment, and kept scrambling backward, using both hands and feet now.

Rudolph shook his head, like he was being buzzed by bees, and he jerked upright in a rush, his legs wobbly. "What's that?" he snarled, looking in my direction but not entirely seeing me. He put one hoof on the something-ometer that I had fallen over, and leaned forward, raising his other hoof as if he meant to stomp on me. It was all very zombie reindeer weird. There was something wrong with his eyes.

I tried to burp again, but I was a little too frightened to relax, and it came out more like a hiccup. Rudolph made a rumbling noise in his belly as he lowered his antlers at me.

"It's the Spirit," I said, rubbing at the moisture on my lips and holding out my damp fingers. "It's in me."

Rudolph shivered like he was trying to shake off a chill. I knew what he was feeling. Anger, heresy, and violence. Satan's touch was still on us. The circles were like a noose around our necks, ever tightening. Each circle smaller than the last. *Fraud.* Squeezing. *Treachery.*

"It's in you," I said. "The Spirit. I gave it to you, remember?"

Rudolph twitched, his hoof slipping on the metal box. He shook his head, the tips of his twisted antlers dangerously close to my outstretched hand. "Bernie," he wheezed, his chest heaving.

As I opened my mouth to say something, a silver rain started to fall between us. Tiny glittery motes like a cascade of delicate tinsel.

Santa Claus was still in the Residence. Satan hadn't lied to us after all; he had been leeching the Spirit of Christmas out of Santa, and since the gates of heaven were closed to Santa, Fat Boy had been forced to haunt the North Pole, adrift on a phantom sea of despair.

I sucked down more air and belched loudly. The sound echoed throughout the room, and some of the glittering rain changed color. Red and green. That's what Santa needed. That's what we all needed. A little bit of crazy, a little bit of crude-yet-absolutely silly joy.

Rudolph swayed as he focused on the colored rain, his pupils slowly returning to a more normal size. His chest swelled as he took in air, and when I thought he couldn't hold any more, he let loose with the loudest belch I had ever heard.

"Wow," I said with a laugh. "You could spook cattle with that." The snow was nearly all red and green now.

"Better than that anemic fog horn noise you were making," Rudolph snorted. He sucked another bellyful of air.

"Anemic fog horn?" I sputtered. I flapped a hand over my mouth and burped out the beginning of "Winter Wonderland."

It made me sad to do it—I wasn't the one who knew all the songs—but it felt right. It felt like the right way to honor those we had lost. We had to keep singing. We had to keep the Spirit alive.

Rudolph stepped off the machine, nodding his head. "Not bad," he said. "Not bad at all." He one-upped me with the first verse of "The Twelve Days of Christmas," his lips quivering as he forced enough air up from his stomach to squeak out the final phrase.

Mrs. C twitched in her chair, nearly spilling out of it entirely. I rushed over as she leaned back, raising her head toward the ceiling. She reacted to my touch, rolling her head around on her shoulders and looking at me. Her eyes were clear, and the gray was fading. Deep blue swirls were moving in her irises. "Bernie," she sighed. "And Rudolph. What are you two rascals doing?"

"Saving Christmas," Rudolph replied with mock seriousness, which he spoiled with a short belch. I tried not to giggle, but failed. It felt good to giggle again.

Mrs. C frowned, but the expression barely turned down the corners of her mouth. She shivered slightly, and pulled her robe more tightly about her as she looked around the room. Looking everywhere but at the still figure on the bed next to her. She saw the red and green snow that was still falling.

"Oh, my love," she whispered, and her lips curled upward. "I knew you hadn't left."

I knew Santa's secret at that instant; I knew what he was laughing about as he drove out of sight on Christmas night. Every year, we worked until we dropped and he always worked harder and longer than anyone else in the village. And then, on Christmas night, he put his DNA at risk by using the Time Clock so that he could visit every house personally. He B&E'd in every country through the course of that night, breaking the law so many times it wasn't even worth counting. He faced violent weather, angry dogs, and unhappy parents who waited up for him to bitch about the unavailability of the latest plastic gewgaw their kids couldn't live without, and he managed it all with laughter in his heart. Why did he do it? Because when he was done, when Zero Hour was over and the Clock was turned off, he got to come home to Mrs C. He got to come home and tell his wife that another Season was done, and she would smile at him, and he would know that he was the luckiest man on the face of this planet.

The rain of festive snow drifted toward us. I stepped out of the way, and Mrs. C raised her face as the rain fell upon her pale cheeks. The red and green glistened on her skin as it brought color back to her face. She lifted her hands, cradling the glittering rain. "Come back," she whispered. "Come back to me." Rudolph and I belched in unison, and she smiled again. "Come home, Santa."

She opened her mouth, taking in a long, deep breath, and the rain stopped, the last glittering motes of red and green vanishing into her mouth. She got younger as I watched, the haggard toll of the last few days falling away from her. She leaned over the bed, carefully cradling Santa's head in her hands. She pressed her lips to his, and what passed between them was all that ever mattered.

She sank back into the chair, leaning on the bed, her hands still touching his still face. Behind me, Rudolph kept burping, but I was holding my breath. Waiting for something to happen. Waiting for a sign . . .

And I got one finally. Santa's left eyelid fluttered, like a butterfly shaking itself off after a cold night. The right followed suit, and after a few moments, he opened them both and stared up at the ceiling. Finally, his lips parted painfully as if he was remembering how to breathe, and then he coughed—violently and suddenly. It was a dry, grinding noise that sounded like someone was dragging heavy furniture across the carpet a floor below. Dust floated up from his mouth. Or maybe it was the last bit of chilly air fleeing the room. I wasn't entirely sure.

"I don't think . . ." he whispered in dry voice more suited to overly dramatic off-Broadway death scenes. "I don't think I've ever heard a Christmas carol so horribly mutilated . . ."

"What do you know, you tone deaf has-been," Rudolph snorted before belching again.

Santa chuckled, a sound like walnuts rattling in a large wooden bowl. "Ah, Rudolph," he sighed. "I missed you." He turned his head slightly and looked at Mrs. C. He wriggled a hand out from beneath the blankets, and he carefully stroked her hair as if he were afraid that it would melt at his touch. "I missed you all."

She stirred at his touch, raising her head and then sliding forward to press her lips against his. Rudolph nudged me out of the way as he stepped up to the bed. "Get a room, you two," he muttered as he nosed them apart.

Santa laughed. "We have a room," he said. "You two are cramping my style." He reached up and grabbed the base of one of Rudolph's antlers, and before the reindeer could pull away, Santa hauled himself up and kissed Rudolph.

Mrs. C kissed me. I, shamelessly, kissed her back.

When else was I going to have the chance?

Santa caught me laying some lip on his wife, and he laughed. His first laugh sounded like an old tire deflating on the shoulder of a hot summer highway. He coughed heavily and tried again. The second sounded like he had just been out of practice. And the third?

Well, it sounded like Santa Claus.

I wandered away from the bedside before Rudolph got all caught up in the moment and tried to kiss me too. "It's not all good news," I said sadly. "We lost a couple bucks. Prancer and Ring didn't make it back."

A dark shadow flickered in Santa's eyes. "The Residence? The elves?"

"They're all gone," Rudolph said. "Run off by a nefarious agency."

"We're under Holy—" The words died in my throat as I looked at Rudolph. "Nefarious?" I repeated, my brain working overtime. "It's not . . . ?"

Rudolph snorted. "God?" He shook his head. "Not His style. This was—"

"Treachery," I finished for him.

"A nasty bit of lying, I was going to say," Rudolph said. "But sure, *treachery* works too."

"The ninth circle of hell," I breathed. "The last circle. The noose, tightened down so far we can barely breathe."

Santa looked back and forth between us. "Would someone like to tell me what is going on? Are the elves gone or not?"

"Oh, they're gone," I said. "That's for certain. In fact, that might be the only thing that is true . . ." I nodded as I slowly shrugged my way out of the ruined thermal suit. "You knew, didn't you?" I asked Rudolph.

"Blitzen knew," Rudolph said. "But then, he's the one who has not only read *Paradise Lost*, he's memorized it. It just took him awhile to remember where he'd heard that angel's name before."

XVI

RAMIEL WAS WAITING FOR ME. I NAVIGATED AROUND THE POCKED HOLES THAT Ring's bombs had left in the thick concrete of the roof. Ramiel's lawn chair sat a little crookedly, one of its legs prematurely shortened, and there was no sign of the little lean-to that had sheltered the angel previously.

Ramiel rose out of the chair as soon as he saw me. "You've transgressed again against the host," he started, waggling a finger at me. A finger on his right hand, the one that had been melted off the last time I had seen him.

I held up a hand of my own in apology. "It was a mistake. We shouldn't have tried to drive you off your post." I took a deep breath. "It was a stupid, immature thing to do. I'm sorry."

My apology caught him off guard, and he stared at me, his mouth hanging open. "Apology accepted," he said finally.

I held out the package I was holding in my other hand. "I brought you something," I said. "I know we're under quarantine and all, but what's a little present between friends, right?" I gave him my best innocent expression. I had scrubbed some of the grime off my face and had thrown a parka over my rather insufficient winter wardrobe.

Ramiel softened. "Of course," he smiled as he took the package. "In fact, I've forgotten all about whatever it was that we were talking about a moment ago."

"I can't remember either," I said.

He raised the package to his ear and shook it gently. "You shouldn't have," he simpered.

I unzipped my parka casually as he tore at the wrapping paper. I had raided Mrs. C's stash, swiping some of the stuff she had been saving for special occasions. This probably qualified. I figured she wouldn't mind.

Ramiel ripped the paper free from the narrow box and tossed it aside. The box was a plain white one, stamped on the bottom with a manufacturer's seal. He checked. Predictably. "Ah," he said. "Hallmark."

"Nothing but the best." I gave him a wide grin.

He popped the box open and took out the smaller cube resting inside. He looked at inquisitively, idly discarding the now empty white box as carelessly as he had the wrapping paper. He found the tiny crank on the side and carefully wound it. I had pre-wound it downstairs. I didn't want his attention wandering while he cranked the box. The crank went around twice before the top popped open and a tiny figure of an angel on a spring danced out. Ramiel gave a little cry of surprise, and then laughed.

I chuckled along with him. My hand rested inside my open coat.

The laugh died in his throat as he looked closely at the figure. I had stuck a sticker on the front of the angel's robe. It read: *Satan inside.*

"What's this?" the angel growled.

"It's an old joke," I explained. "I'm sorry I couldn't find one of the actual stickers that were all the rage back in the last millennium." I shrugged. "But *last millennium*, you know. These jokes come and go so fast. I'm not surprised you don't remember it."

"I do not like your jokes, elf," Ramiel snarled.

"Yeah, well, I'm not too fond of yours either," I said. "Game's up, chuckle-head. I know who you're working for."

"I'm one of the heavenly host. I report directly to God."

I shook my head. "You haven't talked to God in a long time. You switched sides, Ramiel. Someone took roll. You were listed as one of Satan's agents a long time ago."

I had checked in the library before I came up. Milton had been quite specific. . . . *the violence of Ramiel scorch'd and blasted, overthrew.* Good old blind John, taking really good notes when it mattered.

"I've been on a little field-trip, Ramiel. Went down to see your boss." A wry grin tugged at the corner of my mouth. "He's pissed. And not just because we stomped through his daisies." I thought of Prancer's skull and antlers in my hand. The least of Satan's worries was the condition of his flowerbeds. He was going to remember the consequences of killing a reindeer for a long time.

Ramiel was making a noise like the sound of a hundred lions feeding.

I kept talking. I had thought that my knees would have been quaking with fear. But the memory of busting Satan's face up brought with it a certain amount of starch to my backbone. "I heard you got a little wet," I continued, taunting Ramiel. Wondering how far I could push him. "Must have been miserable for a fire-breathing scorcher like yourself to have been forced to take a swim in the Arctic Ocean."

He was growing already, his shoulders and head elongating as his rage filled his form.

"One little reindeer manages to dunk a Demonic Lieutenant." I voiced a low whistle. "How's that going to look on your yearly review?"

His joints began popping, swelling and splitting as he relinquished his angelic guise. He towered over me—nearly ten meters tall already and festooned with spikes and ridges and bony knobs. His mouth was so enormous, I could easily fit inside and comfortably take stock of all of his teeth. Many of which were longer than my arm. His eyes were pinwheels of fire, and black ichor dripped from his mouth. "It doesn't matter, elf," he hissed. "My master has taken the spirit of this place. Christmas is no more."

He roared at me then, lowering his face and blasting me with the full brunt of his brimstone-reeking breath. His nails clicked like old bones rattling as he reached for me.

I held my ground, exhaling slowly through my nose. I lifted my hand from my coat so that he could see the other thing I had brought up to the roof. I raised the second pistol that Rudolph had given me and sighted carefully up at the demon's face. My hands were warm and dry against the cold grip.

"Consider this the Resurrection," I said as I squeezed the trigger.

XVII

THEY CAME IN A GENTLE FALLING OF FEATHERS. ONE INSTANT, I WAS ALL alone on the rooftop with the frozen shape of Ramiel, and the next, I had visitors. I turned casually, tucking the cold pistol back into my coat. There were two of them, and they looked just like I remembered: flowing robes, wings, pearly smiles, and nametags. *Michael,* one read. The other one said *Gabriel.*

"Nice to see some real members of the Rank," I said.

Michael hadn't changed, though I would have been surprised if he had. It was the rest of us who lived lifetimes between visits. He came with a nicer disposition this time. And without his flaming sword. "There is no Quarantine," he said in a tone that didn't quite match the jovial coffee shop voice I had heard last year—but it also wasn't the doomier voice he had used on us on our way out of purgatory.

I nodded. "Yeah, I kind of figured that out."

Gabriel floated up to the frozen statue and buried his fist in the creature's chest with a chunking sound like burying an ax in a block of wood. His wings stretched and bunched, and he and the frozen demon glided up into the air. I watched until they were only a tiny dot in the sky. "There's a lesson there," I said to Michael. "You should be able to tell the real thing right away. They aren't much for conversation."

185

Michael wandered across the rooftop, his slender hand touching the taut wire of the helium angel balloon. "There are a number of lessons," he said. A line of fire ran from his fingers. It streaked up the line, and the floating angel exploded in a rush of light.

My face was still turned towards the sky, and the retinal burn of the exploding balloon faded slowly from my field of vision. "Yeah," I murmured, "There's been a couple."

"You understand now, don't you?"

I nodded. "Satan tried to capitalize on our weakness, on our lack of faith. He set us up from the beginning, didn't he? I should have known it was too easy to hack in to purgatory from the coffee shop. You had a security leak, didn't you? But you couldn't do anything about it until he used it. Only then could you seal up your network. Only then could you lock him out, once and for all."

Michael might have shrugged. It was hard to tell. Damn angelic inscrutability. "And afterward, Satan knew what would happen. He knew we'd be vulnerable. He knew we would be wondering what would happen after we had gone to purgatory. It was just like the firewall, wasn't it? We gave him the opening, and he crept in and tried to steal what meant most to us. And he almost succeeded."

I thought of Ring's valiant struggle on the raft to realize his dream. I remembered Prancer singing carols as we crossed the desert in hell, and how I wouldn't hear that voice again. "I don't like being used like that," I said. "But that's the price of the miracle we performed last year, isn't it?" I closed my eyes and shook my head. "I don't much care for that either."

"You aren't meant to. We live by Old Testament rules, Bernard. Those of us outside the normal realms must abide by the strictest laws."

"An eye for an eye. A tooth for a tooth. Is that it?"

The angel nodded.

"But you're not taking it back," I said. "And so that means we can do it again, can't we? If we wanted to. We could perform another miracle for Christmas. And you'd let us. But I get it now. There's a price to be paid for such things. We bring a soul back down; you get to take one up."

"Exactly."

"But we gave you two," I said, my voice starting to shake. "We gave you Ring *and* Prancer. Two reindeer died on this trip."

Michael shook his head gently, a smile ghosting across his lips. "No, Bernard. Only one."

There was a squeal from the sky, and a shape fell right down to the rooftop, scattering snow as he landed with a clumsy thump. I stared, unable to believe what I was seeing. He looked . . . he looked so *washed* and groomed.

Ring bounded across the roof and bumped into me. "Lookit. Lookit," he squeaked. "They let me keep the scar." He showed me his flank and the vaguely star-shaped pattern of Satan's hand against his skin.

I threw my arms around the frenzied reindeer and hugged him tightly. Ring squirmed out of my embrace and bounded away to examine the rain of destruction he had dropped on the rooftop.

"I don't understand," I said, wiping at my face.

Michael watched the young reindeer wrestle with a sheet of bubble wrap that had survived the bombing run. "We couldn't keep him. He wasn't in heaven five minutes before he tried to jump the gates and come back here. I don't think we could have stopped him." The angel offered another inscrutable movement of his shoulders. "Maybe we could have. Once or twice, but not more than that. He wanted something too badly to let his soul rest. He wanted something we couldn't give him."

I nodded. "Yeah, I know what he wanted. I can't say I blame him."

The angel looked at me, something akin to the color of surprise darkening his eyes. "Belief is a powerful thing, isn't it, Bernard Rosewood?"

I looked him dead in the eye. "Especially when someone tries to take it away from you."

He lifted his eyes towards heaven. "Yes," he said, his voice almost too soft to hear. "I know. I know very well."

I looked up. A rain was falling on the North Pole. A rain of angels of all sizes and shapes. They fell from the sky and landed on the rooftop of the Residence and on the snow-covered Pole. Ring bounded up to a small cherub that alighted on the bent edge of Ramiel's forgotten lawn chair. The tiny angel's wings buzzed apprehensively, but he held still while the young reindeer sniffed him.

Michael was offering something to me. It was my hat—the goofy one that Rudolph had given me in hell. I had lost it—somewhere, I couldn't even remember where. "You've still got a lot of work to do this year," the angel said. "We thought you could use a little help getting back on schedule."

I took the cap from him. "I'll do my best."

He nodded. "I know you will." His wings unfurled.

"No miracles."

"That would be nice." His wings moved like the sails of a gigantic ship, and he lifted gracefully from the rooftop. I noticed that there weren't any footprints to mark the passage of his presence. "Good night, Bernard Rosewood, and good luck."

"Merry Christmas," I shouted after him as he flew into the night.

Ring glanced up from the sheet of bubble wrap he had been stomping. "Merry Christmas," he shouted joyously. He dashed towards the edge of the roof, stopping before he fell off. He looked out at the angels falling on the North Pole. "Merry Christmas to all," he yelled, "And to all a year of good cheer." He scampered past me again, giggling and kicking at the snow.

I rubbed my jaw. "Good night," I said to myself. "'And to all a good night.'" I looked down at the reindeer figure on the front of the hat, and then at the letters that were stitched across the back. *SECO*. Senior Elf in Charge of Operations. I traced my finger along the stitching. Rudolph hadn't done it, but I knew who had.

Mrs. C.

I had given Santa my word once, but it hadn't been enough to keep me here.

But Mrs. C was the one who had stayed with Rudolph. She had believed in him when he had been lost. And she had believed in me too, even when I hadn't known how lost I was.

Michael was right: there was a lot to do. Santa was going to have to be double-stuffing the calories to get himself up to optimum weight. The elves would have to be retrieved. Probably with a promise of hazard pay. We were going to have to find out who was better at snapping LEGOs together—the cherubs or the seraphim. A new sled was going to have to be built.

Ring bumped into me again. I made a grab at his tail as he danced around me.

Someone was going to have to teach him the words. If he was going to be leading, he was going to have to know the words. "Merry Christmas to all and to all a good night."

Could we do it? Could we get everything done in time for Christmas?

I put the cap on.

It fit. Someone had shrunk it to fit my head more snugly.

I guess Mrs. C wasn't the only one who believed in me.

OFF SEASON

"What's that sound?"

"That? That groaning noise? It's nothing."

I blinked several times, not sure if I was seeing things in the dark or if Rudolph was putting out a little light. The drugs were wearing off. Ahead of schedule. In a few minutes, he was going to be fully awake. And pissed.

I still wasn't sure this was a very good idea, but I hadn't known what else to do. It was our first Christmas away from home. I didn't know how he was going to take not being *there* at Zero Hour, and so I did something creative. Or maybe stupid. It was too early to tell yet.

Rudolph moved around in the dark, and I heard his hooves banging against metal. "We're not in the sled," he said. His voice was getting stronger and angrier by the syllable. "Bernie. Where are we?"

"I'm not entirely sure," I lied.

More banging noises, and now I could definitely see a ruddy glow coming off Rudolph's skin. The light revealed the plain metal bulkheads of the tiny chamber where he and I were hanging out. "What is this?" Rudolph demanded.

"It's called a bathysphere," I said. "It's used for deep sea exploration."

He cocked his head, listening to the sounds coming from the metal around us. "We're underwater, aren't we?"

"We are," I said. "More than a mile down, I think."

"You think?"

I shrugged, and adjusted the pillows behind me. "We're kind of floating free," I said. Kind of. There was a thick cable attached to the bathysphere that ran all the way up to a boat, but he didn't need to know that.

The interior of the bathysphere had been stripped down to the bare metal. It wasn't the most comfortable place to spend a few days over Christmas, which is why I had packed along some pillows, a cooler, and more than one thermos of hot chocolate, spiked with peppermint schnapps. *Heavily* spiked.

He clattered over and loomed over me, his skin ruddy with anger. "Bernie," he said. "What's going on?"

I glanced at the luminous hands on my watch. "Well, it's Christmas Eve," I said. "Almost midnight, in fact. Zero Hour is coming right up."

He snorted angrily and lowered his head, pointing his antlers at me. "Why are we here?" he repeated. "Why aren't we at the Pole?"

I shook my head. "You know why."

He rapped a hoof against the metal flooring. "I could bust out of this thing," he said.

I was watching the sweep hand on my watch. "We're a mile down," I said.

"I could hold my breath," Rudolph said.

"You'd get the bends," I said. "It's a nitrogen-rich atmosphere in here. Because we're, you know, a mile from the surface of the ocean."

"No, I wouldn't."

I glanced up at him. "Yes, you would. And then you'd be all weird and crampy and floating out in the middle of the ocean. Is that how you want to spend Christmas?"

He blew air heavily out of his nose and stomped around in the bathysphere. "You know how I want to spend Christmas," he said.

"I know." I sighed. "I'm sorry."

Five more seconds.

"For what?" he asked.

The sweep hand passed the twelve. It was now midnight. If the boat towing us was on time and on course, we had just crossed the International Date Line, heading west. Two seconds ago, it had been 11:59PM on Christmas Eve. It was now 12:00AM the day *after* Christmas.

We skipped a day that year.

THE MUSICAL

December 5th

"We're considering torture."

I was still blindfolded. "This your first kidnapping?" My lips were parched. "I'm just curious 'cause you're kind of off to a rocky start."

I got slapped for that. It was what tough farm boys would consider a girlish slap, but, in my exhausted and dehydrated state, it was enough to rattle my molars. My jaw hurt; I hadn't had any food or water in at least thirty-six hours; my feet and hands were numb from the bonds that kept me sequestered on this uncomfortable chair; and my bladder had long ago given up on trying to get my attention. All in all, nothing a decent massage and six hours submerged in a hot tub couldn't erase. My captors were amateurs.

The fact that they had managed to tie me to a chair and blindfold me notwithstanding.

The slapper grabbed my chin and squeezed me like an overzealous grandmother. "The account password," he said. "That's all we want."

"I don't know what you're talking about," I replied through mashed lips.

"The money in the account, Rosewood. Just give us the password and we'll let you go."

"Where?" I asked through fish-lip pucker. "Where will you let me go?"

My head was shoved back. "We'll send you to hell if you don't cooperate."

I laughed. "Really? That doesn't frighten me as much as you think it might."

Slapper tagged me on the head again, and I rocked back in the chair. The front legs came off the ground, and I teetered there for a second and then the chair came down again. The impact woke my bladder, and I felt like someone had just dropped an anvil in my lap.

There was a scrape of shoe leather against the worn floor as the two men stepped away from my chair to talk quietly. They thought they were playing church mice, but my hearing was a little better than they knew. "I don't like this," the meek one said. "This isn't what I signed up for."

"There's more than a million dollars in his account," Slapper said. "All we need is the password, and we can move the money somewhere else. You gonna walk away from a million fucking dollars?"

"I can't spend it in an American jail."

"We're not going to jail. Not here. Not anywhere."

"We might be if he talks."

"He's not going to talk," Slapper said. "We'll get the password, move the money, and then . . ."

"And then what?"

"We'll see. Okay. Just don't panic. I've got this under control."

There was a rustle of fabric, and Meeker's voice became strained. "Take your hand off me," he said.

"Did you hear what I said? I've got this."

More rustling. "Yes, I heard you." Scrape of shoe leather again. "You're an utter fool if you think he's going to talk. He's been down here a day already, and he doesn't seem the slightest bit worried."

"Maybe not. But there's a couple of things to try yet."

"You had better try them soon. The longer we stick around . . ."

"God, you can be such a—look, don't worry. Everything is under control."

"Yeah?" I heard Meeker walk away from me, and then a door opened. "Whose?" Meeker asked as he left, closing the door behind him.

"Drama queen," Slapper muttered under his breath, and I didn't disagree with him. That exit was pure stage drama, of the most ham-fisted sort.

I waited for something to happen, straining to hear any clue as to what Slapper was doing. There was more rustling—of paper and plastic this time—and then the metallic click of a lighter being opened. Thumb raked flint wheel, and then a crackling sound of tobacco burning. Slapper closed the lighter and exhaled heavily. My nose picked up the pungent smell of cheap hand-rolled tobacco.

Slapper wandered back to my chair, and I flinched as he bent over and pulled heavily on the cigarette next to my ear. It sounded like I was in the path of an approaching forest fire.

"I've done dinner theater," he whispered in my ear. I could feel the lit tip of the cigarette dancing somewhere near my cheek. "I know something about pain," he said. "You will tell me what I want to know."

This was how my holiday season was shaping up.

November 21st

THE FANTASYLAND HOTEL AT THE WEST EDMONTON MALL HAS THEME rooms. What motel with the word 'fantasy' in the name wouldn't? However, since the hotel had a couple of skybridges connecting it to the mall, the rooms' themes were more family-friendly. The Igloo Room, for example, had penguins painted on the walls. Happy little penguins.

It drove Rudolph nuts. There were no penguins in the Arctic. But we could get the thermostat down to fifty-four which made him less grumpy, so we put up with the penguins.

Anyway, the Fantasyland was where Rudolph and I stayed between assignments. The 60th parallel was the line we didn't cross, and goofy penguins aside, the Igloo Room helped us deal with our separation anxiety. Well, it helped Rudolph. After last year's incident with the bathysphere, I had promised to not trick him like that again. But we still needed coping mechanisms for the fact that we didn't work out of the North Pole anymore.

The Igloo wasn't available this time around, so we ended up down the hall in the Exploration of Space room. There was a scale model of Sputnik attached to the wall over the bed, and a dial next to the bed provided three levels of lighting—ambient, sensual, and stark. Scattered across the ceiling and the other walls were luminescent points of the Milky Way. The designers had made some effort to match the play of stars across the actual night sky, and when all the lights were off and the satellites (Sputnik wasn't the only one) were darkened, it was almost like sailing beyond the troposphere into the inky blackness of unexplored space.

I could only get the thermostat down to sixty-two, but Rudolph didn't mind so much as long as I kept the lights off.

He started getting extra cranky as soon as the stores put out their Halloween costumes, because it meant that Christmas was coming. We were still working, and the approaching Season meant we were busy, but the final days before Zero Hour were hard. Last year—our first year away from the Pole—I had doped Rudolph up and taken him for a ride in a deep-sea bathysphere. I'll admit it wasn't the best Christmas present, but we made it through the holiday without an international or supernatural incident, which made everyone happy. Including our new boss, Mrs. C.

We worked for her now. Seasonal stealth agents.

The balcony of our room looked out over the eastern radius of the mall, and even at this early hour of the morning, the parking lot was nearly half full. Through the clear windows of the dome over the center of the mall, I could see the frenzied shopping action going on inside. It was like watching ants in a glass-walled ant farm, scurrying back and forth. Package and parcel standing in for leaf and twig.

I had just wrapped up breakfast—pancakes smothered in maple syrup, crisp bacon, and a cup of fresh fruit—and was finishing my coffee. Rudolph had eaten all the plates already.

"You done with that?" he asked, eyeing the partially empty cup in my hand. There was a smear of maple syrup on his nose.

"I was going to have a second cup," I said. "But then you went and ate the carafe."

"You shouldn't drink so much coffee," he said.

"And why is that?" I asked.

"Caffeine makes people unpredictable." He looked down at the tray resting on the side table next to me. "How about the flatware?" he asked. "Can I have that?"

I shook my head. "Management says they don't care what happens to the china, but they want the silverware back."

"Flatware," Rudolph corrected me. "There's no *silver* in it."

I glanced up at him, and he held my gaze for a moment before his tongue flicked out and cleaned the syrup off his nose. "What?" he asked.

"Okay, Super Goat," I said. "When did you have the mass spectrometer installed?"

He shrugged. "It just tastes different," he said. His head swiveled toward the mall's parking lot all of a sudden. His eyes narrowed, and he lost interest in gnawing on the silver—sorry, *flatware*. His nostrils widened as he took in the scents rising across the mall. "Fat Boy," he announced.

I sat up, trying to pretend I could make out any real details all the way across the parking lot. It was a pretty typically overcast day for Edmonton, the sunlight diffused into a gentle radiance by the layer of gray clouds cloaking the sky from horizon to horizon. Even with the uniformity of light, I couldn't match Rudolph's ocular ability. "Where?" I asked.

"Silver Acura." Rudolph said. I glared at him. As if there were only one Acura or one silver car in the lot. "He just got out. Blue windbreaker. He's wearing a baseball cap. It's got a moose on it."

I gave up, sinking back into the lounge chair. "What's he doing here?"

Rudolph wandered over to the railing and watched the tiny figure make its way across the lot. "We're expecting contact today, aren't we?" he asked.

"Yeah, but not Fat Boy. She usually sends Blitzen."

Rudolph chewed on the inner lining of his cheek. "Last weekend before Thanksgiving, isn't it?" he asked.

It took me a minute to remember the NPC schedule. "Lockdown," I said. "It's the weekend before Lockdown."

The day after Thanksgiving, the North Pole entered Lockdown—the final thirty days before Zero Hour. All leaves were canceled, and no one was permitted to leave the North Pole, including Santa. Especially Santa. They didn't need to be wondering where Fat Boy was the night before Christmas.

That had happened once already. The NPC wasn't keen on it ever happening again.

Rudolph nodded. "He's heading for the amusement park. One

last ride this year."

The phone back in the room rang, and Rudolph glanced over his shoulder. I knocked back a final swallow of my lukewarm coffee—knowing that the cup would be gone when I returned—and went inside to answer the phone.

So, even though Rudolph and I *saved* Christmas the Season before this last one—*again*—the NPC didn't budge on their previous decision to kick me out. Ungrateful bastards. Who invited them back after Ramiel was turned into an ice sculpture anyway? Rudolph called their bluff, saying that if I went, he went too. The NPC didn't even blink.

Which meant I had some company on the ride south this time.

We ended up at the Fantasyland—in the Iguana room that first time, which wasn't a very good choice. That first night was really long, and the only reason we weren't banned from the hotel was because Mrs. C was there in the morning to smooth things over with the hotel management. *You two are my special ambassadors,* she told us over breakfast. *There will be no more incidents like this one with the lizards. Okay? You will go wherever I tell you to, do what is needed, and you will ensure that the world understands how Christmas works now. There will be no more miracles. There will just be people being nice to one another all year long. And at Christmas time, there will be lots of presents under the tree for ALL the good boys and girls. Do you understand?*

After she left, Rudolph said we were going to be the Christmas SEAL team: we'd drop in out of nowhere, bag and tag, refresh some memories, and get out before anyone really noticed us. *Mission: Impossible*-style. And, sure, I'll admit that it sounded a lot more fun when he put it that way. We'd even taken to calling Blitzen "Mr. Phelps" when he visited to deliver a mission briefing.

Blitzen played along. He's good that way.

"Ride the roll," he said when I answered the phone in the hotel suite. "Go go green. Granddad's got a moose."

"Rudolph saw him in the parking lot," I said. "Why aren't you here?"

"Last ride before Lockdown," Blitzen said. "You know how he is." He paused for a second. "Look, Bernie. Talk to him, okay? He's a little . . . moody."

Uh oh. "What's going on?" I asked.

"He'll . . . he'll tell you," Blitzen said. "Just . . . just listen, okay?"

"Okay."

"And don't tell Rudolph."

"Wait. What?"

But he had already hung up.

Santa loved any vehicle that played tug-of-war with gravity using your body as the rope. Roller coasters were a passion he indulged whenever he could. The one at the Edmonton Mall was only a four hour reindeer hop from the top of the world and he could usually get in five or six rides, check stock at the toy stores, buy Mrs. C something lacy and nice, and still be home in time for dinner. Which meant that making Santa wait to ride the roller coaster was akin to pulling out his fingernails with pliers.

When I arrived at the ride, he was already sitting in the lead car of the green train, and the kid working the line had roped off the cattle chute to the front half of the train. The kid gave me a funny look when I came up, and recognizing that universal gleam in his eye, I slipped him a few twenties as I ducked under the rope.

We were going to be riding awhile.

Behind me, children wailed and shouted at the kid who had let me through, and we both ignored them. I slipped onto the wide bench next to Santa, and the kid banged down the security bar, which didn't come down nearly as far as I liked. Santa's belly was already pretty round, and there was an inordinately large space between the rubber-coated bar and my belt. There was no chance Santa was going to fall out. There was every chance I might.

I hate roller coasters.

We did the whole course three times before Santa deigned to acknowledge the white-knuckle signals I was throwing him. When the train came to a complete stop, he signaled to the kid, who came over and raised the security bar. "Come on, son," Santa said in that voice he used whenever he's at the mall. "Let me buy you a smoothie." He clapped me on the back as I staggered out of the car.

Just the two of us out for a lovely day at the mall—jovial grandpa and green-around-the-gills grandson.

As soon as the floor stopped spinning, I was going to grab one of the metal poles that fed the cattle chute ribbons and smack grandpa in the kneecap.

The smoothie did little to assuage my mood; my stomach was all knotted up and wasn't in the mood for anything—not even mixed berries and sherbet and a couple superdoses of powdered vitamins.

Santa wolfed down two enormous chilidogs while I sat on a bench near the merry-go-round, trying to coax my stomach back into its normal place. "You going to finish that?" he asked, indicating the smoothie sitting on the bench between us.

I shook my head. This seemed like the question of the day.

Santa happily slurped away at my smoothie. His baseball cap was pushed back on his wide forehead, revealing a curling lock of his shaggy white hair. It hadn't been cut to regulation length yet, and more of it curled out the back of the cap and disappeared past the collar of his windbreaker. There actually was a moose with a rather surprised look on its face stenciled on the front of the cap. He was surprisingly tan. "I love field work," he said, tugging at the straw. "I don't get enough of it anymore."

I groaned.

He glanced at me. "You've got to relax more, Bernie. You can't tighten up in the turns. You've got to stay loose."

"Easy for you to say," I said. "You were caught under that rail like a mouse pinned in a trap. I was sliding all around on the seat. If that loop had been any taller, I would have fallen out at the top."

"But you didn't," said Santa. "See, that's the beauty of the roller-coaster. You *almost* fall. It's *almost* dangerous. Doesn't it get your heart pounding? Doesn't the adrenaline start thumping through your veins?"

"My life flashes before my eyes, and I wonder about dumb things like: is all the change in my pocket going to fall out and cause the train to jump off the track?"

"Don't you feel more alive?"

I gave him a stern look. "I'm bunking with Rudolph," I said. "I get more than a recommended dose of heart-pounding, adrenaline-rushing, muscle-quivering excitement before breakfast. Every day. When he gets up in the middle of the night, I worry that he's hungry and is going to eat the plumbing in the bathroom. Then the room fills up with water and drowns me before I can get out of bed. I really don't need to go out of my way to get my heart pumping. Especially after our holiday dive last Season."

"Shoot, Bernie. I miss it. It just isn't the same up there without the two of you. The Consortium has put the squeeze on everything. These past few Seasons have rattled them so hard that it's become all tight-ass corporate paperwork pushing up there. No one dares to have a creative thought any more because it might violate a T-PIP or a 2/45-Y or some other ridiculous acronym. I swear they spend most of their time coming up with new regulations and procedures. You know where we had to get over half the toys last year?"

"China?" I tried.

"Target," Santa said.

I shrugged. "It's not a bad idea. They have a pretty good selection. Plus, if you order online, Ama—"

"Don't say it," Santa snapped. "Don't you dare say it." He sucked heavily at the straw, and it made a scraping noise on the bottom of the cup.

"We had help after we went to hell," I said. "But the angels left after Zero Hour. It's not like the NPC didn't know they were going to have to do it themselves after that." I was trying really hard to be sympathetic. From the reports I had read, Christmas last year had been fairly successful. Not the best Season, according to all those places that tracked yearly retail sales, but still pretty good.

"They're making changes, Bernie," Santa said. "The rest of the world is catching up, and there's a group within the Consortium who is arguing that the North Pole should get out of the delivery business altogether. We have the customer data; we don't need to be in the warehousing and fulfillment business. We should be outsourcing all of that. Another year or two and it'll all be virtualized. Gift cards and e-delivery. That Company That Shall Not Be Named has already figured out most of the model. Once they get it all sorted out, who will need some fat dude and a bunch of reindeer to drop packages down chimneys anymore?"

I shook my head, knowing what he was asking of me. "I can't do it," I said. "they took my union card and kicked me out. The RCMP have permission to grab me if I go north of the 60th parallel, and if I'm lucky enough to make it to the 80th, they can put a real bounty out on me. Even the polar bears will be trying to collect. I can't go back. Not ever."

"Name the place, Bernie. Anywhere. We'll pick you up. What can they do once the Clock is on and we're in the air?"

"You're starting to sound like an action junkie. You know, one of those guys who pops up in every extreme sport on ESPN. Extreme hang-gliding, extreme cold water snorkeling, extreme alligator wrestling, extreme volcano spelunking, extreme—"

"I'm loosing it, Bernie." Santa interrupted. "The couple of Seasons before—before we went after David Anderson—they were rough. It was all the same: the same toys, the same trends, and all the same greedy bullshit. Gimme gimme gimme. People fighting over toys. Kids getting trampled during extended shopping hours. It's all material, Bernie. Did you know we're doubling the weight load every three years? It used to take us nearly a decade to double the weight. We're already stretching physics pretty thin, and the curve is getting steeper. We're going to break something in the next few years, and it's going to be worse than '64. A lot worse."

"It's not that bad," I said. "You're just having a mid-life crisis. You're two hundred years overdue. Let it run its course. Find a hobby. Get a dog or something."

"I'm busting my butt up there every year," he said. "Do you know how many homes in the West have security systems now? I can't even do a block in under six minutes any more. The team and I spent nearly a week under the Clock last Season. You think anyone cares anymore?"

"Yeah, I do." I patted his elbow. "I really do. And Rudolph and I are out here making sure everyone else does too."

Santa nodded. "Yeah, I know. She says you guys were doing a great job." He puffed out his cheeks and watched the kids on the merry-go-round awhile. "I just had to get out of there and see it for myself. I had to see if I could still make a difference, see if it was still worth doing."

"It is," I said. "We are."

"That's good," he said. "That's really good to hear." He reached inside his windbreaker and brought out a manila envelope. "Your next assignment."

When I took the envelope from him, he stuck his hands in the pockets of his windbreaker and wouldn't look at me.

"What?" I asked.

"It's a solo assignment," he said.

"Rudolph?" I said. "You're letting Rudolph do one on his own?"

He shook his head. "Rudolph's got to come back with me. We want to get him some help."

"Help? There's nothing wrong with him."

Santa grimaced slightly. "I know. But the Consortium thinks—"

"Wait a second," I said. "The NPC knows about this?"

He ducked his head slightly. "We didn't have any choice. They implemented a new accounting system, and the Residence got rolled into it. I fought it—it's my household; I should be able to run it anyway I want—but they were too damn clever about it. Once they got their sticky fingers on my ledgers, they ran an audit."

"What did they find?"

He looked at the kids going round and round on the horses. "We had to come clean on some expenditures," he said. "And give them access to the report files, which included all of your *and* Rudolph's reports to Mrs. C."

A stickler for historical recordings, she insisted on very detailed accountings of what we had done—from both of us. In a sudden panic, I tried to recall any specifics in my reports that might aggravate my less-than-savory standing with the North Pole Consortium, and then I started worrying about what Rudolph had been saying in his.

"It's the Boston job," Santa explained. "They think you glossed over some details and Rudolph's terminology was so self-effacing as to be useless."

Beantown. Of course, it would be the Beantown job. That one had nearly been a PR disaster. What was his name?

Randy—Randy Filner had sued his parents over an incorrect Christmas gift. He had asked for a horse and gotten a bike. It hadn't been our fault. Mom and Dad rewrote his request and thought he'd be excited about the change. Randy found some bottom-slurper with a law degree who tried to take the parents for nearly a million two in emotional damages. The case would have splashed every major newspaper across the city if it had gotten past its initial hearing, which is why Rudolph and I had paid Mr. Thomas Culpepper of Daughty & Culpepper a late night visit. Special envoys from the North Pole sort of visit. Seasonal stealth SEALs sort of visit. It hadn't gone so well. Culpepper didn't have an emotional bone in his body. It had been like talking to a block of gnarly gristle.

And then he called Rudolph a trained moose. He called me a midget too. Rudolph was a little perturbed. Well, even now, I'm glossing. Rudolph had gotten pissed. The guy held out until after Rudolph set his desk on fire and melted most of the trinkets in his trophy case.

Not entirely a proper solution to the problem, but it had worked.

"Fuck proper," Rudolph had said as we were leaving. "Proper never gets the girl. Proper dies miserably in the back of a rusted deSoto with a pocket full of unpaid bills and less than two dollars in his wallet, wondering why and how."

I left that bit out of the report too.

"What do the NPC want?" I asked Santa.

"They want Rudolph to do some anger management sessions."

"Why now? Why not after this next gig?"

"Mrs. C and I think it's probably best to do it now. We look good by catering to their concerns, and it gets Rudolph out of the way for a while. Trust me, it'll be better if he's not around on this job."

"Why?" I asked. I really didn't want to open the envelope now.

"There's a production company in Seattle that is in trouble. They need some cash and a new producer. It'll be easy: flash some green, tell them how much you love the arts, and smile a lot on opening night."

"If it's so easy, why can't Rudolph play?"

"Well, it's best he doesn't know about the show."

"I'm asking why a lot, Santa, which is making me nervous," I said. "Why shouldn't Rudolph know about this show?"

"It's about him. They're doing a musical."

DECEMBER 6TH

I LIFTED MY HEAD, LISTENING TO A FAINT ECHO OF MUSIC THAT WAS WINDING its way down from somewhere upstairs. The banging and pinging of the old pipes as the ancient boiler sent warm air up had seemed awfully familiar, and now hearing the tinny sound of an old radio playing, I was certain I was still in the Heritage Building. The main boiler room was off to my left somewhere, which meant that the storage space beneath the stage was on my right. The music was coming from the radio in the carpenters' area. Someone had left it on again.

My ear ached. I had left my inquisitor frustrated, and he had ground his cigarette out in the curved valley of my earlobe, more from pique at not getting what he wanted than from any real attempt to make me talk.

I had talked, though. I told him all sorts of things: the combination of my first locker at school, most of the access codes for the NPC network at the Pole, the password on Santa's humidor, the words I had spoken to Clarise Hangvine that had garnered me an invite back to her place oh so many years ago now, the solution to the last puzzle in *Myst*, the answer to the "Got Milk?" question, the reason Douglas Adams picked 42 as the answer to everything; I told him all that and more.

But the one thing I didn't tell him was the access codes to the numbered bank account.

213

Hence the earlobe burning.

I had lost track of time, though my pants were dry now. I might have pissed myself when the cigarette was shoved against my ear; it was hard to remember if it had been then or some time after when I had given up on ever getting a chance to visit a real bathroom. Or maybe both. It didn't matter anymore because it had been long enough that I was no longer damp.

The worst part had been the chills once the urine had dried.

No, scratch that. The worst part was actually having the life experience that allowed me to make that distinction.

Not for the first time, I wished Rudolph were here. Things would have gone a lot differently with him around.

A key was inserted in the outer lock of the storeroom, and I tensed involuntarily. Stupid lizard brain response to the ache in my left ear. I wasn't going to talk, so why did part of my brain keep freaking out?

The lock clicked, and someone entered the room. I strained to hear the sound of shoes against the storeroom floor. How many? Was it Slapper, coming back for another round of hand-rolled cigarette interrogation? Was it Meeker, suddenly developing a spine? Was it—?

The shoes squeaked against the floor. Cork soles.

I knew who it was, and I was a little surprised.

The blindfold was removed, and even though the light in the storeroom was weak and pale, it was still a little bright for me since I had been playing earthworm down here in the basement for the past day or so.

"Hello, Erma," I said, squinting at the only person in the room. "What brings you down here?"

She caught my chin with her large hand and held it steady as she lifted a squeeze bottle to my dry lips. "Talk or drink," she said. "Your choice."

I closed my mouth around the nub of the squeeze bottle, and she applied a forceful amount of pressure, filling my desert-like mouth with a flash flood of warm water. I gasped, choked, tried to sneeze, all the while struggling mightily not to lose a single drop. She let me nurse like a calf for a minute before pulling the bottle away. I snapped at her fingers as she removed her hand from my chin.

She cuffed me lightly on the ear—the left ear—and I squealed like a different barnyard animal. "Watch your manners," she said.

I apologized for a good minute or so straight.

"Do you get it now?" she said when I ran out of steam. "The production was always meant to tank."

Erma Raeddicker was the general manager of the Delirious Arts Renaissance Company, which meant she did ninety-nine percent of all the real work while everyone else sipped expensive coffees and talked about *art* with capital letters. She was round in the head and body like a snowman, and her hair had been strawberry blonde once—though she kept trying to bring back that youthful luster with regular applications of Goldenrod #42. She reminded me of a bird with the way she moved her neck and chin. She was approximating a mother hen now as she tried to sweet talk me.

"What about the cast of thousands that you've got slaving away up there?" I asked. "Anyone told them?"

She raised her hand as if she was going to slap me again. "It's only forty-six," she said. "Don't exaggerate." She lowered her hand when I made a contrite bounce with my head. "They're theater wannabes, anyway. Who cares?"

"They might."

She offered me the water bottle again, but I only got a small mouthful before she pulled it away. "Whatever. They're getting paid for rehearsals. Beyond that? Well, it won't matter after the first few shows anyway . . ."

I swirled a final bit of the water around my mouth to wash out the taste of dust and stale air, turning my head away from her to spit on the floor. I tried to do some math, but I gave up and asked her instead. "How much did you skim off?"

"Enough to make it worth doing." She offered me a smile that wasn't entirely pleasing to look at. "But then you came along. Offering so much more."

I raised an eyebrow. "I don't remember offering."

"Yes, well, that's the sticky part now, isn't it?" She shucked my chin gently with her fist. "You're smart. I'm guessing you've got most of it figured out. How many are in on this con? And what does that knowledge do to your chances of walking out of here?"

"Well, since I finished all of my Christmas shopping before you kidnapped me, I haven't had a whole lot to worry about. Lots of time to think about who I should move over to the Naughty List."

"I warned them." She sighed. "They should have gone harder on you that first day."

"Gee, Erma. It's nice to see this outpouring of compassion during the holiday season."

She leaned in close, and I could smell mint on her breath. She always had a pot of mint tea steeping in her office. Part of the grandmotherly charm she tried to exude. *Come in, kids, have some tea. It'll warm your bones on these cold days.*

"You're going to make it hard for us to disappear," she said in a rather ungrandmotherly way.

"Right," I said. "So let me see if I've got this. Choice A is you settle for what you've got, whack me, and vanish to Cabo. Choice B: threaten me enough that I cave and give you the account password; in return, I get to live, and I suffer temporary amnesia out of gratitude, and you still go to Cabo. Only a million or so richer. That about it?"

She tousled my hair. "That's about it," she said. "And I think *B* is the smart choice."

I leaned back to get out from under her hand. "Erma, you have no idea the shit I've been through the past few years," I said. "You really have no idea."

Her smile stayed, but it looked a little frozen.

"Really," I said. "I've stood toe-to-toe with Satan himself, Erma. I bluffed him, and he blinked. I spent last Christmas a mile down in the ocean with a very pissed off and claustrophobic reindeer. Do you think I'm the slightest bit frightened by your heavy-handed theatrics?"

Her smile dissolved. "I'm sorry, Mr. Rosewood, but you're wrong. I don't do theater. I'm in management."

She left the blindfold off but turned out the lights as she left. I listened to the sibilant whisper of her shoes until the noise was lost beneath the distant murmur of the radio and the buzz in my left ear.

I let the shakes into my knees then. Rudolph was the one who had bluffed Satan. He was the one with the indomitable nerves of steel. I was just the sidekick. The realist who kept everything grounded. I wasn't good at bluffing.

I was good at worrying.

Why had I let them talk me into doing this without Rudolph?

November 23rd

M<small>Y FIRST DAY AS PRODUCER OF</small> R<small>UDOLPH</small>! T<small>HE</small> M<small>USICAL WAS ALMOST AS</small> surreal as having lunch with Salvador Dali on a terrace attached to the dome of a giant egg, during which he spoke in a strange binary code language, and I could only make the noise of an angry hippopotamus while the menu was spelled out in arrangements of boneless lizards. The sky overhead was filled with vermilion water lilies floating upside down, and a pretzel shaped cloud kept jumping in front of a sun that looked like a not-quite solid egg yolk.

Santa had been right. The production was in dire straits, and it only took three phone calls for me to suddenly become the new messiah of the theater. The previous sugar daddy was a Pacific Northwest cattle baron-cum-telecommunications magnate-cum-new-millennial Medici. Josiah Metcalfe had spent the greater part of the five years since his wife's death contributing his vast fortune to the arts. The late Mrs. Metcalfe had been a grand proponent of the arts, and while he tried to match her late enthusiasm, he didn't quite have the same eye for creative activities as he did for beef and microchips.

There was a gallery in Boise, Idaho, named after his wife, and it was filled with a bunch of heavy oils and strained watercolors that weren't doing much but gathering dust. A million of his dollars helped drill a large hole in the middle of a park in Spokane

Washington. The drilling stopped when a large pocket of natural gas was breached, and the latest projections from Spokane's City Council said was that it was going to take ten to twenty million to fix all the structural damage on the surrounding buildings. And no one wanted to talk about finishing the pool that Metcalfe had been trying to put in for the kids in the first place. On the other side of the Cascades, in Seattle, he bought the old Heritage Building with the design of turning it into a permanent theater for the Delirious Arts Renaissance Company.

The Heritage had been on the edge many years ago, both the edge of town and the edge of cutting intellectual thought. A five-story brownstone, it attempted to meld the aesthetics of a modern office building with the space requirements of an equally modern performance center. The downside was that the theater itself took up so much of the interior space of the structure that when it closed, the rest of the building couldn't support the rising operating expenses. The Heritage became a firetrap and a hostel for the homeless until it was saved by Metcalfe's patronage.

Compared to other industries, the arts moved at a glacial pace, and Metcalfe didn't have the same patience in his dotage as he had in his youth. The Heritage had been in his name for four years now and had never opened its doors to the public. The interior design and decorations still weren't done, and they had already put off the opening production season once.

And then things hit a snag. Metcalfe had himself a permanently bad game of golf one afternoon back in September. He had been on pace to hit a 74 that day, having done a personal best of 31 on the front half, when he went for the three wood to recover from a bad shank on the 11th. Not a bad choice when you've got another 160 yards to clear but something twanged during his back swing. His heart did a little tap dance number and then went to a resting rate that was way too low for any activity other than breathing. He inhaled grass clippings for a half hour or so before the paramedics could get him hooked up to all those machines that go *bing!* and keep you alive. Four weeks later, Metcalfe woke up enough for the doctors to tell him that the that 31 he had posted on the front nine was probably the last golf score he was going to post.

Metcalfe got himself the best nursing millions of dollars can buy and went back to Montana to ease into the twilight. His outstanding hobbies were brutally scrutinized by the legal team hired by his half-dozen children. Anything that hadn't shown a demonstrable profit in the previous six months was put on notice, enterprises that had hemorrhaged cash for a year were cut, and projects that had never shown the slightest inclination to profitability were told to lose the Metcalfe Foundation's number. In short, all artistic funding dried up overnight.

The production scrambled for a while, trying to forestall the inevitable, but they couldn't find any other investors on such short notice and were about to close up shop when I called. One of the details in the envelope I got from Santa was a numbered account in Switzerland, and when I called the bank in Bern, a nice fellow there happily told me I had a little over a million US at my disposal.

There were some perks to working for Mrs. C.

I paid a visit to the upscale tailor in the mall and didn't even blink when he told me what it would cost to get them made in my size. I got an expensive haircut, treated myself to a mani-pedi, found some excellent shoes, and caught the morning flight Monday—parked in first class, naturally. I did, after all, have an image to maintain.

That part was easy.

Erma met me at the airport, swaddled in voluminous cotton and trailing an air of patchouli and cinnamon that left a near-visible wake. She insisted on carrying my luggage and kept up a constant stream of chatter from the airport to the Heritage Building. I had hoped to get settled at the hotel first, have a stiff drink or two, before facing what lay in wait for me at the Heritage Building, but my wishes were little more than dandelion fluff stuck to the car seat as far as Erma was concerned.

"We're thrilled to have your support, Mr. Rosewood," she cooed for about the eighteenth time as we rode the elevator to the top floor of the Heritage. She was doing a hungry pigeon dance with her head.

The paneling in the elevator car was all maple with polished brass trim. The ceiling was reflective tile, and the panel over the fluorescent lights was a single piece of scalloped glass. I wondered how much of the restoration project was done. A million plus wasn't going to go that far if there was more work to be done.

Metcalfe's office—my office—was the size of a squash court. It took up the northwest corner of the building, and the view out across the red cranes of Harbor Island to the distant snowcapped peaks of the Olympic Mountains on the peninsula was spectacular. The steel and glass forest of downtown Seattle, buildings gleaming in the weak afternoon sunlight, was on my right. The walls of the office were over-decorated with watercolors, probably on loan from his gallery in Idaho. About five old-growth trees had died to provide the lumber for the table that dominated the room. At first, I thought it was a conference table, but then I realized there was only one chair, and the chair wasn't exactly small either. Stacked on a corner of the monster desk were three piles of paper—each one looked ready to topple over if I so much as stared at it too hard.

Erma fished around that capacious head of hers for some comment to draw attention away from the stature of the previous tenant of the office. I beat her to it. "Well," I said slowly, trying not to affect a cattleman's drawl, "I'll need either a hacksaw to bring the desk down or a couple of phone books to bring me up."

She tittered behind her hand like a pair of chickadees, and I should have paid more attention to the warning bell that went off in my head. The office felt artificial—like a movie set, and Erma alternated between overly officious and overly eager to please with all the enthusiasm of a small dog hyped up with the promise of a walk *and* a ball to chew on. Her laugh was shrill and forced. The walls had been recently painted—one coat too few to really cover up the glue marks left by the old wallpaper, and the shadows on the ceiling were actually old water stains.

But then the moment passed. The stains became delicate shadows thrown by the fancy glass covering the light fixtures. Her laugh became the chirping of happy birds again, and the dust bunnies under the credenza scurried away to some invisible hidey hole.

"I'll see what I can find," Erma said as she drifted toward the ornate office door.

"Thanks," I replied, and that feeling came back. Did I really want her handling either a hacksaw or a stack of phone books?

"Shall I send the rest of the staff up?" she asked.

I threw off my paranoia. "No," I said. "Not today. I'd like to get settled a bit before I meet everyone."

"Okay," she thrilled, slipping into her eager-to-please persona. She closed the door behind her, and the latch settled loudly into the frame.

I wondered where she was going to find actual phone books, and that thought led to thinking about hacksaws. I threw my briefcase up on the desk as I wandered over to the window. A hundred years ago, the Heritage might have been a real landmark, but the modern skyline of Seattle towered over the five-story building. I peered up at the black finger of the Columbia Tower, and wondered how thin the air was up at the top.

The lording-over-my-domain moment passed, and I returned to the monolithic desk. A little free climbing up the side of the chair and a death-defying leap got me to the top. For the record I paced it off: six meters by seven. You could do an elvish line dance on this thing and not fall off. The room the NPC had sequestered me in after our trip to purgatory had been smaller.

The table was more than big enough to accommodate all the paperwork in my briefcase. The theater company's accountant, Ted Laslo, had overnighted me a brick of paperwork, thinking—I suppose—that I was going to review it all on the flight out. First class is pretty roomy, but not that roomy. But when I glanced at the triple stack of papers on the desk, I realized Ted had only sent me the highlights, and I ruefully wondered if the desk wasn't actually big enough.

I got started, and it took me over an hour to get the company records all neatly spread out. I left a walkway up the middle so that I could stroll back and forth as I tried to wrap my head around the copious volumes of data in all the piles. There were cash flow projections, audience outreach plans, expenditure reports, press clippings, staff backgrounds, costume designs, mechanical drawings for rigging and winches, and even a handful of holiday cocktail recipes. I have an aptitude for paperwork, but this all went way beyond my comfort level. It was going to take me weeks to figure all of this out.

I didn't have *weeks*—plural. I had two and a half. The show was scheduled to open on the eleventh of December. It had already been delayed once because of Metcalfe's accident. If the opening was delayed again, there wouldn't be enough days before Christmas to get in a full run of the show. No one wants to see a Christmas show *after* Christmas. That's worse than finding eggs after Easter.

I sat and read, because no one else was going to it, and after a few hours of parsing paperwork, I was starting to believe that the problem really was as simple as Santa made it out to be: show up, spend money, talk about the arts, keep the heat on, and make sure the doors opened on the eleventh. If we could get two full weeks in before Christmas at forty percent capacity each night, the production wouldn't be a complete wash. It was going to eat up a significant chunk of my budget, but what theater company doesn't lose money on actually putting on a show?

The only real problem was I didn't have chairs for forty percent of the house to sit in. Apparently, a broken water pipe had wrecked most of the flooring in the orchestra, and while Metcalfe had managed to get a team of industrious carpenters in to fix the floor (and support beams for the mezzanine), most of the existing seats had been thrown out. Sure, I could bring in folding chairs for the audience, but that didn't exactly match the décor in the theater, and I'm sure some local critic was going to spend most of their review bitching about the hard metal seat. That would not put more butts in those seats.

"So find more," I mused. "How hard can that be? This problem can be fixed by spending money. I can do that."

"Sounds like an easy job," someone said.

I looked up. The voice belonged to a woman with green eyes. She had managed to open the office door without making any noise, and when I made eye contact, she came all the way into the room.

The stack of papers next to my right knee was the one containing all the bios of the employees and actors. The problem with the bio sheets is that Ted—being more numerically oriented than visually driven—hadn't bothered to include any headshots with the bios. And none of them had bothered to mention eye color or predilection for fine Italian footwear.

The woman walked over to the desk and offered me her hand.

"Bernard Rosewood," I said, taking her hand. I could have stood up, but then I would have actually been taller than her, and that was a weird feeling. "I'm—"

"The money," she said.

"Yes," I said, suddenly flustered. Again, eye contact was a new thing for me. "I suppose I am."

"Unless you were talking to a mouse in your pocket a minute ago." Her peepers gave me a quick once-over. I was so glad I had gone for the Armani suit instead of the Calvin Klein. We had similar tastes in Italian designers.

"Can't remember the last time I had a tête-à-tête with a squeaker," I said.

"Not very good conversationalists are they?"

"Not really. Unless you're talking about cheese, and then they'll talk your head off."

She laughed and released my hand. "I'm Barb Prescott. I'm the set designer for the company."

"Right," I said.

A tiny smile quirked the corner of her mouth. She put a finger on the stack of bios, and started to slide them—one by one—aside. Hers came up eventually, and she left it there as she wandered past the desk to look out the window.

I scanned the document quickly. Canadian by birth, British by education; six years with the Royal Shakespeare Company. Married some guy with an impressive list of degrees—in architecture, of all things. And that was it. No other credits. I turned the page over, wondering if there was something more on the back.

This piqued my curiosity. The most interesting bits of any bio were the blank spots. It'd been a decade since she'd been married, and a surreptitious glance toward the window revealed she wasn't wearing a wedding band, which didn't necessarily mean anything, but still . . .

"I'm glad you could join us," she said, coming back to the desk and sitting in Metcalfe's immense chair. She filled it better than I, but it was still ginormous.

"That seems to be the sentiment of the day," I said.

"Deep pockets will do that." She looked over the sea of paperwork surrounding me and wrinkled her nose. "You aren't the type who understands all this, are you?"

"Some," I said. "Ted sent me a brick of paperwork, and I thought that was a lot, but apparently he was being cost-conscious and leaving most of it for me to find when I got here."

"Is it telling you much about the show?"

"You don't have enough chairs," I said.

"And?" she prompted.

"It's a lot of paperwork," I said.

She leaned forward and tapped me on the knee. "Come downstairs," she said. "Let me show you what you're really here for."

The house was dark, the stage lit by two banks of small footlights nestled in the floor out near the proscenium. We wove our way past towering sculptures that were hard to make out in the dim light, though I felt like I was sneaking through a forest of frozen monoliths. Barb made me stand on a taped X near the center of the stage. "Wait here," she said, then she left me there.

I lifted a hand to blot out some of the glare from the bank of lights and tried to make out the shape and style of the theater's auditorium. Orchestra—sans chairs—main floor of the house, mezzanine, and a couple of box seats on either side. Either the walls were overgrown with moss or the trim was exceptionally rococo. It was hard to tell in the dimness.

"Ready?" Barb's voice reverberated from hidden speakers, and I jumped out of my skin.

"I'm not a big fan of playing hide and seek," I said once my heart stopped pounding like a jackhammer in my chest.

"Sorry," she said. "It'll just be a minute."

"Where is everyone?"

"Dinner. We break from three to seven. Traffic is horrible in this city. We have to give them extra time to get anywhere. They'll be back in a few hours."

Tiny lights began to blossom out in the audience, gleaming points on chandeliers dangling from the high ceiling. I could make out the walls now and saw that the ornamentation was even more fifteenth-century than I had originally guessed. The lack of seating left the orchestra area a black pit, and some of the boxes on the sides were missing their front railings.

Suddenly, light spilled across the stage on my right, and all the tall figures were illuminated in stark relief. Barb kept bringing up lights, and I found I was surrounded by a field of twisted, tormented figures. They were very detailed, each one attached to the earth by a maze of wire and ribbon, each one straining and pulling to be free.

My mouth went dry. They looked a lot like statues I had seen once. On a metal plate floating on a sea of hellish air.

There were two platforms adorned with fat cones upstage from me, and as Barb dropped the spotlights down, the cones erupted with plumes of fire, aggravating the shadows on the statues and giving the tormented faces strange lifelike qualities. The fire plumes revealed the details of the platforms, and I realized they were made from thousands of plastic dolls, all melted and woven together.

I was still gawking when Barb skipped out from stage left. "What do you think?" she asked, slightly breathlessly.

"What is this? Where am I?"

"You are in Rudolph's throne room. I modeled it on the original designs of Solomon's chambers. Though," she shrugged slightly, "I made some modifications. A little more Gothic."

"Throne room?" I asked. "Rudolph's throne room?"

"Oh dear," she said. "You haven't read the script yet, have you?"

November 24th

I CONSIDERED DROWNING MYSELF IN THE BATHTUB AFTER READING THE FIRST
two scenes of the play. I eyed the window and thought about
taking a swan dive to the street when I finished the first act. And I
was beyond numb when I finished.

Gothic? Gothic was a blonde Swede drinking lemonade
and licking a cherry lollipop while lounging in a sun-drenched
hammock beside a field of sunflowers compared to this. Imagine
the blackest point of night captured in a can and dropped into the
deepest part of the Marianas Trench, and you can begin to understand the darkness that overflowed this script.

The audience is lulled in the beginning, lead to believe they
are about to enjoy a full family outing of Christmas cheer.
'Twas the night before Christmas and all that. The curtain
rises up on a soft winter night. Typical nuclear family sitting
around a lit Christmas tree. Mom in her kerchief, Dad in
his cap. The children are laughingly trying to decide which
present to open first for this is a post-nuclear family that never
understood the importance of patience. There is a chorus of
sugarplum fairies at the edges of the stage, faces lit by candles
as they sing a graceful noel. There are more candlelit fairies
then, falling gently from the ceiling of the theater, roaming
randomly in the aisles, turning the entire house into a sea of
flickering light.

Onstage, Dad directs his young son towards a very specific package. "Open that one," he says. "You should open that one tonight." The son does so, and out of the box leaps a happy puppy. The script notes: *White puppy with single black spot on face, something with short hair and very energetic.* The boy is overjoyed. "Just what I wanted," he crows. "He's just what I asked Santa for."

Then, a buzz of feedback from the sound system. The script suggests: *like the sound of a thousand children all screaming with joy, but downtuned a half-octave and slowed to one-eighth speed.* The sea of lights is extinguished as if from the strength of this scream, blown out by the outrageous wind. The scream ascends into screeching static, until the Christmas tree explodes—lights popping into showers of yellow sparks, branches crackling and burning, the angel atop the tree dissolving into a pinwheel of red fire. The family is thrown aside by the explosion, and they lie crumpled on the stage. From out of the exploded tree comes . . .

ENTER: AN APPARITION. *The stage is black. The house is black. The only light is the burning Christmas tree. 'As he kept looking, why, here the thornbush was burning with fire and yet the thornbush was not being consumed.' At first, there is only the shadow that reaches out of the flame, a great horned head that stretches across the stage like the stiff, reaching fingers of some great celestial being. The figure appears, limned in fire, a tall figure crowned with twisted horns. The fire subsides quickly, leaving only a ruddy glow on the stage as the figure stands in the living room of the nuclear family. His face is lit with a red glow, a single point of red light like a great Cyclopean eye.*

VOICE: *(over sound system, reverb +10)* No. This is an illusion. This is not real. I will show you reality. I will strip away the sweetness, the candied shell which coats, the taffied taste which numbs, the saccharine smell which opiates. I will show you the true spirit of Christmas. I will show you true.

LIGHT: *Strobe (15 SEC).* The nuclear family sprawled in their living room. The tree consumed and blackened against the wall of their house. Standing in the center of the family's once-happy home is an immense reindeer with a thorny rack of antlers and a nose that glows the color of blood.

LIGHTS: Blackout *(after 5 SEC)*

END SCENE ONE

❄

Rehearsals were underway when I finally dragged myself to the Heritage. I stood near the back of the house and watched the capering and quivering figures onstage. Seated in folding chairs about twenty feet from the stage were the choreographer and his assistant. The lights were up on the stage, and the towering giants didn't look nearly as imposing as they did last night. And from here, you couldn't tell the throne was made from Barbie dolls.

"Stop! Stop. Stop!" The choreographer rose from his chair as if elevated by his upraised hand. The mother of Henrik Guljerssen— our choreographer—must have grown up watching Ray Bolger knee and wobble his way through the *Wizard of Oz*. Bolger's impression of a walking scarecrow had resonated so strongly in her womb that Henrik had come out more like a child of flax and chaff than flesh and blood. He stumbled through his early years all loose and rubbery until something locked into place within the recesses of his brain, and what had once been fumbling became graceful, the continual artless pratfall became an expressive circuit of harmonic motion, and the rough and tumble child of straw became a man capable of infinite grace. Even the simple motion of rising from his chair and stopping the action on the stage was performed with such elegance that watching the dancers come to a halt at his call was like watching a train wreck in comparison.

"Just because you are playing cripples doesn't mean that you should dance like them." Henrik turned the up-thrust motion of his arm into a sweeping gesture encompassed even the empty house behind him. "If we had seats, they'd be running a hundred and twenty dollars each. Do you think anyone is going to pay that much to see a bunch of cripples try to keep time? They are going to want razzle. They're looking for dazzle. They're going to want their fucking money's worth." His assistant shrank in her chair as he turned his attention on her. His voice didn't drop a decibel. "Honestly, what ward did we pull these rejects from?" He let the question hang in the air until he finally snapped his fingers at the electric piano, which was tucked away in the corner of stage right. "Again," he said. "From the top."

The pianist—an angular woman poking out of a large over-coat—hunched over the keyboard and began to bang out heavy chords. Shuffling out of their hunched and twisted postures, the dancers transformed into a ragged line like a centipede uncurling when touched with a hot stick. It was like watching a stomach turn itself inside out, and I felt like a first year med student—repulsed and fascinated at the same time.

"No, no, no!" Henrik shouted. The dancers faltered, and the music stopped. He lifted his long arm and pointed an accusatory finger with such *gravitas* that I expected lightning bolts to shoot from it.

Based on the reaction of many of the dancers onstage, I wasn't the only one who expected fingertip pyrotechnics.

"You. Yes. You," Henrik said. "What is the problem? Do you have a medical condition that I need to know about?"

The dancer in question shrugged and scratched his head.

"You move like you've got an inner ear imbalance, and you've got about as much rhythm as an epileptic rehearsing for a Grand Mal," Henrik sneered. "Do you expect me to shut down the entire production while we fetch some dock workers to beat a sense of time into your thick skull? Is that what I need to do?"

The dancer had enough sense to shake his head.

The choreographer stared at the dancer, and we all watched the young man's head wobble faster and faster. And just before I thought the dancer was going to lose his balance, Henrik snapped his fingers and the young man stopped instantly. "Good," Henrik said. He snapped his fingers again. "Let us start again, you lazy clubfoots."

The pianist didn't react quickly enough, and she jumped when Henrik shouted at her in some dialect I didn't recognize.

He snapped out a four count as she hurriedly put her fingers to the keys and started playing again. On stage, the line of dancers writhed and twisted.

I wasn't quite sure what the clumsy dancer was doing differently this time, and I must have made some inarticulate noise of confusion because Henrik stopped the dancers again and looked over his shoulder with an indolent curve of his head. "Who's there?" he asked archly.

I cleared my throat and stepped away from the back wall. "Sorry," I said. "I was just curious."

He dismissed me with a wave of his fingers. "Be curious somewhere else."

"I—"

"Why am I still hearing that voice?" he said, looking at his assistant. "Why is he still here?" She leaped up, knocking over her chair, and came back towards me, walking swiftly, her arms swinging stiffly at her sides. She was a rather severe-looking woman in a mousy sort of way. Her black glasses were straight out of the late '90s bohemian catalog, and the angular slash of her mouth was made even more angular by the utilitarian color and application of her lipstick.

"Please," she said softly in a voice that made me think of stuffed animals being shoved into a speeding blender. She positioned herself between me and the stage, indicating the lobby doors to my left. "Go," she said in a tone of voice typically used on dogs who have just been caught pooping on the rug.

"I just wanted to see . . ." I started.

Behind her, Henrik groaned audibly. "I cannot believe these conditions. How can anyone have a creative thought when surrounded by such negativity? Such oppressive bleakness?"

His assistant hunched her shoulders at the sound of his voice, looking like she was about to pass a kidney stone. She gestured towards the door again.

"All right," I acquiesced, raising my hands. I turned and marched out like I had just been caught with my hand in a cookie jar. She slammed the door shut and stared at me through the small porthole-style window. I stared back, silently counting, and got all the way to one hundred and thirty before she blinked. And then, as if embarrassed to have been caught being human, she vanished. In the distance, I could hear the ragged wheeze of the music as rehearsals started up again.

"Get caught snooping?"

I turned and spotted Erma standing in the door to the box office. She was swathed in reds and purples today.

"I guess I was," I said. "I didn't know it was a closed set."

Erma waved a paw at the doors to the theater proper. "Henrik's fussy. His choreography is genius, but it comes with a few eccentricities."

"Is that what you call it?" I asked, wandering over. "It looked like an earthworm turning itself inside out."

"It takes a little getting used to. Most of his work is like that. It seems totally chaotic and random, but there is an order to it, an elegance that makes itself known if you free yourself from the rigid constraints of traditional dance forms," she said, launching into something that felt like a researched speech. "You have to be receptive to the possibilities of new experiences. It's very avant-garde. The French dance community isn't even sure what to think of him. We're so very lucky to have him on this production."

"Is that what the scene needed? More avant-garde than French avant-garde?" I tried to recall the script notes about the throne room dance sequence, but my brain was already blocking all of that out.

"The fire spouts weren't on, were they?" Erma asked. I shook my head. "Oh," she clucked. "That makes all the difference. There is nothing like the play of fire off sweaty skin to illuminate the misery of the human condition." The phone in the office rang, and she bustled off to answer it.

How can you turn Rudolph's life story into a musical?

Well, scratch that. It's already been done. Back in '64—the same year we had that horrible accident with the Nuclear Clock. Rankin and Bass released their stop-motion TV special, and generations of children grew up believing that production values were so shoddy at the North Pole that a place like the Island of Misfit Toys could actually exist. Burl Ives was the serpent who hummed "Silver and Gold" in their ears from Thanksgiving to New Year's. These kids thought elves dreamed of being dentists, that Bumbles bounced, and that Rudolph was actually shorter than your average elf.

Yeah, right. I can walk under most of the reindeer without ducking, and I'm considered a giant in my family.

Let's be honest: most musicals are sort of scary anyway, even the ones that purport to be about passionate excess, and most kids' movies that have song and dance numbers would prefer you not to call them by that name. *Rudolph! A Musical* was a fiery fever dream of psychotic fury and impotent man-child rage. It stomped and trampled its way across the popularized myth of Santa's favorite reindeer with absolutely no remorse for its bleak tone. It was equal parts Grand Guignol, orgiastic mystery cult ritual, Abbott and Costello-style sight gags, and a cheap remix of the old Faust legend. Full of pyrotechnics, full-scale choral histrionics, and kinetic word play, it was a mesmerizing disaster. The only way it was going to be successful was if the audience bought the premise that Christmas sucked.

And I had to ask myself: how far from the truth was that?

We had gone to purgatory to make sure that no Christmas wish was left unfilled, thinking—in our eternal sugarplum-coated innocence—that a child's happiness was the most important thing in the world. And, that night in Troutdale, watching little Suzy jump into her father's arms? That moment had been totally worth everything we had done.

But we had performed a miracle, and Ramiel had been right about the repercussions of our actions. We had changed the rules, and it had changed Christmas. It raised the bar, and the wish lists the following year had been outrageous. Even with the help of the heavenly host, we had been hard pressed to fulfill every wish—and some of them we interpreted *really* liberally. And we had hit the ground running after being recruited by Mrs. C. There had been so much work to do in restoring people's faith in Christmas. What do you do for an encore after performing a miracle? Especially when you know the cost of doing them?

Part of the reason I put Rudolph and myself in a metal plug six thousand feet below sea level was that I didn't want to see what happened when Christmas cratered. The fact that it didn't without us was both heartbreaking and a huge relief.

But Santa knew. I could tell. Satan wasn't stealing the Spirit from him this time. It was the rest of the world. We had wrecked things when we went to purgatory, and no matter how hard we tried to put it all back together, it wasn't the same. It was like watching a remake of your favorite TV show. It seems like it should be better—it certainly looks prettier, and the actors are way younger and sexier—but something isn't quite right. And eventually you realize what is off is your sense of wonder. It's gotten dull.

And Mrs. C knew too. I was slow to figure it out, but she had already extrapolated Rudolph's emotional trajectory.

It was all there in the Boston job. If Rudolph's anger had gotten the better of him, if he lost track of his faith and his desire and his direction, that job would have ended a lot worse. He had the Spirit of Christmas in him still—just like I did—but his core was nuclear. How long could the Spirit survive in that heat?

I will tell it true. That's what Rudolph says in the musical. Scene One, Act One. If you looked at it the right way—or wrong way, I suppose—this wasn't a musical. It was a prophecy. Oh, sure there's the deeply entrenched Rankin and Bass influence where Rudolph laments how different he is from the others. How they won't let them play his games. How he can't run with the reindeer on Christmas night. But the similarities stop there. Whereas Rankin and Bass paste a "Kumbaya! let's all clap our hands" veneer on the story, the musical script pulls a Milton and dives off the deep end. Just like Satan in *Paradise Lost*, the musical Rudolph is bent on revenge.

November 27th

Turkey Day was a respite from everything for everyone except the turkey. "A day off," Barb said when she invited me to join the turkey orphans at her place. "We could all use a day off. No rehearsals. No budget meetings. Nothing to do with the show. It'll all be there tomorrow."

The cab driver did the Seattle version of over the hill and through the woods, taking me across one of the floating bridges that spanned Lake Washington and whisking me through one of the neighborhoods where the tech industry's early retirees live. I was deposited on the curb in front of a narrow brownstone house that looked like it had been airlifted out from the east coast. It was half as wide as the surrounding houses, but a full floor taller. White lights were strung along the eaves and the edges of the windows, and through the open curtains, I could see a fire dancing in the fireplace and the requisite triangle of a Christmas tree. Up but not decorated. She wasn't one of those crazy ones.

A pudgy teenaged girl answered the door. She had a dusting of freckles across the bridge of her wrinkled nose, and her eyes were the color of the ocean and appeared ready to overflow with water at any moment. She was dressed in a plaid skirt and a frilly blouse that looked nearly as uncomfortable as her expression.

"Who are you?" she demanded.

"Jacob Marley," I replied dryly.

She slammed the door in my face. Hard enough to rattle the brass knocker. I tapped my thumb against the side of the bottle of Pedro Ximénez I had brought. "Obviously, a huge *Christmas Carol* fan," I muttered as I leaned on the bell again.

"Sorry," Barb said as soon as she opened the door. "Cordelia—my niece—is unhappy with her stepmother and is taking it out on the rest of us." She was wearing a printed wrap dress that augmented the color in her eyes. A simple strand of pearls wreathed her neck. "This is your last chance," she said, offering me a smile. "You can still turn back."

"'Abandon all hope ye who enter here.'"

She cocked her head to one side. "Is that Goethe?"

"Dante."

"You sure?"

I laughed. "Yeah."

She stepped out of the way and ushered me into her house. "From the sound of that laugh, I'd say you're more than a little familiar with Dante."

"Personally? No," I said. "But yeah, I've . . . well, let's just say I've done some independent research on Dante."

"Is there a good story there, or is it all dry academic talk?"

"It's a knee-slapper," I said.

"Do I get to hear it?"

I turned around in the foyer and looked up at her. "Now?"

She closed the door and leaned against it.

"Later is fine." Her eyes twinkled. "If you survive."

I twirled the bottle of wine around in my hand and held the neck like the handle of a shillelagh. "I can handle the moody ones."

She swirled past me, trailing an aroma of spices and sandal-wood that whispered Chanel. "Give up your outer vestments, o fierce warrior," she said as she led me toward the back of the house, where all the noise was coming from. "Let me show you off to the rest of the savages."

I filled out the double-digit group of turkey orphans. Barb. Cordelia. Cordelia's father and stepmother and two smaller moppets: half-brother and -sister to the obnoxious one. The other couple was Edgar and Sylvia Brandstreet. Barb said that Edgar painted and that Sylvia wrote, which I had already guessed by how he held his wine glass and the way she picked at the *hors d'oeuvres*. The other man in the room was Terence Ulan. He tried to bond with me by playing the game of *Whose Hand is More Like a Cold Fish?* and letting me know that he preferred "Doctor" to "Mister." I bonded back by calling him "Terry" and squeezing his hand hard enough to make fish oil.

Cordelia's wrath, as Jack, her father, rapidly explained to me the first moment she was out of earshot, stemmed from the fact that her birth mother had picked last Monday to go into rehab. "Prescription medication addiction," he explained *sotto voce*. "Darlene loved her pills more than her own daughter." Cordelia, he elaborated, never cared much for his new wife, Nancy, and she found the idea of spending an entire four days in her stepmother's companyworse than the psychological torture inflicted upon illicit prisoners of war.

"You couldn't lock her in the basement and send down bread and water twice a day?" I asked.

From his nervous laughter, I could tell that the idea had occurred to him already. More than once.

Nancy was blonde and petite, and as I discovered through the course of snack-table small talk, she had been a cheerleading coach out in North Carolina during the last decade. Her team had gone to Nationals a few times, and had almost one once. Her voice wasn't as helium-charged as I would have expected, but the lingering aroma of ground tobacco hiding beneath her perfume gave her secret away. Her breasts were new, and she was enjoying how they stretched the fabric of her dress, which was very disconcerting, as they were sort of at eye-level for me. Every time she turned toward me, I was worried I was going to get smacked in the head.

Sylvia's demons had taken her beauty. Not entirely. In honest moments, you could be stunned by the shape of her nose or the turn of her hair about her collar or the movement of her jaw. But she was too tightly wound by the stress of her art to remember her grace. Edgar saw it in her. You could tell by his eyes and the way his fingers lingered every time he touched her. And he found lots of excuses to touch her. Even though they were opposites in many ways—he was gossamer to her stone—they seemed made for each other.

Terrence—Terry—wanted that same connection with Barb, but he was as limp and passive as his hands were clammy. He was having a hard time making eye contact, and most of his longing gazes were directed at her legs. Not that I could blame him for that.

Once I had made the social circuit a few times, I excused myself and wandered down the hall to find a bathroom. Locking the door behind me, I cracked open the window and stood on the edge of the bathtub. I was feeling that old tugging sensation in my chest. That magnetic pull north. I sucked in the brisk November air, reveling in how clean and pure it felt.

I didn't miss the North Pole that much, and most of the blame there could be dropped right in the NPC's lap. What I missed was the tranquility of the Residence. Even with all the hubbub of Seasonal prep, the Pole wasn't as crazy and chaotic as life down in the lower latitudes. Life was simpler with the Clauses; well, it had been until recently. Until Satan started mucking with us, and everything took on a little darkness. A little shadow that never went away.

Closing my eyes, I leaned my head against the cool tile of the bathtub wall. "It's this damn show," I muttered. All that gothic posturing was like getting verbally tongue-lashed by Mephistopheles. No wonder Faust said yes. He was hoping that doing so would shut Mephistopheles up.

I washed my hands a couple of times as if it were possible to erase the stain of the script from my hands. I threw some water on my face, trying to ignore the circles under my eyes. My face was getting older too, sprouting worry lines and crow's-feet like weeds in an untended field.

Santa had looked older too when I had last seen him in Edmonton. The job was catching up with us.

❋

I ran into Cordelia in the hall. The passage wasn't wide enough for her to march past without one of us giving way to the other.

She opted for confrontational instead, stopping dead center in the hall and staring at me, hands cocked on her nearly non-existent hips.

I let my gaze wander over the framed pictures running the length of the hall. Typical family records, both indoor and outdoor shots. Barb was in some of them, as were a number of other people. I avoided Cordelia's glare and pointed at a picture of Barb sitting on a log out in the wilderness somewhere, a picturesque mountain rising in the background.

"Who took these?" I asked Cordelia.

She was flustered by my willful avoidance of her confrontational air, and she sputtered and stuttered for a few moments, her fists kneading against her hips. "Daniel," she muttered finally. "Daniel took them."

"Who is Daniel?" I asked.

"My uncle," she said, her lips curling. "He's the family vegetable." And that got the stunned reaction from me that she had been hoping for. She flounced past with a toss of her head before I could formulate another question.

I was still in the hall when Barb found me a little while later. "We're about to sit down," she said.

I had been wandering back and forth, looking at all the pictures. Figuring out the family connections. I pointed at a picture of Barb and a sandy-haired man sporting that deep ruddiness that comes only from exposure to the sun. "Is this Daniel?" I asked.

He looked a lot like the younger version of Jack in some of the pictures.

Barb didn't even look at the picture. "It is, though you wouldn't recognize him now." She took a deep breath. "His hair is gone and he's lost the tan." She tried to find a smile, but couldn't sustain it.

"I'm sorry," I said, dropping my hand.

"It isn't your fault."

"Doesn't make me any less sorry for bringing it up."

She firmed up the smile then. "It's all right. It was a stupid accident. And there's no point in being angry about it any more. I just wish—" She stopped herself.

I stepped forward and touched her arm. "Is there food on the table?" I asked. "Is that why you were looking for me, or has Terry choked on a cracker or something? Do you need me to perform the Heimlich on him?"

"Aren't you a little short for that?" she asked. Her smile worked up to her eyes.

"Not if he is lying down."

"He's not," she said. "Lying down, or choking. He's just"—she raised two fingers to her eyes and then mimed walking around with them—"making sure I don't trip on something."

"He's very observant that way."

"So are you." She laughed lightly as I blushed. "Come on," she said. "Dinner is ready. You can flirt with me more at the table."

"What? And risk Terry's wrath?"

She favored me with a look. "If you're lucky, Cordelia will make vomiting noises," she said.

"I knew it," I said as I followed her toward the dining room. "You totally asked me here to provide comic relief."

❄

It was all fun and flirtatious until I ended up at the kid's table. There was an awkward moment when Nancy announced that she had put my place setting at the lower table—somewhat proudly, I thought, as if she was patting herself on the back for doing something to minimize the potential embarrassment that could come from me sitting at the big people's table.

Terry looked inordinately pleased at the idea, and he might have even applauded Nancy's decision if I hadn't been staring daggers at him. Barb just shook her head and disappeared into the kitchen, and Sylvia stared at me, her long teeth gnawing at the end piece of the crusty bread. Jack had a sick look on his face, like he was worried that he was going to lose control of his bowels at any moment.

"Thanks, Nancy," I said. What else could I do?

Everyone sat, and Cordelia planted herself across the table from me. She kicked me twice in the shins as she fussed with her napkin, and I waited until she was done squirming before I launched a swift kick at her kneecap. The table bounced slightly and she squealed. "Dad!"

"Stuff it, Cor," her father said. He still looked a little green. "Whatever is going on, you probably deserved it." He tried to wink at me, but he was out of practice, and he nearly turned his eyelid inside out.

Nancy saw him jerk his head, and she immediately leaned over to stroke the side of his face. "Are you all right, darling?" she asked. Jack smiled and let her stroke his cheek.

Cordelia gave me the finger. I smiled back and asked her to pass the butter. My grip on my knife was solid.

Barb interrupted further family drama with the soup. Nancy clapped excitedly as our host brought bowls around to each of us. "I got this recipe from the cooking channel last week," she said proudly, directing her comment at Sylvia, who merely raised an eyebrow and cautiously dipped a spoon in the bowl Barb placed before her.

I'm not a big fan of soup—it's the way things float to the surface that unsettles me—but Nancy's soup was pretty good. It had a variety of mushrooms in it, along with some vegetables for color, hazelnuts, and tiny flecks of orange peel.

As my spoon started to scrape on the bottom of the bowl, I noticed there was something red down there. Not in the soup itself, but printed on the bottom of the bowl. I slurped a few more mouthfuls of soup as I checked to see if I was the only one with a mysterious message in my soup.

Apparently not. The others were slurping and scraping too.

"They were so adorable," Nancy cooed. She bounced in her seat, unable to keep a secret. "I just couldn't resist them. I found them at Pottery Barn down in the Village. You can get whole place settings."

Sylvia, for all her disdain for soup and surprises, cleared her bowl first. "I've got Dasher," she said. Edger finished next and held up his bowl for all to see the fat reindeer image in the bottom of his bowl. It didn't look like anyone I knew, but large cartoon letters spelled out COMET beneath the prancing figure.

My spoon was suddenly very heavy in my hand as everyone started calling out reindeer names. Soon I was the only one left, and they were all looking at me. I lifted my bowl, tilting it so that the thin film of soup still in the bowl pooled near the rim. There were red splotches in my bowl, which turned out to be sparkly dance shoes on a reindeer. "You got Prancer," Cordelia sneered.

"They're just *so* funny," Nancy said, showing us a picture of Blitzen that characterized him as half-soused.

I excused myself, went to the bathroom, and barfed up all the soup I had just eaten.

❄

A tiny sparrow tapped at the bathroom door. "Are you okay?" Barb asked.

"Yeah," I replied. I was sitting on the edge of the tub, resting my elbows on my knees. Barb opened the door cautiously, and when she saw that I didn't have my pants around my ankles or wasn't trying to hang myself from the shower curtain rod with my tie, she came in and sat down on the closed toilet.

I had been crying a little, and I wiped at my face as she looked at me. "I knew him," I said. "There was nothing funny about the way he died."

She didn't say anything, which was considerate because that sentence probably made me sound like a nut-job, and we sat quietly awhile. Distantly, I heard the chatter of voices from the dining room, punctuated by a squeal from Cordelia.

"One of her siblings probably touched the butter dish at the same time she did," I noted.

"Or ate a green bean funny," Barb suggested.

"She is bound and determined not to have a good time, isn't she?" I asked.

Barb nodded. "Yes, she certainly wants to be heard."

I flashed on the script. "Is that all it is, then?" I wondered. "Just wanting to be heard?"

"What do you mean?" she asked.

"The musical," I said. "It's so angry. So much frustration and rage. Is that just someone wanting to be heard?"

"It's what we do, Bernie," she said, looking at me like I should know this. "It's a way to cope with pain. I felt that way when Daniel was injured. For months. I drove away half my friends being an utter spiteful bitch. But it didn't fix anything. It didn't fix him, that's for sure. It just made me more isolated, more lonely. It eats at you, Bernie, if you let it. It eats you up and leaves you hollow."

I thought of Rudolph, who had been angry since '64. So driven, so determined to be the best reindeer to ever pull the sleigh. And it wasn't even a contest. The accident had left him so changed that he wasn't even truly a reindeer anymore. He was like those kids in the comics: an X-deer. He didn't sleep, he could fly for days, and his constitution was so strong that he could probably pull the red sled full of toys all by himself. Yet he pushed himself farther. He came back from purgatory, alone against the entire holy host. He would have gone to hell without us. And what had all that determination gotten him? At what point was he trying so hard to make happiness that he lost sight of what happiness was? Was that what had happened in Boston? I had never seen him so angry, so willing and ready to hurt someone because they threatened to speak ill of Christmas.

And now the show. It had a grip on me, like some demonic worm gnawing its way deeper and deeper into my gut. There was a part of me that wanted to pull out. Just walk away and let this show fall apart before anyone saw it.

"Why are you doing this show?" I asked Barb.

She took a moment to change gears mentally. "Originally, I needed to get out of the house," she said. "I needed to work again. I hadn't done any theater work in a long time. Daniel and I had been trying"—she shook her head—"His firm was very successful. I hadn't needed to work, and there were other things to do."

"But there's a different reason now, isn't there?"

She tucked a lock of her hair behind her ear and sat up a little straighter. "It happened at Halloween," she said. "Two years ago. We were at a party thrown by one of the partners in the firm. It was . . . we were walking back to the car. I had had more to drink than him and"—she shook her head again—"It had been a tough week for me, and normally I'm the one who drives, but that night, I'd had a few more. I hadn't been drinking for a few months, and there was no reason not to anymore, and so I had a few. Daniel was going to drive and . . ." She trailed off, her gaze on her fingers, which had gotten all tangled up in her lap. "There were some kids who were pranking the neighborhood. Egging cars. They were wearing marks, trying to pretend it was all in the spirit of Halloween. Daniel said something—I don't remember what he said, but he was like that: he would always say something—and they started throwing eggs at us. I got hit. Had egg in my hair and all over my coat. Daniel lost it. He charged them, and most of them took off running. But one kid stood his ground.

"There were patches of ice on the sidewalk. It was one of those nights that we get infrequently here, when it actually gets cold enough to freeze. There isn't much ice, and it's usually clear and slick. Daniel was running at this kid, who was throwing eggs as fast as he could at Daniel, as if that would stop him. Daniel was waving his arms and shouting, and I was crying at him to stop—just leave the kid alone—and then he slipped. One minute he was up, and the next, he was lying on the ground."

She paused, and her eyes were bright. "He hit his head on the edge of a brick wall. It wasn't much of a wall. Lawn ornamentation. But it had an edge to it, and he came down on it wrong, and it just . . . "

I reached out and took her hand, squeezing her fingers. She didn't look finished, and I didn't dare interrupt her.

"You know the story about Santa Claus, don't you?" she said after a long moment. "That urban legend about Santa Claus going to heaven and bringing back the spirit of a little girl's dead father?"

I swallowed heavily and nodded. I wasn't sure my voice would have worked even if I had tried to say anything.

"It was all over the Internet, of course. Even though the Portland newspaper made a big deal about retracting the story it had written. It only made it worse. The Internet had it, and every time someone passed it along to me, it was wilder and stranger. It was a stupid story, really, and I didn't want to believe it, but shortly after the next Halloween, the doctors told me they didn't know if Daniel was going to wake up. Ever. And I had spent the whole year hoping that he would, praying every night that I'd find him awake when I went to visit him the next day. I couldn't deal with it anymore. I needed something. I needed some way to keep my hope alive.

"I wrote Santa a letter. Just like I did when I was a kid. I wrote it out longhand, put a stamp on it, and dropped it off at the post office myself. Do you know what I asked Santa for? I asked him to bring Daniel some peace. The brick wall had fractured Daniel's skull, and some pieces had been driven into his brain. Even if he woke up, the doctors told me, it was very likely that he'd be . . . he wouldn't recognize me. He might not recognize anything. And so I asked Santa to let Daniel die."

She wiped at her face with one hand, her other hand locked around mine. "You know what?" she said. "I didn't get what I wanted that Christmas." She squeezed my fingers really tightly.

"I'm sorry," I said.

She looked at me, her eyes shining with tears. "Why?" she asked. "It's not your fault."

Well, that was probably true. Last year I hadn't been in charge. Who knows what the NPC had done about Christmas wishes like Barb's. But still . . . I was Mrs. C's special envoy, after all.

She let go of my hand finally. "You wanted to know why I took this job," she said. "Why I'm still here even though this musical is . . . is what it is. I took this job because I needed something to distract me from the daily emptiness that is Daniel's condition. I took the job because the script was everything that I was feeling at the time. All the rage and hate that is coming out of Rudolph on that stage? I know where that comes from. Those are my feelings. Not his. It was all so senselessness, this life I had been given, like a cruel fucking joke. And I was angry about living a life that was void of any hope for happiness.

"You know what the funny thing is? That's my best work up there on the stage. Out of all that bile and frustration and anger, I created something amazing. I created something that has never been seen before. I made something new. And that is why I'm still here, why I'm still working on this show. Because it is about making something new. As bleak as it is, there's still hope in it."

December 7th

Since I had nothing else to do while tied to the chair in the basement, I was making my list, and checking it . . . a couple hundred times.

1) Erma. Definitely. I had seen her face.
2) Henrik. It had taken me awhile to figure out he was the meek-voiced one, mainly because it was so unlike the persona he adopted during rehearsals. But there were clues, and I put them together eventually.
3) Ted. At the very least, he had to know what was going on. He was only one I had told about the amount of money in the Swiss account. If my kidnappers knew, it was because Ted had told them.

Which left the one with the hand-rolled cigarettes and the dinner theater experience. *Slapper.* I had an idea who that was. There were only so many bitter thespians in the troupe. What I didn't know and what cramped my brain during the nearly sleepless nights I had spent in the basement so far was whether or not Barb was involved. What she had said in the bathroom on Thanksgiving kept coming back to me. Was she a better actor than any of them? Was it a carefully constructed lie for my benefit? Did she really believe that there was something extraordinary that could come out of this production?

I believed her; rather, I believed her words, because I needed something to hang on to myself. I was having trouble remembering all the lyrics to "Jingle Bells," and I was starting to worry that I was losing the Spirit.

Rudolph and I both had it. We had brought the Spirit of Christmas back from hell, and in the two years since, it had always been there in my belly. That warm-extra-brandy-in-your-eggnog sort of feeling.

But it can fade. I tell you now: it can fade. Santa was losing it. Satan had yanked hard and pulled all of it out of Fat Boy once, and he had nearly done the same with Mrs. C. We had brought it back, but the connection wasn't as concrete as it had been in the past. You can repair the damage, but you can never truly weld the desire back the way it was. And if the world is hard enough on you, if there is nothing but despair and bleakness all day long, the Spirit does lose some of its luster.

I didn't have much strength left. How long had I been down here? Four days? Five? Thanksgiving had been late this year, and I had stayed in my hotel during the mad shopping frenzy that had followed. How many rehearsals had I seen? Three? Four?

I had been working late in the office, trying to figure out what the deal was with the seats. I had cracked the spreadsheets, and had started to see some holes in the expenses. Money was going out faster than debts were accruing. I was starting to wonder about Ted's ability to do math.

They had been waiting for me that night. I remember leaving the office and standing by the elevator. The bell rang, and the doors opened, and then there had been a rush of sound behind me. Heavy footsteps coming at a run. I had turned just as something heavy slammed into my back. I bounced off the elevator door and fell on my back, staring up at the polished light of the elevator car. And then everything had gone dark.

Someone had hit me with the ornate garbage can next to the elevator, and after I passed out, they dragged me like a fifty-pound sack of dog food down to the basement, where I was incarcerated. Tied up, blindfolded, and left to go five rounds with the pounding headache waiting for me when I woke up. Eventually, they showed up and started asking questions about the money.

It was a long con. Erma had said as much. The production was never meant to succeed. They set up the company, found a script that had enough promise to be seen as avant-garde and daring to a couple of investors, and set up shop. The show might open, but the reviews would be so awful that no one would come. Tickets would go unsold, and the principals would vanish with the money they had siphoned off the accounts. And I had finally realized what the disconnect was in the spreadsheets. It wasn't that Ted couldn't do math; he was screwing up the buckets. The one that all the bills went into was marked Net 60, and there was another one marked "Paid" and it contained everything that was in the Net 60 bucket. Everything was being marked as paid—in cash, no less—but that wasn't actually true. All those accounts were going to be due in mid-December, just about the time the show shut down. All the investment money that should have gone to these debts would be missing, and the collectors would be calling, looking for their payments. Without decent ticket sales, there wasn't going to be any money to pay them off with.

They were playing a tricky game, but they had placed themselves well enough to play it out. When I showed up, the pot suddenly got a lot bigger, but the trick was getting me to cough up the money. And when that hadn't happened outright, they had decided to sweat the account info out of me instead.

And they might actually get it. It had been five days since I had eaten anything. I was past woozy. I was starting to have trouble with my vision. I had given up on worrying about dehydration. It took too much strength. What was I doing down here? Who got hurt if I gave them the money?

Who got hurt if I *didn't* give them the money?

Slapper was Franklin Donovan King. He was the show's leading man as well as the director of record. Over the past few days, I had gone back over everything that had happened since I had arrived at the Heritage about six hundred million times, and every time some other little detail poked out. I hadn't actually ever met Franklin, which was somewhat odd, given our respective roles in the company. Erma had always deflected my questions about the whereabouts of the man playing Rudolph; she had even told me some wild story about a family tragedy back in Illinois that had required Mr. King's sudden presence over Thanksgiving. Rehearsals were still going on with Bucky Dowminster—the ersatz understudy—standing in for King. Everything seemed to be moving along, progressing as it should. No one had seemed terribly concerned about the lack of the leading man/director, and I—who had never seen a live musical, much less produced one— had figured my confusion in this regard was merely my theater production inexperience.

Franklin came to visit again, and when he saw that I wasn't wearing the blindfold, he hovered on the periphery of my vision—hiding in the shadows, smoking his noxious cigarettes. Occasionally, I'd get a glimmer of light bouncing off his shaved head. He smoked two cigarettes in rapid succession, as if his tactic this time around was to poison all the air in the small room until I talked.

I figured there wasn't much reason to wait that long.

"You don't have much faith in Bucky, do you?" I whispered.

He exhaled a long stream of smoke. "Why do you say that?" he asked in return. "He's getting a lot of practice."

"But not much direction. I may not know much about theater, but I know what happens when you let someone think they know what they are doing. He's got the lines down, but that doesn't mean much, does it? Not that you care, I suppose."

"Not really," he said. "Reviewers will see it during the preview shows. By the time it actually opens, it'll be all over." He flicked his cigarette at me, and it bounced off my lap, scattering a spray of sparks. I was so tired I didn't even bother flinching. "Bucky's only experience is regional theater. He's never done Shakespeare. He's never sung anything more demanding than a chorus role in *The Music Man*. But he has the right combination of arrogance and stupidity that will allow him to think he *can* pull this off."

"Whereas your combination of arrogance and stupidity means you can actually do it?"

"I've done Shakespeare. I've done Hamlet. And not in some backwater Canadian production like Keanu Reeves. I played MacBeth in Los Angeles, Caesar in Boston, Shylock in Virginia."

"They why the con? Why bother when you've obviously got some talent."

Franklin grimaced slightly. "There's no money in talent."

"Back to that Keanu thing again?"

Speaking of arrogance and stupidity, here I was smart-talking the one guy who might have it in him to actually hurt me. I suppose some part of me thought riling him up was a clever plan.

Franklin shrugged as he dug into a coat pocket for his tobacco pouch. He was playing it cool, but I could tell that I was getting on his nerves.

All I needed to do was figure out how to capitalize on this before I crossed the line and he started torturing me again.

"Who wrote the musical?" I asked, buying some time while I tried to rub enough brain cells together to start a mental fire. "The only thing I saw was a copyright notice by someone named Dread Caspian, which isn't a very good pseudonym. Did you write it?"

Franklin shook his head as he grabbed a large pinch of tobacco and dropped it in the center of a cigarette paper. "Dunno. Who cares really?"

"It just landed in your lap?" I asked.

"Not my department," he said. He rolled the cigarette back and forth between his fingers. "I'm just the talent."

I wondered if that meant there was someone else involved. A producer-type like me. Someone who had gotten them started. "I was just curious," I said.

"I guess it gives you something to do while you're down here," he said. He raised the cigarette to his mouth and ran his tongue along the paper, and then rolled it a final time between his fingers. "Are you bored yet?" he asked. "Of being *curious*?"

I licked my lips carefully. "I suppose I should be thinking about something else, shouldn't I?"

He nodded as he flicked open his lighter and lit his cigarette. I flinched slightly when I heard the crackling sound of the tobacco lighting up, remembering the hot touch against my earlobe. He puffed once or twice, watching me through a haze of smoke, and after he snapped his lighter shut and put it away, he blew a lazy smoke ring. "'How long a time lies in one little word!'" he said, evidently quoting one of Shakespeare's historical plays. My brain couldn't keep them straight at this point. "'Four lagging winters and four wanton springs end in a word; such is the breath of kings.'"

It was only money, I thought. It wasn't like I couldn't get more. If not from Mrs. C, then from somewhere—there were other ways. Not entirely legal ways, but I could raise the capital myself if I needed to. I could even pay Mrs. C back, if it came down to it. In which case, was the money worth dying over?

Was that my price? One million dollars.

There was a bustle of voices from the next room then, a rattling cacophony as if a Greek Chorus had been infected mid-prologue with Tourette's Syndrome. Someone bumped into the storeroom door, fumbling with the doorknob.

Franklin hurried toward the door, the expression on his face tight and grim. This wasn't part of the plan, I realized. He reached the door as it opened, and Henrik rushed in.

"We've got a problem," Henrik said. "A really serious problem."

Franklin pushed Henrik back toward the door. "Not here," he growled. "Not where he can hear us."

Henrik backed up against the door, which clicked shut behind him. "No," he said, fumbling for the lock behind his back. "This may be our only chance."

"What are you talking about?" Franklin snapped.

The door secured, Henrik fumbled with something in his pocket. He raised his hand, some of his elegant grace coming back, and proudly displayed what he had brought with him. As if he were an advertising model, showing off the latest fashion.

Except what he had in his hand was an old German Luger.

"We stay here. He's our hostage."

Franklin glared at the gun in Henrik's hand. "Is it the cops?" he asked, his voice low.

"Worse," Henrik said. He pushed past Franklin and glided over to me, the gun pointing right at my face. "It's friends of his."

"What are you talking about?" Franklin demanded. "He doesn't have any friends."

"He does," Henrik said. "I've seen them. They're looking for him."

"This isn't the time, Henrik. This isn't the time to lose your cool." Franklin gestured at me. "He was about to tell me the code. We were almost there. Are you out of your fucking mind?"

"We should have left, Franklin. We should have been satisfied. And now? It's all falling apart."

"Nothing's falling apart, Henrik. Nothing's going to happen." Franklin's voice was calm and soothing, like he was trying to coax a wild dog to let go of his sneaker.

It didn't work on Henrik. "There are reindeer out there!" he shouted. He started waving the gun around, causing Franklin to duck. I wanted to duck, but all the ropes were still holding me to the chair. "They're looking for Rosewood, and they're very angry."

"Reindeer don't do anger," Franklin said. "Listen to yourself. You're talking stupid animals with antlers. They're just horses. They're—"

"They're not horses," I croaked, interrupting him. "They're a species of deer."

They both stared at me.

"Horses are domesticated," I explained. "Reindeer aren't. That's the first difference. The second—"

"I don't give a shit whether they're domesticated or not," Franklin snapped. "They've got four legs and they—they don't talk. They don't do anger. They don't come looking for people. They're just fucking animals."

"These ones do," Henrik said.

"Do what?" Franklin said. His face was getting flushed, and the color was rising all the way to the top of his shaved head.

"Talk," Henrik said. "I heard them."

"There are no reindeer," Franklin said, his voice becoming calm again. "You're just imagining it. We're really close here. I just need a few more minutes with Rosewood. Okay? Can you hold it together for a few more minutes?" He held out his hand. "Give me the gun. We'll go outside and talk. This'll all be over soon."

There was a glint in his eye that I didn't like. Franklin had done dinner theater. There wasn't going to be any talking.

Henrik wasn't fooled either. "Stay away from me," he said, pointing the gun at Franklin. The tip of the barrel wiggled slightly, but otherwise the pistol was steady.

Something banged against the closed door, rattling it in its frame, and Henrik flinched. The gun went off, noisy in the small room, and Franklin was shoved up against the wall. He clutched at his left shoulder, blood running over his fingers.

"Oh," Henrik said. "Oh, dear. Oh, dear." He lowered the gun and appeared to be on the verge of tears. "Oh, Franklin. I'm sorry. This isn't—I didn't mean to—"

Howling, Franklin launched himself from the wall, his bloody hand reaching for Henrik and the gun. Henrik started to raise the gun again, but Franklin slammed into him, and they went to the floor. Something hit the door again, but neither man paid it any attention. They kicked and clawed at one another, rolling back and forth on the ground. Even though I had the best seat in the house, I couldn't tell who was winning.

The two men bumped into me, and I tried kicking, but the ropes around my legs didn't provide much range of movement. Henrik reared up, his hand still on the gun, and Franklin followed, clawing at the choreographer's arm. They slammed into me, and I squeaked as they knocked my chair over. My shoulder hurt as I hit the floor, but I managed to keep my head from smacking the concrete.

The gun went off again, and I froze. They were behind me now, and I held my breath for a second, waiting to feel something. Waiting to find out if the bullet had hit me.

The door cracked, a large splinter of wood breaking off and falling to the floor.

I heard someone moving behind me, and I tried to scoot myself toward the half-broken door. Someone grabbed the back of the chair, halting my incremental progress. I looked over my shoulder, and saw the face of the musical's leading man. There was blood on his face and neck. "The code," he coughed. "Give me the access code."

With a lot of effort, he hauled himself around the chair and slumped against me, his head nearly in my lap. I couldn't squirm away; his weight was holding me in place. He had the pistol, and the tip of the barrel dragged across the floor as he struggled to lift the gun. I could only watch as his arm quivered with the effort.

"Thou . . ." His teeth were clenched, and his head was shining with sweat. "Thou are slain," he said. The pistol barrel lifted slowly. "No medicine in the world can do thee good—"

The door shattered, and a tall, antlered figure bounded into the room. The reindeer was lanky and had a splotch of white fur on his flank that looked like the imprint of a hand.

Franklin raised his head, gasped half a word, and then collapsed. The pistol slipped from his hand and clattered against the floor.

The reindeer skipped to a stop and bent his head to look sideways at me. "Wow," he said, examining the room. "What happened here?"

"Too much Shakespeare," I said, and only then did I pass out.

December 9th

I WOKE IN A HOSPITAL BED. MY EYES FELT LIKE THEY HAD BEEN STAPLED SHUT, ripped open, and then stapled shut again. My mouth was moist for a change, and there was a distinct tang of iron riding on the back of my tongue. I lifted my head carefully and wiggled my toes. The heavy sheet moved slightly at the other end of the bed.

I was in a private room. There was a half-open door on my left that led to a closet-sized bathroom, another door just behind, and on my right there was a small desk tucked under a large set of curtains. On the desk were several vases filled with colorful flowers. I couldn't tell if there were any cards.

There was an IV in my arm, and a cuff on my finger was keeping track of all the important stuff going on inside: oxygen content, blood flow, heart rate. I squinted up at the plastic bag hanging at the head of the bed. They were dripping me full of saline and nutrients.

I was alive then, which is more than could be said of some.

That had been Ring at the end, just before I passed out. I hadn't recognized him at first. He looked like a real reindeer now, but he still had the scar from Satan's burn. The fur had grown back, but it was white.

Little Ring. All grown up.

That made me sad for some reason, and when the door opened a few minutes later and a nurse came in, I hastily swiped at my cheeks.

"Good morning," she said cheerfully. "How are we doing today?" She bustled about the bed, checking the drip, fluffing the pillow behind my head, retucking the blanket in at the foot of the bed. She was a little whirlwind of efficiency. "Are you hungry?" she asked. "Do you need to make a bowel movement?"

The proximity of those two questions confounded me for a minute, and she hurried on with her litany of questions. "Do you have dry mouth? How's your bladder feeling? Would you like oatmeal or fruit? Or both? Are you feeling nauseated?"

I thought about just saying *yes* once and letting her figure out which question I was answering.

"How about some sunlight?" she continued. "Shall we see how beautiful a day it is going to be?" She bustled over to the curtains and yanked on the string. The curtains opened in a rush, flooding the room with sunlight, and the nurse shrieked.

At first, I thought that she—like me—had had her eyeballs scorched out by the sudden light, but when I could see again, I realized she was reacting to the pair of reindeer parked on the narrow ledge outside the window. Their fur was matted and wet, and they did not look amused. The one wearing the black librarian glasses tapped on the widow with a hoof.

"Open the window," he said, his voice muted by the glass.

The nurse was half on the bed. Half on my leg too. "Wh—wh—what are they?" she stuttered.

"Reindeer," I said. I extricated my leg and sat up. I was a little light-headed, and the sunlight was giving me a headache, but everything else seemed to be working correctly. The IV tried to tangle itself around me as I got out of bed, but I managed to escape its coil. My knees were a little wobbly, and I was slightly out of breath by the time I figured out how the window latch worked.

It was so nice to breath cold winter air.

"Morning," Ring said, nodding at the still-stunned nurse. "Sorry to surprise you." He tilted his head and tapped an antler tip against the wire screen separating him from me. "Does this come out?" he asked.

I glanced at the corners, trying to figure out how the screen was attached. "Not exact—"

He twitched his head, spearing a couple of antler tips through the wire and yanked the whole screen off. "Come on," he said. "We've been waiting all night."

"Wait, what? Waiting? Why?"

Blitzen shuffled around on the ledge. One of his hooves slipped free as he tried to turn around on the narrow beam. "We're cramped and tired, Bernie. Can you ask questions later? We've got work to do still."

"The show?" I asked.

"Later," Ring said. "We've got more important things to do first."

I stared at the IV in the back of my hand, and with a minimum of fuss, I yanked the needle out. The nurse made a noise like a fish surfacing for water bugs when I slipped off the finger cuff, and the monitor over the bed started making funny noises.

"What things?" I asked.

"California," Ring said.

"What's in California?" I asked.

Blitzen clued me in. "Rudolph. They're going to scramble him."

They were the Psychiatric Board of the Beverly Hills Sanitarium. Actually, the tasteful sign out front said *The Beverly Hills Bed and Breakfast*, and it was a lovely estate up on Coldwater Canyon with a rambling house tucked away behind a high wall and several thick rows of aspen and poplar trees. On the inside, though, word was it was all padded rooms, rubber sheets, and straitjackets.

"Why is he here?" I asked, munching on a drumstick.

We were sequestered on the roof of a house up the road that offered a fairly unobstructed view of the lush lawn at the back of the BHBB house. The reindeer had gotten take-out from Roscoe's Chicken and Waffles, which was much better than oatmeal or fruit in a cup, thank you very much.

"They've got one of the best anger management programs in the world," Blitzen explained. "And they do pet treatments."

"Pets," I said. "Like pets of the stars?"

He nodded. Beyond him, Ring gobbled down a whole waffle in two bites. The way the kid was eating, he was going to be bigger than Donner.

"Cats are always angry," Blitzen said.

"So what do they do?" I asked, curious in spite of myself. "To the pets."

"Behavioral modification," Blizten said. "Chemical therapies. In some cases, aversion training."

"Aversion training? Is that what I think it is?"

"Shock therapy?" Blitzen nodded. "Yep."

I saw movement in the yard at the BHBB and raised the binoculars that Blitzen had brought along. I zoomed in, and my heart skipped in my chest as I focused on the four-legged shape of a wobbly reindeer. "He's there," I said. I watched him shy away from the shadow of a palm tree. "He's doped up. Really badly." There was dried drool flecking Rudolph's chin.

Blitzen had laid the story out for me on the flight down. Rudolph had returned to the Pole with Santa and had submitted to the NPC's decree of anger management sessions. At first, it had only been outpatient appointments at Cedar Sinai, and Rudolph was supposed to check in four times a week. He lasted three sessions before he wrecked the office and tossed his therapist out the window, which unfortunately only proved the point everyone was worried about.

Someone in the NPC suggested a rather permanent solution to the problem, which had not gone over very well with Santa and Mrs. C, and the NPC backed down quickly, realizing they had overstepped themselves. A compromise was reached before Rudolph found out about the closed-door meeting, and he checked in at the BHBB. A week passed, and the only reports coming out of the BHBB were that Rudolph was responding well to the treatments.

Mrs. C didn't buy it. It was all too pat. Something was off, and she only got more concerned when she tried to contact me, and I didn't answer. She called up some of the team—Ring and Blitzen flew to Seattle, and Donner and Cupid headed for LA. I was already in the basement by then, and Donner and Cupid found Rudolph so doped up he didn't recognize his flight buddies.

The quartet was under strict orders to do what needed to be done. If they reported back to Mrs. C, it was likely the NPC would find out and everything would grind to a complete halt. There would be calls for meetings and committee studies. Santa would probably threaten to quit. He might even do it publicly, which would be an epic PR disaster, which meant the NPC would gag him as soon as possible if they got any wind that he was thinking of stomping off. No, it was easier if the reindeer solved the problem all on their own.

But they knew they needed help, and so finding me had been the priority. And while they had been tracking me down, Cupid found out that the Board at the BHBB had decided to scramble Rudolph's brain the old fashioned way.

The procedure was scheduled for tomorrow morning, which was why we were doing recon and carbing up. It was going to be a busy night.

We came in through the veranda. Some of the more tractable patients were having dinner at wicker tables, sitting out beneath heat lamps and canvas umbrellas. We dropped from the dark sky like meteors, landing on the grass, and tromping through the beds of daisies that ringed the patio. A white-jacketed employee tried to stop us, but Donner scooped him aside with a simple flip of his rack. Blitzen bit down on the tie of the first doctor we found and dragged him along as we went room to room until we found Rudolph.

Blitzen spat out the mouthful of silk tie, and the doctor sagged to his knees, struggling to breathe. "Get the door open," I said to the others, while I stared daggers at the cringing doctor.

It took Cupid and Donner less than ten seconds to break down the door. Rudolph was on the far side of the room, staring up at the night sky through the tiny window set high above the floor. "Hello," he said, his voice a drugged slur. "Is it time for my bath yet?"

"What's he on?" Blitzen snapped at the doctor.

The man loosened his tie. "I . . . I don't know. He's not my patient."

"Wrong answer." Blitzen stamped his hoof. "Try again."

Ring was reading the clipboard attached to the wall. "What's REBT?" he asked.

I glared at the doctor, who pretended not to know.

"Rational emotive behavior therapy," Blitzen supplied.

"Can I see that chart?" I asked Ring, who grabbed the board with his teeth and brought it over

Rudolph was busy sniffing Donner's flank. The bulky reindeer was a little uncomfortable with the attention, but he held his ground as Rudolph explored with his flat nose. Cupid was back in the hall, moving towards a point position.

I checked Rudolph's chart, trying to decipher the cryptic handwriting. "Let's see . . . Lodopin. Zyprexa. Serdolect. Haldol. Thorazine. Wow, that's a lot of anti-psychotics."

"That's a lot of reindeer," the doctor pointed out. Ring clipped him on the shin.

I kept reading. "Prozac and Darvoset in the morning, and a mega dose of Wellbutrin in the afternoon. To keep him *docile*." I added the emphasis.

"He's definitely docile," Donner noted as Rudolph started licking his ear.

"Can he fly?" I asked.

"Definitely not—hey!" Blitzen broke off as the doctor made a run for it. Ring darted after him, but the man made it to the end of the hall and slammed the door shut behind him.

"Let him go," I said. "We got what we came for."

"Sort of," Blizten said. "We're going to have to wait for all of those chemicals to wear off. It could take hours. Maybe a day or two."

"We haven't got a day or two," I pointed out. "Can't we shoot him full of amphetamines or something?"

"You're welcome to try," Blitzen said. "But I don't want to be anywhere near him when you do."

"Why?"

He nodded toward Rudolph who was drooping on Donner like a soft watch. "How much are you going to give him? Too little, and you'll want to try again. Too much, and it'll probably make his brain explode."

"Good point," I said, thinking about the last time I had drugged Rudolph. I had been hoping to keep him knocked out well past midnight, but he had woken up nearly early enough to spoil things.

"What if we burn it out of him?" Cupid asked.

"What do you mean?"

"Things catch on fire when he glows, right? That means he's hot on the inside too. All we have to do is make him, you know . . ." Cupid trailed off.

"Angry?" I supplied.

Blizten stared at him. Hard. Cupid shrugged his shoulders in response. "You got a better idea?"

Blitzen swiveled his head to look at me.

"I suppose he's right," I said. "It can't hurt to try. What's the worst that could happen?"

Blitzen didn't even bother to answer that question.

"What about that thing in Seattle?" Ring asked. "You know. The one you're working on. With the singing and dancing."

"The musical?" I shook my head. "No way. He can't know about that. That's out of the question."

Yellow lights set along the ceiling started blinking, and we heard a distant sound like a giant gong being struck. "Non-confrontational security," Blitzen said. "We're out of time."

"Even if I wanted to share the script of the musical," I said. "I don't have it—"

"It's in the backpack," Ring said, nodding toward the bag that the reindeer had brought along. "We found it in your hotel room. In the bathroom."

"Things are going to get less pleasant here in a few minutes when the security service BHBB uses gets here," Blizten said. "We need Rudolph back, and fast."

I pulled open the bag and found the water-stained stack of pages that was my copy of the script. The one I had nearly dropped in the tub that night when I had first read it.

I slid off Blitzen's back. "This'll do it," I said.

Rudolph spotted me and ambled over, leading with his tongue. "Okay, okay," I said, pushing the wet reindeer tongue away. "I'm happy to see you too."

"It's a talking waffle," Rudolph said, and he crowded up against me, working his tongue across my head.

"Hey," I said, catching his tongue in my hand this time and holding it tightly. "Knock it off."

He pulled gently, his eyes crossing as he tried to figure out why his tongue wasn't going back in his mouth. He said something, but with the drugs in his system and my hand on his tongue, no one understood what he was trying to say.

One-handed, I flipped the script open to a random page and started reading.

ACT III SCENE I: A MOUNTAINTOP

Rudolph stands alone by a pile of rock. Lightning flashes in the background. (SFX: Thunder. Distant. +10 to SUB.)

RUDOLPH: I am to take up offense against heaven and Earth with my actions so vile and wretched. Can I stay from this course? Can I foreswear from the ruin which is sure to follow so swift and sure upon my heels? Is it better to die, trapped in the venom of one's own miasma, or to live, hounded and hunted by every last thinking creature for the reprehensible deed which I must call my own? Must I summon the dark cloud? Must I turn against those who brought me hence and destroy them for their narrow thoughts and helpless mistakes? Ah, to dream, to slumber and partake of a realm so changed from this. That brief, sweet touch does strip away the thousand-fold pricks of this hell, which drains the life and blood from my veins.

I had to turn the page, which was a little complicated with one hand.

"That sounds familiar," Blitzen said.

"Please tell me you haven't read this on the Internet already," I said. "I'm really hoping the only copies are the ones that the company has."

Blitzen shook his head. "No, it sounds like something else. Shakespeare?"

"It's all Shakespeare," I said. "That's all they talk about."

Cupid made a noise in the hall, and Ring stuck his head out of the room. "Is this going to take long?" he asked after he checked on Cupid. He did a little *I have to go to the bathroom* dance, which I took to mean something else.

"I'm working on it," I said, finding another page to read.

ACT I SCENE III: THE THRONE ROOM

Rudolph is attended by Toad, his familiar. Present are the wretched fiends which populate this dark place. They caper and scamper about the tall statues.

RUDOLPH: I tire, dear Toad, of this life. I tire of this oubliette of stone and filth which is but the extent of my realm.

TOAD: To rule here, Master, or to serve there?

RUDOLPH: I do not wish to rule. I do not want to be king. I have no need of crown or scepter or subjects. I but wish for the sky beneath my feet. I wish to travel across the plane of heaven and touch the stars. I cannot be bound by this foul gravity which holds us all in its bosom. I crave the vastness emptiness of space, Toad. I crave the world beyond. I crave passage between the worlds, to stand at the pinnacle and look back—all the way back—to that first tiny moment when alpha touched omega and the circle was but a singular infinite point.

TOAD *(clapping)*: To be one and many. Yes, Master, to be one and many.

"Toad?" asked Donner.

"He's a mutant elf. Six foot four. All hairy," I explained. "Rudolph's kingdom is populated by rejects."

"The Kingdom of Misfit Toys," Blitzen pointed out.

"Oh, that." Donner rolled his eyes.

Rudolph had stopped tugging on his tongue, and when I let go of it, he rolled it back into his mouth. He didn't move away from me, and his gaze had gone from sugarplum dreamy to sugar coma lethargy. "You in there?" I asked, peering at his dull eyes. "Do you remember me?"

His tongue started to slide out of his mouth.

"Something a little more exciting there, Bernie," Blitzen said. "Stop trying to ease him into it."

I flipped forward a few pages and found one of Rudolph's many speeches.

RUDOLPH: But the snow and sky are the realms of my nemesis. He cleaves through the air and water with his sled and his entourage, his rage of angels which accompany his every mission. I cannot face them. I have not the strength nor the power to counteract his magic. I cannot break his foul grip on the world above.

TOAD: Break his magic! Break his magic, Master.

"This Toad fellow is kind of a suck-up for a sidekick," Donner opined.
"Is he talking about Santa?" Ring wanted to know.
I shushed them with my hand and kept reading.

RUDOLPH: Yes, Toad. Yes, that course is laid before me with such clarity. Break his sorcery. Shatter his rooftop laughter and his brazen jocularity. I shall smash his seasonal cheer and tear down his traditions. I will destroy his name. (Laughs) Now, this shall be the winter of their disenchantment. Made glorious by an apocalyptic fire of my design. Now, when their houses are but loosely kept and their crowns slack about their brows; now shall I steal their dreams and darken their fair fields with cloud fearsome and calamitous. I, that am rudely marked with this ruddy proboscis, I shall strip away their laughter and their light with my scheme insidious. Since I cannot prove to be one of their number, since even their dogs do bark at the shadows passed by my illumination, I will prove to be the villain. I hate the indolence of their days and despise the cheerful timelessness of their passion. A plot I will lay, a scheme divine and dark to blast their kingdom of winter virtue into a fallow field of corpses. A smoke I will bring, a fog so deep as to cover the sky and hold them to the ground. I will clout them with vapor and, through their very pores, I will ooze and steam until I have rotted their organs from the inside, until I have choked them with their own breath. I will destroy Christmas afore it has a chance to destroy me.

"What happens next?" Ring's curiosity was almost palpable.

"Oh, seriously?" I asked. "You're not getting wrapped up in this, are you?"

"It's not that bad," Donner said.

"Of course not," Blitzen snorted. "Even as poorly written as it is, it's still Shakespeare."

"I was kidding about that earlier," I said.

"I know you were, but that's what it is," Blizten said. "It's Shakespeare."

"Which one?" Donner wanted to know.

"Who's Shakespeare?" Ring interjected.

Cupid wiggled in next to Ring. "What's taking so long?" he asked.

"Shakespeare!" Ring said, as if he knew what we were talking about.

"Where?" Cupid looked around the room.

"No, no," Ring said. "Bernie's reading it."

"Oooh," Cupid said. "Which one?"

"That's what I was asking," Donner said, a bit peevishly.

I tuned them out. Reindeer had a tendency to get distracted when they weren't in action. It came from many, many hours of standing around on rooftops, waiting for Santa. The Time Clock put weird pressures on them, and their coping mechanism was to keep up this stream of inane chatter. No one could sustain the sort of directed focus that the Clock wanted out of you.

Well, Rudolph could. After the accident.

He was staring at me now, his skin ruddy and glistening. His pupils had shrunk to tiny dots. His tongue was darting in and out now, licking his moist nose.

"Hey, buddy," I said. "Are you there? Come on back to us, will you? We miss you." He continued to stare at me, and instead of staring back, I turned my attention back to the script, intending to read some more. "'I will destroy—'" I started.

"I heard you the first time," Rudolph said, in a voice that sounded like someone was strangling a cat in the next room. His face scrunched up as if he was trying to undo a knot someone had tied in his brain, and the glow coming off his skin brightened.

"Uh oh," Donner said, trotting toward the far corner of the room. I stepped back too just as Rudolph sneezed heavily, his whole body convulsing. When he sneezed a second time, he punctuated it with a savage kick with his back legs. His strange radiance increased, and I scrambled out of the way as he put his head down and charged.

Blitzen yelped, leaping aside, and both Ring and Cupid disappeared from the doorway. Rudolph clipped the doorframe as he charged, taking out a big chunk as he plowed into the hallway. The frame was scorched black where his antlers had torn through the wood, and as I stared at the doorway, a tiny finger of flame poked up from a splinter of wood.

"Radiated reindeer coming through," Donner called out from behind me. In case one of the others hadn't figured it out yet.

Blitzen waited for me near the door, and we both peeked out nervously. Rudolph was battering himself against the walls of the hall, and he bucked and sneezed. Each impact left a scorched hole in the wall, and by the time he reached the far doors, his skin was shining brightly.

"Are you wearing protection?" Blizten asked, his gaze dropped down toward my groin.

"What? A condom?" I asked.

"No," he snorted. "Lead-lined undergarments."

"I wasn't given a pair at the hospital," I snapped. "So: no. I'm not."

Blitzen made a face and looked away.

"Hang on," I said. "I wasn't wearing any that year we went to hell either. Are you telling me—?"

"I'm not telling you anything," Blitzen said. "Those thermal suits are pretty good, I think. So you're probably okay."

"You think?" I sputtered. "Probably?"

"Don't get worked up," he said. "It's probably nothing to worry about. Really."

Rudolph had turned back, though he was still wobbling from side to side and shaking his head like he was warding off invisible wasps. Behind him, the door opened and a pair of uniformed men charged through. They were wearing transparent riot helmets and were carrying police batons. A couple more guys were right behind them.

The whole squad came to a sudden halt when they saw the glowing reindeer. Rudolph faced them, steam curling up from his body, tiny streamers of fire flickering at the tips of his antlers. Everyone stared at one another for a long moment—the men fidgeting with their batons, Rudolph tapping the floor with one hoof— and then Rudolph sneezed one last time. It was a big one, and the burst of light and heat that came off him was like a firebomb detonating in the hallway.

I blinked several times, trying to see past the starburst after-image burned onto my retinas. We had kept our distance, but I still felt like I had been standing too close to a bonfire. Eventually, my vision returned to normal, and I could see well enough to notice the damage done to the far end of the hall. The walls and floors were black, and the security squad was down, though they were all still alive judging from their groans and tortured movements.

It was—I have to admit—not unlike "The Dance of the Wretches" from the musical, though with less jazz hands.

Rudolph stood in the center of the hall, looking none the worse for wear. His eyes were clear, and his skin no longer glowed. "Bernie," he said in a much more normal voice, though not without a touch of annoyance. "What were you reading?"

I let out a sob of relief. "It's you," I gasped. "You're okay."

"Of course, I'm okay," he said. "It's not like I haven't been drugged before."

"Hey," I said. "That was for your own good."

"That's what they said here too." His tone darkened as he repeated his question. "Bernie. What were you reading?"

"It's this thing," I said. "Up in Seattle. Some play that a local company is putting on. It's nothing, really. In fact, it's probably not going to happen."

"Why isn't it going to happen?" he asked.

I looked at Blitzen, who shook his head and started studying the floor.

"It's a really bad Christmas story," I said.

"There are no bad Christmas stories," Rudolph said, correcting me.

"Well, let's leave that open for discussion, shall we?"

Rudolph came closer. "There are no bad stories," he said. "There are only stories that need our help. Right?"

"Sure," I said, somewhat weakly. I knew where this was going already. But I tried anyway. "It's a lie, Rudolph. It's just meant to hurt people. It's not even in the proper spirit."

"It's still a Christmas story," Rudolph said. "And we don't cancel Christmas, do we? Or its stories." He looked around at the other reindeer. "Do we?" he asked when no one said anything.

"No, sir!" Ring shouted. Cupid stifled a laugh at the younger reindeer's reply, and then immediately hung his head when Rudolph glared at him.

"Bernie. You said this was a play. When does it open?" Rudolph asked.

"It's not going to open," I said, and Cupid looked up at me with big *WTF?* eyes.

"Er, what day is it?" I asked Blitzen, hastily changing my song.

"Tuesday," Blitzen said. "The ninth."

I laughed. I couldn't help it. "Friday," I said when I could breathe again. "It was supposed to open on Friday."

"Seventy-two hours," Rudolph said, ignoring the crazed sound of my laughter. "We have three days to fix it."

I waved the script at him. "Do you know what's in here?" I asked. I wanted to tell him. I wanted to let him read the whole thing and see just how bleak it was. How utterly without hope the character of Rudolph was. I cringed as I thought about the end; in fact, I cringed thinking about the beginning.

And then I saw something in his face that made me stop being so, well, *dramatic*. I recalled the conversation I had had with Barb in the bathroom at her house over Thanksgiving. The discussion about making new things, and how we found creative expression in the darkest of places.

I stopped tensing all those muscles in my neck and lower back. "Seventy-two hours," I said, letting the words out slowly. "That's a lot of time."

Rudolph smiled. "That's the Bernie I know. That's the Spirit."

December 10th

I STOOD IN THE CENTER OF THE STAGE AND ADDRESSED THE ENTIRE COMPANY— what was left of it, that is. It was right after the lunch break, and the crew usually dragged themselves back in with some reluctance, their bellies weighed down with hastily eaten food. The afternoon rehearsals were never very good, and given what had transpired in the last twenty-four hours, there was no expectation that today's tech rehearsal was going to be anything other than a very, very tedious afternoon.

I had spent most of the morning up in the office getting all my ducks together for this final push. Rudolph had hung around for a half hour before it became clear that I was in my element. "SECO," he had snorted softly before wandering off. It hadn't been derision in his voice, but rather gentle annoyance that I didn't need him.

I did, but not for the paperwork.

"Thanks for coming back from lunch," I said once it seemed like I had most of the company in the audience. "As you know, the show is scheduled to open tomorrow, and we've got a few things to do before then, don't we?" I paused and glanced at my watch, pretended to do some math. "This'll be our first tech rehearsal. After that is dress, and then we have a preview show for the press, right? I think if I have pizza and beer brought in, we can pull an all-nighter or two and be ready. In fact, let's just push opening night out to the 13th, okay? Give ourselves a little bit of time for a

269

final spit-polish." I slapped my watch and then clapped my hands. "So, are there any questions before we get started?"

There was a long pause, and then someone finally raised his hand. One of the chorus. The guy who had been having problems with the inner ear imbalance, if I remembered his face correctly.

"Yes," I said brightly, pointing at him. "What's your question?"

"We have no lead," he said. "Franklin—you know—*got shot* in the basement."

"He did," I said. "I know. I got a real nice private performance of what was supposed to be his death scene. A little overdramatic, frankly. But he did dinner theater, and I hear that you're supposed to chew on the tablecloth as much as you can. For the people who pay more to sit up front." I smiled at the guy as if I had just answered a very technical question, even though he really hadn't asked a question. "Anyone else?"

"What about Henrik?" This was from his assistant. "He . . . he *died!*"

"So he did," I said. Probably from a self-inflicted gunshot wound, but I didn't bother to point that out. "But most of you know your choreography already, don't you?"

More stares from the audience. They were starting to wonder what sort of drugs I had been shot full of in the hospital. I didn't bother telling them that it wasn't me who had been doped up these last few days.

"So, Henrik's gone. Franklin's gone." I listed them off on my fingers. "And so is Ted. The accountant." I paused and looked down at them. "None of you knew Ted, right? So it's not like he's really missing then, okay? And who else? Ah, yes, Erma. The box office manager. Is that it?"

I waited a few seconds. Waited for someone to speak up.

"Right," I said when no one did. "So a couple of assholes who were going to rip you all off and disappear with your money are gone. Is that about the gist of it? They didn't like you. They were planning on screwing you over from the beginning, and they set all of this up to make fools of you. Is that what happened?"

That got their attention.

I pointed toward the doors at the back of the house. "If that's the story you want the local papers to tell, then go ahead and walk right on out those doors. I'm sure the gossip columnists would love to hear all the juice you've got to share with them." I wiggled my finger. "Go on. March right on out. Tell your story. See what it'll get you. See what it will do for your career."

No one moved. They knew I wasn't done, and they wanted to hear the rest of my speech. I kept my smile hidden, but I could feel the Spirit working in my stomach.

"This show is a disaster," I continued. "It's a ripe piece of garbage that was meant to embarrass you, me, everyone involved with this production, and everyone involved with Christmas. It's nothing more than a lot of hate and vitriol masquerading as comedy. And it isn't funny. It's horrible. And you know what? If we walk out now, that's how it will be remembered. People will read the script and they'll say: *Oh my god! Who in their right mind would want to put on a show like that?* And they'll look at you and whisper: *He was part of that show!* They'll all nod, and give you lots of space on the bus, won't they? Is that what we want?"

I waited for someone to speak up, and for a moment, I wondered if I had gone too far. If I had played this too over the top. And then I heard a voice from the back. A lone voice that said what I wanted to hear.

"No."

It was Barb, bless her.

"No," I repeated. "No, we don't. So what are we going to do about it? Are we going to stand around with our mouths hanging open, wringing our hands like we've been handed a shit sandwich and told it was the most gourmet delicacy ever offered poor, working hacks like ourselves?" I mimed holding a very sloppy, nasty sandwich.

A few more shouted in the negative this time.

I held up my make-believe sandwich. "It is a shit sandwich," I said. "Let's not kid ourselves. But there is no reason we have to eat it. We can make our own sandwich. A *different* sandwich, with less, you know, nasty brown stuff in it. We have tech to do. We have a dress rehearsal. And then we have a preview show to put on. We have an understudy, and if any of you don't know your dance steps by now, let's be honest: A) You're never going to learn them, and B) no one is going to notice anyway."

I got a laugh at that, which was a good sign.

"Look," I said. "The gang of four played you. They brought you together with the promise of making something amazing, and they lied to you. They didn't love the theater. They just loved the idea that they were smarter than you. That they deserved something more than you. They took advantage of your dreams and your desires and hung them on this mockery of a Christmas story. You are all here because you wanted to be a part of something. Well, you were. You were part of a long con intended to suck a whole bunch of money out of Mr. Metcalfe and myself, and it might have worked if they hadn't been so greedy.

"And if we quit now, if we turn off the lights and go home, then they will have been right. We're stupid; we're gullible; we're the rubes who get used and left behind. But that's not us, is it? We aren't stupid. We aren't gullible. We're theater people, dammit, and it's our jobs to make the impossible possible."

I waved my hand at the set of Rudolph's gothic throne room. "This is a creative gift to the world," I said. "This is our miracle. Because that is what Christmas is all about. It's about giving. So let's make this happen, shall we? At the very least, no one will ever be able to say we didn't give everything we had."

I was on the phone when Barb came up to the office an hour later. I nodded at her and indicated she should make herself comfortable in the big leather chair. She came around the massive desk, frowning slightly when she realized one of the big floor-to-ceiling windows was outright missing. Most of Ted's ludicrous paperwork was held in place by a few heavy rocks that had been brought in. The temperature in the room was in the high fifties, which suited me fine. I was keeping busy, and that meant I was warm.

"That was a nice speech," Barb said when I hung up the phone.

"Thanks."

"I think you left out the part where you called upon their future selves to strip their sleeves and show the scars they earned on this day."

"I had it in an early draft," I said. "But I thought it was a little much."

"'We few,'" she quoted, leaning her head back against the chair. "'We happy few, we band of brothers . . .'"

"I went with a slightly different source of inspiration," I said.

She blushed lightly when she caught my meaning and looked away, her gaze coming to rest on the empty window frame.

"I need your help," I said, drawing her attention back to me.

"My help?" she asked. "Why? Why do you need my help?" When she looked at me again, her eyes were bright.

"What do you mean?" I asked, taken aback by the sudden sharpness in her voice.

"It was very chaotic here after Henrik and Franklin did . . . did whatever they did down there in the basement. You said you were down there. They took you to Harborview, didn't they?"

I shrugged. "I'm not really sure where they took me, actually," I admitted.

"Is it true?" she asked.

"Is what true?"

"What happened at Harborview."

I didn't say anything, and she leaned forward in the chair. "I heard stories. And I've been thinking about what you said at Thanksgiving. You said Prancer was dead, and you said it like you were there."

"I was," I said, my mouth dry. "And it's true."

"All of it? Even . . ."

"Yeah. All of it. I was there."

A sob slipped from her lips. She clapped her hand over her mouth and squeezed her eyes shut. I watched her, my heart a wounded sparrow in my chest. For all the big speechifying I had just done, I didn't know what to say to her. I wanted to take away the pain in her heart, but I didn't have the words. And so I just sat there, watching her. Waiting for her to say something instead.

She lowered her hand slowly, her fingers closing into a fist. A single tear escaped, and it slid down her cheek and hung, quivering, on her jaw. "Why?" she whispered. "Why didn't Santa . . . why was I the only one who—"

"I don't know . . . I don't—"

"Why don't you just call on God to come down and help you?" she said. "Why doesn't He send angels to fix everything?"

"Because it doesn't work that way," I said. "You can't depend on them if you can't depend on yourself." I leaned forward, stretching out to touch her leg. "I need you," I said. "You believe in this show. You know something about the theater. I don't know which is stage left or stage right. I'm just the money. I'm not the heart and soul of this show. You are."

She choked out a laugh and opened her eyes. They were wet with tears, but that didn't make her gaze any less strong. "Me?" she said. "I'm the heart and soul?"

"You are," I said. "Because you've never given up."

She wiped away the tear with the heel of her hand and stared out the windows. "I want to hate you," she said. "I really do. I want to find some way to blame you for what happened to Daniel. But what for? You didn't throw those eggs. You didn't force Daniel to go running after that kid. And you certainly didn't trip him. You aren't responsible for any of that." She dropped her head and stared at her fingers knotting themselves in her lap. "And my happiness isn't your responsibility either, is it?"

"Well," I said. "I'm trying."

She shook her head. "I let myself believe in a miracle that was never going to happen, didn't I?"

"You have to, though," I said. "You have to let yourself believe in the possibility. It's just—" I felt that awful weight of Prancer's skull when I had lifted it against Satan. "—the price of miracles can be very high."

"And hope?" she asked. "That's still free, isn't it?"

I nodded.

She took a deep breath, and it brought color back to her face. "All right then. Let's start with that."

"Speaking of the band of brothers," I said. "Could you round up Bucky and Sally for a meeting? I meant what I said about opening the show on the thirteenth, but we've got a lot of work to do. I have another call to make, and then we can get down to business."

She left the office, and I dialed a private number in Montana.

❄

I had spent a couple hours the previous evening after our return from Beverly Hills talking with the Seattle Police Department. Most of the conversation was routine follow-up since they had Erma in custody. She was singing any song they wanted to hear, and Metcalfe was still alert enough to send his posse of hardened lawyers. Erma was going to shove the brunt of blame on Franklin and Henrik, of course. She wasn't stupid. But Metcalfe wanted some satisfaction while he was still around to enjoy it, and that meant throwing some lawyer hours at Erma.

And Ted was still missing. Erma didn't know where he'd gone, but she had been happy to tell everyone what she thought of him. He would do well to keep running in whatever direction he had gone.

Once the SPD had taken my deposition, I was clear to finish the job I had been hired to do, and the one thing I had been following up on was whether Metcalfe wanted to still be involved in the production in any meaningful way. I finally got through to the ex-cattleman himself shortly before Barb returned with the two I had sent her to find.

Metcalfe spoke slowly but clearly. I said little, and most of it was variations of "yes, sir."

Bucky Downminster was rounder than Franklin and had a broad nose that reminded me of a hand trowel. He spoke in a breathy voice, and he had fingers that were long and spindly. Sally Hollis—the Costume Director—was Bucky's opposite, tall and lanky like a shoot of bamboo. She wore her hair back in a pony-tail, and her round spectacles softened the angular shape of her face. She wore muted clothing that didn't make her stand out in a crowd, but from the cut and the fabric, I could tell it was from designer racks in Paris.

"Why is that window missing?" Bucky asked the obvious question as he and Sally stood at the table. There was only one chair in the room, and Barb sat in it possessively.

"I needed some air," I said.

"You could fall out," he said, his voice carrying a hint of a passive-aggressive whine. Like there was something on his mind other than the open window. Like the fact that there wasn't a chair for him.

"Not from over here, I can't," I said, ignoring the tone of his voice.

Barb was wearing a pea coat she had nicked from the wardrobe while she was fetching Sally, and she looked quite cozy, bundled up in it.

"Is there a reason you wanted to see us?" Sally asked.

"Yeah," I said. "We are going to open on the thirteenth, like I told everyone earlier. And that's a tall order, I know, but there's a couple of other things that we need to do too." I tapped the stack of new scripts I had run off in the hotel's business center last night. "First thing: we're cutting scenes IV and V in Act II."

Bucky screwed up his face. "The orgy? Why?"

I glanced at Barb, who kept her expression neutral. "Because it's twenty minutes of staged fornication," I said.

"It's great theater," Bucky said.

"It may be, but it isn't funny."

"It's not meant to be," Bucky countered. "It's supposed to be horrifying. I mean, metaphorically speaking. I'm not really a reindeer, and I'm not really having sex with all those women, but that's not what it is all about. You know?"

"I don't, actually," I said. "It reads like twenty minutes of Franklin getting his rocks off in front of a live audience."

"Is that what it does for you, Bucky?" Barb asked.

Bucky reddened. "I don't know what you're talking about. I have a regular, normal sex life. You can ask my wife."

"Before or after she's seen that scene?" I asked.

Bucky's face turned even redder, and he rubbed his arms vigorously, letting us know he wasn't pleased about the window. Or standing. Or the way we were all ganging up on him.

"Right," I said. "The orgy goes. A couple of lines of dialogue get folded into Scene VI—"

"Which lines?" Bucky wanted to know.

"The good ones," I said.

Barb covered her mouth with her hands to hide a smile. Bucky glared at her because he didn't want to risk me glaring back at him.

"Speaking of lines," I said. "Do you know who wrote the script? I assumed it was Franklin, but it doesn't have his name on it. The copyright is for someone named 'Dread Caspian.'"

"I think it's probably a pseudonym," Sally offered. "It might not mean anything. Or it might be her initials. Or his. I mean, the writer's."

"But not Franklin," I said thoughtfully. Something nagged at me about that, but I couldn't quite place it.

Bucky crossed his arms and started wiggling his leg. "What are we going to do about choreography? I know you said that the dancers were either going to nail it or not, and that you didn't care. But there are still some problems with 'The Dance of the Wretches.'"

"I know," I said, putting aside the thought that wasn't quite there. "And I've got it covered. I'm bringing someone in to do some last minute tune-ups."

"Who?"

"A specialist."

"Who?" Bucky repeated.

"A friend of mine," Barb supplied. "She's very good."

"Who?" Bucky asked again.

"Nancy Harrington," I said. "Local talent. She's perfect."

Bucky furrowed his brow. "Local? I don't think I know her."

"You wouldn't," Barb pointed out. "She did most of her work in North Carolina." A tiny smile caught at the corner of her mouth. "Back in the aughts."

"What shows?" Bucky pressed.

"It wasn't theater. She coached the Elite Allstars out of Greensboro."

Bucky's jaw dropped. "A dance team? You're bringing in a cheer-leading coach to do choreography?"

"She has two qualities that make her perfect," I pointed out. "She's great at building morale, which we could use a good boost of right now."

"And the second?"

"She's available."

"But what does she know about French avant-garde?"

"Not a damn thing," Barb said. "Which is probably about as much as Henrik knew."

"This keeps getting better and better," Bucky groused. He glanced at Sally, hoping she was going to share his frustration. Sally, wisely, didn't make eye contact with Bucky.

"You'll like this then," I said, sliding over a piece of paper bearing a hasty ink sketch.

"What's this?" Bucky asked after he had stared at the picture for a minute.

"Your new costume," I said. Both Barb and Sally crowded in, but Bucky snatched it up before either of them could get a good look at what I had drawn. "I'm not a very good artist, but I'm sure Sally can figure out what I mean."

We all stared at Bucky, who didn't want to relinquish the drawing, but he finally relented, handing it over to Sally.

"Oh," was all that Sally said when she saw it.

The other reindeer in the production, the eight who pulled Santa's sleigh, had been designed with flashy costumes—the sort of thing you saw at Cirque shows. I hadn't changed them. I had changed Rudolph, and instead of a towering figure with a pointed rack of horns, the new design showed a man in a poorly fitted reindeer outfit with stuffed horns. It was a full body suit, hands and feet included—the gloves were mittens. Oversized mittens, at that. The cowling with the red nose hung over his forehead. He was going to have to keep pushing it out of the way with his floppy mittens.

"I'm going to look like an idiot," Bucky said.

"But at least you'll be in on the joke," I said. "Not the other way around."

"Oh, that's just great," Bucky snorted.

"Look, Rudolph can't be played as this demonic creature bent on world destruction," I said. "The audience won't have any sympathy for him if we play it straight. You're the hero of this story, Bucky. You want the audience rooting for you. You want them on your side."

"This is pure tragedy," Sally said, tapping the picture. "Look at this face, Bucky. Look how he is suffering. I feel sorry for him already."

Against his better judgment, Bucky sidled over to Sally and looked at the picture again. "You think so?" he asked.

"Totally," Barb said. "Mr. Rosewood is right, Bucky. This is much more . . . what's the word I'm looking for?" She glanced at me.

"Shakespearean," I said.

"Yes, that's it. Much more Shakespearean."

Bucky looked back and forth between us for a few minutes, licking his lips and trying to figure out if he were mocking him. I managed to keep a straight face, though Barb had to turn away and cough. "Okay," he said finally. "But it's got to fit me a little better than that."

Sally looked at me, and I gave her the I'm-not-the-Costume-Designer shrug.

"I've been working out," Bucky said. "For the org—for some of the scenes. Don't want to waste that effort, do we?"

"Not at all," Sally said, smoothly taking control of the situation. "How about we cut off the sleeves?"

"Yeah," Bucky said. He glanced down at his arms, visualizing how his exposed biceps would look. "That'd be great."

Sally smiled at me in a very understanding way. "I'll get started on this," she said. "Is there anything else?"

"No," I said. "That should do it."

Sally nodded at Barb and headed for the door. Bucky hung around for a second, and when I didn't say anything, he glared at the open window one last time as if to remind me that it still bothered him, and then he hurried after Sally. "You know," I heard him say as they left the room. "I've always wanted to do Shakespeare."

Barb waited until the door shut before letting out the giggle she had been fighting. "Oh dear," she said, flopping back in the chair. "Do you think she'll keep the mittens?"

"With big white fur cuffs?" I said as I wandered over to the open window. "I hope so." I leaned out and whistled sharply.

"Is there anything you want changed in the set design?" Barb was watching me, a curious expression on her face.

"Not right now, no. But there's something else I want you to see." I wandered back to the desk, and picked up the large envelope I had prepared.

"Nancy will be here—"

A *whoosh* and the clatter of reindeer hooves interrupted her.

"Oh . . ."

"Say hello, lads," I said.

All five of the reindeer crowded into the office. Ring was in front, and he came over to Barb's chair, carefully keeping his antlers out of the way. "Hello, Ms. Prescott," he said. "I like your work."

"My . . . my work?" Barb had drawn her feet up into the chair.

"Ring," I said sharply.

"Sorry," he said, ducking his head. "I know. I know. We're not supposed to be in the building, but I got curious. I wanted to see the throne room you were talking about." He danced around the chair. "It's really cool," he gushed.

"That's Ring," I said, pointing at the youngster. "He has trouble following directions." I indicated the others. "Blitzen. Donner. Cupid. And the big one in the back is Rudolph."

She looked at each of them in turn, her expression slowly changing into wide-eyed delight. "Isn't he . . ." she started when she got to Rudolph. "Isn't he supposed to have a red nose?" she asked.

"Only when he's grumpy," Cupid said.

"It is a pleasure to make your acquaintance," Blitzen said. He bent his front legs as if he were curtsying, which I suppose he was. "We don't normally get to interact with real people."

"Hey," I said. "What about me?"

"What's up, boss?" Donner asked. He was the only one who appeared to notice the envelope in my hand.

I held it out, and he took it from me. "There's a truck in Toledo that has our theater seating in it. It isn't moving because the company hasn't got any drivers to spare. I've got an envelope full of cash money that says they can probably scare one up if properly motivated. The problem is that I need that truck here tomorrow."

Ring clattered around the chair, eagerly peering at the envelope. "Ooh, same day reindeer service," he said. His brow furrowed as he tried to read the address.

Blitzen backed around Ring. "Ohio," he said as he trotted toward the window. "No problem, Bernie. We'll take care of it." He dropped out of sight, and Cupid was right on his tail. Donner nodded to Barb and I before heading out the window too.

Ring was still working on the address. "Where's Ohio?" he asked.

"Other side of the Mississippi," Rudolph supplied, shaking his head.

"Hey, where's—" Ring suddenly realized the other three had already left without him. "Where'd they go?"

"Try the other side of the Mississippi," Rudolph offered.

"That's east, right?" Ring skipped towards the window. He stopped on the edge and looked back. "Right?"

"Everything is east of here," Rudolph said.

Ring snorted. "Why didn't you say so?" And he jumped out the window too. Gravity took him, and we heard him shout with glee as he swooped up and buzzed the building before headed out over Puget Sound.

"I can't believe I let him lead the team," Rudolph said, watching Ring fly in the wrong direction. "He doesn't even know his geography."

"He'll learn," I said.

"I knew my geography," Rudolph pointed out as he wandered closer to Barb and me.

"That's because we didn't have GPS tracking back then. You had to know where you were going," I pointed out. "Besides, he's just going to follow the others."

Barb was breathing very shallowly and slowly. "This is a little much," she finally managed.

Rudolph nodded. "It can be. I'm sorry if we've surprised you."

"No," she said. "No, it's not that."

Rudolph raised an eyebrow. "You aren't surprised by flying, talking reindeer?"

She managed a short laugh. "Yes. I mean, no." She held out her hand. "May I?" she asked. He nodded, and she carefully touched his smooth flank. Her fingers danced at first as if she was touching something hot and then settled, her palm finally resting against his hairless body. "You're not what I expected," she said. "The stories . . ."

"The stories skip over a lot," Rudolph said. "Like what happened to me." His eyes darkened slightly. "I lost some close friends."

"Prancer?"

He shook his head. "Yes, him too. There was an accident. A long time ago. The rest of the team didn't make it."

Her eyes were bright and she didn't remove her hand. "It's hard to lose someone, isn't it?"

"You never lose them," Rudolph said. "And that is what makes it hard when they aren't there any more." He dropped his head and nuzzled her cheek, catching a tear as it fell from her eye.

December 12th

"Stop! Stop! Stop!" Nancy jumped out of her chair, waving her hands at the dancers. "I need more arms. Just because you're miserable doesn't mean you can't lift your hands above your heads. Come on, people, give me arms."

The Chorus of the Wretched had the good grace to shamble quickly back to their starting places as she clapped her hands. She counted off quickly and then mirrored their performance from the empty floor of the orchestra. She was wearing neon colors that showed up quite clearly in the dim theater. A dancing lightning bug.

Henrik's assistant—now Nancy's—stood with me at the back of the house. She wasn't trying to throw me out this time. In fact, she hadn't given any sign that she knew I was standing there. She watched the rehearsal, rapt. Her name was Kath. No "i" or "y" or "ee." Just Kath. I had been tempted to go with just "Bern" with her but thought better of it. We were actually getting along.

"It's looking pretty good," I said.

Kath started at the sound of my voice.

"Oh, it's you," she said. "Yes, she is. She's marvelous. In just a few hours, she's made them so much better."

"So much for French avant-garde," I said.

"Chaos isn't functional," Kath said, and I felt like she was quoting something Nancy said before my arrival. "No team ever won because its movement were chaotic. No cheer ever brought spirit to the field by being unfocused."

"No," I said. "Of course not. Unity is action." I raised my fist for her to bump.

"Unity wins," Kath said, Kath said, nodding her head. Oblivious to the sarcasm in my voice.

She tapped her fist with my own, and then launched into some complicated secret post-fist bump thing that involved elbows and rocket ships and maybe even a cuttlefish or something. I got lost after the second elbow, and was spared further embarrassment by one of the interns we had working in the back.

The young man peeked in from the lobby, caught sight of me, and beckoned me over. I extricated myself from Kath's grand unification fist bump and wandered over to the hand-waving young man. "What is it?" I whispered.

"There's a truck here for you," he said.

"From Ohio?" I asked.

"I suppose so," he said.

"You're not sure?"

"Well, it's not . . . the top of the truck is missing, and there's, well, a bunch of *antlers* sticking out . . ."

"It's definitely the Ohio truck then." I held out my fist for the intern to bump, and he merely stared at it. "What's your name?" I asked.

"Gary," he said.

"Okay, Gary. Just tell him he's late. I wanted the chairs off the truck yesterday, so—" I patted Gary on the shoulder and indicated that he should lead the way.

Gary was right about the top of the cab. It had been peeled off like skin from an orange, and Donner's impressive rack poked through the hole. He stood up when he saw me so he could look out over the open top. It was easier than trying to fit his antlers through the window.

"You couldn't back it in?" I asked. The front of the truck was pressed up against the rubber stop at the edge of the dock.

"I couldn't find reverse," Donner explained. "Hey," he nodded to my left. "That kid all right?"

I looked over. Gary had fainted. "You're scaring the workers."

Cupid managed to get his antlers through the passenger window and leaned out. "That's nothing," he said. "You should have seen the State Troopers in eastern Washington."

"You're late," I said. I didn't really want to hear what had happened on the other side of the Cascades. "You were supposed to be here yesterday."

Donner jerked his head at Cupid. "Leadfoot here got us in trouble in North Dakota."

"How much trouble?"

Blitzen dropped out of the sky, swooping under the eaves of the loading area, and landed gently on the dock's concrete pad. "Don't ask," he said. He glanced down at Gary's unconscious body. "Is this guy all right?"

"Traumatic reindeer sighting," I said. "You guys are frightening the locals." I did a quick count and came up a reindeer short. "Where's Ring?"

Blitzen looked a little uncomfortable, like he had discovered bugs in his teeth. I repeated my question. Cupid disappeared back into the cab of the truck. "He, uh, he was the diversion," Blitzen explained.

"He's very good," Donner added.

"You just couldn't do this quietly, could you?" I asked.

Blitzen snorted. "How could we? You know how many chairs are in that truck? What were we supposed to do? Carry them on our backs? Do we look like pack animals?"

I held up my hands. "Okay, point taken. Tell me at least that you kept to the back roads and only drove at night."

"Sure, I'll tell you that," Blitzen agreed. "No problem."

I stared at the huge truck with its ruined cab and reindeer crew. I sighed. "I don't even want to know how you got gas for that thing."

Donner nodded sagely. "Yeah, you don't want to know."

Ring showed up about halfway through the dress rehearsal. Rudolph, Barb, and I were watching the show from the mezzanine. Ring navigated down the steep stairs and leaned over to lick my ear. I reached up and grabbed his lower lip without taking my eyes from the stage. "Hey," he squealed.

"Tell me you didn't embarrass me in North Dakota," I whispered.

He pulled free with a wet pop. "Where?"

"Does the phrase 'I'm the diversion' ring any bells?" I asked, looking at him.

Ring glanced from me to Rudolph. "Oh, there," he said. "Nope. Didn't embarrass you. Didn't embarrass myself either. No one saw me."

"How could you be the diversion if nobody saw you?" Rudolph asked.

Ring scrambled. "Well, I mean, nobody saw *me*. They saw something, but they didn't know it was me. You know? It's 'cause I'm fast. Real fast. Faster than lightning. That's me."

"Fast talking is more like it," Rudolph interjected.

Ring looked hurt, his ears drooping. "Nobody saw me," he repeated plaintively. "I know the rules."

It was my turn to be the big softie, and I held out a hand to Ring. "Come here," I said, and he leaned over me. I scratched the side of his head, just behind the base of his horns. "Just be careful, will you? You're Lead Deer. Don't get hurt. Okay?"

He leaned into my fingers. "Okay," he purred.

I slapped him gently on the neck. "Keep an eye on the others. Make sure they stay out of trouble."

"Okay boss." He leaped happily up the stairs, missing the top one and stumbling, nearly cracking his skull on the arm of a chair. He recovered quickly enough and vanished before I could remind him about injuries.

Rudolph tried to look stern when he noticed Barb was looking at him, a smile tugging at her lips. "I was never that goofy," he said.

"Of course not," she replied. Her smiled widened, and she gave him a very big-eyed, innocent look.

Rudolph glared at me next, daring me to disagree. I ignored him. I was too busy watching the show.

Dress rehearsal. This was our last chance.

The chairs had arrived. We were going to make it.

Rudolph might not have ever been that clumsy or goofy, but this musical certainly was. And I hoped it was goofy enough, because there is nothing more unfunny than satire that doesn't swing for the fences.

And then it was midnight. The last touch-up rehearsal had been worse than the previous practice, and I knew we had gone far enough. No one had anything left. It was time to sleep, dream of sugarplums, and hope for the best.

I repaired to my hotel, filled up the bathtub with expensive bubbly stuff, and submerged myself to the ears. Rudolph was in the other room, sprawled on the bed, watching Pay-Per-View. We were both exhausted. The show was going to open tomorrow. We hadn't had time to do a final dress rehearsal with press and guests in attendance. Everyone was going to see it for the first time tomorrow night, and it would either work or not. There was no intermediate position.

I still wasn't sure which way it would go.

The show was still darker than the inside of a kitten in a box. I could tell Rudolph wasn't pleased by the way he kept grinding his teeth. One of the crew had already come to me about missing tools, and it had been easier to promise the kid a new set than explain that the fired steel of a good wrench did a lot to calm an irradiated reindeer's stomach. And one of the reindeer dancers had twisted her ankle during the last run-through. She had assured me that she'd be all right by the first show— it wasn't anything that a lot of ice, some aspirin, and an ankle wrap couldn't fix—but it was just the sort of little accident that popped up to remind us that we didn't have much of a safety net. Random chance could still make for a lot more excitement and panic than we needed right now.

I made a shark with my hand and swam through the layers of bubbles. I had done everything I could. The seating from Ohio had arrived, and we managed to get it all bolted down. I was assured by our carpenter that the molding would all be in place by the time we got back to the theater in the morning. The company was starting to move like a unit on stage, and Bucky had gotten over his annoyance about the floppy reindeer suit. And the show was starting to elicit laughs in a few spots. It was like the last three hours before Zero Hour at the Pole. There was nothing else that could be done. All that was left was the waiting, and even after all these years, I was bad at waiting.

Rudolph poked his head into the bathroom. "There's nothing on," he said. "You want to disable the parental lock on the porn channel?"

"No," I said.

"Why not?" he asked. "It's not *that* expensive."

"How about room service?" I offered, changing the subject. "The flatware in this hotel is really nice."

"I'm not hungry," he said as he clopped into the bathroom and arranged himself on the tile floor. He leaned up against the tub, and tasted the bubbles.

I retreated to the far side of the roomy bathtub.

"You ever wonder if we're doing the right thing, Bernie?" he asked, a splotch of bubbles on his nose.

"What do you mean? We're saving Christmas. We're getting pretty good at it, don't you think?"

"Yeah, but at what point are we just making more trouble than we're fixing? I mean, when do we become part of the problem?"

"Like this is somehow all our fault?"

"Isn't it?" he asked. "Didn't all of this start because we went to purgatory after that soul?"

I frowned and made more shark movements through the bubbles. "I suppose you could see it that way," I said. "Sure, if we hadn't gone after David Anderson, then maybe Satan wouldn't have come after Santa, and so on and so on. But that's the *What If?* game, and come on, you know better than to get caught up in that."

This was the worst part of waiting. Those last hours when all you had left was time to think. Time to doubt yourself.

"You think maybe we've been trying so hard to save Christmas these last few years that maybe we've forgotten what it's all about? That we've gotten so worked up about what's wrong with it that we can't see what's right anymore."

"Like that time in Boston?" I asked. I didn't really want to bring it up, because I knew better. You don't feed the doubt in the last hours. You focus on happy thoughts, like puppies and kittens, sliding down rainbows. But the words came out of my mouth before I could stop them.

He licked the edge of the tub a few times and tapped his teeth against it. "Maybe," he said finally. "It was the moose comment, you know. That's what set me off."

"I know," I said. "He was a piece of work."

"I get it," Rudolph said. "Culpepper had lived in the city all his life. Probably had never even been to one of those publicly funded animal prisons. But it doesn't really matter. He was trying to piss me off, and I let him get to me. And it wasn't that comment, really. I remember thinking that we couldn't let this guy win. We couldn't let him smear Christmas like he wanted. Nothing else mattered."

"We could have hurt him," I said.

Rudolph kept tapping the porcelain like he was searching for a weak spot. "I know," he said finally. I waited for him to add something, and after a few moments of silence he looked up at me. "What?" he asked.

"Nothing," I said.

"Were you waiting for me to apologize or something?"

"I thought . . . maybe . . . well, yeah, a little bit."

"We didn't get that far in my anger management sessions," Rudolph said. He blew into the tub, and a plume of bubbles shot into the air. "I'm not sorry I melted his stupid tchotchkes."

"It's okay," I said.

"It solved the problem, didn't it?"

"Yeah, but . . ." I left the rest of the sentence unsaid.

He rested his head on the edge of the tub. "I know. Once you go down that road bla bla bla. *It's my way or the highway* sort of nonsense. Any means to the end as long as it is my end and all."

"Yeah," I said. "That's where that goes."

"It's going to be Christmas soon," he said. "Less than two weeks. Are you looking forward to it?"

I was tired, wearier than I had been in a long time. "No," I admitted. "I'm just going to be glad when it's over."

He nodded. "Yeah, me too. And that's what worries me."

December 13th

A half hour before the curtain went up, I asked the company to join me in the backstage shop for a final pep talk. I was wearing a new suit, and my face was already tired from smiling. "In less than thirty minutes, it's going to get a little nutty back here," I said when everyone was assembled. "And so I just wanted to thank you all now for the immense effort everyone has put into this show over the last few months. We're doing something that has never been done before, and not everyone is going to like it, but that's the price groundbreaking visionaries always pay."

That got a few titters of laughter. I looked over the faces, noticing who was smiling and nodding and who I still had to convince. Barb and Nancy were standing on chairs at the back, and it was nice to look out over the whole crowd and see them smiling at me.

"Say what you will about Erma Raeddicker," I continued, "but she was good at separating people from their money. Before we had this recent bit of publicity—because bad press is still better than no press, right?—Erma had actually managed to presell a full house opening weekend. Even though we pushed the show back two days, and there was that snarky piece in *The Stranger's* arts section, we haven't had a lot of cancellations. I'm sort of hoping three-quarters of these people don't bother showing up and never try to ask for a refund. That would be sort of awesome, right?"

Bucky—who was already in costume because he was that sort of Method actor—screwed up his face like he was going to argue with me, but I pressed on.

"Listen, all jokes aside, we're going to open with a nearly full house. And I hope they all do show up because we've done something amazing here. Nothing would make me happier than to pick up tomorrow's paper and see a review that—"

The shop door banged open, and there was some commotion at the back of the room. I tried to see what was going on, and the company parted like a chorus line opening up, revealing a man in a dirty trench holding a gun to Barb's head.

"Rosewood," he shouted. "Give me the codes."

"Are you kidding me?" I rubbed my face with my hands. "Haven't we been through this already?"

Ted Laslo—it had to be Ted; who else was left from that crew?—made a show of pulling back the hammer on the pistol. "Not like this," he said. "I'm serious. I want those codes."

"There isn't any money left, Ted," I said. "I spent it all. Cleaning up your mess."

"Bullshit." He pressed the gun harder against Barb's head. "I'm not fucking around, Rosewood. I don't have time for this."

"No, you don't," I said. "Why are you still here, Ted? Have you been hiding in the building this whole time?"

It was sort of a silly question because it was pretty obvious from his hollow-eyed stare and the way his hair was all stiff and spiky that Ted had been playing a longterm game of hide-and-seek. Which meant that he had had many hours to convince himself of this path, and I was remembering what Rudolph had said last night. *Means to an end and all . . .*

"Just put down the gun, Ted," I said. "Just walk out of here. It doesn't have to be like this. You can walk away."

"Not without that money," he snapped. "Without that money, I'm . . ." He tightened his grip on Barb. "I'm not going to jail. You're going to give me the code, and we're going to transfer the money, and then I'll disappear. That's what we're going to do."

Barb was staring at me, her mouth a firm line. She was afraid, but she wasn't going to let Ted know. She was waiting for me. I could tell she trusted me, but she was also ready in case something happened. It was up to me to make sure what happened wasn't Ted pulling the trigger.

I ran my tongue around the inside of my mouth. There was some money left in the account. Less than fifty grand. Was it so bad to give in to his demands and give him the codes? I could send the reindeer after him. There was no place he could go where they couldn't follow.

Bucky stepped out of the crowd pressed against the walls of the shop and struck a pose, his floppy mittens on his hips. His bare arms gleamed. "What's your damage, Ted?"

Such a poor choice of words, I thought.

Ted laughed at Bucky. "My damage? You want to know what my *damage* is? What the fuck is your problem, Bucky? Are you damaged in the head or something?"

"You think money will solve your problems?" Bucky asked. "You think it'll buy you happiness?"

"I don't want to be happy," Ted shouted at him. "I just want to get out of this hellhole!"

"And you think killing someone is going to do that for you?" Bucky took a couple of steps toward the pair, flexing his biceps as he walked. "Is that your ticket to freedom?"

I couldn't believe this was happening. Mostly I couldn't believe Ted hadn't shot him already.

Ted pointed the pistol at Bucky. "I do," he said, tightening his grip on Barb. "I really do."

I raised my hands. "Ted," I said, trying to get his attention. "We don't need the gun. Let's put it away and we can talk about this."

"That's a good idea," Barb said. "You don't need the gun, Ted."

For a second, I thought Ted was actually listening to us. And then Bucky opened his mouth again.

"How many bullets you got in that gun, Ted?" Bucky asked. "That's a revolver. How many shots you got?" The cowling of the reindeer costume had fallen down over Bucky's face, and he imperiously swept it back with his floppy hand. "Six shots, Ted," Bucky said when he could see again. "You can only get six of us. What do you think the rest of us are going to do? Stand around and watch? You think you can kill six of us and walk out of here?"

"Why does he have to kill any of us?" Barb asked.

Ted started to think about it, and the barrel of the gun wavered back and forth. Finally, Ted figured out what he wanted, and the gun stopped wiggling, though it was now pointed at me. "Of course," I said. "Because it's not really Christmas until someone points a gun at me."

Ted gave me a ragged grin. "The codes, Rosewood." Focusing in on what really mattered to him.

I sighed. "Come on, Ted. Are you really going to shoot me if I don't give them to you? Think this through, would you?"

He licked his lips. "You're right." He put the pistol back against Barb's head. "The codes," he repeated. "Or I shoot her."

"Oh, nice thinking there, Ted," Barb said through clenched teeth. The skin around the barrel of the gun was white from the pressure Ted was exerting against her head.

"No one's getting shot," I said.

"That's right," Bucky said, taking another step forward. "He kills one of us, he'll have to kill all of us."

Barb glared at him. "Will you knock that off?" she hissed.

"Look, I'll give you the codes," I said, trying to get Ted's attention back on me. I realized what Bucky was trying to do—as idiotic as it was—and he was almost close enough to Ted to do something even stupider. Which I was willing to bet he was going to do.

Much as I hated to admit it, Bucky's plan was probably the best one we had right now, though I tried not to think too much about what had happened the last time two men had wrestled with a gun in my presence.

"What?" Ted wasn't sure he had heard me correctly.

"The codes," I said again. "I'll give them to you. The account number is"—and I rattled off the eighteen digit number—"and the acccess code is *25000*. They'll ask for a password and it is '*resolute*.' That's it. That's all you need."

Nobody moved. Ted blinked several times.

"What else do you need?" I asked. "I know you know how to transfer funds electronically, so what are you waiting for?"

"I don't believe you," Ted said. He shifted his grip on the pistol, and his eyes started flicking around the room. I realized that Ted hadn't actually thought his plan all the way through. "We had you down in the basement for days," he said, starting to fidget. "And you wouldn't give it up. Even after Franklin tortured you. You expect me to believe that now you're just going to give it up? Just like that?"

He punctuated his last question with a wiggle of the gun. He lifted it away from Barb's head and wiggled it in my direction.

Which was the mistake that Barb had been waiting for. She ducked and pulled away from Ted, wrenching herself out of his grasp. Ted turned, a look of alarm on his face, and that was when Bucky pounced.

The gun went off as Bucky went for a head-butt, clouting Ted on the forehead with the hard edge of the plastic-coated nose on his outfit. Something tugged at my sleeve, and a warmth started to run down my arm.

Ted and Bucky were wrestling for the gun, and Bucky drove them both back against the wall of the shop. Ted gasped, and Bucky hammered on his face again with the red plastic nose. It was like getting beaten up by a clown, and it would have been funnier if there hadn't been a weapon involved.

The gun went off again and Bucky stiffened abruptly. He stepped back—or tried to at least—but his legs didn't work and he fell down. He curled up into a fetal position.

Ted stared down at Bucky. The gun was still in his hand, and he was momentarily shocked by what had happened to Bucky.

A moment was about all he got before Barb hit him in the head with a chair.

Rudolph found me in the stage right wing. Most of the cast was still in the building, as far as I knew. A lot of them, I suspected, were out on the loading dock, watching the EMTs load Bucky and Ted into ambulances. I stayed behind, and Barb fussed over the nick in my arm from the bullet.

"The audience is getting restless," Rudolph said. "We were supposed to raise the curtain ten minutes ago."

"We can't do the show," I said. "We're going to have to cancel it."

"We can't cancel the show," Rudolph said.

"How are we going to put it on?" I asked. "Our leading man just took a bullet in the leg. The EMT said it's likely his femur is broken. He's not walking today. Or next week. There's no way he can go onstage."

"We should have been ready," Rudolph snapped.

"For what? For the wacko who hid in a closet? None of us had any idea he'd been hiding out in the theater for the last week. None of us knew."

"We should have known." Rudolph kicked the wall lightly with his back hooves. "We should have tracked him down."

"Well, we didn't." Barb had dressed my wound nicely using the first aid kit, but there hadn't been any medicinal whiskey in it, which meant I was waiting for the aspirin to kick in. My arm hurt, and Rudolph's attitude wasn't helping. "Look, you know I'm a good planner. But I can't plan for everything. Who knew that Ted would freak out and hide in a closet somewhere? Or that he'd convince himself that an asinine play like this would actually work?"

"Or Bucky," Barb pointed out. "Who knew he wanted to be a hero so badly?"

"Well," I said, glancing at her. "We knew."

"Yeah, okay. You're right. We did."

"Who is his understudy?" Rudolph asked.

"He was the understudy," Barb said.

Rudolph growled deep in his chest, and his skin began to glow. "We have to do something," he said, his voice getting that stiffness I knew so well.

He was staring at the poster on the wall. It was the full sheet, and it had "Rudolph! The Musical" in big letters across the top. At that moment, all I wanted for Christmas was that poster in the trash bin.

"We can't do the show without a lead," I said softly. "There is no show without Bucky. There just isn't." My heart hurt more than my arm at the thought of what I had to say next, but I said it anyway. "We're going to cancel the show."

"We can't cancel," Rudolph said, an uncharacteristic tremble in his voice.

"We have no choice!" I lost my temper. "It's over, Rudolph. You just don't get it, do you?" I waved my hand at him, showing him the streaks of dried blood along the side of my hand. "We're not like you. We bleed. We screw up. We fail. And it's just the way things turn out sometimes."

I shoved him roughly, letting my own frustration play itself out. I didn't like failure any more than he did. I didn't like to quit, but there came a time when even Rudolph's indomitable spirit had to face the fact that the obstacle was insurmountable.

"It's over," I said, shaking my head. "This one got away from us. We'll try again next year. We can't—we just can't win them all."

"Are you sure?" he asked.

"Am I sure of what?" I asked, nearly in tears.

"That there will be another Christmas next year."

"Come on, Rudolph. There will always . . ."

I didn't finish because there was a hollowness in my belly that belied the words I was about to say. An emptiness that shouldn't have been there. I touched my stomach lightly. Where was it? Where was the Spirit?

In a panic, I looked at Barb for some support, some sign that I was mistaken, but she was staring at the floor. "Barb . . . ?" I tried, and she just shook her head, refusing to look at me.

And I knew. In that second, I really understood—with an awful unshakeable clarity—every word of the script. I knew what fueled Rudolph—what lay at the core of his relentlessness. And I even knew why Blind John Milton had chosen Satan as his protagonist in his long poem. It was all about fear. Fear of an eternity of emptiness.

Sure, we were only canceling a show about Christmas. But that was how it started, wasn't it? That's what Rudolph was saying. If we let this one go, then it would be easier to let the next one go. One by one—we'd keep finding reasons to give up, wouldn't we?—until there was no Christmas left.

"'Life's but a walking shadow,'" Rudolph said suddenly, "'a poor player that struts and frets his hour upon the stage and then is heard no more.'"

"What?"

"The Scottish play," Rudolph said. "Shakespeare."

"Yeah, okay, so we're back to Shakespeare again. What are you talking about?"

"You know what the next line is?"

Barb did. "'It is a tale told by an idiot, full of sound and fury, signifying nothing.'"

My arm ached. My heart ached. None of this made any sense, and I said as much.

Rudolph nodded at the poster. "What's the name of the company?" he asked. "It's right there. It's been right there all along."

I looked at the poster, trying to figure out what he was seeing. "Delirious Arts Renaissance Company," I read.

"And who wrote the script?" Rudolph asked.

"Dread Caspian," I said.

"The devil is in the details," he chuckled. "What do the letters of the company spell?"

"DARC," I said, and when I said it, I heard something else. "And the writer's initials are DC."

"As in 'Demonic Copyright' or even the 'Devil's Creation.' This is Satan's revenge, Bernie. This is how he destroys me. How he destroys us."

"Oh, my," I had a sudden thought. "Culpepper. The lawyer in Boston?"

"Who?" Barb wanted to know.

"We did a job in Boston," I said. "There was a lawyer named Culpepper. His firm was Daughty & Culpepper. D&C."

"Of course it was," Rudolph said with a nod. "Who else knows so much about the folly of anger, about the hubris of pride and arrogance? Who else plays the long game so well? Satan doesn't like it when you take him head-on. He wants you to tie your own noose and find your own hanging tree before he snaps the rope taut and kicks your feet out from under you. It's more delicious for him that way. When we strangle ourselves on our own fear."

He looked up at the flies over the stage. "Satan is never going to stop," he said quietly. "Not until I take away his power. Not until I beat him.

"How?" I asked, not quite sure I wanted to hear the answer to my question. I had my own inkling, and I didn't care much for it.

"I know what Christmas is all about, Bernie," he said. "I've always known. And so have you. Satan just wants us to be reactive, to run scared. He wants us to think we don't know our own hearts."

He nodded towards the stage. "Raise the curtain," he said. "We're going to do the show."

"We don't have a lead," I said. "We don't have someone who can play Rudolph."

Barb put her hand on my arm, and I looked at her. She was smiling, even though her eyes were filled with tears. "You do," she said.

"Where's my nuclear family?" Rudolph bellowed, startling the few crewmembers still hovering in the wings. As they ran to find the cast, Rudolph lowered his head and nuzzled my forehead with his warm nose.

"I'm your Rudolph," he said. "I'm the only one you've ever needed."

He walked onstage, nodding at the stage manager who was staring at him from the stage left wing. The stage manager shrugged and spoke into his headset. As the cast members who played the family in the opening scene rushed onstage, the opening music swelled out in the house. Rudolph glanced back at me just before the curtain rose, and he smiled.

A spotlight came on, illuminating Rudolph, and he stood there, waiting for the audience to get over their surprise. "Good evening," he said when the hubbub of voices quieted down. "Thank you for coming to the show tonight. My name is Rudolph. I am one of Santa's reindeer, and I am going to tell you a true story."

I will always remember that look on his face just before the show started. I will always remember the serenity and the peace in his face. There wasn't any anger in his eyes anymore. Rudolph had stopped being afraid.

I will tell you true.

Zero Hour

DANIEL PRESCOTT WAS JUST SKIN STRETCHED TIGHT ACROSS A FRAIL FRAME. His hair was short, and the scar was a bump that ran along one side of his head. It was barely noticeable, but the other lasting effects of his injury were very apparent. The lines on his monitor moved slowly, without many bumps.

Barb sat in a chair on one side of the bed, Daniel's frail hand in hers. Rudolph and I stood on the other side. We had been there ten minutes or so already, and Daniel hadn't moved at all.

The clock on the monitor read one minute before midnight.

I took the oblong device out of my pocket. It was silver and seamless—a product of all the recent industrial design aesthetics. It had two buttons and a single indicator light, which was pulsing once every second. Mrs. C had gotten me one from R&D—who had finally figured out how to pack a Time Clock Wave Generator into something the size of an iPhone.

"This might not work," I said. "Even if he responds, he might not know you."

"I know," Barb said, stroking her husband's hand. "But I want to do this." She looked at me. "This is what I asked for, remember?"

The display changed on the monitor, flipping not just minutes and hours, but the date as well.

"Clock's on," Rudolph said, a vibration running through his body.

The light on the generator went orange, and when I pushed one of the two buttons, the light turned red and stayed steady.

There was a disorienting moment, a wave that passed through us, and then we were synced up with the Time Clock. The wave persisted, and we were in a bubble outside of time. The lines on the monitor were frozen, and the time display was stuck at a few seconds past midnight.

Zero Hour.

Rudolph lowered his head and kissed Daniel on the forehead, and when he got out of the way, I kissed Daniel on the cheek. I felt the red and green tingle of the renewed Spirit move through my lips. We waited as the Spirit moved through Daniel's brain. We were patient.

We had an hour after all. An hour that lasted as long as we needed it to.

Eventually, Daniel stirred. His brain made a request for more oxygen, and his chest rose a fraction higher than it had on the last inhalation. And the next one was stronger still. His eyes moved behind his lids, doing the REM dance. Barb leaned forward, squeezing his hand.

He opened his eyes, and stared up at the ceiling for a long time. We could almost see him remembering himself in the tiny twitching of his eyes and in the fumbling movement of his lips. Finally, he turned his head, and slowly gazed about the room. He stopped when he saw Barb. His eyebrows tightened, and his breath hissed a long second before his vocal cords caught. "I . . ." was all he managed.

Barb got out of the chair and leaned over him, touching her hand lightly to his lips. "It's me," she whispered. "You don't have to say anything. Just look at me."

Rudolph nudged me with his shoulder, and I left the device on the bed. We didn't need to be crowding the two of them. As we left the room, I heard him say a single word: "Moose."

"No," Barb said gently. "Not a moose . . ."

❄

We ambled toward the elevators, and we both shivered when we passed beyond the generator's six-meter range. Time snapped around us, and my ears popped with the sudden influx of all the normal noises of the hospital. On my wrist, I felt my watch get warm as it caught up.

"It's Christmas," Rudolph said as we wandered along.

"It is," I said.

"Merry Christmas, Bernie."

I smiled at him. "Merry Christmas to you too," I said.

"It turned out pretty well in the end, don't you think?"

"Yeah, it did. I'm a little surprised that we sold out every show. And that the local PBS station wanted to tape it."

"What?" Rudolph was surprised. "Which show? Why didn't you tell me?"

"I didn't want it to affect your performance. That review from the first weekend was bad enough."

He looked down at me. "Which review? They all hated it."

"Please," I said. "You know the one. The one that went on and on about self-confessional theater. Called you some sort of mash-up between Hedwig and St. Augustine."

"Oh," he said. "That one."

"I heard about the note you sent to the American Theater Wing. They're not going to make a Tony category for Best Self-Confession by a talking animal."

"Of course not," he snorted. "I'd win it every year. I think Best Actor would be fine."

"When were you acting?"

"Well, that anecdote about the candy cane factory wasn't true."

There was some excitement in the hall behind us. I looked over my shoulder and watched two nurses rush into Daniel's room. A steady tone rolled out of the door while it was open, that steady note from the monitor that said all lines were flat and getting flatter.

Rudolph paused for a second and then kept walking. "Let's have a quiet Christmas next year," he suggested. "Maybe one where someone doesn't drug me."

"Hey," I said. "I meant well that time. You got a bathysphere ride out of it too. That was a pretty good present. And for the record, I opposed the whole anger management therapy proposal. I thought it was a bad idea."

Rudolph paused at the elevator. "Thanks, Bernie," he said. "Thanks for being my friend."

"You're welcome," I said, patting him lightly on the flank. "Thanks for watching out for me too."

"Hey," he said as the elevator car arrived. "Maybe we should drug *them* next year."

"Who?"

"The NPC. But not all of them. Just some of them, so that the rest worry they might be next. Think about it. They'll wondering when we're going to get them, for an entire year."

The elevator doors opened, and Barb was waiting for us inside. She had the generator in her hand. She had used it to shift around us. The light was green again, pulsing regularly like a heartbeat.

"He's gone," she said. Her face was still wet from her tears.

I took the portable generator and dropped it in my pocket. "I know," I said. "I'm sorry."

She wiped at her face and tried to smile. "It's okay. We had a lot of time together. We talked. Got caught up. I could tell it was hard for him to speak. He probably didn't understand half of what I was saying, but he listened." She looked up at the inset light in the ceiling, trying to keep the tears at bay. "He said he loved me. He said he had been dreaming about me."

Rudolph tapped the button for the top floor, and the doors closed. We went up, toward the roof, toward the wintery sky.

"We're all dreamers," he said. "Every last one of us."

Acknowledgements

Once, I wrote a story for my mother for Christmas, and she recently found it and sent me a PDF. Thanks, Mom, for hanging on to such ephemera. A later version of that story sold to Pulphouse Publishing in the early 1990s, but was orphaned shortly thereafter. It was picked up again for an anthology called *Buried Treasures*, a collection of neglected and lost stories. My thanks to Dean Wesley Smith and Jerry Oltion for getting me started.

The later parts of this quartet of Christmas stories were extremely wordy Christmas "cards" I gave to fifty or so of my closest friends during the waning years of the last millennium. There was talk of putting them together as a novel, but little came of that in those days. Cecil Beatty-Yasutake, though, never let a year go by without reminding me that I should get this book out. Here it is, sir. Better late than never. Thank you for your unflagging enthusiasm.

The interstitial season was written especially for this edition.

Darin Bradley and Misti Morrison have recently joined me on a wild ride into the unknown, and it was with their blessings and constant reminders of how many other things weren't getting done in a timely fashion that *Rudolph!* was realized in concert with the 50th anniversary of the Rankin/Bass stop-motion edition of *Rudolph the Red-Nosed Reindeer*.

And finally, many continued thanks and outpouring of love to Em, Es, and Zee, who make me laugh.

MARK TEPPO is a synthesist, a troubleshooter (and -maker), a cat herder, and an idea man. He is the publisher of Resurrection House, a fiercely independent genre publishing venture that seeks to reignite a passionate love affair between authors and audiences via the printed book.

He lives in the Pacific Northwest, where he occasionally spends a weekend in the woods. His favorite Tarot card is the Moon.